FEW
and
FAR

Dear Philipa,
Thanks for your interest and
support during this interesting
time. I hope you enjoy stepping
back in time with Florence,

FEW
and
FAR

a novel by
Allison Kydd

Allison Kydd

Stonehouse Publishing
www.stonehousepublishing.ca
Alberta, Canada

Stonehouse Publishing Inc. is an independent
publishing house, incorporated in 2014.

Cover design and layout by Anne Brown.
Printed in Canada

Stonehouse Publishing would like to thank and acknowledge
the support of the Alberta Government funding for the arts,
through the Alberta Media Fund.

Government

National Library of Canada Cataloguing in Publication Data
Allison Kydd
Few and Far
Novel
ISBN 978-1-988754-01-7

A writer I know once said blue eyes are too obvious, like a man in a white Stetson or riding a white horse, but that writer never looked into my father's eyes. So I dedicate this book to two men with blue eyes: my father and a young man named Dougie Macpherson, both of whom died too soon.

Chapter 1

-

HUMILIATION

My invitation to the wedding of my cousin, Mary Humphrys, a resident of Cannington Manor in the district of Assiniboia (part of the North West Territories of the newly minted Dominion of Canada), arrived at a most opportune time in my twenty-third year. While I had not been jilted—not precisely, since there had been no formal engagement—I had recently suffered a most unhappy romantic adventure.

Mr. Frederick Corby was a gentleman who lived on a neighbouring estate in South Norwood, near, but not part of, the sprawling metropolis of London. When my story begins, Mr. Corby had, by marked attendance of no less than two-and-one-half years, indicated his attachment to me, which had encouraged me to care for him in return. Being a properly instructed young woman and conscious that Mr. Corby, though an elder son, had yet to come into his property, I did not press him into making definite plans. I had no doubt the discussion of marriage would take place in due time, when his family affairs were settled.

By the time my prospects changed, it was the year 1892, and I had waited—with remarkable patience, if I may give myself such credit—for the gentleman to make his offer. Lest the reader think me too patient, I can only say that I believed myself the object of Mr. Corby's sincere affection. And, though I lacked the security of an engagement, what could be of more import than mutual regard?

Still, with the last twelve-month having recorded the death of the said gentleman's father—making Mr. Frederick Corby the head of his household—and finding me still in a state of anticipation, I began to have apprehensions whether the event would ever take place. In fact, I had hinted at the particulars of my situation, and my distress at the same, in a letter to my cousin Mary the previous September. When her reply arrived a mere six weeks later, she advised I bring him to the point without delay.

"After all," she wrote, "though an eligible and eminently pleasing young woman, you must still be wise. There is no profit in spending your best years neither available to other suitors nor betrothed to the one who attends you.

"I have," she continued, "decided to address a similar matter with a gentleman of my acquaintance. Mr. Ernest Maltby has been attentive to yours truly at all the community functions. Not only does he seek me out for quadrilles, but he is at my side during race days, cricket matches (when he isn't engaged on the pitch himself), and other entertainments. In fact, he seems desirous that I approve all his exploits, in business as well as sport. My good will, not to mention my affection, he has secured already, though I once thought him plain, awkward and too much my senior. I was mistaken on all those counts, and my only regret is that he may be rather too partial to games. Admiring a sporting fellow is all very well, but would he make a good husband?

"Nonetheless, I find his company most pleasant, and I am impatient to know whether his intentions are serious. My parents and I are of one mind on this—an uncommon occurrence for my dear mater and myself. We agree that marriage—if it is within her power—is the duty of every young woman, especially in this country, where women are scarce and young men without the inducements of home and hearth are inclined to wander or waste away."

My cousin Mary, who is one year my junior and lovely in face and manner, has a disposition both courageous and practical. While I could not match her confidence in her powers of attraction, I was encouraged by the similarity in our situations. If she could ask her Mr. Maltby to "know his own mind or she would think no more of him," then surely I could hint to my own Frederick Corby—I thought him mine at the time—that I "wished him to offer his love in terms of more substance."

When, however, I made cautious reference to the conveniences of marriage as opposed to lingering courtship, Mr. Frederick Corby's reaction was dramatic. His face blanched alarmingly, his complexion becoming paler still from the surprise, and his expression was that of one seeing me for the first time. He immediately moved from my side to take up a position by the fireplace, where he gazed intently into the flames (previous to this, we had been blissfully shoulder-to-shoulder, looking over a magnificent volume on horse husbandry that my father had just received).

It may indeed have been those fine specimens that induced me to speak at that particular instant of my desire for matrimony, for Frederick Corby—it must be admitted even at this less-indulgent date—had always struck me as a fine figure of a man—tall and definitely masculine in form. Even my mother and Penelope, my sister, commented on his many graces. They did so with some puzzlement, as if it were difficult to account for the attentions of such a paragon to one such as me. No doubt in their eyes I was, at nearly three and twenty, not only past my prime, but a bluestocking as well. I *read*, you see.

Because of Mr. Corby's reaction, I immediately fell into a flutter of regret and self-doubt. I made as if to follow him across the room, but was arrested by the coldness of his expression. Indeed, both his face and figure had taken on a haughty stiffness that filled me with alarm. Regretting my most unmaidenly initiative, I thought to clarify my meaning without distressing him further. Yet once I had offered him the choice, there seemed no graceful way to remove it.

In a voice as unbending as his manner, Mr. Corby professed himself deeply hurt. He had thought his situation perfectly understood—his income was insufficient to support a wife and family at present, since he had just come into his property.

"But," I persisted—somewhat haltingly, I confess, but it was too late to do other than persist—"I would be content with a modest establishment. It is your affection that means the most to me."

"She speaks of *affection*," he remarked to the stag's head mounted above the mantel, as if calling upon it to join him in indignation, "surely with affection must come trust?"

Then, though still quaking, I reminded him that I was not without resources. I was fortunate to have a modest inheritance from my father's aunt that afforded me an allowance. The principal would be available to me in the event of marriage, and my future husband would have the benefit of it.

Mr. Corby waved that protest aside as well, and with rather less respect than it deserved. Yes, he had been *informed* of that—by whom, I wondered, since I had never before mentioned it—but *he* would not wish to live off his wife's income. Not even for the few years it would take for his estate to be modernized and profitable again.

"You deserve so much more than I can give you at present," he said, his kind words belied by his sudden inability to look at me. "Please do not press me further, as it hurts me deeply to discuss it."

Naturally, I promised to refrain from making further reference to the subject and repeated what I had averred so many times before, that his excellent company and his regard for me were all that was needed to assure my happiness.

"You are indeed a dear girl," he said, returning to my side, apparently much relieved. He pressed my trembling fingers between his hands, which—though larger than mine and of masculine proportions—were still very fine hands. I thrilled to the contact. My face flushed and my heart swelling with relief, I hoped he might take the opportunity to kiss me, as he had done on a few previous occasions, but he did not. Perhaps he still thought to punish me.

In spite of my relief to see him no longer distressed, it did flit through my mind that his resistance to altering his state might not be for *my* comfort, but for his alone. Everyone in my father's house set great store by him. My mother had the cook reserve the best mutton haunches and gooseberry pies for dinner in anticipation of his visits, and my father paid more gratifying attention to Mr. Corby than he had ever paid to me, the eldest of his two daughters. Perhaps the gentleman in question, since he tasted already the benefits of attachment to my family, may have felt marriage would not improve—and might even endanger—his felicity. Setting up his own household would almost certainly deny him the opportunity of dining so frequently at the expense of my father.

In spite of my doubts about Mr. Corby's motives, I did not perceive that the tide of my future had already turned. The gentleman and I soon bid each other a tender adieu. I remained bravely cheerful, though my lips remained un-kissed and I saw him beckon for his horse and ride down our avenue without a backward glance. Saddened as I was by his lack of display, I had no inkling of what was to come.

It was not long after this awkward interview, however, that the gentleman ceased to be a regular caller at my father's house. At first I was mystified not to see him, and I feared he might be ill. Then I overheard rumours—the serving-maid telling my mother and sister (when I had stepped out of the room)—how Mr. Corby's horse and hound had frequently been seen on the road to Plymouth Grange, home of the Bentley-Kydds. That family was famous in the county for the excellence of both table and cellar, and at least one daughter was of marriageable age. Neither was it of any comfort to recall that they were a family reputedly short on propriety, though blessed with high spirits and affluence.

But enough of such unkind thoughts! Suffice it to say I was mortified by this news, both overhearing it and then having it immediately served up to me by my mother; she, lacking the humble serving maid's sensitivity, did not consider how the report might wound me. It appeared that Mr. Frederick Corby's gentlemanly, but not kind, attentions had been accepted elsewhere as eagerly as they were by me.

To add to my misery, my family—at least my mother and sister—evidently held me responsible for this defection. Had I been attending those disgraceful women's suffrage meetings again? Some new eccentricity of mine seemed the only possible explanation for this strange turn of events. Though it was hard to bear this additional unfairness, I left them in ignorance. It was humiliating enough to admit that I, a woman of good family and some pride, had welcomed the attentions and believed the empty posturing of a man who now seemed to have had no intention of marrying me. Of even greater shame, however, was the fact I had been so bold as to make what was essentially a marriage proposal—a proposal that was rejected.

What my father thought of my suitor's defection I did not know, since he kept his distance from domestic concerns, even those pertaining to the marital prospects of his daughters. In fact, I would have been more surprised had he made any inquiry, than I was to find him silent.

Chapter 2

-

HOPE

But now I return to my cousin Mary, who, I was elated to hear, had found an *Ernest* more honourable than my faithless *Frederick*. Soon after our first exchange on the subject of lingering courtships, Cousin Mary wrote to me—Miss Florence Southam—of her upcoming marriage. Her letter was enclosed in an envelope addressed to my father, Mr. Reginald Southam, Esq., Grandin House, S. Norwood, England.

I noted the envelope and Canadian postmark in the tray with the other mail one morning when I was at the sideboard choosing my breakfast. Naturally, I was impatient to know the contents of the letter and whether there was any word for me. The recipient of the letter came into the room a few minutes later, made his own selections, then carried his plate and his mail to the head of the table. Some minutes later, when he had scanned his message from my uncle, my father handed me Mary's pages.

"Here is something to cheer you up," he said.

I was then impatient for my parents to finish eating so I could leave the table. When they finally pushed back their chairs and departed from the morning room, they went as usual in separate directions, while I retired to my own chamber to enjoy Cousin Mary's letter in peace.

Mary first gave the particulars of the wedding. It was set for the first of June, and Mary desired that I might attend her in her preparations—*if*, that is, my own situation had not changed and *I could still be spared*.

"As you know, I have an abundance of sisters," she wrote, "and they must play their part by being my attendants in the performance. But I long to have a friend to confide in—someone with whom I can be myself and not always concerned with having to set a proper example."

Mary went on to inquire about my "negotiations" with Mr. Corby. "Unless you have immediate plans to change your situation," she wrote, "an absence of a few months might be quite strategic. Furthermore, as I have mentioned before, there are a great number of young bachelors in these parts—many of good family, some very industrious—but all of whom would happily settle down to populate our little community if given the proper inducement."

She then explained that Mr. Maltby was somewhat more mature, having previously been established in India and now the postmaster for Cannington Manor. He and her father (and two other gentlemen) were also business partners in an enterprise known as the *Moose Mountain Trading Company*.

In case I might think him too serious, Mary quickly added a codicil: "mature as he is, on occasion, Mr. Ernest Maltby still has the grace to blush and be at a loss for words."

After more gushing on the subject of Mr. Maltby and his blushes, and further description of their courtship, Mary continued her letter by pleading for my immediate acceptance of her invitation. She suggested I make my preparations so as to arrive no later than May Day, as the banns would be read soon after.

"In a community such as this," she added, "everything is at the mercy of agriculture, while agriculture itself is at the mercy of the weather. By the beginning of June, the crops should be greening the fields, and we will be praying for rain and tending to all that has been set aside for the sake of the planting—surely an auspicious time for a wedding."

She had spoken in other correspondence of the Canadian climate and its effect on agriculture. If I were permitted to accept her invitation, I meant to search for those letters and reread them. In this way, I would prepare myself and show due respect for the family's concerns. I did recall her mention of long, severe prairie winters, the reason why work in the fields could not begin until May. By then the snow would be melted, baring the ground to the drying winds, which, according to Mary, blew lustily most days of the year.

Though these details seemed to interest her mightily, I could not have judged the differences between agricultural practices in England and those in the colonies, as I had never paid much attention to that aspect of country living. Nor was it expected that I should, the practical matters of running estates and overseeing farms being as much a man's province as the marriage of daughters was the responsibility of a mother.

So I mused as I continued to read, but it was evident that Cousin Mary could not refrain for long from mentioning her Mr. Maltby.

"He talks of hiring my brother Ernest to enlarge his house, which is nicely situated at the east end of town," she continued. "Yes, there will soon be two Ernests in the family, not to mention the others in the community. *My* Ernest, Mr. Maltby, intends to enlarge his parlour and kitchen and to add two or three smaller rooms upstairs.

"'For what purpose these rooms, pray?' I long to ask him, but I do not know him quite so well as that. Besides, if hinting at potential offspring, my blushes would surely add to his, and we would both be undone. (And I should doubtless not speak in this manner to another unmarried lady.)"

I felt my face heat up as understanding came to me, but I did not hesitate in my reading.

"As you remember," Mary's letter went on, "my father owns a substantial piece of property and has livestock as well as crops and gardens to worry over. Even Mr. Maltby has fields beyond his tennis courts, though his few acres have been shamefully neglected due to his other interests; not only tennis, but, as I have said, cricket, hunting, and all the other gaming pursuits hosted by the Didsbury folk, the Becktons.

"The Beckton brothers are both the blessing and curse of our little settlement. But I will introduce you to that family, and all our neighbours, when I see you—see how confident I am that my dearest wishes will come to pass! As I said, *when* you arrive, you will no doubt be anxious to form your own opinion of all our neighbours.

"Now I must go, as my dear Mr. Maltby waits patiently on my father's doorstep for me to finish this epistle so I may slip it into my father's envelope. If Mr. Maltby were to despair and return to town before I am done, my letter would miss the weekly post.

"As to Mr. Maltby neglecting his acres, I have become a true farmer's daughter and will take charge of that oversight. Unless, that is, he intends to begin filling up the additional rooms of his house immediately upon our marriage and leaves me no peace to think of anything else." (More blushes while I tried not to imagine his eagerness and my cousin's welcoming response, but I read on.)

In spite of its promise to end, the letter continued, "but, seriously, I am sometimes relieved Mr. Maltby supports other enterprises than farming, though even in town our livelihood will still depend somewhat upon agriculture. If the farmers prosper, we prosper. If they fail—but they will not, and that is all there is to it."

I paused again, marvelling at the knowledge of and passion for farming my cousin had gained in scarce four years. A short time ago, as befitted the eldest daughter in a family with some claim to station, she had been in Germany studying music and art. No doubt she—like her father—knew how to use every part of her experience to advantage. My parents, on the other hand, were nothing if not cautious, and had often congratulated themselves on their prescience when not a few of my uncle's schemes proved overly optimistic.

I turned back to my cousin's letter, where but a few lines remained.

"But now I wish you good-bye. Please go this instant and consult your parents, so that I may soon be able to embrace you in person, well before lady May ends her reign and June finds me a bride.

—Your affectionate Mary."

There was yet a post script: "Our honeymoon trip is to Winnipeg and Lake of the Woods. We expect to be away for a full six weeks. Oh, my fluttering heart!

—M."

In spite of my recent disappointment, I read (and would re-read) my cousin's letter with great interest. Who would not be curious to see this untamed country she described, this place where people regularly placed all their dreams and prayers in the hands of capricious Fate and the weather?

Though several years had elapsed since I had seen my cousin Mary, our lively exchange of letters—the liveliness primarily Mary's, though on occasion mine—made the time seem shorter. It was like her to spin her tale as if she alone were putting plough and seed to stubborn land. When her family had lived on a neighbouring estate in South Norwood—before the greedy fingers of Croydon and London annexed much of the good farmland (as my father complains they now have done)—and we saw each other regularly, I had known her to be restless. She was easily bored with *women's duties*. These consisted—in her world as well as mine—of visiting, distributing charity and taking lady-like exercise; of practicing womanly arts such as light reading, drawing, music and embroidery; and of overseeing younger brothers and sisters—in her case not mine. (Penelope would not have needed nor tolerated any management by me.) Also unlike me, Cousin Mary took over the management of her parents' house and servants during her mother's rather frequent confinements and absences.

When last I saw her, she was preparing for her study in Germany. But even that she had viewed as something of a duty. Such study would increase her marriage prospects, prepare her to teach her younger sisters and brothers or—if need be—give her the means to earn her keep as a companion or governess. That is, if the family fortunes worsened—which has happened to many a young woman in these uncertain times. Though she was realistic about her options, I knew Mary would always make use of her opportunities.

But now my cousin appeared to have found a life and a partner that suited her, and duties that stirred her passions. I confess I envied her for it. With the small part of me that could see beyond my cruel defection by Frederick Corby, I wondered if some similar fate could possibly be in store for me. The mere thought of such a thing caused a stir of excitement within me that my cousin would have found gratifying.

Chapter 3

I TAKE LEAVE OF MY FAMILY
AND BEGIN MY JOURNEY

Soon after receiving my cousin's letter, I was on my way to Liverpool. There I would meet the Pierces, who would be my companions, and the steam ship *S. S. Sarmatian*, which would take us across the Atlantic Ocean to the port of Halifax, in the new dominion. The ocean voyage, as I understood, would take ten or twelve days, perhaps even a fortnight. From Halifax, about which I had read a little, I would take the Canadian Pacific Railway into the thinly populated Canadian North West, to a frontier town called Moosomin, also in that district known as Assiniboia.

I was grateful for the enterprise, as it took my mind off my disappointment—though, if the truth were told, I thought arrangements for my leave-taking made with almost too much ease on the part of my family. Could it be they welcomed my absence? After all, Penelope would become "Miss Southam" during my absence, and my mother could focus her energies on putting forward the more promising, younger daughter.

My sister was then only eighteen, while I, nearly five years her senior, had failed to secure myself a husband, which appeared to be the only situation available to me. Since I had my inheritance, there was no need for me to search out a position—which was fortunate, since my qualifications were few. Neither was I particularly suited to being a companion to one of our few elderly female relatives. How fortunate for all that my cousin was to be married and that Uncle Humphrys had arranged an inexpensive passage for me in company with a reliable Cannington Manor family!

I had brought up the subject of the visit as soon as possible—at supper on the day I received my cousin's invitation—it was the only time I could be certain of finding my mother and father in the same room. It turned out my father was already aware of the invitation, for that was the substance of his letter from my uncle. In spite of this courtesy, my father's words on my uncle's arrangements were disparaging as always.

"Humph," he said, "since they are so eager for your company, one would have thought your uncle would pay your passage rather than relegating that honour to our family. No doubt his farming experiment in the Canadian prairies is not so profitable as he would have us believe. But then, Jim Humphrys could never make a success of anything."

I thought this comment most unkind towards my uncle, and I regret to say the theme was not unfamiliar.

"But, Father," I interjected, "I had expected to pay for my passage myself. Is this not exactly the purpose my aunt intended—that I be able to act independently?"

For a moment my father was silent, and I feared he might be angry.

"But only if you approve," I added, noting as I often did, how he drew his brows together and seemed to scowl when he looked at me. I could not remember many occasions when he had looked at me with pleasure.

Since he still said nothing, I ventured on. "I had thought to return at the end of June—a mere ten weeks—if I could be spared."

My choice of words surprised me. Had not Mary used the same phrase referring to a lover's inability to tolerate a long absence? I could only imagine how wonderful it must be to know oneself so valued.

My mother had also waited for my father to speak, but then she shrugged and signaled for the serving-maid to clear the dishes and bring dessert.

"Since it is for such a short time," she said, "I cannot see any difficulty, unless you require a new wardrobe. And it is proper your cousin should ask you to attend her."

I assured her I had no need of a new wardrobe (a decision I was to regret when I found how inappropriate my English costumes were for most colonial activities; of course I had no way of knowing this at the time).

Since my mother seemed to favour the plan, my father made no further comment, though he later insisted on paying my fare and gruffly spurned my thanks. When he had arranged the financing and confirmed the time I would meet with the Pierces, the affair became *women's business* until two days before my departure. He then offered to accompany me to Liverpool, but both Mother and I protested that I had travelled on my own before, and he withdrew on that point as well. To tell the truth, I was touched by his offer, but as we had never spent much time in each other's company, I could only imagine so much time alone together would be uncomfortable for us both, and I felt he greeted my decision with relief.

My solitary trip to Liverpool allowed me time to ponder my parents' relationship with the Humphrys. The families were not close. Mary's mother and my own were sisters, though they had chosen somewhat different paths in life. When she was twenty years of age, Aunt Jane's marriage had been a love match with a man in the same business as our ship-builder grandfather, and since then she had been much occupied with bearing and rearing their children. (Mary had both four—no, five—brothers, and four sisters, at my last count.) My mother, by waiting until she was two and twenty, had managed to secure a landed gentleman. Though she deigned to bear him two children, she had consigned our care to nurses and governesses as much as possible until we were of age.

These differences in temperament and instincts, plus my uncle's tendency to move his growing family about the country, as a result of changes in employment or other unsuccessful enterprises, meant the sisters had spent little time together in recent years. Long before my uncle moved to the Canadian North West, built Humphrys House and embarked on his various entrepreneurial activities in the new agricultural community of Cannington Manor, Mother and Aunt Jane were accustomed to seeing each other no more than once every few years. Cousin Mary and I, by virtue of regular letters and occasional visits, had maintained a closer acquaintance, even when she was studying in Germany.

It was from observation, therefore, that I knew it had been Mary's duty—as behooved an elder daughter—to replace her mother in the domestic capacity as Aunt Jane recuperated from her various pregnancies. My cousin also managed the household when her mother was away from home, and apparently Aunt Jane would be absent during my visit. (She would be in Yorkshire visiting our grandmother and an aunt with whom she was a favourite.)

Perhaps it was these demands on Mary's time that had prevented her from establishing her own household before the age of twenty-one, despite her being an extremely comely woman with lustrous dark hair and eyes, so much more distinguished than my fairness. Or perhaps customs were different in this raw new country, and women were not so readily seen as spinsters if they failed to secure early marriages. Whatever the truth of it, this was the country for which I too was destined—at least for a short time.

Now that I had the opportunity, it would have been impossible for me not to respond to the lure of such an adventure. I was not the pioneer my cousin was, but neither was I totally without spirit.

Chapter 4

I LEARN THE ORIGINS OF CANNINGTON MANOR

As my first evidence of spirit during the trip across the Atlantic, I was reduced to tears over the unkindness of Mr. Frederick Corby as seldom as I was confined to my cabin because of violent seasickness—on one occasion only. My companion, Mrs. Lydia Pierce, widow of Captain Edward M. Pierce, Cannington Manor's founder, suffered more than I, though she had made this trip before. I strove to be sympathetic, since her suffering was not only physical. She, after all, had lost a husband, while I had merely lost a suitor, and an undeclared one at that.

During those times when Mrs. Pierce was not seasick, she spoke at length about her family's removal to Canada. She also told me of Captain Pierce's connection (through his mother) to William of Normandy. An ancestor had come to England with "the Conqueror," she said, and the Duke of Normandy had given him the manor of Cannington in Somerset. Her husband did not recall precisely who the ancestor was nor where the bloodlines entwined, but he still treasured the connection.

When Edward Michell Pierce was born, the story still figured in the family legend, though the property was in other hands. This was the origin of the name *Cannington Manor*. Captain Pierce would have preferred simply *Cannington*, like the legendary estate, but a town by that name already existed in Canada.

"Ah," I said, "I had wondered about the name." I settled myself more comfortably in my deck chair and adjusted my lap robe to protect me from the incessant, salty wind and spray. It was clear by this time that Mrs. Pierce was an inveterate story teller, but I was still grateful for her company. One could not spend all one's time reading, dozing or staring seaward without sometimes entertaining loneliness or other unwelcome thoughts. Though I had not found a kindred spirit in my companion, listening to her was not an unpleasant way to occupy the daylight hours.

"In the year 1880," said Mrs. Pierce, "Captain Pierce, having retired from the British army, was a wine merchant and one of the directors in a bank. The failure of his bank that same year left him with few resources, as the directors were obliged to cover the bank's losses. Fortunately, however, I was the former Lydia Bishop Bowdage, with connections and some money of my own."

Though I did not recognize her family name as she seemed to think I might, I felt "Bishop Bowdage" had a respectable ring.

"The captain," continued Mrs. Pierce, "though fifty years of age, was desirous of making a fresh start, and advertisements for free land in the Canadian North West provided the opportunity for which he had been waiting. Not only could he claim a homestead, but each of our adult sons could as well."

At this point I ventured a nod and a modest "How fortunate," as some response seemed appropriate.

"Alas," said Mrs. Pierce, "our move was not accomplished without separation, hardship and even heartbreak."

"Ah," I said again.

"It was in 1882 that Captain Pierce and our son Harvey travelled to Canada, where they leased a large house in Toronto. Our eldest son, Duncan, stayed in Devon to help me settle family finances, pack remaining belongings and make other arrangements for moving. Though we had been forced to sell our beloved Strawberry Hill and much of our antique furniture and other valuables, we had many loyal friends, some of whom bought pieces of our furniture in order to return them later as gifts."

"How extraordinary! Such kindness!"

"Indeed. But such was the loyalty inspired by the dear Captain—" And here Mrs. Pierce was overcome by her memories and must locate her handkerchief.

After my companion had composed herself, she explained that the process of locating desirable areas to homestead was almost as unwieldy when in Canada as it would have been writing letters from England. Consequently, the captain had done little more than settle on the district of Assiniboia when the rest of the family arrived. Things moved more quickly then, as Duncan felt all long distance efforts were ineffective and determined to see for himself what was available.

"To do this, he must take the train all the way to Fourth Siding, now called *Moosomin*, at the end of the line."

I nodded again. Cousin Mary's letters had introduced me to the town that was once the railway terminus. It was also the closest business centre to Cannington Manor. Mary had described it as a "dirty, noisy place," but I did not repeat this to Mrs. Pierce.

Once at Fourth Siding, Duncan Pierce "made good use of his wits," according to his fond mother. He located a group departing to look at land that had recently been surveyed, and hired a horse and buggy to travel with them.

Somewhat to my surprise, Mrs. Pierce named the members of Duncan Pierce's party of explorers.

"There were two sets of brothers," she said. "Spencer and William Page and Harry and Frank Sayer. The Pages were acquainted with the Marquis of Lorne, the Canadian Governor General, and had dined at Rideau Hall." She paused to allow me time to note this piece of information before she continued. "Also in the party were Mr. and Mrs. Frank Taylor and two Scottish guides, Malcolm Mac-Neil and Donald MacDougal, the former of whom would one day teach my girls how to cook porridge."

I smiled at this image of a rough and ready Scotsman giving

instruction on cookery to three young English ladies. I was also amused by Mrs. Pierce's habit of dropping the names of distinguished people into her conversation. She had obviously told her stories many times and perhaps embellished them a little, yet her enthusiasm was infectious—to a point—and I would possibly have use for the names in future.

After Duncan and the others journeyed southwest for forty miles, an adventure that included crossing the Pipestone River and one or two smaller creeks, the group arrived at its destination. I may have looked alarmed at this point, as Mrs. Pierce hastened to assure me the Pipestone only became a river when in flood and the trail was much improved, with more stopping-houses now available along the way.

"Was their trip successful?" I wondered, anxious to dispel any hint of cowardice on my part.

"Oh yes. Duncan found a site that would suit our family's needs and hastened back to Fourth Siding— Moosomin—to telegraph the news to his father. Then Captain Pierce and Duncan's brothers must come and see for themselves, which they did, and approved the location, as it was on high ground and had a pleasant aspect."

"And this is where the town—?"

But Mrs. Pierce had her own method of telling her story. "Of course Ted selected his own quarter, but Duncan and Harvey, having less interest in farming, agreed to take whichever quarters remained. So all seemed decided until, back in Moosomin, they found they could not file for the homesteads. That particular tract of land wasn't yet open for settlement!"

"But how can that be? Were they not able—?"

Mrs. Pierce preened a little. "Captain Pierce, of course, was not one to be easily deterred. He immediately sent a telegram to Ottawa and was able to make an appointment with Sir John A. Macdonald, and he and Duncan travelled immediately to the country's capital."

"Sir John A. Macdonald—the Prime Minister, was he not?" My reading of history was showing its usefulness, and I was suitably impressed by the Pierces' determination. Mrs. Pierce meanwhile continued her story with the air of one confiding a piece of momentous information, which no doubt it was, especially to her family.

"The Prime Minister, though he did not have time for a conference himself, introduced them to Sir David Macpherson, the Minister of the Interior. No sooner had they all shaken hands most civilly than the Minister asked about Captain Pierce's middle name, Michell. So it was that the Captain and Sir David discovered a good friend in common, none other than Brigadier Michell."

I wondered nervously whether I should also know the Brigadier, for I did not. Mrs. Pierce let it pass.

"After a few reminiscences about that excellent fellow, Captain Pierce was able to explain his hope to make part of our homestead the site of a town. This interested Sir David very much. He excused himself to speak to the Prime Minister. Before long, Prime Minister Macdonald had arranged what is called an *order in council* and opened the area for the filing of homesteads, but only for twenty-four hours."

"Oh my," I said, "so little time. But what gratifying attention on the part of the Prime Minister!"

Mrs. Pierce nodded. This was undoubtedly the response she had sought, but she also sighed, possibly reliving the hardships of that time.

"It must have been very trying for you," I said, "waiting to hear what would transpire, not knowing what to expect."

"It was—difficult—but my two girls helped to keep my spirits up."

"Two girls—did you not mention *four* daughters and four sons—what happened—?"

At this point Mrs. Pierce was silent. I suspected she might be weeping and regretted having been the unwitting cause. When I leaned over to pat her hand, she attempted to smile. After a time, she was able to explain that one dear daughter, Annie, "had succumbed to typhoid fever"—perhaps contracted during the ocean voyage—soon after the family arrived in Toronto. Because there were rumours of a more widespread typhoid outbreak in the city,

Captain Pierce insisted they send their youngest daughter, Frances, to live temporarily with relatives of the family in Buffalo. Mrs. Pierce's recent loss had made her desperate to keep all her dear ones close to her; however, she reluctantly agreed.

"It must also have been a great trial to be separated from your husband and sons," I said, anxious to demonstrate my sympathy.

"Indeed it was. The Captain wished us to stay where we were until he had built us a proper house, but the children and I would have none of it. We chose to brave blizzards and frigid weather for the sake of being together."

"So you followed immediately?"

"Yes, though we stopped three months in Winnipeg, with our friends Captain and Mrs. Tinning, who had immigrated to Canada some years earlier. My precious Frances took the train from Buffalo to rejoin us, and in January, it was convenient for Duncan to come to Winnipeg and take us home. Spencer Page accompanied him, as he had business in the city.

"Spencer Page?" Had I already heard this name?

"He would become my son-in-law," said Mrs. Pierce, proudly. "An educated man—with political ambitions. He met our Frances in Winnipeg and was immediately smitten."

How easily such things were accomplished. I also found it interesting that of the three sisters, Mr. Spencer Page chose the youngest as his object. But then, I reflected with chagrin, this was often the case. Men were illogical. Older sisters had taken time to develop the ladylike and domestic arts, and they certainly had a broader knowledge of the world, which should make them better companions. Still, men tended to choose younger sisters—*for their bloom*—and, it often seemed, the younger the sister the better.

With this reflection on the mysterious ways of men came an unwelcome thought. It struck me that some part of my attachment to Mr. Frederick Corby might have been gratitude—for he had chosen me over my sister. Penelope was but fifteen years of age when he first started to call, so it is possible he had never seen her as a romantic possibility—presumably that is what he had considered me—yet I had been foolishly grateful, and that troubled me. It was neither a happy glimpse of my relationship with my only sister, nor of my own character.

The garrulous Mrs. Pierce may have been conscious of my sudden distraction, for she paused in her description of the trip from Winnipeg to Moosomin.

"Oh, please continue," I said. "You mentioned that it was a one-day journey?"

She nodded, then declared with evident satisfaction that it was "late at night, blizzardy and bitterly cold, 48 degrees below zero"—a temperature I could scarcely imagine—when the train arrived at Fourth Siding. Cold as it was, the family had spent a comfortable night at the town's new hotel, and I was glad to remember that she and I were also to overnight there.

That first winter, the Pierces and Mr. Page travelled the last leg of the journey in the company of the same Scottish guides who had escorted Duncan's party the previous spring. It was January, what they soon learned was the coldest month of the Canadian winter. Furthermore, the winter of 1882-1883 was particularly harsh.

"When we finally gazed on what Duncan described as our new home," said Mrs. Pierce, "we were convinced the guides must be in error or Duncan was playing a trick on us. There were no buildings, only a huge mound of snow. Then our men-folk emerged, one by one, like moles, from the mound. They were scarcely recognizable and wore ugly, evil-smelling clothing: fur caps with ear flaps, fur-lined mitts, heavy overalls and boots and jackets made of raw skin."

Mrs. Pierce stopped to shudder at the memory, while I gasped in sympathy at the scene she had painted.

"It did not take long, however, for us to appreciate the need for such unlikely garments. We women had no proper outer wear and, consequently, spent most of the winter underground, unable to venture out for more than a few minutes at a time. Even the men sometimes had difficulty getting in and out, as snow would drift against the doors during blizzards, and then they had to make a door in the roof to get out to feed the horse and to clear paths and doorways."

It was truly a daunting picture, and again Mrs. Pierce must have read my feelings on my face.

"Oh, yes, I admit it. Whatever charm there might have been in these rough accommodations soon waned, though we tried to keep up our spirits. Fortunately, after that first difficult winter, conditions improved. We managed with a tent through the spring and summer, and in the fall, our *Great White House*—large enough for a family of nine and a total of six agricultural students—was ready."

"Agricultural students—?"

At this point in her story, Mrs. Pierce paused again and looked at the timepiece pinned to her bosom.

"Oh, my," she said, "it is time to dress for dinner, and we mustn't be late."

I could understand her urgency, since her previous indisposition had meant missing the opportunity to dine at the captain's table. For my part, I could have foregone the pleasure and was disappointed to have her story end. Not only was I touched by the family's adventures and their desire to be together, but I wanted to know what came later. Had Captain Pierce's dream truly captured the imagination of the Prime Minister and caused him to take a special interest in the community? What form did that interest take in the building of the town? It seemed I must wait for the answer to those questions.

Chapter 5

-

ALSO ON THE VOYAGE

We saw little of Mrs. Pierce's son Ted, though he was our official escort, except at dinner. I had learned from his mother his reason for travelling back to *the old country*—it was the first time I had heard England, my home, described thus, though I was to hear the expression frequently in the future. Apparently Mr. Ted Pierce had been responsible for a large shipment of live beef cattle from Cannington Manor to Glasgow, Scotland. Since he had also been commissioned to purchase livestock while there, and he and the new stock were to take the English route home, it had been convenient for Mrs. Pierce to travel part of the way with him in order to visit friends and relations. And so it was that I had the opportunity to accompany them both.

In answer to polite inquiries from the ship's captain, Mrs. Pierce retold much of what I had already heard. In addition, I learned that the oldest son, Mr. Duncan Pierce, now lived on an "Indian" reserve in the Qu'appelle Valley, where he was secretary to the "Indian" agent. Harvey, the Pierce's second son, had moved back to Toronto, having been much impressed with that city during the family's brief stay a decade before. Two daughters—not only Frances, but Jessie as well—were married and settled in Cannington Manor, while the eldest daughter and the youngest son still dwelt at home.

Mrs. Pierce did not mention the marital status of her sons, but Mr. Ted Pierce, whatever his situation, would not have fluttered maidenly hearts, possibly because he paid them no attention—at least, he paid *me* no attention. However, he shared his mother's fierce devotion to Cannington Manor. From their descriptions, one might assume their community offered all possible beauties of flora and fauna, combined with pure air, unlimited space, opportunities for investment and, of course, *the best kind of society*.

This measure of loyalty was perhaps not surprising, since the Pierces must ensure the legacy of father and husband. Not only had Captain Pierce founded the community, but he had also been mentor to a large number of young Englishmen who came to learn Western farming methods at his Agricultural College. In time, some of these young men registered their own homesteads, becoming members of the community in their own right.

I was moved by the Pierces' devotion to their cause, though many of the names they mentioned meant nothing to me. I did, however, feel somewhat put upon when Mrs. Pierce asked more than once about *my* situation, curious to know the length of my visit with the Humphrys, and finally asked directly whether I was *unattached*. When I admitted my status, she promised to introduce me to the two or three young men on board who shared our destination.

The Captain cleared his throat, I flushed and dropped my fork, the steward replaced it, and she went on as if there had been no interruption.

"Ted and I always make a point of meeting other passengers," she explained, "since there are farmers in Cannington Manor who continue in Captain Pierce's footsteps and take on agricultural students."

So little was I interested in the young men she offered, however—no doubt most of them must have seen fewer than twenty summers—that I was tempted to invent a suitor, merely to still her matchmaking efforts. It is not that I was disinclined to marry—as

I have indicated, spinsterhood was not a choice—but neither was obtaining a husband the purpose of my visit, and I found her efforts more than a little embarrassing.

I might have been gratified had Mrs. Pierce's own son shown an interest in me. Though he was tallish without being distinguished and tended to baldness—surprising in one not much my senior— he seemed energetic and had a certain air of authority about him. Furthermore, as my cousin Mary would have said, it is better to have admirers—even those whom one does not want—than to have no admirers at all.

As it turned out, Mr. Ted Pierce was not only married, but also a father, so I was glad I had paid him no more attention than he had paid me. Moreover, his passions seemed limited to his own farm, his late father's fledgling community and the town's Moose Mountain Trading Company. As he told the captain and company one evening, the store had been formed in 1884 and had a number of worthy investors. I then remembered that Mr. Ernest Maltby, my cousin Mary's fiancé, was part owner of the store.

It was not until later that I discovered the village of Cannington Manor was even then at a crossroads. The death of its founder and a series of failed crops resulting from late thaws, drought, prairie fires or hail *all* had dealt their blows upon the community. Most importantly, the fact that the railway's trunk line through the village—which the Pierces were convinced had been promised by Prime Minister Sir John A. Macdonald himself—had not materialized was yet another sign of hard times ahead for the whole English experiment.

Chapter 6

-

WE REACH OUR DESTINATION

As I have said, I managed well enough for the 12-day passage (which the captain told us covered 2,660 miles of ocean), as I was somewhat accustomed to travel by water. After all, I had spent part of a summer with the Humphrys family on their houseboat ten years before, not to mention semi-frequent crossings from England to the continent with my own family. Perhaps because of this experience, I found the barren ocean vistas, the dipping and rolling of the vessel and its various squeaks, swells and whistles quite calming, even cleansing. The sensation of leaving my old life and sorrows behind—at least for a time—and of having new worlds open before me was tangible, even as the expanse of ocean between the ship and my home grew daily.

In time, we reached Halifax, were disembarked, recorded as immigrants, citizens or visitors and received into various waiting rooms. There was no opportunity to survey the town, as—typical of most port cities—there were few places unescorted ladies could walk without courting impudence or even more dire consequences. Mrs. Pierce and I had only each other for company, as Mr. Ted Pierce was too much occupied with transferring his livestock from ship to train to attend to our edification or entertainment.

Neither can I say I enjoyed the trip overland. Train travel for short jaunts is all very well, but very confining for long distances. Rocking along those rails day and night became an ordeal long before the end of our five-day journey: first, from Halifax to Quebec City; then through miles of forests with only occasional lakes and rocky outcroppings to break the monotony; and finally, across the flat treelessness of the prairies. Though I had had my fill of barren landscape and uncomfortable seating arrangements long before the train pulled into Moosomin, the worst was yet to come.

It was near midnight when we reached the ramshackle collection of tents and temporary houses—or so it seemed to me at the time—of what the locals still referred to as Fourth Siding. Because of the resources that had been available to me through my women's reading group, I knew the town's present appellation was very recent. It was, in fact, a tribute to a heroic "Indian" chief who had refused to fight against the Great White Mother during the recent troubles between the *Métis* people—those of French and Native ancestry—and the Government of Canada.

As promised, we had an adequate rest in Moosomin's only hotel, a wood-frame building of some size and consequence, and in the morning we were invited to take our places in a caravan comprised of several wagons of various kinds, pulled by teams of either oxen or horses. There were as well several of the squeaky contraptions they called "prairie schooners" or "Red River carts."

At first I was puzzled by this means of travel—whether passengers could not have been accommodated in a more comfortable fashion—since I had learned there was now a daily stagecoach from Moosomin to Cannington Manor. Of course the stage served other communities as well, so its route would have been less direct. The most important consideration, however, seemed not to be *our* comfort but that of the quantity of supplies and livestock the Pierces were bringing back with them. I later regretted blaming the unfortunate livestock for my discomfort, as it turned out many of the creatures, including a prize Shorthorn bull, a boar and two sows, each of the latter with a litter of piglets, were on their way to my uncle.

Such a cargo obviously could not be accommodated by stage-coach. Therefore, we joined the supply train to the shops and businesses of Cannington Manor; at least I expected shops, and Mrs. Pierce and her son did nothing to disabuse me. My aunt, they playfully informed me, would be fetched home in her own carriage when she returned from England, but they had not such affectations. Given this information, I was bound to keep my counsel if I had expected any such concession. I, therefore, allowed myself to be wedged in beside Mrs. Pierce—who was not of slender proportions—on the high seat of one of the wagons.

On the other side of Mrs. Pierce was the hired driver. Swarthy and taciturn—so much so that I avoided glancing in his direction—he paid little attention to his passengers throughout the trip. He was, however, conscientious about the well-being of the various barrels and boxes that were also in his charge. Perhaps he anticipated some fit reward for the protection of this other cargo.

If I had looked more closely at the wagon's contents, I would have realized the bulk of what was being conveyed was for the benefit of farmers, carpenters, hotelier, miller and blacksmith. There was, for instance, a millstone, and fifteen cases of whiskey (marked "Proprietor, Mitre Hotel and Resting House")—these no doubt would have interested our driver. Even the numerous boxes and barrels labeled *Moose Mountain Trading Company* would have only a limited selection in the way of fabric, notions, imported foodstuffs or other items designed to soften a woman's lot. As it happened, there was also a crate containing two dozen Church of England prayer books and finally, several barrels of dried fruits, sacks of potatoes and other root vegetables, plus two cases of claret, the latter destined for Humphrys House.

Meanwhile, Ted Pierce continued to take his responsibility for the livestock very seriously, though travelling with them might mean he would not reach the village until the next day. In fact, while Mrs. Pierce and I were partaking of our breakfast at the fine new hotel, her son and a number of other men had been attempting to load the Shorthorn animal into one of the wagons, but the animal had balked. It seemed he too had had quite enough of uncomfortable travel arrangements. Furthermore, though only a little over two years old, the animal was large enough that there could be no arguing with him. Finally the men anchored him securely behind one of the slower wagons, which was pulled by a team of oxen. Since oxen travelled at a more lumbering pace than horses, these wagons would possibly spend the night at one of the stopping places along the way.

Mrs. Pierce seemed not at all troubled by this change of plans. To my surprise, since she had been such a bad sailor, she appeared to do very well overland. As soon as we were underway and had left Moosomin behind us, she began to point out the beauties of the landscape. I, on the other hand, could see little but a rutted trail in a sea of mud, tall grasses and uninspiring bush, all of these bordered by an upside-down bowl of mercilessly blue sky. Twice in our journey, we were forced to climb down from our uncomfortable perch and walk to lighten the load, so men and animals could negotiate the mud.

In other particularly boggy parts, we encountered what Mrs. Pierce called "corduroy" roads, where poles had been laid side-by-side and two or three layers deep to give wagons and hooves some purchase in the muddy patches. For passengers, the result was such a bumpy ride it might have been preferable to walk. I, however, could not be comfortable with either alternative, as I had already discovered my shoes and other attire, considered sensible at home, were pitifully unsuited to my surroundings.

We also encountered a valley and a river. This was the Pipestone Creek that Mrs. Pierce had mentioned before—though it seemed more than a creek or stream to me. Though not overly wide, it was deep enough at this time of year that wagons must be hauled across on a makeshift ferry. I watched in wonder as the Red River carts were quickly stripped down to become miniature boats themselves. The oxen and cattle, including the Shorthorn animal, had to wade or swim, with their snouts pointed carefully at the sky.

It was late that night when our caravan reached the end of our journey. Mrs. Pierce had nodded off against my shoulder, and I was so numbed by weariness and the constant bumping and rocking of the wagon that I scarcely comprehended our moment of arrival. Gradually, however, I realized everything had creaked to a halt. For an instant, I felt the enormous silence of this vast, strange country and was overcome almost to the point of tears.

Then the clamour rose up even louder than before. Voices shouting, horses and men grunting and the crunch of heavy objects on solid ground all indicated the unhitching and unloading had begun. Mrs. Pierce was now awake and our monosyllabic driver—who turned out to be William Page, brother of her highly educated son-in-law—stricken apparently with a belated sense of gallantry, scrambled to the ground in order assist her descent.

At the same time, hands touched my elbows, and as I looked in that direction, I felt a flutter of surprise when a man's arms slid around my waist and lifted me without apparent effort or ceremony out of the wagon. Responding I suppose to that surprise as well as to my weariness and the constant motion of the day, my knees immediately buckled under me. I was forced, therefore, to cling to the warm, rough shirtfront of this stranger, and to suffer the strength of his arms, until I was steady on my feet. In that moment I caught the dusty but not unpleasant smell of a working man and sensed as much as saw his blue-eyed gaze upon me.

Then my cousin's sweet face and dark eyes appeared and put him out of mind. "You must be exhausted, my dear," she said.

I nodded, running my hands clumsily over my dusty face and straggled hair. My hat had fallen askew many hours since, and my mouth was too dry to speak. I let Cousin Mary take my arm and lead me away.

Though it was still a distance of some two or more miles to Humphrys House, I had no recollection of that journey, as I spent it dozing against Mary's shoulder. I did not remember having her brother Billy, now eighteen, but still a scrawny youngster in short pants when the family left England, presented to me. Neither did I register my introduction to Lionel Cuthbert, their blue-eyed hired man, though it was Cousin Billy and Mr. Cuthbert who conveyed us, along with numerous boxes, barrels and packages of domestic and farming supplies, to the Humphrys estate.

When the same man reached up and lifted me down from my seat, I was able this time to stand on my own as soon as my feet touched the ground. However, the memory of his brief glance from under the peaked brim of a well-worn woollen cap stayed with me rather longer than I would have expected or wished.

It was by then too dark to gain an impression of the exterior of Humphrys House, though the front door was bright with welcome. Once we were inside, I trailed after Mary down a long hallway, up two seemingly endless flights of stairs and down another hallway. This one bordered an opening to the main floor, rather like a loge or balcony at the theatre, and I felt a touch of vertigo again as I realized how close we were to the edge of the opening.

Finally reaching what was to be my room, I was touched to see the commodious accommodation set aside for me, no small accomplishment for such a large family. There was also warm water in the wash jug, one of Mary's bed-gowns laid out on the patchwork coverlet and a hot water bottle beneath the covers. I was numbly grateful for all these things, for the room was surprisingly chilly after the heat of the day.

When I had washed my face and hands, Mary helped me into the bed-gown, tucked the soft sheets and blankets around me and kissed me on the cheek. I could not remember having been treated with such tender care since I was a small child and still attended by a nurse.

Chapter 7

-

FIRST IMPRESSIONS

Waking the next morning, my first at Humphrys House, I felt some soreness in my joints, as could only be expected, considering the rigours of my journey. In spite of that, I was in good spirits, perhaps due to my cousin's kind ministrations of the night before. The activities of the previous day also offered much to occupy my mind, and I could have dallied even longer in my cosy nest of quilts had I not been curious to see the estate in daylight.

First, I scanned the chamber where I had been sleeping. It seemed a regular shape, solidly built and, I noted, of larger dimensions than our guestrooms at home. There, the bedrooms on the second floor were fitted into the slant of the roof, with ceilings low to accommodate the maids' rooms in the attic above. Even the second-floor sitting room was cramped, and the nursery and school-room that survived my childhood and that of my sister were pokey, angular rooms now essentially unused. My father's house was also of sprawling construction; rooms and even wings had been added as needed over several generations, with no overall plan and little attention to real comfort and convenience.

Humphrys House, on the other hand, was built to my uncle's own plan, and much of it had the same pleasing proportions as the room where I had spent such a comfortable night. When I became accustomed to the interior balcony, I found the house as a whole more appealing than other houses I had known, for the shape and regularity, as well as the views from various rooms, seemed a testament to my uncle's training as a ship-builder. As such he would have been able to fit many small enclosures within a solid shell, without their looking and feeling cramped. He also knew the value of space and the importance of comfort over long journeys—at least for ships' officers. Though I was to discover that not all the rooms in my uncle's house were finished to the same degree—the third floor, for instance, had the appearance of a project started and forgotten—the ambitious scale and high ceilings gave a feeling of spaciousness even there.

As the official guest room, mine must have received particular consideration. It was, as my cousin had told me proudly when I followed her graceful form up the stairs on the previous night, *a pretty room*. The morning light through the south-facing windows touched the rose-papered wall with a warm glow, and a froth of sheer curtains softened the effect of heavy drapes. The sills were deep and crammed with potted geraniums. The floorboards must have been recently oiled, for they too glowed in the early light, while colourful braided rugs inhabited convenient positions on that polished floor. One close to my bed was worked in green and rose, and in front of the tidy commode table with its basin, water jug and looking glass: was another, in green and white.

When I noticed steam rising from the jug, I realized it must be later than I had thought. The family—or at least the maid—would be up and about. (I naturally assumed the presence of a maid and that it was she who had brought the water for my morning ablutions.) I also thought that person responsible for fetching my travelling cases, which were piled neatly just inside my door, and beside them, the woebegone footwear I had abandoned last night, now freshly cleaned. Along with these observations, I finally comprehended that I had been hearing voices—mostly female, but occasionally male—for some while.

I didn't want to appear a laggard on my very first day, so I pulled back the bedclothes and planted my bare feet tentatively on the bedside rug. Before I made use of the warm water, however, I could not resist peering outside. From my window, I saw the bright green of grass and thickets of young saplings—aspen, I thought, newly in leaf, though it was already May. Other leaves had a darker hue—perhaps maple or lilac—were there lilacs in this country? How lovely for my cousin to marry in lilac time!

I could also see, beyond the fringe of trees (none a great height), wide stretches of black earth where sod had been broken. These must be fields newly-planted or waiting to be sown, unless they had some other purpose, for they seemed to encircle what I could see of the yard. And beyond the cultivated areas were undulating meadows, which I was now disposed to see as beautiful and possessing infinite variety, since they were part of this domestic setting. Already I had forgotten the barren expanse of the previous day, the miles and miles of rippling grass and slightly rolling hills that had seemed so unfriendly under that blazing dome of sky.

In an easterly direction—if I judged correctly—and as far to the left as I could spy from my window, there appeared to be a series of pens for domestic animals or fowl. These no doubt extended beyond my vision, and there would possibly be stables and other outbuildings as well, none of which I had noted on the previous night. I saw no actual livestock from my present vantage point, though both domestic and wild creatures might have been present in the meadows in the distance.

Surely each window in the large house would present a new scene. In my eagerness to explore, I regretted my promise to return to England at the end of June. Because my time would be short, I was filled with determination to learn as much as I could about this unfamiliar terrain and vibrant civilization before the end of my visit. I also hoped to prove I was no *fragile English rose*, in spite of my less than stalwart performance the previous night.

It so happened that the scene before my eyes was not comprised entirely of trees, fields and fence-rails. Two or three masculine persons rounded a corner of the house and appeared to be having some manner of conference not far below my window. I thought I recognized my uncle, though he was clad—most democratically—in his shirtsleeves, with casual hat and vest; the other two were slighter in form and might have been my cousins, but I could not be sure. I drew back into the shadow of the draperies, not wishing anyone to behold a figure at the window in only her nightgown. Even with these precautions, I feared I might still be visible, so I moved away from the window altogether, though reluctantly.

When I had washed myself in the now lukewarm water, scented with a few dried rose petals, I selected my simplest waist and skirt—I didn't wish to appear overdressed. Descending the main staircase, I followed the sound of voices down the hallway and found my cousin Mary in the kitchen. Observing her, I discovered I was still overdressed. Mary, busily clearing up after the breakfast and supervising one of her younger sisters in the setting of bread, was wearing a plain wool skirt that seemed a patchwork of several pairs of gentleman's worn wool trousers. For her bodice, she wore what must have been a man's shirt, with the cuffs rolled up and threatening to reveal her elbows. Her hair was also loosely dressed, a dark tendril or two falling onto her collar, and her cheeks flushed from the heat of the kitchen.

She looked girlish and charming, but also a little unkempt. To tell the truth, I was embarrassed for her as I understood a loosening of concern for appearances generally led to a certain laxness in other matters. Anxious to think no ill of my cousin, I surmised that some proprieties might be relaxed in the colonies. After all, we three women were alone in the kitchen, and no gentlemen except her father and her brothers would be observing Mary in such disorder.

I also remembered belatedly the name of the cousin who was starting the bread. She was called Nettie by her family, though her actual name was Janet.

My assumption that only members of the family were in the vicinity almost immediately proved to be false. The kitchen door opened without a warning knock, and a young man entered who was not a brother to Mary and Nettie.

"You will remember Lionel Cuthbert," said Cousin Mary. He apparently was the man of the night before, the very one who had lifted me from the wagon and steadied me when I was momentarily too dazed to stand. I was mortified to feel my face heat up as I recognized his light-coloured eyes and sandy moustache and remembered how I had accepted the comfort and support of his sturdy body. Not wanting my flush to be misconstrued as pleasure, I stepped back a little and lifted my chin.

For his part, Lionel Cuthbert stepped forward. He tugged off his woollen cap, revealing a crest of thick, sandy hair and a line of white forehead between it and his sun-burned face. His rough appearance and attempt to close the gap between us was imposition enough, but after a mere moment's hesitation, quite without invitation from me, he went so far as to thrust forth his right hand in welcome. For an instant, I looked at the strong, square palm he was offering and was nonplussed. Because of his apparent connection with the family, I did not wish to ignore his gesture completely, though it was obviously what he deserved. Finally, I settled on a small nod to acknowledge him but encourage no familiarity. He must be the son of simple country folk not to realize it was a lady's prerogative to initiate such a greeting.

When I ignored his outstretched hand, Lionel Cuthbert's cheeks reddened until they matched the sunburned neck above his collar-less shirt. It was his turn to draw back, and he did so with exaggerated dignity. Though he was not tall, certainly not as tall as Frederick Corby, he straightened what height he had. I also noticed that Mary and Nettie had been watching this little interaction with interest, and Mary found it necessary to put her hand on Lionel Cuthbert's arm and smile at him in a sisterly fashion.

"Thank you again, Lionel, for fetching and carrying for us last night. I often worry that you neglect your own acres for our sake, and yet we could scarcely manage without you. Will you sit at least and have another cup of tea?"

"No, Miss, thank you." Lionel Cuthbert lost his stiffness when he looked at my cousin. He had a mellow, not ill-bred voice, with a hint of a brogue, and his expression was both fond and respectful. In fact, his gentleness almost made me regret my own cold response. After glancing quickly at me and my younger cousin, perhaps to ascertain if he were intruding, he continued.

"Your father has remembered your mother's rose garden, but not where she had a mind to put it. It seemed a good time for breaking ground, as I'm about to plough the east meadow."

"Of course," Mary began. Then she hesitated, seemed uncertain, started again. "I believe I remember my mother's wishes," she said, "but the laying of the flower beds should be up to Nettie in Mother's absence. After all, in less than a month I am no longer under my father's roof."

As she said this, Cousin Mary's colour—even considering the heat and bustle of the kitchen—seemed heightened, and Mr. Cuthbert's no less so. Nettie was now seated at the table, much befloured and resting her head on one hand. At the mention of gardens, she spoke up quickly.

"Oh, Mare, you decide. I have no notion. And Mother and the others don't much care. It's only you and Daddy who think about gardens."

Mary bent over her sister and gave her something between a shake and a hug. "I too wish Mother were here to organize these matters for herself, but she won't be pleased if you let things fall apart. What will happen to you all when I'm gone? You mustn't expect to dine at my house every night of the week."

Nettie grinned back at her. "Maybe Cousin Florence will stay on and look after us until Mother returns from Gran's."

I gasped a little at this, and Mary beamed at me over her sister's shoulder. "That would be nice, wouldn't it? But we should perhaps let our cousin know us better before we ask such things of her. I'll help Father with the rose garden, you silly thing—since you find it so difficult."

Mary then untied her apron and was draping it over the back of the chair when she remembered my breakfast. I insisted I couldn't eat a bite, though my first good night's rest in over two weeks had actually given me a healthy appetite, and I had already looked in vain to see what was offered. No matter. I could wait. I did not want to miss out on any adventures, and this process of cultivating flower gardens promised to be one.

Chapter 8

-

A LOVING FAMILY

As I followed Cousin Mary out the kitchen door, which appeared to be on the west side of the house, I marvelled that this Lionel Cuthbert and my cousin talked so freely together. Who was he to the family? His manner did not suit my idea of a farm labourer, and yet he seemed to be in my uncle's employ.

Because there was a slight self-consciousness between the two of them, I was also bound to ponder my cousin's feelings for him, and his for her. He was undoubtedly well formed, with that romantic hint of Scots in both appearance and voice. This could place him as a refugee of the Scottish potato famine and enclosures or a transplant from Upper Canada. I also understood that many Scots had made their homes in the Eastern Provinces, because of the similarity between its rocky coast and their homeland.

Were he from a wealthy family, though this seemed unlikely, he might be one of the "remittance men" of whom my father had often spoken—younger brothers and ne'er-do-wells sent to the New World to make their fortunes, but still dependent on regular postal notes from home. Somehow, because of Mr. Cuthbert's manner, which seemed both modest and independent, this too seemed unlikely.

Whatever his origins, I could not but be struck by his appearance. He didn't have Frederick Corby's fine height and elegant bearing, but his facial features were pleasant, and he carried himself with a plain, manly dignity. If Lionel Cuthbert were, in fact, well bred, Mr. Ernest Maltby must definitely be a superior sort to have won Mary's heart away from such a comely fellow.

As I accompanied Mary and the mysterious Mr. Cuthbert across the yard to where my uncle was holding a horse harnessed to what I supposed must be a plough—I had never seen such an implement at close quarters—I could not avoid observing the young man's face in several animated expressions. (My cousin walked between us, so my gaze was turned quite naturally in his direction.) I noticed again that his eyes were very blue, while his eyebrows and eyelashes were dark. It was an arresting combination, and I hastened to look away periodically, for fear that I was gazing too intently.

Fortunately, the awkwardness of the arrangement was short-lived. We soon reached my uncle, who gave up the horse's reins to Mr. Cuthbert and greeted me in a manner appropriate for an uncle.

"Uncle James!" I cried enthusiastically as I was folded against his waistcoat, cheek pressed against his rather dusty beard.

"Little Flossie," he chuckled and held me at arm's length. What he beheld I could only guess, as looking glasses have given me little help in forming a clear impression of my appearance. They show me a rather colourless young person both shyer and more graceful than I imagine myself to be, rather like a captured doe. My uncle's regard, however, was more generous than either looking glass or my own family.

"Very pretty," he said. "Far too pale, but don't worry; we'll get you out in this prairie sun and repair that."

"Father, we'll do no such thing," protested Mary, taking my hand protectively. "We'll put her under a hat immediately. That fair skin will burn the colour of Lionel's here if we're not careful."

I was blushing from all the attention which caught Lionel Cuthbert's eye in spite of myself. He too was observing me, though not with Mary's kindness nor my uncle's admiration. I felt chastened by the coldness of his expression and turned quickly back to my uncle.

My uncle's skin too was reddened by the sun—that which I could see of it, since much of his face was covered by his beard. Judging from his appearance and manner, I would have said he was happy, prosperous and full of life, even though ill health had prevented his coming into town himself on the previous evening. Suffering as he did on occasion from gout, he often found it difficult to ride or walk long distances. Still, if my own father had seen his evident vigour and enthusiasm, he could not have spoken so easily of "that wastrel, Jim Humphreys."

When I regretted aloud that I wasn't able to give my compliments to Aunt Jane, my uncle looked distressed, so I didn't pursue the point. In fact, my aunt's absence and Mr. Lionel Cuthbert's coldness were the only flaws in the perfect tableau. Though Mary had obviously adapted easily to running her father's household and looking after her younger siblings, I wondered if my aunt was frailer than I remembered. Or did her absence have some other significance? Was she perhaps unable to share my uncle's enthusiasm for the adventure of living in this largely uncharted country? From what he and Mary had said, it was already obvious my uncle poured most of his waking hours into either civic responsibilities or farm enterprises, and they appeared to be many.

It was he who had given the handsome book on horse husbandry to my father, the very book that was displayed on the desk in the drawing room at home and had so interested both Mr. Corby and myself. The book's owner, however, seldom looked at it without a snort of derision. Though kind enough to his daughters in the little he saw of us, my father was not—I regret that I must say it—a man of generous instincts.

"Does Humphrys now plan to go in for horse breeding as well as his pork-packing pipedream and his market gardens?" my father had scoffed. "It's no wonder your sister must spend so much time courting your Aunty Peg."

My mother had sighed. She did not take part in these rants of my father against her family, though neither did she defend her sister and her sister's husband. As I was fond of the Humphrys family, this hurt me, but what indeed could my mother say? My father was a rich man who had married her in spite of a dowry that was less than what he might have expected. Neither had my mother made any efforts to invest and therefore increase her assets since her marriage. In fact, there was no need. Still my father seemed to resent the possibility that James Humphrys might gain where he did not. What a relief it was to be free of both my parents for a few months!

When I had finished my exchange of greetings with my uncle, Mary again praised Lionel Cuthbert and Cousin Billy for meeting the supply wagons on the previous evening. Then she seemed to remember the reason for our stroll and led the way through grass somewhat in need of the scythe to a spot ten yards or so south of the house. As she walked, she talked with her hands, drawing the specifications for the rose garden in the air. Fortunately, my uncle and Mr. Cuthbert appeared to have no difficulty understanding her, and I too found myself imagining the finished product with pleasure. Again she protested that she should not have the responsibility for it, as she would not be around to tend it.

"Perhaps you should not be so hasty in giving any garden away," said my uncle teasingly. "'Tis likely the only one you'll have to enjoy this season. Unless you have already bullied poor Maltby into planting his wee acre in town to satisfy you."

Mary's glance caught mine, and her expression told me she had not overlooked that detail.

Soon our entourage had reached the chosen location. Though he limped a little and favoured his gouty leg, Uncle James had tucked my hand in his arm in as courtly a manner as any drawing-room gallant. I was so touched by the gesture I ignored the possible damage to my cambric sleeve from its contact with his rougher, work-soiled woollen. In fact, I would not have thought to resist him. He was my uncle, after all.

My uncle seemed desirous of including Lionel Cuthbert, who was bringing the team and plow along behind us, in the conversation. In doing so, he made a remark that was obviously well intentioned, but no doubt as discomforting to Mr. Cuthbert as to me.

"We'll be only too happy to have another young lady to squire about the country, won't we, Lionel?" he said, "especially after the defection of our Mary."

Mary was the only one who laughed besides my uncle, and even she evidenced a slight discomposure, though no doubt for reasons more complicated than mine. I was by now convinced a romantic attachment or possibility of the same had existed between her and Mr. Cuthbert, though perhaps long before Mary brought her Mr. Maltby to the point.

My uncle continued in a more serious tone, but like the good stockbreeder he was. "The sad fact is there are never enough healthy and pretty young Englishwomen in a rural community such as this," he said. "Our town won't be established properly unless our young men settle and start families. Already there are rumours of new gold strikes in the Klondike, and that will lure our lads away for sure unless they have a strong inducement to stay."

"Father," said Mary, hands on her hips and darting an anxious look at me. "You mustn't treat poor Cousin Floss" (no one but Mary and her family ever thought to shorten my name, and I rather liked it) "as if she were some likely heifer on the auction block. She is here for my wedding and to experience this lovely country for as long as she likes. If she finds other projects that interest her, so be it, but we must not burden her with our concerns."

Then Mary turned to smile at the man who was bringing up the rear of our procession. "Besides," she said, "some young men will make up their own minds about such things. Here is Lionel, for instance. He won't be marrying *or* following after some gold rush unless it is his own idea."

"Aye, that's right enough," said Lionel Cuthbert distinctly, and again I thought I saw something peculiar, even knowing, in the look that passed between him and my cousin.

My uncle held out a hand to his eldest daughter, while keeping mine tucked beneath his other arm. Mary came warmly to his side and lifted her lovely cheek for his kiss. "Oh, Mare," he said, "what will I to do without you? You with your good sense and loving heart."

I shot another glance at Lionel Cuthbert. He too was watching the embrace between father and daughter, and on his face I read something like the yearning I felt in my bosom. If only Mary were free and his situation more independent, I thought. Then he could make an offer where his heart was obviously leading. To my surprise, this flickering thought caused me a foolish and totally unwarranted twinge of loss.

Chapter 9

A MAN OF MYSTERY

As Uncle James, my cousin Mary and I stood back and watched, Lionel Cuthbert prepared to start his ploughing. I watched with interest and some nervousness. Not only had I never been so close to a plough, but neither had I been so close to a horse of this size. It was larger than a dray-horse, most likely one of the breeds of draft horse pictured in my father's illustrated book, yet it was one thing to look at such a large animal in a glossy drawing and quite another to stand in close proximity. I took yet another step back from the horse's magnificent haunches.

Mr. Cuthbert and my uncle had earlier attached the plough to a contraption of wood, rattling chains and leather that were attached in turn to the horse's harness. Mary had named some parts of the harness, but there were too many for me to recall all of them. Now Mr. Cuthbert adjusted the long leather reins or "lines," which were fastened on each side of the "bit." My uncle had already pointed out that this piece of molded iron with a ring on each end went through the horse's mouth and was attached to its halter in much the same way as the bridle on a riding horse, though this seemed to be of sturdier construction and size.

Up to this time, the lines had been looped over Lionel Cuthbert's arm, but now I noticed that the ends were actually knotted together. Mr. Cuthbert dropped this knot over his head and across his shoulders and back. Next, he planted the blade of the plough into the sod at the corner of the patch Mary had selected. Finally, he clucked to the horse and threw his weight down on the implement just as all the straps went taut and the implement started to move. The result was a tufted ribbon of black earth spilling out beneath his feet. When he had gone about fifty feet in one direction, he yanked the reins to stop the horse, tipped back the blade of the plough, reset it, and then finally turned the horse so he could cut a furrow back in the direction whence he had come.

The rows seemed admirably straight, perhaps a special effort because there was an audience, but I found my eyes drawn even more to the man himself. When his back was turned and our eyes naturally focused on him, it was rather easier for me to take his measure than it had been at any time previously.

I noticed, as I had before, that he was of merely average height. Neither was his breadth imposing—in fact, he appeared to be rather on the thin side, since his trousers billowed about his legs as he moved. His shoulders, however, were broad, broader I think than Mr. Corby's, for all that the latter gentleman was considered such a fine specimen. I had also noticed Lionel Cuthbert's forearms; these were also sun-burned, and corded with deep veins, bared when he pushed up the sleeves of his shirt and combinations before starting to plough. It gave me an odd sensation to observe Mr. Cuthbert's forearms.

By the time he started ploughing, Lionel Cuthbert's brimmed cap was clapped on his head again, pitched forward somewhat over his brow to protect his eyes from the sun, revealing the sandy hair at the nape of his neck. The fact his hair was somewhat in need of a shearing did not detract from the agreeable picture he presented. Not only was he well proportioned in both face and frame, but he had a sturdy vitality in his bearing that was even more appealing. He and the horse seemed fortunately matched, strength against strength creating the physical tension necessary to do the job, with the plough prying up the earth between them.

It was with some regret that I finally turned my eyes away from the team of man and horse. Mary had linked her arm in mine, and we started back to the house with my uncle. I was deep in thought. It had occurred to me that while I had always found Mr. Frederick Corby's height and bearing acutely agreeable to my eyes, I had never seen him engaged in any physical activity other than riding and dancing. Furthermore, in recent months—before his defection to the Bentley-Kydds—even the exertion of hunting to hounds had increasingly given way to sitting at table and exchanging port and pleasantries with my father.

My uncle soon departed from our threesome, as he was overseeing the raising of a large stone building to the east of the house. This could have been either the barn and piggeries or the pork-packing plant, since he had mentioned all of them. When Mary and I were alone, she seemed to withdraw as well, and I wondered whether her distraction had as much to do with the comely Lionel Cuthbert as with her impending marriage. Not wanting to encourage any such folly, I initiated some conversation myself.

"How long does my aunt remain in England? It seems particularly unfortunate if she shouldn't be here to see you wed."

Mary sighed. "There's no chance of that now," she said. "It was rather expected that her elderly relative—that everything could have been settled before this—"

Slightly embarrassed, I wondered if she had forgotten for a moment that the relative and relationship to which she referred was one we had in common. A moment later, I was certain she had forgotten.

"But Aunty Peg was never one to consider anyone's convenience but her own. I must admit this constant need of my family for funds, which means Mother must be at Aunty's beck and call to stay in her good graces, can be frightfully awkward."

Not only had this confession caught me by surprise, but I also felt complicit because she revealed so much. In a moment, however, perhaps regretting her frankness or remembering to whom she spoke, she hastily cheered herself and continued in a far more buoyant manner.

"Let us talk of happier things. You will know our worries soon enough. Do you not admire our Lionel? My father and the boys—all of us, in fact—quite dote on him. Had I not already too many brothers—not to mention sisters—I think my father would adopt him!"

This playful speech did not suggest she harbored an ill-considered romantic attachment to the person described, therefore, I did not change the subject again, and she coaxed me into admitting Mr. Lionel Cuthbert was not unpleasant to look at and seemed strong and capable. I did not mention that I had noticed his fine features and the earthy grace in his movements, nor even that his concentration on his work made the picture he presented even more attractive. Mary obviously found my response lacking and turned her teasing gaze full on me.

"Pleasant? Capable? My cousin is stingy in her praise. Why, our Mr. Cuthbert is not only the bonniest man, but also the best farmer in these parts, and we are very fortunate to have him working for us. Of course, my father had hoped our advertisement would have brought us a young man from England—one whose parents could pay a premium, you see, to settle him in a good situation. As you have possibly heard, not only the Pierces, but also the Pages and many of our other neighbours, have agricultural students. Such a premium would have been welcome in our present circumstances."

My face must again have registered my concern, for Mary shrugged and smiled in a way that would deny the existence of any need.

"Lionel himself makes up for the loss of a premium, of course. He is a Canadian—from Upper Canada—so he has experience of farming in this country. When he can take time away from his own homestead, we offer him slim wages—little more than meals and a bed in the bunkhouse. Yet my father says he is worth three of any others he could hire or has hired. My brothers work hard when they put their minds to it, but this kind of work is still strange to them."

I was about to ask what sort of family Lionel Cuthbert had back in Ontario, what class of people they were, but Mary had less sensible things in mind. "All the misses in the county, from Fourth Siding to Grenfell at least, are casting sheep's eyes at him, but Lionel will have none of them, except . . ."

(Here Mary lowered her voice.)

"My parents thought for a time he might be responsible for our Nurse's trouble, him being so bonny and she known for teasing the lads . . ."

Another mystery. I vaguely remembered the family's nurse. "Didn't your family have a nurse by the name of Ruthie Ford . . .?"

"The same . . ."

"And is she—compromised?"

Mary nodded.

"Not . . ."

Mary nodded again. "With child," she said gravely, though her face was less serious than might have been appropriate in such a circumstance. She actually seemed to take delight in my horrified expression.

"Almost at her time," she added.

"My goodness," I said in a feeble voice, too overwhelmed to ask what seemed the obvious question.

Fortunately Mary offered the information without my having to inquire. "It turned out the man in question is a widower with children who also worked here for a short time. Naturally Mother made Father let him go—but he's been less than a gentleman about it. Says he is a poor man and can't afford to marry poor Nurse, has difficulty caring for the children he has. Would that he remembered his circumstances before he took advantage of her warm heart and lively spirit."

Mary's face became serious for a moment before she continued.

"Indeed, she was a great comfort to all of us when we first arrived. While we hardly knew how to manage, Nurse could find the humour in anything. But now we must keep her—and the baby—until McClure does his duty and Ruthie is recovered from her lying-in and able to travel to his homestead near Pipestone Creek. Father is certain the man will relent in time, but until then, that's more mouths to feed."

"My dear Mary . . ." I began in some dismay. I'd had no idea the family was experiencing such financial and domestic hardships, and I was not sure her parents would want such information general knowledge. Not only that, but I was keenly aware of being yet another drain on their economy while I stayed with them.

"Oh," Cousin Mary blushed and quickly contradicted herself. "I just mean that it's a worry. One mouth more or less does not make a great difference."

At that moment, however, I resolved not only to earn my keep, but also to see if there was anything else I could do to ease the family's burden.

Chapter 10
-
VIRTUE LOST

We were back at the kitchen door by now, and Mary turned to me and put her finger to her lips. "Nurse may be about," she said, "though she keeps as much as possible to her room. She still does all our mending and sewing. And keeps us in cakes and pastries—which, in my opinion, is a very good exchange for her keep."

As it happened, we found the woman in question hovering over a cup of tea at the kitchen table when we entered the house, and I was surprised to see how much Mary Jane Ford (known as "Ruthie" or "Nurse" by the family) had changed. Though pretty still, she was no longer the carefree young woman from the Humphrys' nursery back in England. The earlier Ruthie had seemed girlish and playful, but I too had been young when last I saw her, in one of a series of Humphrys establishments. (The fact that the Humphrys never stayed long in one place was one reason my father gave for disapproving of my uncle, but I had never before connected these changes to financial stress.)

As I have said, I was young then. And so was Cousin Mary, who must have escorted me to the nursery to see whatever baby was the newest member of the family. While Aunt Jane tended to the baby, the spirited Ruthie diverted the other young ones with various games and plays. For this task she was admirably suited, since her lively manner made her appear not much older than her charges.

How different was her situation and appearance now. Not only was her uniform rumpled and worn, but she seemed in low spirits—understandable considering her unfortunate condition. When we appeared, she heaved herself to her feet and seemed about to hurry from the room.

My eyes were drawn in spite of myself to the bulge camouflaged only slightly by her apron and shawl. I knew very little of childbirth, since it was never discussed at home and I remembered little about my sister Penelope's arrival. There had remained only the impression that my mother spent her waiting time reclining, either on the settee in the morning room or in her chambers, where I can remember visiting her only once. I was banished on that occasion because I misbehaved. First I wriggled and pouted, then I cried because my mother wouldn't stir herself to play with me. Finally, when I was taken back to the nursery, I screamed and kicked out at my own Nurse.

After Penelope's birth—which must have been a difficult one, since it justified my mother avoiding repeat performances—I found my mother too much occupied both with my sister and with her own health to give attention to me. I was, after all, at that awkward age of five years: all bony angles in place of baby curves, earning scrapes and bruises from my desire to explore the world, yearning to be heard yet too young to put words to my needs and ideas. In fact, there was little about me for my mother or anyone else to find appealing. Even my Nurse, the one I went to for comfort during those anxious years, complained of my restlessness and found greater satisfaction in caring for my baby sister.

Neither had I the compensation of a closer relationship with my father. I have already mentioned that he was not a generous or particularly discerning man. If he too felt banished by my mother, he used it as an excuse to avoid all domestic attachments, including his children. It is possible—probable, in fact—that he found solace elsewhere, but he was discreet, and his household was not disturbed. All I noticed was that my parents avoided each other except on public occasions and for the most part avoided their children, though in later years, my mother and sister have discovered interests in common.

For all these reasons, I had a lonely childhood and thought myself unlovable as well as unloved. Any admiration I earned in later years for my physical attributes caught me by surprise and simply made me even more awkward than usual, though I yearned for a lover who would find me beautiful and awaken my love in return. For a time, I thought Frederick Corby was to be that lover, until he too had shown himself less than devoted.

So, at the age of three and twenty, I was unschooled in love and little understood the physical aspects of marriage and childbearing, though my awareness of my own innocence frequently made me blush. I was unable to fathom how my cousin Mary could make light of Ruthie's uncomfortable condition or gaily anticipate it for herself, as she appeared to do.

Now, Mary smiled kindly at the woman and put a hand on her shoulder. In spite of being the younger of the two—Nurse must have been around thirty years of age—my cousin naturally assumed the role of benefactress.

"Do finish your tea, Nurse," she said. "There is no need for you to spend all your time in your room."

Ruthie looked from Mary's face to mine and then back again. Finally, she dropped her gaze to the floor and sniveled, "But Miss, your mother . . ."

"She was upset . . ."

"She said I shamed my family."

"It was the surprise of realizing your condition. And she was distressed—for your future and that of the child."

"You and your father have been so kind." Ruthie sighed deeply, as if she were grateful, but not yet comforted.

"And so have you to us. All these years . . . Letting us take you so far from home."

"Where else would I have gone? And with Master James a baby.

But now I'm ruined, Miss. I don't know what will become of me."

Cousin Mary patted her shoulder again. "Dear Nurse," she said, "you mustn't go on so. We've talked about all of this before. My father will speak again to Mr. McClure. No doubt he will come for you after the baby is born and you are both well enough to travel. Until then, you know you have a home with us."

"Oh, Miss," Ruthie was again heaving to her feet, "I beg your pardon . . ."

"Well, hurry then . . ."

The woman then sidled away, her hand hidden in her apron, just below the mound in her middle.

"Is she all right?" I asked in some alarm.

"Oh dear, yes—poor thing. She just needs her chamber pot. The child presses against her—well, you know. In a minute, I'll take her tea and a scone, when she's had a chance to tidy herself up."

In fact, I had no idea what might be pressing on what, but judged it not a question I should ask. Again Mary was confidential. "The whole business threw Mummy into quite a tizzy, you know. She was sure nothing like this could have happened in England. And now she wants all of her daughters out of harm's way as soon as possible."

"Out of harm's way?"

This time it was Mary who blushed. "Safely married," she said.

I was suddenly emboldened on the subject that interested me most. "What does your mother think of Lionel Cuthbert? Of having him . . . almost as one of the family?"

"Oh, that. I always intended to marry Maltby. Things just sped up considerably is all."

And whether that mystified me further or answered my question, I was not sure.

Chapter 11

SOCIAL OBLIGATIONS

With so much to see and hear—all the sights and sounds of the country, not to mention the stories the family seemed compelled to share, that first day at Humphrys House passed quickly for me. By mid-afternoon tea, I was grateful to Cousin Mary for suggesting I take a nap.

"I notice your eyelids drooping, Cousin Floss, and shudder to think how you must have suffered over all those miles. Whenever my mother travels, she is shut up in a darkened room for days. . . You needn't make any heroic efforts for us, you know."

"Has Aunt Jane been back to England on more than one occasion, then?" I asked.

Mary sighed, as she seemed inclined to do whenever my aunt was mentioned. "On one other occasion, but she sometimes accompanies Father to Moosomin as well. And this business with Nurse rather spoiled her leave-taking this spring, which probably made the trip that much more difficult for her. She seemed very low in her first letters back to us. And I know my father is anxious that all be settled quickly, that there may be no more heartaches for her. Poor mother has had a rather bad time of it here from the first . . ."

Yet another mystery it seemed.

I didn't ponder it long, however, as I had scarcely removed my skirt, waist and stockings and loosened my stays before I was overtaken by sleep. This was unusual for me; I seldom took to my bed in the afternoon, though it was a practice of which my own mother was fond. At home, with the rest of the household abed, afternoons had always been a time of uncustomary freedom, when I could explore and imagine worlds beyond what I knew.

Usually, I had spent my afternoons in my father's library, discovering volumes of Dickens and Hardy, Sir Walter Scott and the Rev. Mr. Jonathan Swift, even Miss Mary Wollstonecraft—though she was not considered proper reading for a young lady. Many of these volumes might not otherwise have been opened, and I sometimes wondered how they came into my father's possession—perhaps from the same great aunt responsible for my legacy. My mother had no interest in reading and seldom entered what was my father's domain. Furthermore, the books that most appealed to me were far too democratic for my father's taste, so I could not discuss them with him.

"Who wants to read about dirty children and thieves and fallen women?" he would snort from his place at the head of the table. "The poor will always be with us, and the poorhouse tax is imposition enough."

"Yes, my dear," my mother would agree, nodding for the maid to remove her half-finished plate of supper or tea. "If they just did a good day's work among them, I would be more inclined to sympathy."

I was never certain when she made such comments whether my mother meant the poor or our illustrious British writers should do a good day's work among them. Neither could I resist wondering if my mother had anything beyond a vague notion of what qualified as "a good day's work." Though her father, my shipbuilding grandfather, had made his own way, by most definitions she had little experience of work herself.

Naturally, I didn't express such un-filial thoughts to either of my parents. While they were lax with their daughters in some ways, I had no doubt impertinence would be punished. In fact, I remembered evenings spent imprisoned in my bedchamber—evenings I would have been without supper if it had not been for the secret intervention of soft-hearted maids and nannies—as a reward for a saucy tongue. The fact is, as I have already indicated, I had few friends in my own family and little freedom to argue against the *status quo*.

When I awoke from my afternoon nap on my first day at Humphrys House, I chided myself again for my laggardliness. With so much to see and do—and so little time before my return to England—how could I waste precious minutes in sleeping?

There were sounds of activity from below and the fragrant smells of cookery. Soon I thought I heard light, womanly footsteps on the stairs, undoubtedly those of Cousin Mary, since they entered the room next to mine. I could hear her rustling about for several minutes.

Much as I did not want to miss anything of importance, I swung my feet out of bed with some reluctance. There was so much comfort in staying where I was. Yet I had scarcely touched my bare toes to the braided rug when I heard a tap at my door.

For an instant, I was uncertain what to do. My stockings and shoes were where I had left them in front of the dressing table; my hair was loose on my shoulders, and my stays untied and twisted oddly around me. It would have been wiser to take leave of them entirely, but that had seemed quite wanton in the middle of the day. All in all, it would take several minutes to create any semblance of decorum about my person.

Another tap and the door opened. I gasped, instinctively covering my bosom. Mary beamed at me from the doorway. "My dear cousin, you needn't start so. Though you do look enchanting, and it's a shame you have no husband to surprise you in such disarray."

"Mary . . ." I gasped. "Please . . . the door."

"Oh, yes, of course, my modest darling." She entered the room and closed the door behind her. I noticed that she was already attired for dinner and looked quite fine. Her hair was neatly dressed;

her linen skirt and bodice were light in colour, as suited a warm evening, and she had pinned a small cameo at her throat. This she fingered as she bent to check her reflection in my looking glass.

"To celebrate your coming," she said, smiling into the glass with apparent satisfaction, "we have planned a dinner party on the lawn. It looks quite festive, though I suspect you may find the actual fare rather humble for your taste."

She turned back to me with a rather appraising eye and continued. "Make sure you choose something pretty, as there may be a gentleman or two eager to escort you—not to mention our Lionel and my Mr. Maltby. Dr. Hardy, alas, could not come. He is a favourite of the whole family."

Dr. Hardy was not someone she had mentioned to me before, and I wondered if there was any significance in her doing so now. Then I chided myself for my vanity. It was simply her playful manner of speaking, and I mustn't read anything into it. Indeed, the doctor had already been forgotten as she went on.

"We also invited the Pierces," Mary was saying, "since they were your close companions on your voyage. But they were otherwise engaged. I cannot say I am disappointed, as Mrs. Pierce can be something of a rattle."

I smiled at the aptness of her description and enjoyed the feeling of being conspirators, though her confidence went only a little way toward dispelling my nervousness. Knowing there might be at least one young man of interest sharing our meal made me uneasy. Besides being something of an oddity in my parents' house, I was not as a rule at ease among strangers. In fact, Mary was one of those rare souls with whom I felt comfortable.

It was typical of my cousin that she countered my confusion of feelings by being practical and offered to help me get my stays and other undergarments in order. She even chose my costume, suggesting I did not want to appear in the same dress for the evening as in the morning. She put aside my two best supper gowns, saying I should save them for a finer occasion, and finally settled on a linen frock of a pale lemon colour with a wide cloth belt.

I thought with amusement that her suggestions were somewhat reminiscent of her father's, though she had scolded him about wanting to put me on display. For my part, I tried to dwell on my duty to my cousin and kinship, but it would have been difficult for any maiden not to feel a flutter of expectation in her breast after such preparation. I was far from being a hardened woman of the world immune to masculine attention.

When Mary had assisted me in my toilette even so far as to suggest cotton stockings—since the tall grasses were wicked on anything finer—and to hand me my garters, she pronounced me a virtual English rose and led me to the landing. Walking downstairs arm in arm, we might have done justice to the children's tale of Snow White and Rose Red, with my complexion so pallid and she healthy and glowing in comparison. Of course her glow, like my pallor, could well have had its cause in the presence of the gentlemen below.

In due course I extended my hand to the three gentlemen who were assembled in the drawing-room, but Mr. Maltby had the honour of being first. Mary showed him a marked preference, and I thought that boded well for their felicity in marriage. Another gentleman was named Mr. Arthur LeMesurier, who was slight in stature and courteous, but in other ways unremarkable. And there was also "one of the famous Beckton brothers"—those were Cousin Mary's words. Which one he was, I immediately forgot, though later I had occasion to remember. For the moment he interested me only because of Mary's stories of the wealthy sporting family, not because his face or physique was in itself distinguished. Curtseying to these gentlemen, I felt Mary had chosen the most sensible of the three.

Mr. Earnest Maltby was tall and thin, with a pleasant face and courtly manner, though he tended to slouch his shoulders deferentially when speaking to anyone shorter than himself. He asked with great correctness about my journey from England, saying it was a good many years since he had spent much time in the "old country." However, it was there he had met Mr. Robert Bird and learned of business opportunities in Canada.

"Mr. Maltby was previously in India, where he spent many years working for the British government and perfecting his tennis," supplied Mary, with a mischievous glance at her fiancé.

He smiled in response but said nothing, making me wonder if he was somewhat overwhelmed by her wit. There was an obvious difference in their ages; he seemed well over thirty and she not yet two and twenty, but such a difference was not unusual. In fact, most believed marriage to a somewhat older man a steadying influence on a young woman, especially if she were prone to willfulness—though I would not have applied such a description to my cousin Mary. Rather, she seemed perfectly in control of her situation and managed to combine playfulness and poise.

Moving towards the chair Mr. Maltby had graciously offered, I noticed there were yet two more gentlemen in the room. They were engaged in conversation and had apparently failed to rise when we entered the drawing room simply because they were unaware of our presence. Now they amended their behaviour, and for all Mr. Maltby's crisp appearance and courtliness, I could no longer say he was the handsomest man in the room, for I now recognized Mr. Lionel Cuthbert. He too was outfitted more formally, having donned a fresh shirt, jacket and collar for the occasion, though it appeared they did not suit him. Even as he rose and gave us a slight bow, he was twisting at his collar.

My cousin Ernest, who had been his partner in conversation, came across the room to greet me. I did not remember Mary's older brother well, as he had been a sullen, studious youth, inclined to either avoid ladies or to scoff at what he called their *silliness*. Though enlisted to work for his father at the Barrow Shipyards when he was still quite young, he had also studied music.

Since this cousin and I were almost strangers, I was grateful he showed no inclination to embrace me, but merely expressed pleasure at our meeting again. His complexion too was ruddy and his manner vigorous. This raw, unspoiled country seemed to enhance the physical attributes of all its inhabitants. I smiled at Cousin Ernest and said I looked forward to being reacquainted.

"There are more than enough of us to remember," he replied, "though we're three short of our number at present—Freda, Jimmy and Mother."

When we were all seated about the room, Mr. Beckton was the first to speak up. "How is your mother faring?" he asked of Mary. "I had hoped to dance a reel with her at your wedding."

"Since we are not Didsbury, I doubt our drawing-room can accommodate a reel," answered Mary. "As for my mother, she is unable to return in time."

I felt there was a hint of reserve in my cousin's voice as she continued. "Her relatives are unwilling to part with her and her aunt so ill she cannot be refused." Clearly Mr. Beckton was not considered family and should not presume too much familiarity.

Mr. Beckton, however, was apparently not easily put off. "Has your cousin heard the story of your mother's introduction to this house?" he asked.

Mary frowned slightly rather than answering his question. I also saw her shoot a warning glance at Cousin Ernest, but if he saw her, he paid no heed.

"The mater's first introduction was to the cellar," said Cousin Ernest to me. "It had to do with a special piece of equipment, a barometer and thermometer built into one case, which father had brought across from the old country when he went back to fetch the family. To keep it safe during the trip, they had wrapped it in blankets and kept it propped upright all the way over.

"Having given so much care to its safety, the mater's first thought when she crossed the threshold of her new home was to find a place to hang it. With it in her arms, she walked across the kitchen to what she supposed was the pantry, opened the door, stepped in and promptly fell right through to the basement. The fall knocked her senseless for a full hour. Naturally, the barometer fared even worse."

"My poor aunt! Did she suffer any permanent injuries?"

"Fortunately not," my cousin Mary interjected quickly, perhaps not trusting Cousin Ernest with the response. "Except a certain willingness to believe our family is dogged by misfortune. Of course, our father does his best to cheer her with all his plans, and especially his successes."

Cousin Ernest seemed to give a derisive snort at that, but I must have been mistaken. He could not have had so little respect for a parent.

Chapter 12

DINNER PARTY ON THE LAWN

At that moment, the parent in question appeared in the doorway. It seemed Uncle James was catering the evening himself, assisted by Cousin Nettie and Cousin Dora. The two younger children, Noel and Cicely, had already eaten in the kitchen and filed in to say good night. They were to go to the nursery to read or play until bedtime, under Nurse's supervision. The older boys, William ("Billy") and Francis ("Frank"), would join us as soon as they were changed, since they had just finished their chores.

Seen altogether, the Humphrys must be a family of daunting proportions, as Cousin Ernest had said, and many accomplishments. Though I resolved to make myself useful by taking some charge of the younger ones during my stay—on the morrow, I would firmly attach the proper names to faces for all present members of the family—I was actually relieved the youngest weren't there on my first evening. Not accustomed to children, I had always found their constant chatter and tendency to leap about quite distracting. The younger Humphrys were no doubt good-natured and accommodating when at their best, but I imagined that the extended absence of their mother must make them insecure and therefore noisy and quarrelsome.

It was when I thought of the children that I first considered extending my visit, if it were convenient for my uncle, and I rather expected it would be. Nettie had already hinted at such an arrangement, so perhaps they had even discussed it among themselves. In truth, I had chosen to depart a week after the wedding with little understanding of the time and effort involved in travelling such a great distance. It also seemed rather a large expense for such a short visit, and I doubted my parents would protest a longer stay. Perhaps I could provide a little stability during what would be a period of adjustment for my cousins, since Mary had been surrogate mother for them during Aunt Jane's absence.

The loss of Mary was not to be the only change in the household. A new maid was coming from England within a fortnight. My uncle had undertaken the engagement of Miss Martha Pritchard as a special treat for my aunt, but the young woman would arrive in time to help prepare for Mary's wedding. She would also take over some of the household duties formerly assigned to Ruthie Ford. In the meantime, poor Nurse's future was still uncertain. Though Mary and my uncle were confident the scoundrel in question would yet be persuaded to make an honest woman of the former nursemaid, I could not imagine that her position was a happy one, and my brief sighting of Ruthie had confirmed this impression.

On this first evening of my visit, however, my Uncle James appeared to have forgotten family hardships and intrigues and played his role as both host and butler with considerable flourish. Following his lead, we processed in style through the house. Mary took first place, of course—on Mr. Maltby's arm. Both Mr. Beckton and Mr. LeMesurier offered me a bow and the crook of an elbow. Since my cousin Ernest, whose prerogative it would have been, had neglected to offer me his arm, I took Mr. Beckton's invitation. For all that she led the procession, Mary missed nothing and turned to cast an arch look on me, which I affected not to notice and, as it turned out, entirely misinterpreted.

Mr. Lionel Cuthbert, I presumed, would follow somewhere in the rear, but I did not glance back to see if that were the case.

We walked from the drawing room and through the dining room, where fine French doors opened onto a view of the lawn, and a covered porch extended along much of the south side of the house. This, I supposed, would be where Cousin Mary and Mr. Maltby would greet their guests for the wedding breakfast, here or in the wide front hall.

In fact, as I had noted before, there were—thanks to the imagination and shipbuilding prowess of my uncle—many unusual features to the house, most of them attractive. Its first advantage, perhaps, was its size and the convenience of having large receiving rooms. In England, many homes were tall, narrow and close together, especially in the towns and cities. Such homes abounded in staircases and many small, inconvenient rooms.

Other English homes were converted cottages, charming certainly, but seldom distinguished in their aspect. True, there were still some larger country houses and estates, such as my father's and those of our immediate neighbours, but they were fewer and fewer because of the encroachment of industry, and not all of them were beautiful. The Humphrys' property was more like the finest English country homes, with grounds expansive enough to accommodate many other gracious aspects, such as the future rose garden and arbor.

My escort commented on this potential. "It's a fair prospect," said Mr. Beckton. "I'm not sure we could boast of a better, even at Didsbury."

I merely smiled in response. Not having seen the Beckton estate—though I was curious about it—I could have nothing to add. Fortunately, the gentleman required no reply and seemed content to admire the view. In fact, the whole procession had halted as if of the same mind. As we stood on the porch, I noticed the air had a fresh, grassy sweetness, something I would come to associate with these prairies of the North West. I also mused on how sufficient rest and a day of pleasant discoveries had increased my own appreciation for such a scene.

I pondered as well the importance of enhancing without destroying the natural beauty of country living; the rose garden, when it was in bloom and not just a patch of broken sod, would surely be such an improvement. The same could be said of the vegetable gardens that framed the rough lawn on the south and south-west of the house. I wasn't certain the tennis court beyond honoured the same principle, but clearly there must also be room for recreation, especially with a house full of youngsters.

At that moment my uncle approached us, and Mr. Beckton took the time to say he regretted "the other beggars" had been forced to send their regrets and that "Florrie" didn't do much these days except lie about with her feet on a stool. No one, however, enlightened me about Florrie's identity or condition at that time. No doubt they assumed I knew. When I had accepted the same Mr. Beckton as my escort to dinner, I thought he was a bachelor simply because no one had mentioned a wife. When I later discovered my mistake, I hoped this original assumption had not somehow been reflected in my behaviour towards him.

Mr. Beckton also regretted that "old Hardy" was not to be there. "Hardy always has some tales to tell," he said.

My uncle nodded politely and then turned to me, "I too am sorry the doctor isn't here to meet you, but he is much in demand. I can't think how we managed without him." I presumed my uncle at least was talking of Dr. Hardy's medical prowess and not of his gifts as a storyteller. However, this second mention of him made me even more curious about someone so generally respected and popular.

Mr. Beckton seemed disposed to be generous. "And we owe his presence almost entirely to you, Humphrys."

"You are too kind," said my uncle and then drew my attention back to the scene. "What do you say, niece? Has your father such a garden stretching before him when he dines?"

Though he was obviously commenting on both the natural world and his own innovations, I suspected the garden might be better developed in his imagination than in reality. The dining arrangements, however, were delightful. Before us was a long table that hadn't been there earlier in the day and a smaller serving table. The dining-room chairs looked only slightly out of place on the grass, and both tables were covered with white linen cloths. These cloths had heavy brass candlesticks to anchor them at both ends, for there was still a mischievous breeze afoot. In fact, I had already noticed there seemed at all times to be some measure of wind ruffling or even buffeting whatever lay in its path.

I smiled at my uncle and replied with all the appreciation he could have wished, for the garden party set against a background of budding trees and grass and sky was indeed an enchanting sight. "I have never seen anything quite like it," I said.

"A lovely setting for a wedding breakfast, do you think?"

"Yes, lovely. Perfect."

I did wonder, however, about the provision for inclement weather. Though both the drawing room and the dining room were of goodly proportions, I doubted the dining table could accommodate more than thirty, even with two or three extensions, and there would almost certainly be a shortage of chairs, especially if children were included.

We had now stepped off the porch and moved towards the table itself. I enjoyed the pull and swish of the long grass against my skirt. At the same time, it was soft underfoot, and I wished Mary had chosen not merely cotton stockings for me, but also more sensible footwear, since the heels of my slippers sank into the earth with every step.

Meanwhile, the bride-to-be was directing the guests to their seats. I could have foreseen a problem, considering the over abundance of men, but she had no qualms about seating two men side by side. She herself would grace the foot of the table, facing her father at the head. On her right was Maltby and on her left, her oldest brother, giving her the opportunity for a light jest about being surrounded by Ernests.

I was to be on my uncle's right, with Mr. Herbert ("Bertie") Beckton beside me. To my surprise and consternation, I heard her place Lionel Cuthbert directly across from me, on my uncle's left, with her brother Billy next to him. I knew it would be difficult to maintain my composure in such an arrangement, especially since I found myself blushing the very first time I met Mr. Cuthbert's eyes across the cloth. This was as my uncle, who had stepped ahead of Mr. Beckton, held my chair for me.

All down the table, my female cousins were being shown a similar courtesy. When we were comfortably settled, the gentlemen sat as well, and I hazarded another glance at Lionel Cuthbert. He was not smiling, nor did he speak, though again he gave me a slight nod. I would have no occasion to fault his manners in the future—that I could see. Neither, it seemed, would I have occasion to feel his friendship or approval—and I was surprised to discover that this mattered to me. He looked away again, as Mary was speaking.

"Father, this is exquisite; I would have just such a meal for my wedding. But do we not have any wine?"

"I do have some claret," responded her father, and I felt his sadness that he could not offer more. "But I had rather thought to save it . . ."

"Oh, please do save it," broke in Mr. Beckton. "We have had far too many spirits lately at the old place."

I presumed he referred again to the legendary *Didsbury*, which Cousin Mary had already described to me at length. According to Mary, the Beckton house, the grandest in the neighbourhood, was built of grey-blue stones from nearby creeks and had been completed only a few years ago—so Mr. Bertie Beckton was being more than a little affected in calling it "old." Mary also said the house was obviously designed by men with bachelors' tastes. Its billiard room apparently adjoined a smoking room, with space for unexpected guests above—perhaps those who were too intoxicated to go home—and the whole west wing was known as "The Ram's Pasture." The wing had been built for the younger brothers in anticipation of the first bride, the former Jessie Pierce, being installed in the main house by the eldest (another Ernest).

According to Mary's description, not everything about the house reflected exclusively bachelors' tastes, since it also boasted a good-sized ballroom, a conservatory, a mahogany staircase, French doors and many gothic-styled windows and gables. In all, again according to Mary, Didsbury House was very elegant and designed to *look* costly; in that way, it was quite unlike the Humphrys' "spacious and practical family home."

The Becktons were also unlike the Humphrys in that they employed a large number of servants and had been able to hire a good deal of labour, both skilled and unskilled, in the building of their home and various outbuildings. I wondered whether their ready money gave them rather an unfair advantage over their neighbours when it came to getting things done. Perhaps this was what Mary had meant when she had described the Becktons as the bane of the community as well as the making of it.

However mixed her feelings about the Beckton family and their advantages, I knew Cousin Mary took part in the hunts organized by the Becktons. I hoped to have an opportunity to visit Didsbury myself, as I had always enjoyed visiting fine houses. Not only were they beautiful in themselves, but they provided so many insights about their inhabitants. Perhaps it was this interest in Didsbury that had influenced my choice of Mr. Beckton as my supper escort, though I was less willing to be impressed by him as the evening progressed. Would the house and the estate be similarly disappointing? I wondered.

While I mused on these things, Mr. Bertie Beckton rattled on, offering a long tale about the drinking and dancing and late hours kept at the wedding of his elder brother in September three years previous. There had been no celebrations since to equal it, he said, and this comment earned him a thoughtful look from my uncle.

"Why, when we lads had emptied the Didsbury cellar," Mr Beckton said, addressing himself to me, but enjoying the attention of the whole company, "we applied to the Pierces. Now, Duncan Pierce, come home to be the head of the family for the wedding, is somewhat tight-fisted, nothing like his father in that way. So we had to sign a note for his bottles. Of course, by the time we had emptied the second cellar of its supply, we were more than a little intoxicated, and none of the ladies would dance with us. Is that not so, Mary?"

Though Mary smiled tolerantly at the speaker, my uncle was looking more and more distressed. I wondered whether he was feeling his claret punch would be a paltry offering in comparison or if he was troubled for some other reason.

Mr. Beckton had not finished his story, however. "So the evening ended with the ladies partnering each other inside the house and the men gamboling drunkenly on the lawn. And this went on, thanks to the music," he spread his arms to indicate both my uncle and my cousin Ernest, "into the wee sma's."

Those indicated nodded their thanks.

"A few of us may not have made it home to our bunks that night," Mr. Beckton went on. "Fortunately, the grass was soft, and the house has a good supply of extra beds. It was a warm night for September, and I seem to recall sleeping on the grass myself. No doubt it was John Hardy stretched out next to me, as he's a man that can out-drink the best of us."

My young cousin Frank, obviously getting caught up in the spirit of Mr. Beckton's tale, though he cast an anxious look at his father, chose that moment to establish that he had been of the intoxicated party. "I slept in the wagon," he exclaimed. "When Ernest found me asleep on the grass, he tossed me in with the umbrellas and left me."

"And a good thing too," declared the older brother, who was close enough to reach around and give Frankie a playful cuff on the ear. "Why should we have you bringing such a display into the house?"

Frankie appeared quite crest-fallen.

Uncle James finally spoke up, though rather ruefully, "I was thinking to have a little claret punch for our Mary's wedding, not expecting to compete with the Becktons and the Pierces."

Mr. Beckton declared—rather belatedly, considering the tale he had just spun—that claret punch would be just the thing for him and repeated what he had earlier said, that there had been far too much drinking and carousing lately.

This speech was followed by an awkward silence. I wondered somewhat illogically where Lionel Cuthbert had been, whether he had been of the house party or the lawn party. But then I remembered he might not have been invited to the wedding party at all, not being one of the gentry.

It was also Mr. Beckton who introduced the next subject of conversation, the Beckton brothers' acquisition of some "Indian" ponies for their stables. With their speed and the bloodline from Jase Phillips, the Beckton's stallion, the brothers felt their colts would offer formidable competition on the racetrack. This subject appeared to restore the men who had found themselves in dangerous waters on the subject of spirits, and they wanted to hear again how Billy Beckton and Tony Purser, the Becktons' jockey, had traveled to Iowa to purchase the prize-winning stallion. Mr. Bertie Beckton was happy to repeat the details and to describe the Becktons' purchase of another horse, this one named "The Leper" because its bad temper made it virtually untouchable.

Meanwhile, the ladies were unable to take aught but a listening role. Horse breeding was something about which we knew little, not that I would have put it past Mary to venture an opinion if she had one. I did notice her whisper an aside to the Ernest who was her brother. He shook his head as if unwilling to take responsibility, and Mary then spoke to eleven-year-old Dora, seated between Mr. Maltby and Mr. Le Mesurier. Dora squirmed self-consciously and made a face at her elder sister, and I noted with an even greater amusement that Mary made a face right back. Again I reflected on the joy of being part of such a large, lively family.

The discussion of horseflesh continued to dominate the conversation for some time, as the gentlemen most involved in it (Cousin Ernest, Mr. Le Mesurier and Mr. Beckton) seemed oblivious that it might be an indelicate subject for the ears of young ladies. Most noticeably, the words "sire," "dam," "stud," and other breeding terms, were being used both explicitly and frequently. My uncle and Cousin Mary continued their half-hearted efforts to change the subject, but the speakers had too much the ear of the whole group for such attempts to be successful. Little Cousin Dora continued to be especially attentive and refused to look in her father's direction even as she resisted her elder sister's efforts to dislodge her from her seat.

For me, the conversation was upsetting for another reason. Whether it was the subject or the experience of being excluded, my thoughts were inevitably drawn back to Mr. Frederick Corby and the fateful discussion that had begun while we perused my uncle's book on horse husbandry. For the moment, I forgot the role that discussion had played in bringing me to my present felicitous surroundings in my uncle's garden, not to mention the many new experiences and feelings of the last fortnight. Instead, I allowed the pain and confusion of being rejected to overtake me even in this new and exciting place. Who was I, after all, but a visiting spinster, an observer only, who must return in time to the scene of her humiliation?

-

Chapter 13

A PAIR OF BLUE EYES

I suppose my disheartening reflections must have had some play on my face, for my uncle sought to know what was troubling me. Was the sinking sun in my eyes, or was there something amiss in the accommodations? As I shook my head, I suddenly noticed Mr. Lionel Cuthbert was also watching me intently. Because of his proximity, I was again struck by the contrast between his blue eyes and black eyelashes, a contrast rendered even more acute because of his sandy hair and ruddy complexion. These observations also brought me quickly back to the present, at the same time almost taking my breath away, so I was unable to respond immediately to my uncle's questions.

"Nothing is troubling me, nothing at all." What else could I have said? "I can't believe I'm really here," I added. "It's even lovelier than I imagined."

It seemed then that I had finally made a remark—or expressed my thoughts in such a way—as to incline Mr. Cuthbert in my favour. He nodded his head in agreement and may even have smiled.

"Aye, it's a fine country," he said and began to talk in a tone so low that it came across as confidential. The subject of his unexpected soliloquy was his family's farm in Upper Canada, near a town called Exeter. He seemed to feel some yearning for his old home and presumed—I suppose—that I too was nostalgic for family and friends. Though my momentary unhappiness had nothing to do with missing my home—I was so wholly engrossed in my new adventure—I would not for the world have denied him any assumption that allied us.

For a few minutes I forgot my reservations about his breeding and his possible romantic inclination towards my cousin Mary. Instead, I took pleasure in watching the play of late afternoon shadows across the bridges and hollows of his handsome face. The angles softened, I noticed, as the light faded, even while the shadows gathered and added mystery. In those shadows, I began to see a likeness to that famously indiscreet Scottish poet, whose name I had for the moment forgotten.

After a time, I noticed my uncle was also watching the transformation in Mr. Cuthbert's face and manner, and observing perhaps how engaged we were in private conversation. Fearing that my fascination was somehow unmaidenly, I strove to listen to and watch somewhat less intently. But still I warmed to his eyes upon me.

It is unlikely our *tête-à-tête* lasted more than a minute or two, with Mr. Cuthbert talking and my giving every appearance of feasting on his words. However long the episode, I do remember that the rest of the company seemed to fade away, until Mr. Bertie Beckton inquired about our subject.

Lionel Cuthbert stiffened in his chair. "I'm sure it wouldn't interest you, Beckton," he said, in a way that told me the two men did not like each other. Neither, it seemed, had Mr. Cuthbert any particular regard for class, and in this instance, I respected him for it.

"Come, now, Cuthbert," said Mr. Beckton. "Don't be a stuffed shirt with me. I'm not the first to notice your success with the ladies."

This comment seemed to silence the whole group. My eyes went quickly to Mary, but I could not see her expression. Yet, in spite of the fading light, I am certain Lionel Cuthbert coloured. He began to rise from his chair. My uncle, however, put a hand on his shoulder and actually pushed him back into his seat. "I have something special for dessert," he said, "if you will excuse me for a minute."

Mary nodded and nearly everyone applauded, so it seemed that whatever ill will had touched the group for an instant did not settle upon it. I dared not look at Mr. Cuthbert to see whether he too applauded, though I think he did not. After a moment he rose and, nodding briefly to me and then to Mary, followed my uncle to the house.

When my uncle returned bearing his delicacy, a delicious trifle pudding made with saskatoon berry preserves (it being too early in the season for fresh berries), as well as slivers of pound cake, vanilla custard and thick Jersey cream, Mr. Cuthbert was not with him.

The dessert portions were generous and left the younger gentlemen so sated it promised to be very late before they managed to wrench themselves from the table. I finally walked back to the house by way of the front door. Mary and Mr. Maltby were my companions this time, and I tried without much success to put myself a few paces in their shadow to allow them some privacy for their farewells. Every time I did so, they would pause to wait for me. Furthermore, when I opened the door, Mary apparently felt no need to linger; nor did her betrothed exercise what surely must have been his prerogative and kiss her cheek. Fearing this delicacy was exercised on account of my presence, I immediately said, "Good night," and stepped inside.

Mary was at my side before I had walked the length of the hall. "Dear cousin," she asked me without a scrap of delay. "What has happened to upset our Lionel?"

I must have shown some of my surprise at what I felt an unseemly interest. Why was Mr. Cuthbert and his concerns uppermost in her mind?

"I am sure I do not know," I answered truthfully, in a tone I hoped didn't encourage further speculation.

She still seemed reluctant to let me go. It was then she mentioned that all the Beckton brothers were married. "We asked them to ensure it would be more than just a family party," she said, "and

Bertie alone was available. Florence, his wife, is in the family way and doesn't go out much at present, so perhaps he was restless. We would much rather have had Dr. Hardy, but he must have been called out to visit a patient, as we could not find him."

She paused again and added in a thoughtful voice. "Perhaps Mr. Cuthbert didn't approve of Mr. Beckton appearing without his wife and paying you so much attention. Lionel is very particular about such things and might have thought to protect you from a bad influence."

Mr. Cuthbert wishing to protect me! I could not entertain such a thought in her company and begged her to please excuse me to her father and sisters and extend my gratitude for a wonderful day and a superb meal. Though she seemed not entirely satisfied with my response, she kissed me on the cheek and bade me good-night.

When I finally reached my bedchamber, I had the opportunity to contemplate the day's events in full. Upon reflection, I felt I had acquitted myself quite properly throughout the evening meal and neither said nor done anything to discredit either of my families—after all, Mr. Beckton had given no indication he was married. Nonetheless, I undressed and donned my nightdress with a keen sense of unease.

It was not Mr. Beckton who troubled me—him I could easily forget—but Mr. Cuthbert. What was the mystery of this young man and his relationship with my uncle's family? Why was he having such an effect on me when I knew his station in life was decidedly below my own?

My behaviour at supper may have been above reproach, but in my dreams it was not. And in those dreams, Mr. Lionel Cuthbert of the blue eyes and dark brows figured most prominently.

Chapter 14

DISTRIBUTION OF LABOUR
AT HUMPHRYS HOUSE

On the days following the dinner party on the lawn, I was grateful for the general activity of the household. Not only did it help to free my mind of troublesome imaginings, but I also gained new insights about the Humphrys family and about pioneer life in general. It would seem that Mrs. Pierce's stories of her family's hardships were less extravagant than I had imagined, since many were echoed by my cousins.

The first hardship I recognized was the absence of maids and other servants working quietly in the background. Nurse still did the sewing and mending, as Cousin Mary had earlier indicated. She also baked an assortment of cakes and puddings. However, her desire to be away from curious eyes and the general acceptance of this decision meant she could be counted on for little more, especially when she was working on wedding garments.

Therefore, it was vital everyone in the family took on a share of the work, whether the arena be domestic or agricultural, and I was anxious to do my part. I had never felt myself a fine lady when it came to my own needs—I had, for instance, bathed and dressed myself from the time I was a child. On the other hand, I had never before lived in a house without servants, or taken account of how many domestic tasks in a gentleman's household were accomplished largely behind the scenes. Nonetheless, I was confident that with my cousins' example before me, I should soon master all the consuming female occupations of the household.

Before long I realized this confidence was misplaced. None of these tasks—cooking and preserving, cleaning, laundering, ironing or sewing—was as simple as I had imagined. Not only did all of them require some skill—Mary and her sisters joked about their own lack of proficiency—but they were dependent on other tasks being completed.

To cook, one needed wood for the large kitchen range, water from a well or from some other source, and meat or game, either fresh or from the icehouse. Vegetables, when in season, were picked or dug from the kitchen garden. In the winter, they were found in storage bins or barrels, or on shelves in the cellar, and in May there were few fresh vegetables to be had, not so much as a handful of young lettuce. My uncle talked of starting a patch of asparagus, but he had not yet found the time.

Some home-grown vegetables from the previous year had been dried, pickled or otherwise preserved, and samples of these could still be found among the rows of large glass containers and earthenware crocks on the shelves in the larder. Also called the "pantry," this was a small windowless room just off the kitchen. Other foodstuffs, including essentials such as flour, sugar and tea, were also stored on pantry shelves or in kitchen cupboards.

Finding the various food components was only the beginning of preparing a meal. All utensils and work surfaces must be carefully cleaned prior to cooking, baking or preserving; otherwise, food could be contaminated and spoil before its time. However hot the day, one must also be on guard against the insects that hovered about windows and doors, not all of which had screens, as flies and various kinds of mites were known to carry diseases.

Mary and the others had their hands full maintaining this regimen of organization and cleanliness, and they admitted they sometimes didn't manage very well. Perhaps this is why everyone seemed to find his or her own breakfast, and not in the way to which I was accustomed. There was no sideboard of dishes from which to choose, though there was generally a large pot of oatmeal porridge on the stove. Other than that, those wishing to break their fast must rummage through cupboards and larder in search of bread, biscuits and jam or, occasionally, the remains of a pudding.

The noon meal also tended to be what was known as a "cut lunch", though for this meal, the bread, butter and other ingredients were generally laid out on the kitchen table. Instead of tea and a late supper, as was the custom in England, there was generally only one evening meal. Furthermore, only my uncle and my female cousins took the time to dress for supper or observe other evening rituals, though there were intimations that things were done differently when my aunt was at home. My male cousins worked at their outdoor tasks as long as there was daylight and were happy to stumble in at the end of the day and have their supper—like their lunch—in the kitchen.

After I had observed my cousins busily cooking and laying out the meals, I wondered whether I might be better placed helping with something more mundane such as the laundry. This job too involved many other tasks, such as carrying water and wood. Some of the water was stored under the house itself. At breakfast one morning, Uncle James had explained that metal troughs along the eaves collected the rainwater and melting snow into one downspout at the northwest corner of the house, a downspout that drained directly into the cistern. This innovation would have been very convenient if there had been a pump installed to bring the water up to the kitchen. This plan, however, had not yet been initiated.

In fact, I was not a little dismayed to learn that the water storage system, like other parts of the house, had been in the same state of incompletion for several years. I could not imagine that being the case in my own home. Loyalty to my uncle, however, made me inclined to be forgiving. No doubt there were many pressing needs in pioneer communities, where everything had to begin from scratch, and new, unforeseen challenges must arise daily. My uncle, in spite of his many abilities and innovations, could not be expected to do everything at once.

Because there was no pump, procuring the water from the cistern for use in the house was an extremely awkward task. Moreover, the concern about water involved more than just the lack of a kitchen pump. However well placed the eavestroughs and cistern, precipitation on these dry plains was not sufficient to provide for all household needs, so the cistern was considered merely an emergency supply. Furthermore, rainwater, even if in greater quantities, was thought too "soft" for drinking or cooking, though it was preferred for bathing and the washing of hair and delicate garments.

What the family most needed was a reliable well, and it was another of Uncle James' regrets that he had yet to produce one, though there had been two attempts to dig one. The stock, fortunately, were served for the time being by the reserves in a pond (what the Canadians called a "slough") below the barn. My uncle also planned to build a "dugout," another quaint and perplexing colonial term. I eventually learned that a "dugout" was simply a large, man-made reservoir for watering livestock.

I also learned that finding a water source was a great difficulty not only for the Humphrys family, but for most settlers in this community and beyond. Until a homesteader was able to dig a successful well, the family must haul water, and for my uncle's family, this meant all the way from Cannington Lake. I might have wondered why the family hadn't chosen to settle closer to a source of water but supposed it must have to do with the terrain as well as the need for a community. Domestic animals and crops thrived on grassy meadows, not on rocky, forested hillsides. No doubt hauling water for a time was easier than felling many acres of trees.

In the Humphrys family, the task of hauling water—like many other chores— seemed to be the lot of Cousins Billy and Frankie. They also cut ice from the lake in the winter and hauled wood to feed the furnace and stove, so the water could be heated for domestic tasks, or the ice melted, depending on the season. Though I worried a little about all the hard work these two young men were obliged to do, they didn't seem overly oppressed, and their labours certainly added to their supply of stories.

"Last winter I hauled wood all day every day in order to maintain the heat," bragged eighteen-year-old Billy. "Each load I brought was practically burned up by the time I arrived with the next, so I must hurry to unload it and go immediately back for the third."

If I thought his story somewhat extravagant—for instance, it made no mention of cutting wood into pieces suitable for furnace and stove—I laughed and liked him the more for it. Such stories gave me insight into his character and suggested the kind of man he would become.

Not only did Billy and Frankie have a store of yarns to share, but they were often the butt of family jokes—as when laundry was discussed. Mary was fond of saying that "given their *druthers*" they would wear their clothing until it could stand up and walk by itself, and this did not seem to be far from the truth. Neither had the boys adopted their father's gentlemanly habit of changing clothes when the workday was finished. Instead, whenever they came inside, they installed themselves directly at the kitchen table and prepared to eat whatever was placed before them. They did remove their boots and wash their hands, but those were their only concessions to domesticity.

Ordinarily, I would not have noted such details, but because I now had responsibilities, I became more aware. I also learned that for laundry—as with meals and cooking—there was a system in place, though one that was haphazardly followed. Everyone in the family was expected to contribute his or her own garments to the basket placed for that purpose near the upstairs landing. Since few remembered to do so, garments must also be collected from the various bedchambers so they could be sorted, soaked and scrubbed as necessary. Because Frankie and Billy most frequently forgot and tended to have the dirtiest garments, Mary sometimes had to resort to stealth—or so she claimed—creeping into her younger brothers' rooms to steal their underdrawers, stockings and *trews* from the floor while they were sleeping. Fortunately, they did remember some of their nursery training and usually shed their outer clothing in favour of pyjamas at bedtime.

I smiled when I heard the story and wondered if I would have the courage to follow Mary's example. The yarn itself was yet more evidence of the comradely feeling that so marked the family. Again I regretted my lack of brothers, that my sister and I had never been close and that my whole upbringing had offered little of warmth or gaiety.

Since I had already noticed the state of my cousins' work clothes, and even, at times, those of my uncle, when they came in from toiling in the fields or managing the animals, I was less than eager to confront their less reputable garments. I didn't wish to appear overly fastidious, but I confess I found this part of the exercise more than a little unseemly, especially when so many of the undergarments seemed pitifully tattered. In fact, they offered so little support or protection that I debated whether I should pass them on to Nurse for mending or relegate them to the dustbin. What if they had no replacements for these vests, combinations and underdrawers? In spite of my doubts, however, I carried on as best I could and tried to hide my distaste.

However the laundry was obtained and no matter how soiled, the fact that these garments were being washed was reason to rejoice. Apparently some hired workers had only one suit of clothes, so one could be certain their garments had little acquaintance with soap and scrub board. When Mary told me this, she did not mention which workers had such a limited supply of clothing, though I hoped the men of the Humphrys family were not allowed such an indulgence. About Mr. Lionel Cuthbert and his laundry, Mary volunteered nothing, though if he was at times *almost one of the family*, he might well contribute his laundry to the family collection! Therefore—laundry being such a democratic business—his vests and combinations might also fall into my care, though I tried to avoid thinking of such things. Still, laundry was another reason to look forward to the coming of the new maid, an event my Cousin Nettie found reason to mention daily.

If laundry itself was democratic—in that its ownership was un-known—there was a pecking order in the way certain kinds of garments were handled. Children's play clothes and men's work clothes were soaked before scrubbing, but the "glad rags" (for so my cousins called their best shirts and blouses) were boiled to preserve their whiteness. When it came to the scrub board, eleven-year-old Dora was my instructor, as she had become quite adept. She preferred scrubbing to ironing, she said, for she always managed to burn herself on the irons.

When I volunteered myself for the latter duty, I quickly began to appreciate the danger Cousin Dora described, as I too suffered many small burns. The heavy sadirons were heated on the top of the stove. When they had been lifted and spit-tested to judge the temperature, they were carried with a special pair of tongs to the pressing surface—either the kitchen table or a smaller surface that doubled as a kitchen shelf and pastry board. It would have been helpful to have a separate space for laundry, and my uncle had plans for a washhouse near the main house, but this too was yet to be accomplished.

For the first few days of my stay, my cousins had sought to exempt me from all domestic duties, but I was anxious to prove myself not above hard labour, and the clothes pressing finally seemed to be something I could manage. My first attempts were disastrous, not only because of the injuries I sustained, but also because of the shocking damage to several of Uncle James' starched collars. I would have relegated *them* to the dustbin as well, but Mary prevented me. He would not want them wasted, she said. Still, it didn't take long for me to appreciate the meaning of the boys' word "botched," for I botched many a collar, and even a shirt or two, before I got the knack of pressing them. Though Uncle James never complained, I shrank to see him dressing for dinner or an evening out, for I never knew when the scorched collars would appear.

Chapter 15

THE DUTIES OF JAMES HUMPHRYS, ESQUIRE— AT HOME AND ABROAD

On another morning, over porridge, soda bread and marmalade, Uncle James spoke of his numerous community obligations.

"It was expected of me," he explained. "Certain roles became vacant upon the death of Captain Pierce, who was my good friend. Nor was I averse to such responsibility. After all, the captain and I had common interests."

Apparently he had been staying with the Pierces when the captain had his first stroke, so there had been many opportunities for the two to share ideas.

"Even before that," he added, "within four months of my arrival in Cannington Manor, I was asked to be Justice of the Peace. No doubt that too was the Pierces' influence. However, when rumour suggested me as candidate for the territorial parliament, I knew— were I asked—I must decline. Fortunately, no such nomination arrived, for I'd have been loath to disappoint my supporters."

I wondered briefly what my Aunt Jane thought of these other claims on her husband's time and attention, whether she was one of his "supporters," but felt it presumptuous to ask. Besides, his efforts were clearly for the good of the community, and if he derived some personal satisfaction from being prominent, then all the better.

Uncle James was also constituted lay reader for All Saints, so he must lead services when the parson was absent, in addition to directing the church choir.

"Your Cousin Ernest, however, has the greater responsibility," he said, "as he is sometimes called upon to accompany the hymns. Ernest also obliges when I am asked to play my golden flute for weddings and other parties—in those houses where there is a piano. Oh, you mustn't think we are so very provincial, my dear niece; we do have our entertainments."

My uncle's community work was to become a common theme, and on other occasions he told me of his farm and business ventures. No detail was too small for his notice. When, for instance, I presented to him the problem of his damaged collars, his response was sadness that he had not yet provided a washhouse and summer kitchen.

Uncle James also had plans for a wood house, a small dairy and a boot-cleaning shed, and hoped to begin construction of these buildings very soon. However, larger tasks—those that affected the family income—had first claim.

I thought of the market gardens both he and Mary had mentioned the first day of my visit. Were these extensive enough to live on?

My uncle seemed to hesitate before answering.

"I am not without hope," he said, finally, "that such an enterprise could be profitable, as there is a great need for a local source of vegetables and fruits. The crate of oranges for Cousin Mary's wedding—oranges are a great delicacy in the West—must come all the way from the State of Florida and may not arrive in time. This reminds me how important it is prairie dwellers become self-sufficient. Not that I expect to grow oranges, but I could at least try some of the hardy apples."

In the comfort of the kitchen, I was emboldened to ask whether Lionel Cuthbert had any expertise to benefit him in this area. After all, Mr. Cuthbert had lived in Upper Canada, where I understood the climate was somewhat milder, mild enough perhaps for fruit growing. I had seen Mr. Cuthbert but a few times since our supper party on the lawn, and only from a distance. Still, I found myself bringing his name into conversations. At first I told myself it was to test Cousin Mary's reaction, until I caught myself doing it when she was absent.

Uncle James nodded in answer to my question. "That might well be," he said, "but Mr. Cuthert's family has more experience in live-stock and grain production. 'Twas Cuthbert, in fact, who persuaded me sheep are unfit for the prairies. One can't keep them in pastures, they tend to get water-logged during wet weather and they die of cold in the winter. Not only that," my uncle seemed momentarily to have forgotten the source of his information, "they are easy prey for wandering coyotes."

"What then did Mr. Cuthbert suggest?"

"Cuthbert said pigs were a better investment, since they can be kept in close quarters and fattened quickly on a combination of chopped grain, food scraps and what they root up from the ground."

"That sounds very—ah—practical."

"Indeed," said my uncle, "and that is why I am determined to finish my pork-packing plant, which includes a smokehouse for preparing hams and bacon for export. That, I believe, is where I will make a name for myself, as a pork producer. Can you see it? Humphrys & Sons. Or should a name be more general, do you think—something on a par with the Moose Mountain Trading Company, for instance?"

I was about to suggest that I had no expertise in the naming of business enterprises when my uncle answered his own question.

"Humphrys & Sons must appeal to some," he said, "as we have just been awarded the contract to supply bacon, ham, lard and Cambridge sausage to an English distributor."

"Oh, well done!" I said.

"Of course, the contract was mostly due to the persuasive powers of H. D. McNaughton & Company, my Moosomin agents, but I was the one that hired them."

At this point, I would have asked whether Lionel Cuthbert had suggested this as well, but I dared not speak his name again. Still, I felt a glow of something like pride that his advice was taken so seriously.

On the other hand, I remembered overhearing Cousin Ernest remind my uncle that filling the order would be difficult, with the smoke house yet to be completed. This had deflated my uncle and suggested the very picture my father had often held before me. Was my uncle an entrepreneur of vision or a rather pitiful middle-aged man facing ruin and loss of yet another dream, someone scarcely able to support his own family? I did not know the solution to my uncle's difficulties, though I dearly wished he might succeed in at least some of his ventures. Neither did I know how I came to be his confidante, though perhaps he sensed I wanted to believe well of him.

Chapter 16
-

THE MYSTERIES OF
THE CELLAR

I had always been somewhat afraid of the dark, so when Cousin Mary first offered to show me the cellar—indeed it was more than a cellar, she assured me—I was more than a little reluctant. In my father's house, the stone cellars smelled damp and musty, and they were never properly lit, though some parts were regularly used by the servants. Even as an adult, I could not help but imagine the many darting and slithering creatures—mice, salamanders and even snakes—taking refuge in dark corners and among rows of dusty jars.

My cousin, however, was not to be put off. She must draw some water and had need of my help. Besides, they had a good basement.

"Many of the village houses sit on dirt root cellars alone—" she let a trace of scorn creep into her voice, "such root cellars are mere holes in the ground and provide no foundation whatsoever. Our cellar, however, is of solid stone construction, and has ample space for cistern and furnace, as well as vegetable storage."

I could never resist Cousin Mary for long and eventually followed her to the pantry, where I held her water containers as she lifted and fastened the heavy cellar door. I was not reassured, however, by the appearance of a dark hole in the floor and no visible stairway. Even at home the cellar was approached by solid steps, while this one depended on a mere ladder for access. Indeed, Mary had to lean into the hole to pull up the suspended ladder and fasten it in place. My imagination was drawn back to my Aunt Jane's misadventure when she first stepped into her new home, fell through a doorway and knocked herself senseless on the fine stone floor that was at the bottom of this dark hole. I could not confide to Mary the tendency of my mind to dwell on the story, but I continued to hang back.

Mary, meanwhile, hitched up her skirts and began to descend the ladder. She would light the lantern, she said, and in less than a minute she had done so. I handed the water pails and jug down to her, and then there was no help for it, I must attempt the ladder myself. I bundled my skirts with one hand, kneeled on the edge of the opening and reached for the first rung of the ladder with my foot. For a moment, it seemed as if there was nothing below me but empty space.

"You're almost there," said Mary encouragingly, though I had yet to locate that first rung. I waved my foot about, and in my fear and excitement lost hold of my skirt and petticoats, so they flapped about my legs. Then I felt Mary's firm hand about my ankle, pressing my foot securely into place on the rung. It took me a trembling moment to secure my balance, then she took her hand away, and I was able to place my second foot beside the first, find the ladder with my hands, and so on.

Mary told me later that my progress was like that of an inchworm, alternately humping then straightening its vertebrae, but at that moment I was far too frightened to see any humour in it. When, finally, my feet were planted on solid stone, my cousin handed the water containers back to me, took the lantern off its hook and turned up the wick.

Now I looked around me, trying to focus on the part lit by the lantern and not on the dark corners. I found it a huge, cavernous place—cool, but not cold and damp, which should have been no surprise, since it was the heating centre for the whole house. When

Mary lifted the lantern to show me the furnace, I noted the huge iron door and the maze of metal pipes surrounding it and marveled at this complicated system that would spew hot air to every room in the house.

Because of the season, the furnace was a resting giant, but I'd have guessed even without Billy's stories that it must consume a daunting supply of wood in winter. (Mary explained that it could be converted to burn coal—were that available.) Also marvelous was the fact someone must go up and down the ladder several times a day to feed the appetite of such a beast! When I said as much, Mary laughed.

"One gets used to it," she said. "My father feels this method is 'most efficient and economical,' much better than fireplaces in every room. He also thinks it keeps the rooms freer of dust, a great nuisance when rooms are heated by stoves." She laughed again. "Trust my father to think of everything."

Next Mary showed me the banks of shelves, and I exclaimed over the quantity of preserved wild fruits still in the family store as well as the size of the storage bins for root vegetables. Each bin appeared to have a thin layer of sand at the bottom.

"That's to absorb moisture," said Mary, "the major problem with storing vegetables is spoilage, so we try to keep them dry." She sighed. "Our efforts aren't entirely successful."

For all my inexperience, I then detected a sweetish, not wholly unpleasant odour of decay permeating the storage area. Sure enough, in some bins, carrots and turnips appeared to have been reduced to mounds of odorous material with only the occasional lump worth retrieving.

Cousin Mary wrinkled her nose. "Remind me," she said, "to have one of the boys clean this up. These bins must be empty and dry in time for this summer's crop."

I no longer wondered that my uncle's dreams of a market garden were temporarily stalled. Even if the problems of vegetable production were solved, the problems of storage must still be dealt with. How discouraging for my uncle, and how difficult for him to climb down the ladder to oversee this part of the enterprise!

Our final stop was for the complicated business of dipping water out of the cistern. In order to do this, Mary had to stand on the ledge against the cistern wall and toss a rope with a somewhat-battered pail on the end over the edge.

We heard the pail bump against the wall before it splashed into the water. On the way back up, however, the pail was too heavy for Mary to lift, so she had to jerk the rope, dropping the pail down again. On the next attempt, the heavy pail caught on some part of the cistern wall. Again, she had to spill the water and start the process all over again. Mary stopped to take a rest.

"With practice," Mary assured me, "one can draw up a sufficient amount of water to fill one's containers without spilling more than one collects. As you will see, I haven't yet acquired Ruthie's skill. Would that she were still able to do it."

I realized then how little I thought of Ruthie, how almost invisible she had made herself, and we did not give her much thought when in the cellar either, as we still had our task to complete.

By the time we had an adequate amount in our containers, Mary's hands were bruised from the rope, we were both dusty and rumpled, and we had splashed a good quantity of water on ourselves. I insisted on carrying one pail and the jug while Mary carried the lantern and the other pail and led the way back to the ladder. However, the containers, though only partially full, were still very heavy and caught in my skirts, spilling yet more water.

Finally Mary had the lantern in its usual place and came back to rescue me. I found it easier to climb up the ladder than down. My cousin, however, had to carry the containers one at a time up the ladder and then go down yet once more to blow out the lantern. Finally, she must lean down and release the ladder so we could close the trap door. All in all, it was a difficult and illuminating experience, but not one I wished to repeat nor one where I appeared in a good light!

Chapter 17

-

REGARDING THE CHILDREN'S EDUCATION

Though I strove to be available and willing when it came to all domestic chores, I found presently that my greatest usefulness and greatest rewards came from spending time with my younger cousins. They were bright and obliging youngsters, though our time together consisted more in my joining their games than in my providing any type of instruction. Cicely, seven years old, was a reluctant reader, but she was adept at finding birds' nests and early wild flowers. She also promised to take me berry picking, and I hoped my stay would be long enough to give her the opportunity. While I saw blossoming trees and shrubs in abundance—one with tiny white flowers and a particularly intoxicating fragrance—there was as yet no evidence of fruit.

In the days Cecily was not in school, we set about making nature journals of wild plants and flowers. I wished to keep mine as a memento of my visit and hoped at the same time to introduce my little cousin to more ladylike pursuits than collecting frogs and earthworms, which she inevitably fondled to death.

First, we pressed leaves and blossoms between the pages of whatever weighty volumes were available. Then we made a flour and water paste. For our portfolios, we made use of a supply of outdated and well-used copies of *The Lady: A Journal for Gentlewomen.* These arrived monthly by post and made the languishing belles of the household—when they weren't too busy attending to household needs—wistful for England and the life they fancied they remembered.

When the samples of flowers and leaves were pressed and dry enough to be pasted on the pages, I would pencil notes in the margins about where such treasures could be found. I was, however, disappointed to discover that the pressed flowers lost much of their rich hue and most of their fragrance when they dried. I had imagined a pictorial record that preserved them in the height of their glory. Because this drying process was somewhat unsatisfactory, I considered watercolour representations. After all, Cousin Mary was very talented with brushes and colour washes, and I hoped the children might have the same inclination.

While pursuing this notion, I was saddened to note that Mary no longer opened her sketchbook or paint-box. At least she did not do so nor make any mention of it in the first week after my arrival. Perhaps this was not surprising, since she was in the middle of wedding preparations as well as overseeing all the domestic tasks of the household. Still, I was puzzled, since I had been of the opinion such artistic talent must be the consuming force of one's life.

In spite of my disappointment over Mary's neglected talents, I did not attempt to take up drawing and painting in her stead, for my skills were remarkably inferior to hers. In fact, to the best of my knowledge, I possessed no artistic talent of any sort, a fact that had never troubled me at home, since no one in my household set any great store by such accomplishments. Here, however, marks of culture were much appreciated. Not only were they a buffer against homesickness, but they brought enrichment to the whole community. Judging from the activities in which he was involved, this was obviously my uncle's thinking, and such efforts appeared to be typical among "the English group."

The feelings of "the Canadians"—the group of homesteaders who had straggled in from other parts of Canada about the same

time as Captain Pierce was setting up his village—were more difficult to ascertain. Mr. Lionel Cuthbert might have had an opinion,
but I had no occasion to speak to him, much less ask him for his
views. In fact, even if such an occasion had presented itself, I might
have hesitated, not wanting to defer too much to his authority, as
the rest of the family seemed more than willing to do. Furthermore,
it was uncertain whether Mr. Cuthbert attended the concerts and
other entertainments organized by Uncle James and the English
group.

I did venture to ask Mary when we were alone one day in the
kitchen whether Mr. Lionel Cuthbert appeared in society.

Mary looked up from scraping pastry dough off the breadboard.
"He is welcome if he chooses," she said. "In fact, he's very popular,
with his fine tenor voice and all, but he often chooses not."

"And I have seen him dance," she added. I waited for more, but
it did not come, and her face revealed nothing. After a moment, she
smiled at me and went back to her breadboard.

Chapter 18

-

A CURE FOR
RECALCITRANT SCHOLARS

Only three of my cousins attended the school at Cannington Manor—Dora, eleven; Noel, nine; and my little Cecily, who was so blithely undiscriminating about the occupations presented to her, whether they be chasing frogs and butterflies or reciting her lessons. When I first asked, I had been heartened to hear there was a school in the village and that my uncle was a strong promoter of education. Having promoted the institution until it came into being, however, he seemed less than determined his own children should have the benefit of it. In other words, he did not ensure they were able to attend in a regular and timely fashion.

The impediments they faced were several, but the primary one was transportation. They could not depend upon being driven to school and fetched afterwards. Neither was it an appropriate distance for the girls to walk on their own. The village—and therefore the school—was somewhat more than two miles from the Humphrys estate. Neither could the children drive themselves. Though both Noel and Dora claimed they knew how to drive, it was of little significance, as there was no horse and cart available for their use. There was also a creek to be crossed, by way of a temporary bridge that was somewhat in need of repair.

If Frankie had still been attending school, this difficulty might have been solved, but he had apparently, though only fourteen years old, excused himself from formal study. This seemed rather young to me, but perhaps his current apprenticeship in barn building and animal husbandry *would* hold him in better stead. With such models as Mr. Cuthbert before him, I could well understand the appeal of learning farming. On the other hand, he may have had little choice, as there was an endless amount of work to be done, and Uncle James was neither equal to heavy labour himself nor in a position to hire a multitude of others—in the style of the Becktons. The semi-regular employment of Mr. Cuthbert was an exceptional case and seemed as much dependent upon Mr. Cuthbert's generosity as on my uncle's resources.

And then there was fifteen-year-old Freda, who had accompanied her mother to England for the specific purpose of going to finishing school for two years, followed by study in Europe, if money allowed. My heart went out to her. For all that it was a fine opportunity for her, I was sure she must miss the warm and lively company of her sisters and brothers.

My greater concern, however, was for the three younger children, and I decided their haphazard attendance was one thing about which I could do something. It would surely inconvenience no-one if I walked the children to school myself on those days when there was no conveyance available.

On the very first such occasion, I discovered my commitment was more substantial than I had imagined, as it required close to one hour both coming from and going to town. There was also the problem of footwear, since I ruined yet another pair of boots in the mud the first day I ventured to be the children's escort. It did seem to me that some kind of paving might have been devised, but again this was not uppermost in the minds of the men folk. Why should *they* notice, since *they* always had some means of transport at their disposal and could drive or ride anywhere they needed to go?

In preparation for accompanying the children to school again, I was able to borrow a pair of work boots that Billy had outgrown and Frankie had not yet grown into. Their appearance was some-what derelict, but I would not let that deter me. I also found them cumbersome and uncomfortable—my feet had no experience with footwear of this nature—but two pairs of men's short knitted hose (what my cousins called "socks") provided considerable relief. After some rehearsal, I found I could stride out quite well in this equi-page. In fact, I rather enjoyed the freedom provided by the loose fit and broad, sturdy sole.

I had also learnt from our previous attempt that we must leave the house no later than eight-and-one-quarter hours in order to arrive safely for the hour of nine. Our destination was the large, new frame building near the far end of the main street, just oppo-site the flour mill and the church. To reach it, we must also pass the carpenter's shop and the Newman's small, neat house—the two so close together that they were almost one building. This I learned was so Mr. Newman could check on his invalid wife while he was at work in the shop.

Neither was the school a schoolhouse alone. While the children learnt their lessons on the main floor, the upstairs functioned as the town hall and meeting room. Fortunately, the hall was seldom used during the day, so this arrangement must disrupt lessons but little.

Of greater concern was the fact that the Mitre Hotel sat across the road from the mill, and a number of young rowdies appeared to make the hotel the centre of their pranks. When we came in sight of that structure on the first day, Noel took delight in reciting some of the adventures that had taken place there, especially the ones hav-ing to do with the hotel stable and large haystack, which was also in the yard of the hotel.

Apparently homemade liquor was stored in the haystack, and the hotel yard was also where the gentlemen who frequented the hotel retired to settle their grudges, grudges that no doubt gained significance as the liquor took effect. These same gentlemen may have had their usefulness—they were either agricultural students or involved in some building project about the town—but as they loitered about in the mornings, they managed to make sport of any likely subject that was in sight.

Sometime later, Cousin Ernest explained that the threatened bouts of fisticuffs were seldom consummated, as there was a general understanding that gentlemen must follow the Queensbury rules, which no one, fortunately, could quite remember. I was relieved to hear that there was seldom any brutality or bloodshed involved. Nonetheless, stories of such rough and ready manners made it even more appropriate that the children be accompanied to school, and I wondered if my uncle was aware of the dangers.

Cecily was but a child, and Noel had the protection of being young, male and of an easy-going nature, but Dora was tall for her age and, though only eleven, threatened to blossom soon into a very pretty young woman. She at least should not be exposed to such uncouth behaviour. Perhaps Aunt Jane had similar concerns and that is why she chose to have Freda finish her schooling in England.

In order for me to deliver the children safely into the hands of Mr. Kent, their teacher, a courtly young man who arrived no sooner than my young charges and myself, we had to pass the gauntlet of stares from outside the hotel. None of the young men, who appeared to have breakfasted but were in no apparent hurry to be on their way, said anything untoward, yet I could feel their bold eyes upon us both going and coming, and I took care to look neither left nor right until well past the unfortunate building. Clearly, I must waste no time in referring the matter to my uncle's attention.

When I had passed safely back along the main street and was in the countryside again, my felicity was as intense as my recent discomfort had been. Surely the season of May near the town of Cannington Manor offered an aspect that rivaled the finest countryside in Europe. I was not a seasoned traveller but had known the pleasures of occasional holidays in France and Italy and had regularly taken the waters in Brighton and Bath. Though the scene that stretched before me may have lacked some of the conveniences of those destinations, in natural beauty I felt it was second to none.

Besides the glories of berry bushes in fragrant bloom and other trees robed in their bright new leaves, the tall natural grasses were fresh and green as they waved in the wind. From the elevation of the townsite, I could see the purple outline of what the Canadians called the Moose Mountains. There—I knew, though I had not seen it myself—were waters and trees in abundance. Indeed, there was nothing lacking in this place, and I was determined to drink deeply of all of its beauty in the short time I had.

Though my hardy footwear allowed me to cover the ground more quickly than would otherwise have been possible, I paused often to admire my surroundings that my cousins were beginning to lay out the ingredients for the noon meal when I arrived back at the house. Cousin Mary looked up from her task to wonder what had kept me.

"We thought you lost or perhaps kidnapped by wandering brigands," she said. I saw from her expression and that of my Cousin Nettie that she was not in earnest; however, it gave me pause to wonder whether there might be dangers I had not considered. I hastened to apologize for my tardiness, but she bade me give it not another thought.

As I have said, the noon meal was never formal at the Humphrys' House. Everyone served himself as his morning tasks allowed, and I never knew whose face would appear over cutlets and pudding. On that particular day, one of those who came to the kitchen table was Mr. Cuthbert. I found myself somewhat abashed over this coincidence, there having been so little intercourse between us since our conversation during that first supper.

Unlike that earlier occasion, this was not a time for confidences, as everyone appeared to be in a hurry to get on with the afternoon's activities. It happened, however, that Mary mentioned my having taken over responsibility for the children's school attendance. Mr. Cuthbert gave me a somewhat speculative glance at that, but he said nothing and before long had eaten his meal and excused himself from the table.

After luncheon, I begged to be allowed to do the washing up, since I had contributed nothing to the preparation. There was no argument, and by the time I had completed that task and shaken the dust and grasses from inside my footwear, I must be on my way again in order to arrive before the afternoon dismissal.

With the sun beating down on me, I found the afternoon much warmer than the morning had been, especially as I was walking quite strenuously. Convinced there was no danger of my being observed on this solitary walk along the wagon trail that cut across wild meadow to the town, I took the opportunity to unbutton my collar and cuffs and to remove the straw hat that was my companion whenever I was out-of-doors.

It wasn't long before my hairpins found themselves unequal to their task, and I made no effort to restore them. Rather, I enjoyed the brush of stray locks against my cheeks and neck. Such, in fact, was my feeling of freedom and abandonment that I had a sudden vision of myself twirling and dancing. Nothing less could express this sensation of being at one with the glorious outdoors.

Fortunately I did not act on that impulse, for in a moment my solitude was broken by the rhythmic beat of hooves on the hard ground and the rattle of a vehicle. I looked anxiously over my shoulder and pondered why I had been so foolish as to imagine myself alone. I turned quickly back in the direction I was headed, clinging to some foolish thought that I might not be recognized, but by the time I had replaced my hat, the conveyance had overtaken me. When it was apparent the driver had stopped alongside me, it seemed perverse to pretend to ignore the intruder.

Soon my colour rose higher still, for it was Mr. Lionel Cuthbert who had interrupted my gambol, and now he was gazing down on me with something very like a smile. I bowed and would have been on my way, had he not addressed me.

"Ma'am," he said. "I am bound for the village. May I shorten your trip for you?"

I protested, while still trying to repair my appearance. He then impressed upon me what my cousins had not, that there were indeed dangers in what had seemed to me a pursuit that was harmless as well as helpful. Was I certain I knew the way? What if a storm came up? Would my courage fail if approached by strangers or by animals larger than the prairie squirrels I had seen? He reminded me that I was new in this country and did not know its ways. Much chagrined, I had little choice but to take up his offer. At that, he looped the reins around a convenient support, sprang lightly to the ground and offered to help me mount the front seat of my uncle's two-seater wagon.

I had a sudden remembrance of his arms supporting me when I first planted my feet on the packed earth of Cannington Manor. This time, however, he offered only a strong hand under my elbow, and with this help I found I was able to manage the wagon seat very easily. Back in his place, he unwound the reins and cast me another quick glance before he hied the horses on their way. Incredible as it was, considering my disarray, I thought I detected admiration in his expression. That realization quelled any conversation I might have summoned to my aid.

He was the first to speak. "I did not mean to frighten you, Miss. 'Tis a fine thing, your concern about the young ones' schooling. But 'tis still a rough, wild country for one—especially a lady—who is new to it."

"I did not mean to cause trouble," I replied sheepishly.

And that was the end of our conversation on the matter. It was fortunate, however, that he had come to my aid, as the children had been dismissed early and were loitering about in the road not far from the hotel. It was also fortunate there were no roguish young fellows about the place at that time of day. Apparently, they had finally remembered they had work to do.

Mr. Cuthbert, who did appear to have business in the town, promised to convey us all home again if we could but wait a few minutes for him. Within an hour, all of this was accomplished and the children and I were deposited safely at the Humphrys' front door. Wanting to show my independence, I did not wait for Mr. Cuthbert to assist me down, but scrambled over the wagon wheel myself and prepared to skip off after the children. If he was surprised by my lack of ceremony, he made no comment, though he did call out and suggest I speak to my uncle about the school situation. Caught in mid-flight, I turned back. Again looking down at me from the wagon seat, he also reminded me to ask for his assistance if ever I had need of it.

My gratitude was great, as was my surprise at his gentlemanly behaviour and expressions, though I hardly knew how to respond to either. Fortunately, he drove off in the wagon as I stood there, and saved me the trouble.

Chapter 19

ALL SAINTS ON THE PRAIRIES

Though sometimes careless about his children's school attendance—he had so much to attend to, and the springtime was so hectic—Uncle James did not neglect his parish duties, nor allow his family to do so. Cousin Ernest—or even Mary—became the organist for All Saints' Church when there was no Mrs. Hanson or Miss Pierce at hand; Ernest, Mary, Dora and Freda sang in the choir; and Aunt Jane was an essential part of the Ladies Guild, of which Nettie was also a member. Even for the younger Humphrys, church attendance meant a break from daily routine and an opportunity to see friends. For his part, as church warden, lay reader and musician, there could be no doubt my uncle was a pillar of the church.

At Evensong on the first Sunday after my arrival, I had occasion to see the Humphrys family play these various roles. I also noted with an emotion oddly like satisfaction that Lionel Cuthbert appeared to be a churchgoer as well. He appeared, again dressed in his suit and uncomfortable collar, just as the family gathered for the trip into the village.

To justify my interest in his habits, I decided such attendance gave credit to my uncle. Furthermore, not only families would be expected to support the Church, and for the bachelors and spinsters in the community, the benefits of regular attendance pertained not only to spiritual welfare. Many might first have spied their prospective spouses in the pews or the choir. This thought also took me by surprise. Surely, with my visit so short, I had no such expectation for myself, yet I was interested to observe the actions of others. Thanks to Mrs. Pierce's stories during our sea voyage, I already knew of links between such leading parish families as the Pages, the Pierces and the Becktons. Not only had the eldest of the Beckton brothers married Jessie Pierce and Spencer Page married Frances Pierce, but they and their families were also instrumental in building and maintaining All Saints. Of this my uncle reminded me during the drive to the church.

Given the nature of the day, my uncle had chosen to use the family carriage and would have Mary, Nettie and I accompany him, with Ernest as our driver. The others—Nurse alone had chosen to abstain from worship—would be accommodated in the two-seater. I thought Cousin Billy a little crest-fallen not to be driving the carriage, but no one argued my uncle's arrangements. I also noticed a few minutes later that Billy held the reins for the other team, which was usually Mr. Cuthbert's prerogative.

The drive was not eventful, and as we approached our destination, I noticed the structure itself was modest in size—smaller than the family chapels of many English estates. It was also built of logs, giving it a rustic air, though the logs had afterwards been carefully chinked and whitewashed. Though not imposing, the church was of standard, cruciform shape and looked neat and serviceable. All in all, I was inclined to be pleased with it. According to information gleaned from my uncle, various cousins and, of course, Mrs. Pierce herself, it had been built in 1884 and was consecrated by the venerable Bishop Anson, in June of 1885. It was also the first church to be consecrated in the newly formed Diocese of Qu'appelle.

I murmured what I hoped was an appropriate response when this information was provided, though I doubted I could retain all of it, not being acquainted with either the reverend gentleman in question nor the structure of the Church of England in Canada. I did marvel, however, that the diocese itself could yet be so young.

Fortunately, my uncle and his family were more inclined towards stories of their neighbours, which were easier to remember. Many in the community had been involved in the church's construction, but it was Captain Pierce who set aside the land for church and graveyard, dedicating it "God's Little Acre." He did this at the request of his daughters, for they were in the habit of strictly observing "the Sabbath" and didn't wish to be cut off from the Church—meaning, of course, the Church of England. They felt there must be a church building, as "outward and visible sign" of their faith and practice.

The inside of the church was much like the outside—chinked to prevent drafts and whitewashed to preserve the wood. Because of its diminutive size and rustic construction, it was unlike the drafty edifices where I had previously worshipped. But I did not miss the high ceilings, echoing spaciousness and rainbows of light filtered through stained-glass windows, for there were other charms to pique my interest. I noted that much of the furniture—pews, altar and prayer desk—appeared to be hand-hewn and polished to a warm glow. Because it was an evening service, the chandelier—consisting of three coal-oil lamps with beautifully decorated globes—hanging in the centre of the transept was already lit, as were the candelabras on each side of the altar. These fixtures and the candles on the altar gave enough light for the musicians to see their music, while other lamps in the porch and the centre of the nave cast a soft glow into even the furthest corners.

Though not all pews were full, by the time the verger had retied the bell rope, it was a goodly congregation for an evening service. There was also a surpliced choir, consisting of animated young women such as Cousin Dora, more mature women and a few men. Among the latter I noted two or three English youths, as well as Cousin Ernest, Mr. Lionel Cuthbert and another mature gentleman. This last, Mary whispered to me, was the famous Dr. Hardy, who had stayed some months with the Humphrys when he first arrived, in 1889. In fact, it was her father who had invited him during the flu epidemic and guaranteed his income for the first year.

I looked obediently at the doctor and saw a pleasant-looking, well-dressed man of medium height. From what I could see, his lively manners must be his most remarkable asset, for all that the Humphrys family seemed so fond of him, but then I reminded myself of my limited knowledge of men. With so little experience, surely I was no judge of masculine beauty and worth.

Uncle James himself cut a fine figure for he stood to direct both congregational singing and the choir's four-part rendition of the Rev. John Ellerton's fine new hymn "The Day Thou Gavest, Lord, is Ended." Because the whole choir sang this offering—and did a creditable job—I could not detect for certain what Mary had described as Mr. Cuthbert's "fine tenor voice." However, I did think that the men—though smaller in numbers—showed rather more musicianship than the women, in spite of Dora's enchanting face and lively expression.

Perhaps the women lacked Cousin Mary's example, for I understood she usually sang with them. It was to be company for me that she had chosen to sit this time in the congregation. Mr. Maltby, however, also had reason to be pleased by her decision, as he was able to slip into the family pew beside her. Mary flushed ever so slightly at this, but she did not appear displeased.

She and Mr. Maltby had more reason to blush when the Rev. Mr. George Nelson Dobie—perhaps because it came to mind when he saw them sitting side by side—announced the banns one week early. Church law decreed that these must be published for three consecutive Sundays before a wedding. Since the Maltby-Humphrys nuptials were to take place on the first of June, the first announcement would properly have been on the fifteenth of May. Nonetheless, there was Mr. Dobie, though a week early, saying from the pulpit:

"I publish the banns of marriage for Miss Mary Jane Humphrys, spinster, of this parish and Mr. Ernest Newcombe Maltby, bachelor, also of this parish. If any of you know cause or just impediment, why these two persons should not be joined together in holy matrimony, ye are to declare it. This is the first time of asking."

While Mary blushed, Dora beamed from the choir and Nettie stifled a giggle. Mr. Maltby's reaction, however, was somewhat more extreme, no doubt because of his shyer nature. He went red to the roots of his neatly-parted hair and dipped his handsome head so that it seemed he would disappear into his gentlemanly collar if he could. Neither would he raise his eyes through the rest of the service, even when Mary held her *Book of Common Prayer* for him to share. He also excused himself immediately after the service and hurried away. Mary handled all of this with admirable poise, as if his bashfulness were nothing out of the ordinary.

The incident did not escape attention, however. First, Mr. Dobie hurried over to apologize for his error in publishing the banns prematurely. Then Mr. and Mrs. Ernest Beckton approached.

"Thought of some impediment did he?" asked the eldest Mr. Beckton. "I didn't think old Maltby had it in him."

Mary laughed in her usual good-humoured way, though I thought the jest in poor taste, and Mr. Beckton's wife rapped him sharply on the arm with her personal Bible. At that, Mr. Ernest Beckton wisely found it necessary to excuse himself and join a nearby group of men.

While Jessie Beckton was apologizing to Mary for her husband's behaviour and for being unable to accept the supper invitation a few days previous, Mary introduced Mrs. Beckton to me as one of those responsible for the existence of the church. At that point, Jessie Beckton became quite poetic. She spoke, for instance, of "walks over sunburnt grass in the cool evenings" as she and her sisters wrestled with the difficulties of building a church in such a wilderness.

"Since, we had no money at our disposal," she said, "the way seemed a little obscure, and the means nil."

Then she described how the Pierce sisters advertised in the English "Little Papers," which were known to be sympathetic to the work of the Church, and especially to its missionary work. I nodded at this point, as I too was aware of the small publications that appeared in the English coffee houses and could be read for the price of a cup of coffee. My father frequently brought one home from his club.

Apparently the advertisements were successful, and financial assistance gradually began to come in. The first donations were from parties who had connections to the new settlement. First, there was a gift from the parish of the Rev. A. S. Page, father of Spencer, William and George Shaw Page; and later there were funds from a Miss Beckton, sister to Ernest, William and Bertram Beckton. The name "All Saints" was given as a tribute to All Saints in Selsley, Glouchester, parish of the Rev. A. S. Page.

Now that she had started on her favourite subject, Jessie Beckton was obviously happy to continue. "Once we had a little money," she said, "the next step was to bring in the materials, and brother Ted cut and delivered the first load of logs from Moose Mountain."

"But wasn't there something about needing permission to cut down trees?" interjected Mary.

"Oh, yes, I forgot. Then as now, one needs must have a permit to cut wood at Fish Lake. As for the furnishings, when Father saw three large trees on Birch Hill, he knew they would meet our needs, even though he had to lease 120 acres of land around Birch Hill in order to cut them. Those three birch trees provided wood for all the furnishings of the church."

"All?" I thought of the altar, a dozen pews in the nave plus choir pews, the bishop's chair, the prayer desk and other small tables.

"Oh, yes, and there was enough for a large desk for my father as well."

I had to agree that the whole project was a tremendous achievement, and I looked around me with an even greater appreciation. Yes, the church was small, but the cosy atmosphere enhanced rather than detracted from the sense of worship and community. When I was back in England, I would surely remember the interior of this church with nostalgic affection, especially when I visited those austere cathedrals that need such breadth and height, as well as quantities of stained glass and all those marble pillars, in order to inspire awe.

Cousin Mary and Mrs. Beckton had by this time progressed to the subject of Mary's upcoming wedding.

Mary sighed, "My gown is finished. The silk with train looks very well, and poor Nurse is doing her best with the rest, but I despair of everything being finished in time."

"Would you like to bring some of the work over to me one day? My Miss Ross has been trained by a professional tailor and is very quick, to boot. She can do last minute fittings and finishing in no time at all."

"Well, I do have a grey travelling costume that may be more than Nurse or I can manage . . . But I don't want Ruthie to think I don't trust her. Her position is difficult enough without my adding more unhappiness."

Mrs. Beckton nodded, and I ceased to listen as they talked a little more on the subject of Nurse and her situation and then settled on a day for Mary to spend with Jessie Beckton and her seamstress at Didsbury. By that time, Cousin Ernest was hurrying us to the carriage. It was now getting dark and we must make haste, he said; with no lamps on either wagon or carriage, we should have to rely entirely on the horses knowing the way.

Mrs. Beckton must then have remembered something, for she hurried after us as much as was possible in her fashionable gown and footwear.

"I bring a message from my mother," she panted. "She was indisposed tonight, but wishes to engage all of you for tomorrow evening—dinner and musical selections. Do you think that would suit your father?"

By this time, we had reached Uncle James, who—owing to his gout—was already seated. He attempted to rise, but Jessie waved him back to his place. He was soon able to satisfy her on the invitation from her mother, so the date was confirmed. Then we were on our way and again travelling over the dark and bumpy trail, though even in the gathering dusk it was now becoming somewhat familiar to me. The wagon preceded us, though from my seat facing the back, I saw very little of it. The glimpses I was allowed showed me that this time Lionel Cuthbert was driving. The rest of the family seemed to be huddled in the box of the wagon with blankets about their shoulders, since at this time of year the evenings were frequently chilly, for all that the days were generally warm and sunny. Perhaps the sight of Mr. Cuthbert's sturdy, purposeful shape silhouetted against the fading light also gave *them* a feeling of warmth and security, a feeling that, in spite of any discomfort and fears they might have, all would be well.

I chided myself for such foolish thoughts and attended more carefully to the conversation between my uncle and Cousin Mary. Uncle James was congratulating himself for the choir's performance, while Mary was pondering the music for the wedding. Cousin Nettie apparently couldn't resist a laughing comment about the premature publishing of the banns, to which Mary responded with a sigh. Uncle James apparently hadn't noticed, so intent was he on his role as music director.

I closed my eyes and again saw Mr. Cuthbert's straight back and strong arms, the set of his head and neck upon his shoulders and the way his sandy hair curled against his collar.

Chapter 20

-

HISTORY LESSONS CONTINUE

If I found myself paying Mr. Cuthbert more attention than I would have expected or wished during the excursion to church, the evening at Mrs. Pierce's taught me the full extent of my folly. But that was later.

First, there were more stories to attend to, as everyone in my uncle's household had some piece of information about the founding family. Many of these stories were recounted during afternoon tea the next day—though the family did not customarily have tea, Cousin Mary had felt we might need some refreshment before going out for the evening. If the Pierces were having a large gathering, the supper would most certainly be later than seven o'clock, which was our usual time.

I was soon disappointed to learn that visiting Mrs. Pierce did not mean an evening at the "Great White House", as the original Pierce house was presently occupied by a Major Charles Phipps, the community's land titles officer. Instead, visiting Mrs. Pierce meant visiting her son Ted and his family, where the former first lady of the village and her unmarried children, Lily and Jack, were currently living. I pondered this. Surely, it must be very difficult for the mother to have descended in the space of a few years to widow and permanent guest in the house of a son and daughter-in-law!

When my uncle—with his usual fondness for genealogy—began to recount the Pierce family background, information he had gained while staying with the Pierces during his first months at Cannington Manor, my mind wandered a little. After all, I had heard these stories from Mrs. Pierce herself. What I did note was how much my uncle had valued Captain Pierce's friendship and the fact the latter had entrusted him with so much of his history. I also noted, but did not mention aloud, the many similarities to my uncle's situation, among them losses of career and resources, dependence on his spouse and the need, in middle age, to make a new start in life. Though the Captain had immigrated to the district six years before my uncle, both men had recognized the potential in the Moose Mountains and had hoped to finally realize their destinies here.

Cousin Ernest, having waited somewhat impatiently during his father's recital, now took the opportunity to set the record straight.

"One might get the impression," he said, "Captain Pierce was the first to arrive, when his eldest son, Duncan, was actually the first to see the site for the town. And there were others as well. An Irishman named Mr. William Brownlee was the first white man to both see the Cannington-Moose Mountain area *and* to come back to settle in it."

My uncle seemed not a little deflated by this revelation, but he allowed his eldest son to continue. Ernest explained how, in 1881, Mr. Brownlee was cook to a party of surveyors responsible for mapping wide stretches of the Western prairies. However, this part of Assiniboia had pleased him the most. Perhaps the hills reminded him of Fermanagh, in the north of Ireland, which he had left at the tender age of fourteen, during the potato famine. He had first come to the United States as a cabin boy on a sailing ship, had learned to be a baker and, by 1879, had owned his own shop in Winnipeg.

Owning his own bakery seemed a settled life and a fine accomplishment for one of such origins—from reading the pamphlets of the Rev. Mr. Jonathan Swift, I knew something of the Irish potato famine and the resulting destitution. Therefore, I wondered why

Mr. Brownlee had not been satisfied with such advancements as he had already made, what taste for wandering had made him leave his business and join with the party of surveyors.

Whatever his reasons, he came back in the spring of 1882 with a group of settlers, and it was this group of settlers, explained Cousin Ernest, who led Duncan Pierce to what became Pierce land and the site for the town. Not only were there other settlers in the district at that time, but one might correctly call all of them, including the Pierces, "squatters" since the area wasn't yet open for homesteading.

I sensed Uncle James was becoming restless at this point.

"Indeed, there may have been others," he said. "But they had no vision for greatness and could not imagine industry or commerce, nor the bustling town and growing concern that Cannington Manor has become. They were content merely to eke out a living by farming a few cattle and growing a little grain."

"I would not say John Turton merely ekes out a living," retorted Cousin Ernest. "With all his stock from Manitoba, I would call his a legitimate cattle business, with his contract to supply meat to the reserve—not to mention to the Becktons and the rest of us."

My uncle interrupted him. "I would not say a word against the good Mr. Turton," he said. "But we were talking of the Pierces. Mr. Turton is more than capable of relating his own adventures."

The others laughed. "That's true," said Cousin Ernest, "though some doubt his veracity at times. But what about Mr. Brownlee? Does not our cousin wish to hear the story of how, in 1885, the Brownlees, then newly-weds, met the train carrying troops to quell the uprising led by Louis Riel? And then there was the occasion when Mrs. Brownlee and the children hid in the attic while a band of renegades from Montana ravaged their belongings."

"Ernest, please, you will frighten poor Cousin Floss," Mary reached over to pat my hand. "Like Mr. Turton and Mr. Brownlee, my brother cannot resist the opportunity to tell a story, and the more harrowing the better."

I smiled at her. I did indeed feel overwhelmed, though I wasn't, as Mary feared, frightened by the stories. Rather, I was impressed by how complicated it all was, this business of establishing home and title in the Canadian North West.

Of course, to do all this, one must also be a man—what would Mrs. Mary Wollstonecraft-Godwin have said, had she survived the birth of her second child? When it came to the harsh realities of pioneer life, there might actually be some logic to the division of the sexes. If it was difficult for a man to manage, it might well be beyond the physical capacity of a woman, for even when one had acquired a homestead, there were requirements for earning the title, requirements such as breaking so much land and building a house. On the other hand, for gentlemen such as Captain Pierce and my uncle, both of whom had several sons—and daughters—to establish while they were themselves in straightened circumstances, homesteading offered a blessed opportunity.

My uncle finally brought the conversation back to the Pierces, and again my mind wandered, though my uncle's distress was obvious when he described the bank failure that had provoked the Pierce family's financial crisis. Listening to my Uncle James get bogged down while describing the kindness of the Pierce's friends, Cousin Ernest again took over.

"The forty-mile trip to this district was much more rigorous ten years ago than the journey you recently experienced," he assured me. "When the first settlers came, there were few good trails, especially in the early spring, when the water in the Pipestone is highest."

When Cousin Ernest came to the Pierces' Ottawa trip, it was clear that even Cousin Mary loved retelling stories, so long as they didn't put her own family in a bad light. After she took up the narrative, Cousin Ernest tried to interject that the Pierces no doubt took this step at the suggestion of the Pages or the Sayers. After all *they claimed* to have obtained *their* homesteads through the intervention of the Governor General, after they had dined at Rideau Hall. Mary chided her brother for his cynicism and continued her version of the story.

"It was the Prime Minister who introduced the Pierces to the

Minister of the Interior," she reminded us. "And it was Sir David who must have persuaded the Prime Minister to open the area for homesteading."

I nodded. Yes, Mrs. Pierce had told me that.

Again Cousin Ernest interjected, somewhat unkindly, "And with this evidence, Captain Pierce was known in the community and beyond as a personal friend of the former Prime Minister."

I noted how the different perspectives revealed much about the three Humphrys. Each storyteller emphasized those elements most interesting to him or her—my uncle, the Pierces' impressive genealogy and the many similarities between Captain Pierce and himself; Cousin Mary, the convenience of aristocratic, powerful or monied connections; and Cousin Ernest, human foibles and less romantic truths. They all came to the same place in the end, however, and the overall effect was basically consistent with the story Mrs. Pierce had told me when we travelled together from England.

"Since it was August by the time the land claims were settled," continued Cousin Ernest, "the Pierce men had to go back and build some kind of winter shelter."

"Yes," I said, "Mrs. Pierce told me about that." But Cousin Ernest had more to add.

"They had already erected a small lean-to barn of poplar poles for Billy, the horse, and their 'Wonder Cow.' But this sort of structure was too flimsy and open to the elements, especially to accommodate women. In time they would build their solid log house, but for the moment, they merely needed something adequate."

I could see Cousin Mary bristling at the suggestion women were less hardy, but she said nothing.

"With the help and encouragement of their new neighbours, the Pages and the Sayers, they dug their shelter, which would be mostly underground. They also designated separate rooms for eating and for sleeping, and others for storage, and they covered the whole with poles and a sod roof."

"That seems very clever," I said. This was not quite what Mrs. Pierce had described.

"It was the best solution under the circumstances—since there was no time to search out and fell enough large trees from the woods around Fish Lake, much less to actually build a house."

I began to despair at this point of ever hearing the story of the Pierces' grander home, completed in 1883, the year after they settled. It interested me even more since I had seen it when I walked the children to school and had noticed how well situated it was to be a manor house, as it was set back from the street and at a slight elevation, yet visible from the school and other buildings.

As far as I could judge from the exterior, *Gitcha Wa Teepee*—the name meant "Great White House" and was apparently a gift from the chief of White Bear Reserve, the Cree community six miles south of town—was a fine establishment. Because it was built of logs, it was not in the grand style of English country homes, but it had a somewhat more finished appearance than my uncle's house. This was not surprising, since my uncle's vision was unusually ambitious, and his house must be finished alongside other demanding projects.

The Pierce's Great White House was not only famous for its location and for its Cree name, but from the beginning it had been the centre of community celebrations. The Pierce Christmas dinners, for instance, were legendary, though the Humphrys could not agree on whom the Pierces invited. Uncle James was convinced "the whole neighbourhood" took part in these festivities. After all, Mr. Pierce had been an astute politician. However, Cousin Ernest and Cousin Mary were only certain of the Sayers and the Pages being guests. They had, after all, contributed a great deal to the family's comfort in their first year. The Humphrys agreed, however, that the centrepiece for that first Christmas dinner was wild goose and duck, along with potatoes and other vegetables the family had grown in their very own garden.

Nor was the Pierce family only hospitable on special occasions; rather, they were in the habit of inviting parishioners for tea after church. In this way, they lived up to the message on the board over their front gate, and all the Humphrys could recite it by heart: "Welcome all who enter this hospitable gate, none can come too early, or stay too late."

After this recitation, there was a momentary lull, and my uncle took advantage of it to consult the timepiece in his waistcoat pocket. It would soon be time to dress for dinner, he said, which ended the history lesson for the time being. Ruthie would clear the table and do the washing up while we dressed.

As I attended to my toilette, I pondered all that I had heard. What if Mrs. Pierce had changed living quarters after her husband's death because of both loneliness and economic necessity? Without her husband, she would need her adult sons to maintain the land. She certainly could not host young, male agricultural students on her own, so there would be no regular income to run a large house. Furthermore, most of her sons and daughters had their own establishments and could not devote their time to her.

I now wished I had shown more gratitude to the very respectable mother and son when I was travelling with them. Unfortunately, there had been too many hints, as if I were a kind of community property. Furthermore, it had seemed that any bachelor who needed a mate would do, and this had offended my dignity. In spite of my parents' rather cynical arrangement and my recent romantic disappointment, I still fantasized about one day being a wife. Furthermore, however unlikely it seemed, I also clung to some idea of being—like Mrs. Wollstonecraft-Godwin, who sacrificed much for love—loved and chosen for myself.

Chapter 21
-
I MEET THE NEIGHBOURHOOD

Since my uncle had been asked to bring his flute to our evening with the Pierces, and I knew the family had a piano and all the misses and young matrons played, a variety of music could be anticipated. Cousin Ernest, his transformation from the gawky boy I once knew perhaps owing to his frequently being asked to help provide such entertainment at parties, would naturally be accompanying his father and others.

Besides being sufficiently rested to look forward to seeing Mrs. Pierce again, I also welcomed the opportunity to meet other persons from the neighbourhood. Though my days with the Humphrys had been full and I enjoyed my household chores, supervising the children—and wedding preparations, of course—they still lacked a certain variety. As for Mr. Lionel Cuthbert, I continued to have glimpses of him, but there had been no new pretext for us to speak. There were no more wagon rides to school, as the children could be conveyed more easily without my presence. My initiative might have reminded my uncle the matter required more careful attention from him, but that was all the satisfaction I could take.

Still, I remembered the delight of my afternoon walk in the wind and sunshine, followed by the awkward pleasure of finding myself alone in the company of the surprisingly civil Mr. Cuthbert. I was now able to admit to myself that the latter experience had been a pleasure, though it would have been decidedly improper to allow it to become a pattern. Still, the walk and the person of Mr. Cuthbert were indelibly connected in my memory, so I could not recall the former without remembrance of the latter.

I most often espied Mr. Cuthbert at mealtimes, where the routine had continued much as I had observed it during my first few days. The "boys" (which included any farm workers) ate most of their meals in the kitchen. The morning meal was very early, at about seven hours, and except on rare occasions, the men were finished ere the women and children began. The same was true for noon luncheon. Tea had been all but eliminated, save on Sunday, the boys seldom took supper in the dining room, and the only formal supper had been the one enjoyed at the beginning of my visit.

It had taken me some time to accustom myself to this unfamiliar pattern, as my upbringing had been traditional, with afternoon tea and a late supper, even when there were no children to be fed and hurried off to bed. Mealtimes at Cannington Manor, however, were in the spirit of the frontier—organized around the men's schedules, which followed the progress of the sun. When the light began to disappear in the evening, it was time to break from heavy labour, but not before. I understood the reasons for this, but nonetheless was often conscious of a ravenous hunger before the evening meal.

Though formal dining such as I had enjoyed on my first day seldom happened when my aunt was away, there was to be a dinner party in a fortnight. The guests this time would be my uncle's potential business partners Dr. Hardy and Mr. Robert Bird, both of whom were unmarried. Not only was my uncle seeking investment for his pork-processing plant—which, after all, had a contract to fill—but other community leaders were considering a cheese factory. (In the colonies, as in England, many new enterprises had their beginnings in social occasions.)

Considering my uncle's financial situation, I was a little surprised he was hosting a social occasion so soon before his daughter's wedding. On the other hand, the dinner party might prepare the way for a financial advantage.

My uncle's situation, however it concerned me, was not foremost in my thoughts as I prepared for the evening at the Pierces'. Instead, I wondered if Mr. Cuthbert was included in the invitation, since he was only a hired man. I suspected not, so I was pleasantly surprised to see him, again in his gentleman's attire, amid the cluster of uncle and cousins already assembled in the hallway when Mary and I, gowned and caped for the evening party, descended the stairs. Mr. Maltby was not in the number; he would meet us at the Pierce house. This absence did not affect Mary's spirits, nor her looks. She was even more lovely and glowing than usual, as befit a bride to be.

I have no doubt that Mr. Cuthbert noticed my cousin's beauty. Whether or not his blue eyes also approved of me, I do not know, since I felt I must avoid looking at him. I did, however, feel the warm, firm pressure of his calloused palm as he handed me into my uncle's two-seater, which he was to drive. In fact, I found myself imagining his hand held mine both longer and more firmly than was absolutely necessary.

After this felicitous beginning, it turned out to be a cramped and uncomfortable journey, as we took the more direct route to Ted Pierce's farm, a hilly, twisting track somewhat off the usual road to the village. My uncle was well enough not to require the carriage, but he must still accommodate his gouty leg. Therefore, he, Lionel Cuthbert and Cousin Dora—since she was the smallest—occupied the front seat of the wagon. That left Ernest, Mary, Nettie and me to find room as best we could on the seat behind them. Cousins Billy and Frankie perched on blocks of wood in the bed of the wagon, and I confess I somewhat envied them, impossible though it would have been to manage a gown in such a situation.

I was surprised that no one thought to put a few comfortable chairs in the back of the wagon. But perhaps there was no way to anchor them, which would have meant a great deal of slipping and sliding on the steeper hills, and there were two or three such on our way to the Pierces. As usual, the two youngest children, Noel and

Cicely, were left at home, in care of Nurse.

My suspicions about the size of the group at the Pierces were correct, as there were already quite a number of people, both young and old, gathered when we arrived. Mr. Maltby was almost immediately at Mary's side, gravely handsome as always and perhaps a little sheepish after his hasty exit from church the night before. Others of my acquaintance were Mr. and Mrs. Ernest Beckton, Mr. Herbert Beckton (again without his Florrie) and Mr. Arthur LeMesurier, and there were many new acquaintances to be made.

Dr. Hardy was introduced to me for the first time, and at close quarters I found him younger than I had imagined. The tales I had heard of his exploits suggested an older—perhaps even dissipated—man. In fact, he seemed properly attentive, attractive and good-humoured—though I might have suspected he was courting Cousin Nettie, were there not such a discrepancy in their ages. He must still have been past five and thirty. Her possessive manner towards him did suggest a special understanding, and I noticed for the first time that she too had taken special care with her toilette that night. On the other hand, this might have meant nothing more than that he was a great favourite with the whole family.

There were also several young married couples, including the third Beckton brother, William, and his attractive English wife, Edith, as well as Spencer Page, now nominated for the territorial government, and his wife, the former Frances Pierce. Frances Page informed me, clutching a young child who threatened to run off, that she had been the first bride to be wed in the Cannington Manor church. There were also affianced couples, not only Cousin Mary and Mr. Maltby, but also the Rev. Mr. Dobie himself and his fiancée, who were to be married in late June. This might account for his fluster and blunder on the previous evening. The Pierces were all lively company, as were the Pages, the Prices, the Troughton brothers and Dr. Hardy. Neither did Mr. Cuthbert, though he tended to stand back with the other unattached men, seem out of place in this jolly company.

The party included a supper, a rather good one, roast pig rather than mutton, to which I was accustomed, and this was particularly succulent, having been basted all afternoon over a spit in the yard. My uncle praised it highly and seemed troubled he hadn't considered such an option for Mary's wedding breakfast. Mrs. Pierce senior, who presided over the feast, for all it was her daughter-in-law's house, begged him to consider the evening a gathering in honour of the upcoming nuptials. Weren't both the bride and groom such favourites of all? It was a kind thought, though perhaps a little presumptuous. I glanced at the daughter-in-law, wondering if it were she who most needed my sympathy. It seemed that Mrs. Pierce senior had retained her position as first lady of the community after all.

After the meal came the entertainment, and Uncle James obligingly brought out his flute and delighted all the company by playing with both flourish and taste. Since it was known that she had studied abroad, Cousin Mary also played—a simple French folk tune that was very pleasing and appropriate. Still, it was obvious Cousin Ernest had become the more proficient musician of the two. In fact, it seemed a waste that his main role was that of accompanist for my uncle. The flute is portable and a showier instrument in some ways, but I have always greatly admired those whose talent is for the piano, as it has such depth and versatility.

Cousin Ernest and Lily Pierce were also prevailed upon to accompany certain singers, and many young ladies sang a ditty or two. I was asked myself, but since I am no more accomplished in music than in drawing, I quickly refused. The undoubted high point of the evening for me was when Mr. Lionel Cuthbert was persuaded to come forward for a few Scottish songs. He chose romantic favourites *The Red, Red Rose* and *Bonnie Banks O' Loch Lomond*, followed by *My Ain Folk*. Though they were familiar parlour pieces, on this occasion they affected me far beyond my expectations.

Such songs are often performed with comic expression and gesture, no doubt when singers are unsure of themselves or wish to show their sophistication, but Mr. Cuthbert had no such affectations. Instead, his rich, sweet voice dipped and soared, and the words and emotions came forth as if from the heart of a true and honest rustic lover. In this he superseded the Scottish poet who penned the *The Red, Red Rose*, since Mr. Robert Burns himself—I now recalled the name that had eluded me when I first met Mr. Cuthbert—was known to be a fickle suiter, for all his other gifts.

Of the three songs, I was most moved by the last. Though Mr. Cuthbert's birthplace was neither England nor Scotland, when he opened his mouth, the yearning seemed to flood from his heart. "Far from my home I wander . . ." he sang, and I knew my own were not the only eyes that filled with tears. I vividly recalled our conversation at my uncle's dinner party on the lawn and felt again the pure magnetism of Mr. Cuthbert's gaze. This time I knew my tears were not from nostalgia, but from a desire to possess that beauty—not only the song, but the man himself.

And the tears on my pillow that night came of my awareness that such a thing would be utterly impossible. Even were I destined to stay in Cannington Manor, the worlds we occupied—save for a treacherous evening when a few Scottish love songs made all seem possible—were not the same. How foolish I knew myself to be, and how I wished I had never set eyes on his handsome face.

Chapter 22

-

THE ARRIVAL OF MISS MARTHA PRITCHARD

After the evening at the Pierces, the next significant event was the arrival of Miss Martha Pritchard, the new maid, which happened a few days later. She was a prim little thing, probably not more than eighteen, and judging from the look she cast upon all of us gathered in the kitchen, she seemed to have an eye for details. Furthermore, her sour expression suggested she was not disposed to be pleased by these details—though her moodiness might also have been due to weariness from her trip.

Whatever the reason, I found myself immediately on guard against her. I supposed her critical gaze about the room—and the fact she was corseted and wearing a striped gabardine travelling garment far beyond the requirements of her station—was her way of giving herself some importance. No doubt she saw every new position as an opportunity for her to improve her prospects.

With such a forceful young woman before me, I immediately feared for my young cousins. Martha Pritchard's presence now was intended to ease preparations for Mary's wedding. But when Mary was wed and established in her own home and their mother still absent, how would it be? With this democratic feeling that everyone depended on everyone else to survive existing in the community and with few privileges to define rank, would Cousin Nettie and the others be able to keep such a maid in her place?

And then there was Uncle James. After all the upsets in their household because of Nurse, he was understandably relieved to have Miss Pritchard finally among us. Yet, I noticed with some alarm that his manner towards his new domestic verged on the courtly. It seemed as if he were actually apologizing that he had not met her in person, just as he had apologized to me a fortnight ago! And hadn't he sent Lionel Cuthbert to pick her up from the stagecoach in his stead, just as he had sent Mr. Cuthbert and Cousin Billy to fetch me?

Though I told myself it was no concern of mine, I could not help but wonder whether Mr. Cuthbert had performed the same gallantries for this young woman as for me, when I practically fell into his arms upon my arrival. Indeed, Miss Pritchard had already cast a few glances in Mr. Cuthbert's direction as she stood there in the kitchen, surrounded by the family as if she were a person of some importance—in fact, she might have guessed we had all stayed up to have a look at her. But perhaps those glances were merely on account of Mr. Cuthbert's comely appearance and not because he had paid her any particular attention. Whether he had or not, I still felt a pang, which sharpened my resolve to establish the necessary distinctions.

If Mary had been at home, she would have understood the situation, but Mary was visiting with Mrs. Ernest Beckton for the day and would be home either very late or perhaps not until the morning. This was the day my cousin and Jessie Beckton had chosen for Mrs. Beckton's ladies maid to help finish a few of Mary's wedding garments.

With Mary absent, Nettie too mild and my uncle too grateful, the responsibility appeared to be mine to demonstrate the appropriate distance between family and servant. I was certain my aunt would be able to maintain the necessary balance when she returned, if someone just laid the foundation. For all that I often discounted my own mother in my heart because I felt she discounted me, I was her daughter, and she would never have allowed a maid to think herself an equal.

"Uncle James," I moved closer to him and touched him on the shoulder, for I could see Miss Pritchard was about to elevate herself further by giving him a recipe for the gout. "You must be anxious to retire after all those hours of work on the new barn today. Nettie and I will be happy to show Miss Pritchard her room. She is to share with Nurse, is she not?"

This brought Martha Pritchard's eyes in my direction. I could see that she had scarcely noticed me before and that I had indeed discomposed her. "Share a room?" That is all she said, but clearly she had hoped for—perhaps even expected—private quarters.

"We felt it most convenient for the moment, as there is no other room available." I was speaking completely out of turn, for I had no idea what space was available in the nursery wing or the maid's quarters. I did suspect, however, that by sharing a room, she would also have to share a bed with Nurse and that this would not please her. I could have mentioned that this arrangement would not be for long—if Ruthie's man finally made good on his indiscretion and married the woman who would soon be bearing his child. However, Miss Pritchard would learn about that business soon enough.

I also had to steel myself not to put out a hand to lift one of Miss Pritchard's bundles for her—she had brought rather a lot of luggage for one who would be a mere housemaid. But I caught myself just in time and was pleased to see my young cousins followed my lead. Meanwhile, the men, including Lionel Cuthbert, had turned away and were queued up to leave the kitchen, either to bed or bunk-house, so Miss Pritchard was obliged to carry her own portmanteaus.

When she seemed unable to manage on her own, I gave Nettie a warning look, for my generous young cousin still seemed disposed to be helpful, and I assured Miss Pritchard that she would be wise to make a second trip to carry all her things. After all, the maids' stair was narrow and turning, not at all like the staircase used by the family. Furthermore—and my tone suggested that I was being ex-tremely magnanimous—nothing would be expected of her on her first evening.

"We are rough and ready here," I said airily, even while doing my best to show that class distinctions would be carefully maintained, "and capable of clearing up a meal when we must. We have saved you a plate, which I will bring up when you are settled."

Then I beckoned to Nettie to lead the way to Nurse's quarters, for I would not have been able to find the room on my own, and Miss Martha Pritchard with her bags and bundles laboured along behind us.

I stepped forward and knocked before entering Nurse's room, where we found to my relief that she was still properly attired. Still, I noticed as a stranger might, how her bodice was stretched unnaturally tight over her bosom, and her apron failed to mask her condition. As she got up to greet us, she also moved awkwardly, in what could be called a *waddle*. All in all, I was sincerely glad she hadn't been appearing in company for some time. Though her appearance was graceless to the point of being comic, I addressed her respectfully, as "Miss Ford," and was careful about my smile. This too was for Miss Pritchard's benefit, as she was eying Nurse dubiously and had clearly taken note of her predicament.

Nurse seemed no more pleased by the prospect of sharing a room than Miss Pritchard had been.

"I had thought with Master Jimmy away . . ." she began.

"But then she would be inconvenienced when Master Jimmy returns with his mother, and we certainly would not want to inconvenience Miss Pritchard," I said with my best lady-of-the-manor smile. I was near to enjoying myself.

There was only one bed in the room, but it was wide enough for two to sleep—uncomfortably. There was also a small cupboard, a shelf and a second chair by the window, where it appeared Nurse' had been sitting. When we interrupted her, she had possibly been making use of the remaining light for sewing. I motioned her back to her chair, and Miss Pritchard, exhausted apparently by her exertions, took that as a signal to sink into the other seat.

"There," I said, "it's nice to see you so settled and able to rest a little before you bring up the remainder of your belongings. Miss Ford will explain the meal schedule to you. And in the morning, Miss Humphrys will be able to acquaint you with the rest of the family's needs."

I noted with satisfaction that Miss Pritchard rose from her chair when Cousin Nettie and I left the room. Though the need to reinforce the message might arise, at least the proper distinctions had been made. Cousin Nettie made no comment as we descended the backstairs to return to the kitchen, but she was uncharacteristically quiet as we worked together to clear up after the evening meal. She too had taken note.

Cousin Mary, however, had no such compunctions and, when she heard of the evening's adventures, teased me about how I had "put Miss Pritchard in her place."

"I had no idea that behind that delicate facade you are a woman fashioned of steel," she said, making a show of saluting me. "We will in future make certain we mind our p's and q's in front of you."

At this Cousin Nettie also laughed. I blushed and started to protest, but Mary hushed me with a smile and an embrace. "Mother will be grateful," she said.

At that moment I could think of no better praise. However, when I retired for the night and reflected on actions that were quite out of character for me, my motivations were less clear. Extraordinary as it seemed, did I see Miss Pritchard as some kind of threat? And what, after all, was my position in the family? Was I not a stranger too and not even anyone useful, merely a visitor, and a visitor of short duration?

Chapter 23

THE TEMPEST AND
THE TEAPOT

Though, as I have indicated, I later had reservations about my actions on the night Miss Pritchard arrived, the incident did make me more aware of Ruthie Ford. Up to that point I had seen little of that unfortunate woman. However, following Cousin Mary's example, I was learning to call her "Nurse" rather than "Ruthie." In fact, I was uncertain why she had ever been called "Ruthie," as it was not her actual name. It may have been a pet name devised by her own family, but more likely it had come from some employer or other. I knew it was customary for many ladies in my mother's circle to give maids the names of former maids, as this saved them the trouble of learning something new. At times they also addressed servants by their surnames or by the surnames of their employers.

In Ruthie Ford's case, the name might have had to do with her former light-hearted manner, for I noticed the younger Humphrys still called her "Ruthie." Whatever her title, she was still the children's nursery maid, plus the family seamstress and occasional housemaid, though her condition kept her out of sight.

In England, her seclusion would not have been unusual. Nannies and nursery maids were seldom seen, just as children themselves were usually confined to the non-public areas of the house. In this environment, however, where the hired man, the chaw boy—when we had one—and the maid ate at the same table as the master—or at least as the master's sons—Nurse's absence seemed an unusual delicacy, especially as she had been the only house servant until the arrival of Miss Martha Pritchard.

On those rare occasions when I did encounter Nurse, the knowledge of her situation made me feel awkward in her company. At the same time, I was curious about her fall from grace. How had she allowed such a thing to come about? What heated desires had made her so reckless of her reputation and welfare? Had her error been one of her own volition, or had the man concerned imposed himself upon her without her consent? And how was it that the Humphrys family had failed to protect her?

The man involved I had not seen, though I had heard his name was McClure; I had also heard that my aunt insisted he leave my uncle's employ. I imagined him a lone wolf—sullen in expression, dark of hair and intentions; encountering the vulnerable girl who was lonely for her English friends and their innocent larks; luring her with sideways looks, the thrill of covert meetings and finally whispers and acts of raw, physical passion.

Though he too kept himself to himself, Lionel Cuthbert was nothing like Mr. McClure. Lionel Cuthbert, though quiet, had an open, honest manner and expression. He was also a hard worker—not easily distracted—and had, I was discovering, a strong sense of propriety. But there I stopped myself. How distressing that he would so often come to mind, when I had no intention of thinking of him.

Whether Nurse's isolation came from her own sense of propriety or was a direct order from my aunt, I did not know. In the middle of the afternoon (apparently she was still indisposed in the mornings) she sometimes made her way down to the kitchen to make the family's cakes and pastries. No doubt this responsibility at least would now become Miss Pritchard's duty and prerogative.

Nurse's main occupation at the moment was basting Cousin Mary's wedding garments. The wedding gown itself had arrived long since from Harrod's, the well-known London clothier and mercantile store; I knew this because Mary had donned the gown to show it to me, knowing no doubt that it set off her beauty to perfection. In fact, if I had not protested, she would have modelled undergarments and nightdresses as well, even though they were unfinished. My protests earned me more of Cousin Mary's good-natured teasing. Modesty has its limits, she said, and my husband would have much to teach me. Then she kissed me on the cheek, to prove it was not her intention to wound me.

The grey, two-piece travelling dress as well as two new tea gowns had also been finished, thanks to Jessie Pierce's ladies maid. However, there was still considerable work to do on the undergarments, as well as on the dresses for Mary's sisters—for they were to be bridesmaids. In fact, I was surprised at how much Nurse was able to accomplish in spite of her condition.

Whenever we visited her in Mary's apartment—where Nurse often worked to make the fittings more convenient—her swollen figure drew my eye, try as I might to focus on the regularity of her tiny stitches. As the wedding grew nearer, this arrangement was satisfactory for all, as Mary's room was large, the twin to my own, and Nurse's own room quite small—it could not be easy for her to be sharing it with Miss Pritchard. But I had not thought of Nurse's convenience on the day Miss Pritchard arrived. I had merely thought about the importance of maintaining class distinctions—or so I had told myself at the time.

Increasingly, I not only questioned my motives, but also felt some qualms about the additional discomfort my interference had caused Nurse. Perhaps there really was no excuse for crowding, with little James in no need of his room while he was in England with his mother. However, no one in the family seemed inclined to criticize or change the arrangements. For the first few days, therefore, the situation remained as it was.

This did not mean the atmosphere was peaceful. The crowded quarters clearly contributed to Miss Pritchard's apparent ill-nature in the mornings, as she frequently commented that she had not slept well. Sometimes she was stiff or suffering from a chill because she had not been allowed her share of the bedclothes, and at other times, she had been kept awake by Nurse's snoring. In fact, we women of the family learned it was wisest not to give Miss Pritchard as much as a "How do ye do?" in the morning. She was inevitably not well, and she implied, even when she did not state it, that her roommate was the cause of her distress.

Though I was disposed to think more kindly of Nurse when her needs and the needs of Miss Pritchard were in opposition, I had to admit the older woman was also somewhat to blame. It seemed clear the two were shuffling for position, and it was Nurse who precipitated the final crisis, which involved a pot of black India tea.

Because she was still inclined to nausea in the mornings—or so we understood— Nurse had taken to staying in bed after Miss Pritchard had got up. This strategy alone seemed designed to cause resentment, but Nurse further fueled the situation when she regularly prevailed upon Miss Pritchard to bring up a pot of tea. On the first occasion, Nurse's ploy that she was feeling unwell might have been forgiven. But once Miss Pritchard had reluctantly accommodated her, it became an established pattern that one considered a right (her having precedence as the longer-standing member of the household) and the other considered an imposition (imagine someone in Ruthie Ford's situation having the effrontery to expect favours!).

This morning tea ritual continued for almost a week, and my cousins and I should no doubt have taken steps to defuse the situation. We had noted the lack of friendliness between the two—in fact, I regret to say it created some small amusement for us—but, until we heard the crash, we had no inkling of the extent of the problem.

It was a weekday morning, the children had been transported to school, and Uncle James and the other men had partaken of their breakfast and gone off to their various employments. Mary, Nettie and I were lingering over our second cup of tea as we discussed the day's activities. It was now little more than a week until Mary's wedding day, and there were a number of things to accomplish. Though we were vaguely aware of Miss Pritchard glowering about her tasks in the background, we had learned to ignore her huffs. Neither did we consider that our lingering might in fact be adding fuel to the flame—as it held up her work—nor notice she scarcely had time to finish her own breakfast before she dashed upstairs with Nurse's tea.

The crash, however, arrested our attention. Mary hurried up the back stairs to Nurse's room, closely followed by her sister and me. Nurse's *time* was getting very near, and we naturally supposed any accident might relate to her condition. Arriving at the scene, we found tea-tray, broken teapot and cup on the floor; soaked bed-clothes and Nurse damp and sputtering on one side of the bed, while Martha Pritchard was hissing on the other. The language coming out of both women's mouths is not fit to report, but it seemed Martha had been provoked to throw the tea things at the other because Nurse had complained her tea was late. Establishing blame at that moment was unimportant, but it was clear interventions were overdue.

Mary was admirably calm in both voice and manner as she suggested Miss Pritchard might wish to remove herself to Baby James's room until Nurse's baby arrived. This would prevent her being disturbed, though she would be close enough to hear if Miss Ford had need of her during the night. In fact, Mary suggested Miss Pritchard might wish to go to the other room right now, to calm herself. She—Mary—would attend to the cleaning up, she said. She did not refer specifically to the broken crockery or the dripping bed linens, though both difficulties would take some effort to put right. I had frequently admired my cousin's poise, but never more so than now. Neither did Mary ever hint that I might bear some responsibility for the disaster, but I felt it nonetheless.

Chapter 24

A DAY'S LABOUR

Though I had claimed centre stage for a few minutes when Miss Pritchard arrived, believing I must intervene for the sake of the family, for the most part I merely observed the dramas of the Humphrys household. When Ruthie Ford's baby chose to be born, however, just seven days before Mary's wedding, of necessity I played a larger part, as Mary and I were near at hand when the unfortunate woman's pains began. It was I that raced for help while Mary undertook the more difficult task of assisting Nurse upstairs to her chamber.

Nurse's travail took place only two or three days after the teapot incident, on a weekday and early in the afternoon, all most fortuitous, as I wouldn't have wished the children or the others present at such a delicate time. Uncle James and Cousin Billy would be fetching Dora, Cecily and Noel home from school when they returned from their trip to town. It also happened that Cousin Nettie and Miss Pritchard were with them—as a special treat for the latter. Though her manner had not improved, the little maid had capably taken on—and performed with ease—many of the tasks managed so awkwardly by the family, so a reward seemed appropriate. Even I could not disagree with that.

Neither did Mary and I suffer for being left behind, for we were also spending our afternoon in the sunshine. Our task was to transplant melons, squash and cucumbers from the hotbeds to the vegetable garden, according to the directions my uncle had left us.

"Be mindful of their tender roots," he had said. "And plant them at least eight inches apart; though they are small as yet, one must bear in mind how they spread and their eventual size. Water the soil after planting, and put a mulch of grass around the seedlings to support them and hold the moisture while they adjust to their new surroundings."

Though my uncle's instructions were specific, I cannot be certain we handled the fragile plants with quite the care he might have wished. I certainly damaged a stem or two in the process of moving them from tray to garden. But we did our best and enjoyed the smell of the warm grass and woodsy soil as we laboured.

Because there was no one in the house to hear her if she called, we had persuaded Nurse to bring her sewing outside. It was a lovely day, and we thought she too must appreciate some fresh air. She had complained of indigestion when Mary checked on her that morning, but had apparently improved as the hours wore on and had eaten a full lunch.

After Mary and I installed Nurse upon a bench, we bent over the rows in our bonnets, gloves and aprons, for Mary was insistent as usual that we try to protect ourselves from the sun. But still she exclaimed when she rolled up her cuffs and bared her wrists.

"Oh, Floss," she moaned, "see how brown I am! Mr. Maltby will think he is marrying some imposter."

"Your colour is perfect," I protested. "And Mr. Maltby thinks himself very fortunate. You know that."

Though we had placed Nurse within call, we were still startled by her cry, as often happens when an event long anticipated finally comes to pass—especially if one is apprehensive about it—we are tempted to disbelief. Nor was it a cry exactly, but more a gasp, expressing more wonder than pain. Mary and I heard it nonetheless, and we dropped our trowels and ran to her. I was embarrassed to see that the unfortunate woman seemed to have wet herself, copiously, since her shoes and stockings were soaked, and a small pool darkened the grass about her feet. Mary's manner, however, suggested this was more significant than poor bladder control.

"I think her water has broken—we must help her to the house. No, I can do that. You find one of the men to go for Dr. Hardy." My cousin hooked her arm under Nurse's, and the two were soon mincing along together, while I stood as one stunned. *One of the men? Was there anyone about? Would I have to search the meadow for them, perhaps get lost and be no help at all?*

"Try the barn," Mary called over her shoulder, sensing my indecision, and I scampered around the corner of the house like a terrified rabbit, careless of stones or pieces of building material that might be in my path.

As I approached the new barn, where construction was then at a standstill, I thought I heard movement, but couldn't gauge its origin. There was no time to lose in searching for the source. My voice came out feeble and breathless.

"Help—someone, help!"

Mortified by such a weak effort that surely no one would hear, I cupped my hands around my mouth, took a deep breath and tried again. "Help, we need help!"

I was too relieved to be abashed when it was Mr. Lionel Cuthbert who appeared. "What is it, Miss?" he called back, then hurried towards me.

A flood of gratitude engulfed me. Of course, if anyone knew what to do in every emergency, it was surely Mr. Cuthbert. I waited until he was at my side, but then blushed at his proximity.

"'Tis Nurse," I said, still breathless. "The baby . . . Mary says her water . . ."

He quickly understood. "I'll speak to Mary, then fetch the doctor."

Not until later would I remember his intimate use of my cousin's first name. Now he strode to the house, and I sought to keep pace with him. He took the main staircase, as it was closer, yet had no difficulty finding the way to Nurse's chamber—perhaps not surprising as it was now the scene of some commotion.

Mary was hovering over the agitated patient, who was half sitting, half lying, moaning all the while. My cousin was more flustered than I had ever seen her. Her hair and apron were both awry, and she was trying to remove the other woman's wet stockings with gloved hands still grimy from our work in the garden. Still, she had time to look up and smile.

"Oh, Florence. Lionel. Good." She tore off her garden gloves and dropped them on the floor. "Florence, can you bring hot water and clean towels, as many as you can manage?" And as I turned, the door closed behind me, leaving Mary, Lionel Cuthbert and the expectant woman inside the room.

For what, I wondered, did we need the towels and hot water? For washing our hands? For cleaning the patient after her ordeal? I hurried down the back stairs to the kitchen. No doubt there would be blood, a lot of blood—even I knew that much—and we would need something in which to wrap the baby.

In the kitchen I found a kettle on the boil, emptied it into a basin, filled two more kettles from the pail of water pulled up from the cistern that morning, put them on the stove and then headed toward the stairs with the basin. I stopped, came back to put the basin on the table, sloshing scalding water on my wrists but scarcely noticing, though I took the time to pull off my wet gloves. I also stoked the fire and added wood—at this time of the afternoon we often allowed it to die down. I then went to the kitchen closet, gathered an armful of clean towels and balanced a bar of lye soap on them, finally took the basin in my other hand and made my way back up the stairs, scalding myself again.

Lionel Cuthbert and Cousin Mary were now talking softly outside Nurse's door, and his hand was resting upon her arm. Mary turned as I arrived on the landing. She seemed a little flushed, and his hand fell to his side. For some reason, the words of *Red, Red Rose* flashed into my mind.

"Lionel is leaving right now," said Mary. "He feels there is still time to fetch the doctor. We are just to stay with her and make her as comfortable as we can, and have her drink lots of water."

"Try not to worry. You will manage." This time his glance included us both. "I'll find Hardy. Tell your brother Francis," this he said to Mary, "if he comes looking for me." Then Mr. Cuthbert disappeared down the stairs again, and we soon heard a team and wagon rattle out of the yard.

Chapter 25

-

A SINGULAR CRY

For all the urgency of those first few minutes, the afternoon wore on with little change. Now that Nurse was settled, she lay quietly for the most part, but every few minutes, she cried out with pain. Meanwhile, there was little we could do but tidy her, wash her feet and legs and smooth the sheets and bedcovers around her. When the pains came, we rubbed her back; and when the tears came, Mary put her arms around her.

"'Tis God's will. On account of my wicked ways," whimpered Nurse.

"Hush such silly talk," said Mary, looking at me over the woman's head as she rocked her gently from side to side. I tried not to remember the sight of Mary and Lionel Cuthbert outside Nurse's room—his hand upon her arm.

But Nurse couldn't lie still for long. Every time the pain came again, she tensed and twisted to escape it. Even when she writhed and appeared to pull away, Mary continued to stroke her back. Perhaps she did not know what else to do.

Dr. Hardy finally arrived and, not long after that, the whole family too, so there was a houseful of excitement and confusion. Dr. Hardy told Mary and me that we had done well, but it was no longer necessary for Nurse to lie quiet. In fact, it would be better if she moved about a little, as that would hasten the birth. He glanced toward the bedroom door, which was slightly ajar, and a number of interested bodies seemed to be clustered just outside it.

"Perhaps she could be helped to one of the chairs," he said.

When he glanced again toward the door and then looked at me, I understood what he wanted. I left the room, closing the door behind me. The whole family, with the exception of Billy, Ernest and Lionel Cuthbert, were hovering nearby, and I knew I must again take charge.

First, Uncle James must be persuaded he would not be needed in the birthing room. Assisting there possibly seemed the most difficult, noblest task, and no doubt he felt he must show himself willing to undertake it. Cousin Frankie, who was young enough to be fascinated by any spectacular event, even when it involved blood and pain, needed but little encouragement to escape with the other men. The afternoon was getting on and there was an evening meal to prepare—Miss Pritchard could take charge of that, with Cousin Nettie's help. Cousin Nettie could also bring the doctor anything he might need.

It seemed my lot, therefore, to distract the children, possibly to usher them straight outside again. I don't know whether I was more grateful or disappointed that this purpose would take me away from the scene—I have already admitted to an un-maidenly interest in the events that were taking place—but it was obviously Mary's place to stay with Nurse and to assist Dr. Hardy as required.

Cecily and Noel were soon off at a run for the swing that had been hung from a sturdy poplar tree beyond the makeshift tennis court. Dora, however, hung back. She looked up at me with her large, beautiful dark eyes.

"Will it hurt her very much?" she asked.

I knew not how to answer, so merely put my arm around her, which seemed to suffice, as she pressed her soft young body against me and tucked her head against my shoulder.

When the children were all happily playing, I remembered to

take Nurse's sewing into the house and to move the bench back to its place by the kitchen door. Noting that the puddle that had formed around Nurse's feet had disappeared, though the grass was still bent where her shoes had been planted, I busied myself by gathering up the bedding plants and returning them to the hot bed to be planted another day.

Even when these tasks were done, I repeatedly found some necessity to return to the house, to passing Miss Pritchard and Cousin Nettie, who were busy in the kitchen, and listening at the bottom of the stairs. Each time, hearing nothing unusual, I turned and went back to my charges. On the last occasion, I found the kitchen empty, with food left uncovered on the table. Footsteps hurried back and forth in the hall upstairs. Voices, and then a cry, that peculiar squalling cry that only an infant or young animal can make. Hearing it, I felt a stab of pain in both my breasts, and, hardly knowing how I came to be there, I was suddenly outside Nurse's chamber again.

Just as I arrived, Mary came out the door with a bundle in her arms. The baby was swaddled in towels, the hair still streaked with blood and mucous and the wrinkled face scarcely visible, but Mary's face was alight, and she lifted a corner of the wrappings so I could see the nose and puckered mouth.

"A boy," she said with a sob, "a lusty little boy!"

I gazed only a moment, then remembered the little ones outside. "I'll tell the children."

It was unlike poised Cousin Mary to show such illogical emotion, to react with tears to a happy event, but I had caught the sentiment from her and must wipe my eyes before showing myself to the children.

Chapter 26
-

A WALK IN THE MEADOW

The arrival of Nurse's baby made surprisingly little difference to our household. The children, it is true, asked many questions—most of which I and their older sisters evaded by setting some small task for them—and fortunately they spent most of the next two days at school. Mary did ask them not to speak of the event to their school-mates, as there might be those who would say unkind things about a child without a father.

Since Nurse did not eat with the family, it was no surprise when she continued to be absent from meals. I believe Mary, Nettie or Miss Pritchard checked on her and her baby quite frequently, as Dr. Hardy had suggested they should, but they did so without fanfare. I also know Uncle James visited her briefly shortly after the birth, almost as if to give his respects, and I thought it very gracious of him.

For my part, I hesitated. Truthfully, I am uncertain what held me back. It wasn't that I felt any distaste for what had occurred; in fact, I was surprised by my level of acceptance and by how the drama had moved me. How extraordinary that so many women underwent this experience regularly, not just once, but often a dozen times! This experience of giving birth bound them together in a way that had nothing to do with class. My hesitation about visiting was more likely due to awkwardness, my fear I might either do or say the wrong thing, or conversely that I might be incapable of giving Nurse or the baby some necessary attention.

From all reports, the child himself was remarkably well-behaved and seldom seemed to cry, though perhaps that was because his mother was constantly in attendance. In fact, Mary felt it necessary to allow Nurse a day away from her sewing. So it was that on the day after Nurse had given birth, Mary appeared to have unexpected time to spare, and she asked if I would take a stroll with her after lunch.

It was a beautiful day and I readily agreed. For some minutes we walked in silence, past the barnyards and pigpens, and into the east meadow, which Mary had told me would soon be mown to make hay for the stock to eat in the winter. At first, Mary said little and appeared to be lost in thought, but I was sure she would in time share what was on her mind, so I was content to wait. We had also to give some care to our footing. I hadn't taken the precaution of using the walking boots I had borrowed from Frankie, and though the earth underfoot was now, for the most part, dry enough that we could walk without fear of mud on our shoes, we must keep a sharp eye out for cow and horse dung.

As we strolled along, I reflected that my cousin and I had not spent much time alone in each other's company since my arrival. Even without the consuming interest of Nurse's successful delivery, there had been so many things to occupy us—at least things to occupy Mary—and I continually tried to be useful, though not always with success. That morning, for instance, I had worked for some time on Nettie's dress for the wedding, as Nettie was afraid Nurse would not be able to finish everything now that she had the baby to care for. Though I lost a thimble and punctured the ends of my fingers and thumbs numerous times, the difference between Nurse's tiny stitches and my own awkward imitation was only too apparent. In fact, I might have created work for her rather than saving her time. Finally, I gave up the task, concerned that my punctures might begin to bleed and stain the delicate fabric.

After this rather unsuccessful morning, I was grateful to have another prospect before me. As I have said, I had begun to feel myself part of the family, and like the others, was aware of how much we relied on Mary and how sorely we would miss her when she was gone. This was in spite of the fact Miss Pritchard was taking on many of Mary's household duties; the house was cleaner and domestic arrangements running more smoothly than I had seen since I arrived. However, Mary's warmth, good sense and lively interest in everything going on around her could not be as easily replaced as her housekeeping skills. She was much in demand at all times, and in light of this, I was grateful whenever she dedicated some time to me.

And what a lovely day it was to be out of doors! Around us we heard the birdsongs in their infinite variety, the buzzing of insects and occasionally the rustle of mice or other small animals in the grass. Besides that, we were still assaulted by the intoxicating scent of choke-cherry blossoms every time we went outdoors. The tiny white flowers seemed to grow most often on low bushes at the edges of thicker stands of poplar and aspen. Their fruit was generally ripe in August, Mary said, but even then they were bitter—hence the name—and the pulp stained fingers and teeth. Still, if boiled with sufficient sugar, they made tasty syrup or preserves, and some more adventurous folks even made choke-cherry wine.

Blending with this sweetness were the perfumes of other flowers—even a few wild roses—as well as the more earthy smell of grass and musky sloughs and other budding trees. The wind—there always seemed to be some kind of wind—was refreshing and for once carried no chill with it. I would have liked to grasp Mary's hand and run across the meadow—as we had done when we were children, before we knew that playtime hours were limited. Yet I sensed Mary still wished to talk about something in particular, and I was reluctant to interrupt her thoughts.

Though I tried to be patient, she appeared to have some difficulty arriving at what was uppermost in her mind. Instead, she commented that I had been close to one month with them and wondered if I had found the visit to my liking. I replied with emotion.

"I have never before felt I belonged to a real family. You have all been more than kind—"

Mary laughed, "It is not difficult to be kind to one such as you, Cousin Floss. And I trust you like the country as well?"

"Oh, yes!"

She then became serious. "But there is something else. It concerns—Mr.—Lionel Cuthbert."

"Lionel Cuthbert!" To my dismay, I found my voice suddenly breathy with emotion.

"I think you admire him, do you not." The phrase was not a question. Mary was calmly describing what I thought had been my secret.

"Oh," I said, "what makes you say that?"

"Your lovely eyes, my dear, that follow him. Your face that glows when he enters a room, even your pretence you don't see him—when it is obvious you do."

My blush deepened, and I covered my face with my hands. Mary gently grasped my wrists and wouldn't allow me to hide my eyes.

"He is a fine man. There is no reason to be ashamed."

"But he is not . . . by birth . . ."

"Not a gentleman? Is that what you think? Are there not so-called gentlemen less worthy of the title than he? What of your beau Frederick Corby? Do you think Lionel less a gentleman than Frederick Corby?"

Numbly, I shook my head.

"Florence, this is not England! What you need here, in this country—if you have the good fortune—is a man who is strong and steady and honest. All the airs and graces of so-called gentlemen make no difference."

"But why ask this of me? Why would you have me admit an attachment—when you do not?"

There, I had said it, the thing I suspected, and I was certain she would be angry with me. For a moment Mary was silent, and she released my hands. Finally she said, "You are right. I did admire

Lionel Cuthbert. And who would not?—His handsome face . . . his strength and . . . manliness . . . When I first heard him sing, I thought I would swoon."

"Why then—?"

"I don't know—yes, I do. There were many reasons . . . first being the question of money. Without any resources of my own, I could not be the wife of a poor man."

I was silent, and she continued. "I do admire and love Mr. Maltby," she said. "At first I thought him too old, too serious. I noticed only that he was tall and thin, his way of slouching his shoulders—some tall people are like this; they seem to slouch as if wishing to accommodate others or ashamed of their height." She laughed. "I called him 'Allys Sloper'—because he—sloped. Brother Ernest says we shall be the 'Sloper family'—sometimes he is incorrigible. Then I saw Mr. Maltby playing tennis, noticed his grace and skill at the game—"

She paused for rather a long time, long enough for me to wonder if some further response from me was expected, then finally continued. "I knew from the first my parents considered Mr. Maltby a good match. Perhaps that accounts for my critical eye. He comes from good English roots and had made something of himself in the Indian civil service—until the heat affected his health. He also came here with resources, unlike our constant struggle. It is no wonder my parents looked kindly on his potential as a husband.

"For a girl of less than eighteen, as I was when we first arrived, those attributes held no appeal. It wasn't long, though, before I began to appreciate him for his sense and his steadiness . . . and he could be graceful, as I have said. There was also his obvious preference for me—even though, as you know, I began to despair that he would ever announce his intentions. Mr. Maltby," she smiled, "is very shy, as perhaps you have noticed."

"In church, when the banns were read early?"

Mary nodded.

"But what—what of Mr. Cuthbert?"

Again Mary paused, as if searching for words. "I feel some shame knowing I may have caused him hurt. For I encouraged his notice—as much as it was . . . notice. There was never much to speak of—looks and smiles only, no talk of love, no time alone together. But such looks and smiles can be where love begins, as you know. And perhaps Mr. Cuthbert hoped for more, was disappointed..."

I still found it difficult to speak. "Cousin, what are you asking of me? Do you wish me to comfort Mr. Cuthbert, who once loved you?"

"Oh, dear Florence, do not look at me so. I simply felt that I must, in honesty, share this knowledge with you—"

"But . . ." I knew my face was flushed again, and I could scarcely look at her.

"—because, if there were to be an attachment between the two of you, I would not want secrets between *us*. And, I did think of Mr. Cuthbert as well."

"What do you mean?"

"I wanted to warn you, if indeed you were attached—and he to you—a man can only take so much disappointment without becoming bitter." There was another pause. "At present, it seems you will soon be leaving, and—and, I would not want him wounded twice."

We were silent then. And as we turned and began to retrace our steps through the meadow and towards the half-finished stone stable, we were wordless still. I had much to think about. First, my suspicions of a previous attachment had been correct. It also seemed clear my cousin had in some way given me her permission, even her encouragement, to care for Mr. Lionel Cuthbert. No doubt she even considered the possibility I would have financial resources she did not—the legacy from my father's aunt—and therefore would have more freedom to follow my inclinations.

I bumped my foot on a stone and almost tripped, but Mary's hand was there to steady me. I looked at her in a kind of wonder, uncertain whether to be grateful or to resent her. Indeed, it was interference of the most dreadful kind. And yet, how could I not be dizzy with the thought of such possibilities?

Most of all, she was my cousin, my dearest Mary, and I could not be angry with her. In fact, I would have liked to embrace her at that moment.

Yet, the thought of Lionel Cuthbert as my husband was impossible. I could not marry a man without breeding, someone of whom my family would disapprove. Such a union would make me the subject of gossip and speculation, both at home in England and here at Cannington Manor—it would be humiliating. I would be much more culpable than Nurse for her indiscretion, as I would also be betraying my birth.

Another thought chilled me. Since Mary had found me so easy to read, I must change whatever it was about my present behaviour that was giving me away. I must not allow myself to lead this good man on, must not even think of him.

And the worst realization was yet to come. If my feelings had been so easy for Mary to read, had Mr. Cuthbert also seen the evidence of my foolishness? Again, humiliation flooded over me. And as playful Fate would have it, the man himself was in sight, against the half-built wall of the new barn. He looked up from what he was doing, then straightened his shoulders and stood watching us. Mary smiled and nodded to him—her usual gracious self—but I would not, could not.

It was not until we were well past the place where the men were working that Mary broke the long silence between us.

"Can you ever forgive me?" she asked.

"Oh, Mary," my voice was husky. "I could never—never *not* forgive you."

But I could not imagine how I would ever face Mr. Cuthbert again, or how I was to treat him if I did.

Chapter 27

-

A LIVELY RACONTEUR

Cousin Mary had previously made reference to money worries, only to laughingly deny them immediately after. I was uncertain, therefore, of the extent of my uncle's financial hardships until I was witness to a telling scene between him and Dr. John Hardy. The occasion was the formal dinner on the following Sunday, and the guests were—besides Dr. Hardy—Mr. Ned Fleming, who lived with Dr. Hardy; Mr. and Mrs. Harry Bird; Mr. Bob Bird—who would also be Mr. Maltby's best man—and Mr. Maltby himself.

Mr. Lionel Cuthbert was not present. He had apparently gone directly back to his homestead after church. This relieved me of concerns that had occupied me since my walk in the meadow with Mary and, therefore, left me free to listen and observe the behaviour of others.

Most would agree it was a successful dinner. Martha Pritchard's presence in the house meant the Humphrys could now all retire in good time to dress for dinner, and the dining arrangements themselves were superior to those previously experienced at my uncle's table. I could not say precisely what particulars of decoration or service embodied this change, other than the vast improvement in the silver—it had obviously been thoroughly cleaned. Yet, there was a discernible difference overall, and I was not the only one who noticed. Mrs. Bird was full of compliments, which Cousin Mary accepted with appropriate grace, as hostess in her mother's absence.

As the person most responsible for such improvements, Martha Pritchard's value was increasing daily. Even I could not but respect her work. She had obviously been well trained at her previous establishments and, for all her youth, was very good at her job. I should say her *jobs*, since her current employment as housemaid involved tasks that in a larger English house would have been consigned to others. Indeed, that might have been the case at my uncle's house as well, had Nurse's time not been taken up by caring for the baby and stitching wedding garments.

My cousins and I still contributed where we could, but Martha had taken on the responsibility for baking, cooking and serving, as well as most of the cleaning. Her manner at times was still less than agreeable, and she was possessive about her tasks, so we were anxious not to oppose her, especially when it came to food preparation. Indeed, she had a particular gift for pie making—applauded by all. Her pork and kidney pies with my aunt's rhubarb chutney had been the centerpiece for this evening's dinner and had earned much favourable comment from our guests.

It was also a lively meal, as any company that included Dr. Hardy was bound to be—so I had been told, and I was seeing the proof of it. He launched into a tale as my uncle and the rest of the family greeted him at the door, and with each course regaled us with more adventures. This capacity to please left me in no doubt why he was such a favourite. It was a quality that had caused me some concern at the Pierces' party, where Nettie had sought out his company with the single-minded devotion of which only nineteen year olds are capable. But now I saw her brothers also vying for his attention, and their interest was just as pleasantly received.

I was already aware Dr. Hardy had arrived at Cannington Manor during the influenza epidemic of 1889. A few years earlier, two young children of the Moore family had succumbed to diphtheria, which had alerted the community to its vulnerability. To calm fears and prevent another such tragedy, my uncle had taken it upon himself to advertise in England for a qualified medical practitioner. In Captain Pierce fashion, he had also gone so far as guaranteeing such a doctor—should he find him—his salary and accommodation. When the agreeable and highly recommended Dr. Hardy responded to his advertisement and subsequently arrived, the doctor was installed at the Humphrys' home. There he stayed, occupying—until he decided to file for his own homestead—the room Cousin Ernest now claimed for his darkroom.

Not only was Dr. Hardy the community's medical practitioner, a merry companion and a welcome addition to the Humphrys household, but he also had some experience with amateur theatricals. In fact, as much as his schedule allowed, he took part in all community entertainments. This included my uncle's glee club and the church choir—as I had discovered on my first visit to the log church. In the style of most robust English gentlemen, he was also a sportsman of sorts, for he played both tennis and cricket and rode to hounds when he had the opportunity.

It was an impressive record, and I smiled with the others as the doctor provided the entertainment at dinner. I could find no fault with him, but neither did I feel any strong admiration. How capricious are the ways of the heart—that the handsome, cultured, amusing and—it seemed—eligible Dr. Hardy did not move me, while another had aroused such uninvited interest!

Mr. Ned Fleming had joined Dr. Hardy on the latter's homestead when the doctor found his practice kept him too busy to allow him time for farming. Between the two of them, they kept a small flock of sheep and had a batch of lambs every spring. Dr. Hardy also kept thoroughbred horses, though on a smaller scale than in England, and had been known to enter horses in the annual race day. In fact, the mare he described as his "most faithful companion" had been bred to race. She—then known as "Susan"—had failed to come to post in her maiden trotting race, and after a few more false starts, it was clear she must make herself valuable to the doctor in more pedestrian ways.

So she did, for it was with the faithful Sue between the shafts of his buggy that Dr. Hardy visited patients over a large territory. Not only did he travel to Moosomin and other towns along the main road, but also forty miles west as far as Broadview and the Crooked Lake reservation to the north. He also went south to the border of the United States and east as far as Manitoba. Though some larger towns boasted their own doctors, the Cannington Manor physician also served most of the rural patients. Such was his renown that on a few occasions he was even called upon to assist surgeons in Winnipeg. He was also the official medical officer for the White Bear Indian Reserve—as well as Justice of the Peace when my uncle was unavailable.

As was often the case, Uncle James and the others had offered most of this information about our guest before the actual dinner. Though, as I have said, I did not feel a personal interest in the doctor, I was touched by my uncle's desire—nay, insistence—on acquainting me with Dr. Hardy's history. Uncle James had told of patients avoiding serious handicaps or even an early demise because of Dr. Hardy's intervention. He also described how Dr. Hardy once traveled 125 miles in 24 hours to make sure he had attended to the needs of all his patients. Though the details were difficult to imagine, I believed the reports to be true, since my uncle must have had them on the authority of Dr. Hardy himself. I felt great compassion, therefore, for both the gentleman and his equine companion, if this degree of service was often expected of them. Beyond compassion and disinterested admiration, however, my feelings did not go.

Other stories about the doctor focused on his somewhat unorthodox methods. For instance, when he was forced to perform an operation outside a hospital, he apparently relied a great deal on whiskey—for its antiseptic properties and orally to dull the patient's pain. In fact, just before we sat down to dinner, Dr. Hardy was telling my uncle of a recent case where he had operated on a young man's foot in this manner.

Apparently, it was a situation that called for desperate measures. The operation could not be put off if the man were to retain any use of a foot mangled in an accident while clearing land. To make matters even worse, it was night when Dr. Hardy arrived, so the operation must be performed on the man's home-made table lit only by two small coal-oil lamps and a stable lantern. Though the patient had friends with him, not one of them could be trusted with more traditional anesthetics. Apparently, too much ether would do more than take away the pain. It could cause many serious problems, including failure of internal organs and paralysis of the whole body.

Dr. Hardy did the only thing he could do. He dosed the man with whiskey and had four men hold him down. This rough-and-ready medicine was re-administered whenever the patient showed signs that the pain was again too much for him to bear. When the operation was finished and appeared to be successful, the doctor had the additional comfort of knowing the patient had enough spirits in him to be pain-free at least until morning. Finally, after charging the young man's friends to keep an eye on the young man and help him with his work until he was back on his feet, the doctor was on his way to his next patient.

Dr. Hardy shook his head as he finished his tale. "It is not the kind of care I would wish to give, but this is still the frontier. And I am glad to say the foot was saved. The man is recovering well and should soon be back to work, with nothing but a slight limp to show for his adventures."

Uncle James clapped a hand on the doctor's shoulder. "But think of it before you came—Charlie Couper with his broken arm . . . John Moore . . . and many others still remember the misery of driving all the way to Moosomin for a doctor's care."

"Speaking of care," interjected the doctor, perhaps a little embarrassed by so much adulation, "I cannot stay long this evening. However, I do have a headache remedy for your Martha. Could I attend to her problems with her teeth another time—next Sunday perhaps?"

The following Sunday would be but a few days after the wedding, and I thought the doctor presumptuous to suggest another visit so soon, especially as patient care and social occasions seemed so entwined. Even Uncle James seemed momentarily doubtful, but his gracious nature won out. "Indeed, we would be grateful, for she suffers—and you and Mr. Fleming must sup with us then as well."

This was further evidence of my uncle's hospitality—whatever the circumstances and his own situation. At this point, everyone being seated, Martha served the meal, and for awhile the conversation was more mundane. My uncle's pork-processing plant was mentioned as was the possibility of a cheese factory. The Birds asked polite questions about both until my uncle returned to the earlier subject, the achievements of Dr. Hardy. This seemed unnecessary, since the other guests were worthy of equal attention, but he must have had some purpose I did not at that moment understand.

When Uncle James again expressed gratitude that Dr. Hardy had made Cannington Manor his home, as there had been some concern he might go further south to establish his practice, Dr. Hardy said he could hardly do otherwise than stay. Not only was there more than enough work to occupy him, but also such gracious hosts and lovely women in the neighbourhood. Nettie tittered nervously when he said this and earned herself a reproving glance from her older sister.

Cousin Frankie, sitting next to Nettie, was apparently so caught up in the high spirits of the occasion that he too felt the need to put his sister in her place, though his teasing was not so discreet as Cousin Mary's correction. He bumped Nettie's elbow and whispered in a voice loud enough for everyone to hear, "Not you, you silly—'tis Freda he fancies."

Nettie blushed painfully, and my heart went out to her. With several cousins between us at the table, there was nothing I could do to comfort her, though she seemed for a moment about to burst into tears and bolt from the table. Whatever her brother's intentions, the comment had been very unkind. Admittedly, Nettie did not have her sister Mary's poised beauty, nor young Dora's guileless bloom, and Freda too must be very pretty—but Nettie was also a wholesome and attractive young woman. No one but a brother would have failed to admire her.

The doctor himself stepped into the breach. "In fact," he said, smiling kindly at Nettie, "there are so many lovely women and so many gracious friends that I could never choose. I am determined therefore to stay a bachelor, that I may enjoy the company of all in good conscience."

At this, Cousin Frankie laughed quite loudly to further demonstrate his manly sophistication. "In that case," he said, "you must continue to wait for rain in order to do your wash!"

"*I* don't intend to have to get up *my* white shirts and collars myself," Frankie went on. "So I suppose I shall have to get myself a wife, to look after me when my sisters are all tired of the job."

Though the doctor didn't appear distressed and indeed seemed about to unbutton his collar to pass it around for the ladies' inspection, Cousin Frankie's comments earned my cousin a stern glance from his father as well as an audible shush from his eldest sister. No doubt he would later be favoured with words from Cousin Mary on the wisdom of bringing kitchen manners into the dining-room, especially in the presence of company.

For the moment, Mary turned to the doctor himself, "We trust you have no regrets then, Doctor, since we understand you left a good practice in Durham County to come to us?"

"And a country house and a stable of pure-bred horses!" added Mr. Fleming.

At that, Cousin Dora piped up, like the devoted student of ladylike deportment she was, "Were you a country squire with many good horses as well, Mr. Fleming?"

Her question and the lovely innocence of her face as she asked it could not but bring smiles to what had been an awkward situation. Everyone had a reply for her, but Mr. Fleming's was most on the mark.

"Ah, no, I am but one son of an impecunious London vicar," he said. "Dr. Hardy and I went to school together, and I sometimes visited his family during vacation."

At this point, Martha was serving second helpings of meat pie, and Dr. Hardy held up his plate to accept one. He also handed the

maid the headache powder and apologized that he would be unable
to tend to her toothache this evening, as a serious case called him
elsewhere when he had finished his dinner.

Martha had the grace to flush slightly at this attention, but she
curtseyed as was proper. I was pleased she knew enough not to
be intrusive in company. It was another sign either that she had
changed or that I must adjust my first impression of her. When she
had slipped the powder into the pocket of her apron and was turning away, the doctor had a final message.

"As I will be unable to earn my supper by wiping the dishes, I am
sure Mr. Fleming will be happy to take my place—having no doubt
had much domestic experience as the son of an 'impecunious' London parson."

Cousin Billy, who was sitting between Cousin Dora and me,
then explained that the doctor always had someone or other's teeth
to "torture" every week and that he almost always helped with the
dishes.

Clearly the doctor's generosity and good humour extended to
domestic help as well to as the family. I compared my own behaviour towards Miss Pritchard to his apparent lack of concern for
social class and was more than a little ashamed. As further proof of
this, when Martha Pritchard came back to the dining-room to serve
the dessert, the doctor invited her to come and see his flock along
with everyone else.

"I've near twenty baby lambs this spring," he said, "and they appear to be doing very well on the prairie grass—provided the fences
hold up and the coyotes keep their distance, as they too like a juicy
leg of lamb, with or without mint sauce."

I noticed Cousin Dora shudder, no doubt more sensitive to the
image of tooth and claw than appreciative of the doctor's wit. Obviously repentant, Dr. Hardy smiled mischievously at her and assured
her there would be no coyotes about when she came to visit him.

My uncle then asked Dr. Hardy if he still planned to purchase
another piece of land—he understood Archie Field's homestead
would be available.

Dr. Hardy sighed. "What I really want," he said, "is a small place on the shore of Cannington Lake, a place to relax, to stay overnight after a busy day—when there are no baby lambs to watch over, of course."

Cousin Dora then favoured him with her glowing smile. He had won over yet another of the Humphys women.

Soon after this, Dr. Hardy excused himself in order to check on Nurse and her baby before leaving to visit other patients. My uncle followed him, as behooves a good host. He also seemed to consider himself something of a guardian for Nurse and no doubt wished to hear the doctor's report on her recovery from her ordeal.

Though the others were still lingering over their rich desserts a quarter hour later, I, too, excused myself, for I had spilled some sauce on my frock and must retire to my chamber to repair it. And so it was that I witnessed the transaction between my uncle and Dr. Hardy in the front hallway. Had I passed by on my way to the stairs but five minutes prior or hence, I would have missed the exchange, and how I wished it were so! As it was, my movements might have seemed especially designed to cause the most embarrassment to all parties.

I had moved towards the gentlemen, you see, as if to join my uncle in his good-byes. The gentlemen must have heard my foot-steps, as they both looked in my direction. It was then I spied the crumpled bills in Dr. Hardy's outstretched hand, while my uncle was reaching forward to take them. For a moment, they were frozen in the telling gesture and I in observing it, and then I turned on my heel and retreated.

The abruptness of this action must surely have implied a judg-ment, and, if the truth be told, I did feel some shame on my uncle's behalf, though I would not have wished to show it. Uncle James had obviously made use of the private interview as an opportunity to ask Dr. Hardy for funds. It was also clear Dr. Hardy was comply-ing with some awkwardness—either out of embarrassment for his friend or because the money represented some loss to himself. Even if the loan were prearranged, such a transaction between friends suggested the extent of my uncle's penury.

As I dabbed my bodice with a dampened cloth, attempting not very successfully to remove the dribbles of pudding sauce, I would have given much to have behaved more discreetly. As it was, I had doubtlessly added to the clumsiness of the interaction by behaving as if I had seen something sordid. Later, I would sigh because of reawakened concern for my uncle and his family; my immediate distress, however, was for my own lack of grace.

This gracelessness suggested a lack of good sense that was of a part with other recent events. First, there was my discomfort over the interview with Cousin Mary a few days previous. Then there was the problem of Mr. Lionel Cuthbert himself. After much painful reflection, I had determined to show him by whatever renewed coldness I could muster that I had no interest in him. Unfortunately, he had frequently been absent from my uncle's estate since that day—no doubt tending to his own property—so it was difficult to test this resolve. In order to show that I did not want to see him, I first had to see him. And such anxiety to see him suggested anything but indifference.

When I had finally done the best I could do with my bodice—or the worst, since I had replaced a couple of small buttery dribbles with a huge wet spot—I returned to the dining room to find the rest of the company had left it. Dora had been sent to bed, and Mr. Fleming was indeed helping Martha in the kitchen, with Cousins Nettie, Ernest, William and Frankie, giving him pointers and quick to see any dish that was "botched." Mr. Ernest Maltby was travelling back to the village with the Birds, and they were pointedly allowing him a little privacy to bid adieu to his fiancé.

It was then that I finally witnessed a lover's kiss between the engaged couple. What had provoked it, I did not know. Perhaps Mr. Maltby wished to appear masterful in front of his friends, or perhaps he was somewhat anxious about how much Dr. Hardy had dominated the dinner conversation—and desired reassurance. Whatever the reason, I was relieved as well as embarrassed to intrude on it, so I retreated in confusion for the second time that evening. I did, however, have time to note that Cousin Mary lifted her face obediently and received the kiss with every appearance of good will.

In a few minutes, Mr. Maltby and the Birds were gone; Mary had joined the others in the kitchen; and Uncle James had retired to the library. No doubt my uncle was writing an account of the evening to my aunt, as I believe he wrote her daily and shared most of the concerns and events that occupied him. I thought to wish him good night but presently decided my interruption might provoke less than pleasant musings on his part, owing to the earlier incident.

I did not for one instant doubt my reading of the interaction with Dr. Hardy. It was only too obvious from the manner of each that my uncle had asked for and received money from his friend, and my uncle's desperation for money so close to the time of his daughter's wedding was painful to see. I wished it were in my power to offer assistance to Uncle James and his family myself, but my aunt's legacy had left little provision for that. Neither could I appeal to my father on my uncle's behalf, as my father would be more likely to see it as an opportunity for recrimination than brotherly love. I did have a small allowance on hand for personal expenses, a few pounds only. Perhaps I could offer it for the family's use, but such an offer would take very delicate handling.

All of these worries left me in no condition to join the lively company in the kitchen. Instead I took myself back to my chamber for a renewed study of my own dilemma and the plight of those around me.

Chapter 28

-

DISTRACTIONS

You may wonder—when Cousin Mary's wedding was my reason for visiting Cannington Manor in the first place—why wedding preparations have taken up such a small part of this account so far. Indeed, I wonder myself, though it is obvious there were many other things to occupy my thoughts and time, especially my own predicament regarding Mr. Lionel Cuthbert. There was also the existence of the unfortunate Ruthie Ford's baby—not that I was expected to help with the child in any way or even to acknowledge his existence, since he was not a part of the family, at least not in the usual sense.

The children were naturally struck with the wonder of having a baby in the house, just as they would have been with a batch of kittens or a puppy. I could picture them hanging about the basket in Nurse's room until she found them too much underfoot and shooed them away. I wondered whether she was now reconciled to her situation. Would she become the laughing girl again now that her travail was over? Somehow, I doubted it, especially when it seemed that Aunt Jane desired her absence.

While I was moved with pity for Nurse and her little boy, I was every day more anxious for the welfare of the Humphrys family, especially since the scene between Dr. Hardy and my uncle. The intensity of my affection and concern for these kinfolk should have caused me no surprise, for I had always believed it in my nature to be affectionate, especially were the affection returned without restraint. (In my own family, the restraint and frequent ill-temper—or, at best, uncertain temper—of my parents generally prevented any strong demonstration of affection.)

The Humphrys, on the other hand, had love aplenty and no reluctance about showing it. Yet their overall situation was precarious. I had in a month seen much evidence that my uncle, for all his splendid ideas, enthusiasm and generosity, was not a practical man. If I still wished to deny this, I must ignore the evidence of my own eyes, and the similarity between my observations and my father's unkind opinion was mortifying to me. Far more important, the evidence suggested the family could be facing still more adverse and humiliating circumstances in the future.

After much deliberation, I did take some measure of action regarding these concerns. I attempted to offer my uncle the whole of the allowance I had brought with me from England. Though concerned about the seemliness of such a gesture, I persuaded myself my uncle must see me—after a month in his household—as a member of the family, a kind of surrogate daughter. Did he not frequently confide in me? And could not a daughter offer help? In spite of my careful planning, it was as awkward and unsatisfactory an interview as I had initially feared.

I had chosen to speak to him after supper on the night following the dinner party, at a time when other members of the family would be firmly engaged in their various occupations—whether retiring to bed, planning meals for the morrow or, like Mary and Nurse, doing last minute adjustments on wedding garments. When he was not going out for the evening, my uncle's activities were quite predictable, and it was not difficult to find him alone in his study.

I knocked and entered at his invitation. He pushed aside his papers and made as if to rise painfully from his chair. I protested and quickly seated myself in the only other chair in the small, poorly-lit room. I had my leather purse in my hand and found myself fiddling with its strings as I spoke. My nervousness also made me more direct than I would have wished.

"I am concerned," I began. "I have been remiss." I paused, drew my five wrinkled pound notes from my purse, smoothed them in my lap, then held them out to him, as I floundered into the speech I had prepared.

"Please allow me to offer some small remuneration for my stay."

My uncle's complexion was always highly coloured, more so when he shaved every day, as he had been doing for the past week in preparation for his daughter's wedding. Now his skin took on an even darker hue, visible even by candlelight.

"My dear niece," he said, and the emotion in his voice said more of suffering than gratitude. For a moment he bowed his head into his hand, but when he raised it, his expression was again that of host and patriarch. "My dear Florence, you are our guest, and have come at our invitation."

I continued to extend the notes towards him, uncertain what else to say, as my rehearsals had not taken a refusal into account. Finally, my uncle folded my hand over the notes and pushed them firmly back to me. The gesture could not be mistaken and neither could his words.

He said stiffly, and still with somewhat heightened colour. "Thank you, my dear, you are very kind, but a young lady has need of her allowance."

There was no more I could say, and I was ashamed. No doubt I had wounded his pride yet again. Perhaps he was even now remembering my actions the night before. I stood up and was about to go, when he spoke.

"Of course, if your father ever wished to invest in one of our companies—I could offer a brother very good terms."

Did he have no inkling then of how little respect my father felt for him? It was my turn to blush.

"Thank you, Uncle. I—I…" I did not know what else to say. "Good night, Uncle."

I closed the door behind me and hurried away.

It was not only my admiration and my concern for their welfare that drew me to all members of the Humphrys family and made me observe them with such interest. I was also building up a store of memories for myself—not only of the family, but of their neighbours, the house and the land itself. These would have to sustain me when my visit was over.

There would have been much to occupy my mind and heart even without the unexpected romantic interest that seemed unwilling to release its hold on me. As to that person—though after my long walk with Mary I tried harder to resist—there were still many times when I could not help thinking of, and frequently even watching for, Mr. Lionel Cuthbert.

Some days, I merely thought I saw him, from a distance—something about the stride or compact height that suggested his person—but I could not be sure it was him. Neither could I be certain if and when he would appear for breakfast or the noon meal. He had not formally dined with us since the evening after my arrival. Nor had the family taken another meal on the lawn, though the grass had been scythed and edged in preparation for the wedding breakfast. Instead, unless there were guests, the men and children continued to eat supper in the kitchen, and the women and my uncle in the dining room. Mr. Cuthbert may have slept in the bunkhouse occasionally; however, since he did not sup with us, it was more likely he drove his horses and wagon home to his own lonely domicile each night.

When I thought of Mr. Cuthbert going home each night, I wondered what manner of house his was. Perhaps it would be a one-room log shanty that sufficed as kitchen, dining-room and workshop, with a ladder leading to the sleeping quarters in the attic above. Perhaps there was not even an attic. No doubt my uncle and any one of my cousins could easily have enlightened me on this subject, but I was ashamed to ask and thereby reveal my untoward interest.

I had heard of sod huts, tents, lean-tos and shelters built into the sides of hills. I had even heard of two men building a log cabin on the boundary line between their homesteads, so each man could get credit for sleeping in his own residence, though they were in one building. For the most part, however, I was certain Mr. Cuthbert would have provided himself with a more permanent home. Not giving adequate thought to such matters or trying in some way to subvert the system would suggest a less practical and capable man than I thought him to be.

On those days when I could not prevent myself thinking of him, I worried about him as well. He spent so much time working for my uncle—had he been able to accomplish all that he must for himself? Was his homestead secure? I remembered Mary having once made reference to these requirements, but I could not recall all she had said. It was unbearable to think that Mr. Cuthbert might put his own property at risk. However, this worry too I was able to allay by reflecting on the character of the man. His quiet strength and ability—his steadiness—suggested he would not neglect his homestead anymore than he would be delinquent in other duties.

In spite of these concerns, wayward and otherwise, it was soon the eve of Mary's wedding, and daytime thoughts at least were occupied elsewhere. Though Mary was seldom exacting in her demands on others, she was particular about her own appearance and dress when in public, so she fussed a great deal about her trousseau and all the other arrangements. More than once she sent Nurse back to redo a seam, and I know that on the night before her wedding, she herself sat up late, pinning and re-stitching, though she let poor Nurse retire, tend to the needs of the baby and try to get some sleep. I was aware of these nocturnal activities because my room was next to Mary's, and I was lying awake.

Chapter 29

-

THE WEDDING DAY

At the hour of eleven on the morning of June 1st, before they spilled out of the house and into the vehicles, the members of the Humphrys family lined up in their wedding-day finery to have their photograph taken. This in itself was an occasion, as Mary had told me that Ernest didn't often bring out his camera, for it was a complicated procedure and required patience on the part of both photographer and subjects. For this reason, he admitted he was rather out of practice.

Though not highly experienced as a photographer, Ernest's artistic eye stood him in good stead here as always. His first photograph was quite naturally to feature Mary in her wedding dress, and his idea was to have her pose in the dining room doorway. It took some time for him to arrange the image—what with camera and bellows, tripod, drape and photographers' plates to contend with. Not only that, but he would find he needed to make some change to her posture or to the folds of her gown just as he had everything else ready. When he had finally completed all this to his satisfaction, he popped the flash, startling the photo's subject and everyone else. Then he must hurry upstairs to his darkroom for another plate before he could set up the rest of the family. By this time, however, my uncle was concerned about the lateness of the hour, so the second photo was rushed and would be less successful.

Whether or not the photographs were wholly successful, I thought it an excellent idea to have such visual reminders for the bridal couple—in fact for the whole family—to enjoy in years to come. Collected together in the hall as they were, I also reflected that the Humphrys were a very handsome family. Whatever their everyday worries may have been, they were now caught up in the excitement of the day and looking their best.

I, too, had taken care with my costume, choosing my best gown and a matching satin jacket, both of a delicate lavender hue. Instead of my usual straw hat, I wore a concoction of net and ribbon. Though both hat and gown were the current London fashion—I had it on my mother's authority—I still felt a colourless wisp beside the vigour of the Humphrys. Fortunately, that did not matter. Neither did it matter that there was not time for me to be included in a family photograph. It was satisfaction enough to look with pleasure on my relatives.

Uncle James and Cousin Ernest were well accustomed to dressing for church and social engagements, so their smartness was no surprise. Nettie was fretting a little. Her new dress had not in fact been finished in time, and she was forced to wear the same gown she had worn to the Pierces' party. She was cheered, however, when her family reminded her how well her old gown became her. Besides, Cousin Ernest hastened to point out, she had put her hair up for the wedding, and this gave quite a different look to her collar. It also meant one could see the curve of her neck, which was a woman's finest asset. Nettie, blushing, then threatened to pinch his ears for his impertinence and to pull out all the pins from the coiffeur she had spent considerable time perfecting. It was clear she was pleased.

Dora and Cecily were very pretty in new matching gowns, though I thought Dora had perhaps outgrown the pattern. Her hem seemed rather short, as befit a little girl and not one on the verge of blossoming into a young woman. It was too late, however, to do anything about this other than to loosen her sash a little, which I did as surreptitiously as I could. I was certain Aunt Jane would attend to the matter of Dora's hemlines, as to the many other matters that needed her attention, when she returned from England.

Cousin Noel was very handsome and very self-conscious, as little boys always are when scrubbed clean and dressed in formal attire. Perhaps the greatest transformation, however, was in Cousins Billy and Frankie, generally so reluctant to waste time on dress. Now they were slicked, polished, pressed and appropriately suited in shiny woollen gabardine and stiff celluloid collars. For all their awkwardness, they looked very well and were more than a little aware of it. I was moved to realize it wouldn't be long before Billy at least would be of courting age himself.

Finally there was Mary, and she was even more breathtakingly beautiful than I had expected. What Ernest had said about Nettie's profile was even more apparent in her older sister. With her glossy brown hair in soft waves over her forehead and piled in heavy rolls on the top and back of her head, Mary's slender neck was free to flow with cameo elegance from her trim shoulders and womanly bosom. The rest of her figure was also elegant, with tapered waist, slender arms and legs, and feminine curves that were just full enough. Though she sometimes complained about her brown skin, its healthy hue was set off very well by the white silk and the many tucks of ivory lace that covered the breast of her gown. Over her wedding dress, she had draped a fringed silk shawl worked in such brilliant colours I thought it must be a gift from her betrothed and a souvenir of his years in India.

Mary's carriage was also elegant. She held her shoulders back and her head erect both standing and walking, and when she moved she planted each step with precision. One could not imagine a more stately, though still graceful, figure. She would not be the first bride to grace the aisle of the village church, but it was difficult to imagine a lovelier one, and Uncle James no doubt had the same thoughts as he moved forward to kiss her brow in tribute. The trace of sadness on his face could only mean that he especially grieved the absence of his dear wife and helpmate at this time. I could not resist stealing a glance at Lionel Cuthbert to apprehend his response to Mary's loveliness. To my surprise, he was no longer standing in the foyer, though I had seen him there a minute before.

Mr. Cuthbert soon appeared again, leading the first team of horses from the barn. He was wearing the same suit—no doubt he only had one—he did for all formal occasions, so his appearance was no surprise, and I could look on him with equanimity. Focused on his task as was generally the case, he did not appear to notice me.

Cousin Ernest would drive his father and the bride in Aunt Jane's Victoria. The original plan had included Cecily and Dora, but that had been abandoned, as there really was only room for two passengers, especially considering the delicacy of the bride's gown and Uncle James's gouty leg. Seldom used, the victoria had been cleaned and polished for the occasion, but still showed signs of wear; no doubt it suffered from the roughness of the prairie trails, having been built for smoother English roads. Still, it was the most appropriate equipage in which to convey a bride.

Since the larger family carriage was not large enough to accommodate all the others, Mr. Cuthbert would convey the remainder of the family in the two-seater. As Fate would have it, after the flurry of everyone climbing up or being helped aboard, I found myself momentarily seated next to Mr. Cuthbert, with Nettie on my right and Miss Pritchard beside her; the others were either in the seat behind us or in the wagon box. Nurse had again chosen to remain at home, still not wishing to parade herself and her baby before the community, it would seem. It was not an arrangement of my choosing, nor one to be endured without awkwardness, since there would inevitably be some accidental pressure of adjoining limbs during the course of the drive. Nonetheless, I found myself quite satisfied to be there.

When Mr. Cuthbert turned sideways to look at me briefly as we were about to depart, I could almost have imagined he had planned the seating. This filled me with equal quantities of pleasure and unease. I also noticed, because of our proximity, that he appeared to have cut himself slightly with his razor, as there was a small smear of blood just under his cheekbone, quite close to his right ear. It took an effort of will for me not to reach up and touch it. At that moment, Cousin Nettie suggested she and I, as well as her younger sisters, should be in the seat behind because that would give more protection to our gowns. As an afterthought, she suggested Miss Pritchard might also be more comfortable switching seats.

Though I somewhat regretted the change, it would have been unseemly to protest, so the shifting and repositioning started up again. This time Mr. Cuthbert stayed in his place to hold the horses steady until the ladies were settled in the back and the men (including Noel) in front of us.

We finally set off, our vehicle leading the way. Though Cousin Ernest had threatened to go ahead if we could not get ourselves organized, Nettie insisted the bridal carriage must always arrive last. She also repeated what she had said earlier, that Mary must not alight or be seen until she, Nettie, was able to rearrange the bridal train and attend to any wrinkles in her gown. In the face of these arguments, Ernest had no choice but to wait, though his horses were champing at their bits, eager to test a load that was lighter than the wagon.

For me, the now familiar road to the village and the church passed beneath us far too quickly; for once, I was grateful that wagon travel was noisy and dusty and prohibited much conversation, for I did not want to converse. Instead, I wished to preserve every moment of this day in my memory. Not only was Mary's wedding day to be the high point of my visit, the very reason for my sojourn in the community, but I must soon afterwards begin to think of my homeward journey. In these few weeks, what was home to the Humphrys had so easily become mine as well, but soon I must return to England—to my father's house and my ordinary life.

As we reached the main street of the village and started up the hill, our drivers slowed the teams to a walk, as it would not do for the bride to be seen too early. Soon we were within sight of the church and noted all the wagons and carriages gathered outside, some teams tied to the hitching rails and others attended by grooms. Still more people were arriving on foot. The whole community, it seemed, wished to share in this happy occasion.

There was a designated space for our vehicles, so we need not worry on that account at least. We reined in behind Mr. Maltby's smart barouche, and Nettie immediately stood up, eager to attend to her sister. In fact, she moved so quickly she seemed about to lose her balance, and Mr. Cuthbert had to spring from his seat with reins still in hand in order to save her. With a less experienced driver, this action might have startled the horses and caused a full-scale disaster, considering how many teams were lined up along the churchyard fence, but as usual his steadiness saved the day.

Mr. Cuthbert then handed the reins to Billy and accompanied Nettie to the bride's carriage, apparently to confer with Cousin Ernest and my uncle. The decision made, Nettie stepped aside and the victoria rolled through the gates into the churchyard. This appeared to be the customary sign that the bridal party had arrived, for it sent the stragglers who were just arriving—or those waiting outside the church for a first peep at the bride—inside to find their seats.

Our wagon did not follow the carriage into the yard. Instead, when it was placed to Mr. Cuthbert's satisfaction and the team secured to a ring on the hitching-rail, we began our ceremony of descent. Though I was watching Cousin Mary's progress in the distance more carefully than my own, Mr. Cuthbert kept me safe by holding my elbow until I reached solid ground. I remembered to turn and thank him before I hurried to my cousin's aid, but I did not stay to see his response. Even so, I was just in time for Nettie to hand me Mary's shawl.

Inside, were it not that someone had the foresight to partition off a pew for the bride's family, there would have been no space for us to sit. As there had been no rehearsal of the proceedings, there was also some confusion about the order in which the family would process. But that too sorted itself out. First, Ernest slipped by, as he was to play the organ for his sister's wedding. He paused to shake the hand of Mr. Maltby, standing at the foot of the chancel with Mr.

Robert Bird, who was not only his best man but also his witness, since Mr. Maltby had no relatives attending. In fact, as far as I was aware, Mr. Maltby had no relatives living, as I had never heard any mentioned—and certainly none in Canada.

Billy, Frankie, Noel and I proceeded next, and I was proud to be seated with these three young stalwarts. Mary's sisters were her attendants. They did not walk on rose petals or apple blossoms, it being too early in the season for an abundance of either. However, someone had thought to pick nosegays of what wildflowers there were, and these sufficed very well for decorating the church and for Nettie and the others to carry. Mary held her Bible in one hand and tucked the other under her father's elbow.

The ceremony itself was surprisingly brief, there being no sacrament of Holy Communion. The family had found the logistics of including it simply too difficult, as they wished to make the whole community feel welcome. Though most neighbours and friends belonged to the Church of England, there were Roman Catholics and Glen Adelaide Presbyterians who would be attending as well.

For all that I knew a wedding was only the outward sign and beginning of the much more important ritual of marriage itself, I was still very moved as the bride and groom made their vows. From my place near the far end of the pew, I could see both of them quite clearly. Mr. Maltby looked very handsome and very serious. Would Mary be able to bring her lively spirits into the marriage? Would the lovely matron still retain the part of her that was a girl? Would Mr. Maltby continue to appreciate her not only for her beauty, but also for her good sense and good humour? I earnestly prayed that it would be so and that both would look back on this day as the beginning of their greatest happiness—for that was what marriage promised, when partners were loving and well-matched. At the same time, it must also be a journey of discovery, the culmination of hopes and dreams.

Quite unbidden, thoughts of Mr. Lionel Cuthbert intruded as I was musing on these things. He must have been seated near the back, not with the family—perhaps near where Miss Pritchard had recognized a friend. Would he too see this union with satisfaction and wish the couple well, or would he see it as a sign of his own dashed hopes? I prayed for the former. He was too fine a man to waste himself in regrets, whatever dreams he might have had. And how remarkable that my feelings for him had changed so much, that I could wish him well and admit my own admiration when once I had seen him as an upstart who did not know his place! How strange too that when I was gone from this place, his handsome face—like all the others I had come to know—would only be a memory.

At that moment, Billy nudged my elbow and gallantly offered me his carefully folded handkerchief. Though somewhat embarrassed, I accepted it gratefully. I had not known until the handkerchief was proffered that tears were running down my face.

Chapter 30
-

THE WEDDING BREAKFAST

Once outside the church, the tone of the day changed. Nettie had just time to smooth her sister's gown and restore her shawl to her before the bride and groom must gather up their finery and run to avoid the onslaught of rice, which appeared from pockets and reticules alike. Even Mary's youngest brother and sister were part of the pursuit, which left off only to allow for a scramble for pennies when Mr. Maltby paused at a strategic distance from the carriages and gallantly tossed several handfuls of coins in the air.

The scramble gave the bride and groom the time necessary to climb aboard their barouche, where Mr. Robert Bird was already waiting, then settle themselves to drive away. Only then did I see the decorations that bobbed and rattled behind their carriage. Among the ribbons, posies and jangling objects, I'm almost certain I spied a cricket bat, a tennis racket and several pairs of old boots. I laughed aloud at the sight. If I had feared that the demands of marriage would dampen my beautiful cousin's high spirits, this playful message—no doubt from friends of the groom—reassured me.

On the wagon ride back to Humphrys House, this frivolous spirit continued, at least among the younger members of the family. Noel, brandishing several pennies, was noisily relating how he would spend them at the Moose Mountain General Store, while Cecily had her own collection and chimed in with a similar story. Nettie had opted to take Mary's place in the victoria, and slender Dora had managed to slip in between her and my uncle, so the older boys, Billy and Frankie, had only to share the back seat with Miss Pritchard. This may have been a mistake, as they apparently forgot their fine clothes and earlier courtly manners and immediately engaged in some kind of wrestling match, which seemed rather dangerous in a moving vehicle.

I had been restored to my earlier position beside Mr. Cuthbert, again through no effort of my own, and this time I allowed myself to simply enjoy his proximity. After all, a wedding day should be a time apart from ordinary concerns. From my seat, I could see the horses' ears twitching back and forth, no doubt puzzled by all the noise and activity. Lionel Cuthbert, as usual the quietest one amongst us, kept us on course through all the commotion while also maintaining our position as first vehicle on the road home. As my uncle and Cousin Ernest had congratulations to accept and last-minute invitations to issue, we had departed earliest from the church, but we could now hear what must be the phaeton behind us.

"Let's give old Ernest a run for his money," hollered Billy, while Frankie warned us that their older brother was overtaking us. Even Mr. Cuthbert, despite his neutral expression, seemed mischievously determined to keep his lead over the lighter vehicle. However, when the noisy contortions in the back seat grew even louder, he signaled suddenly to those behind us, reined in the horses and brought us to a standstill in the middle of the road. Billy and Frankie immediately protested, and Mr. Cuthbert mildly invited them to walk for the remainder of the distance.

"I do not wish to endanger the ladies, or the wagon," he said.

I suggested—enjoying the feeling of being in league with Mr. Cuthbert—that perhaps Noel or Cecily would like to sit between their brothers. Cecily immediately volunteered, which had the desired effect of calming the older boys. They might show off for young Miss Pritchard, but they would be protective of their little sister. Sensing that Noel might also want a change, I relinquished my place—though with regret—so he could have the seat of honour beside Lionel Cuthbert.

All of this rearranging had taken a little time, which meant our position relative to other conveyances was seriously threatened. In fact, Ernest seemed about to go off the beaten track and pass us, rather a dangerous move in a light carriage even though the ditch was shallow and comparatively dry. This, however, didn't suit Mr. Cuthbert, for he immediately chucked the horses into a slow trot, then a faster one. I was grateful that the little ones were both safely anchored between their elders, for I must focus on protecting my hat and clutching the edge of my seat. In this position, I could not see Mr. Cuthbert's face, though I imagined he might be smiling.

When both vehicles were finally reined in by the front door of the house, the men were all in high spirits after the friendly competition. The children and Billy and Frankie raced for the house, while Ernest and Mr. Cuthbert clapped each other on the back in a way that suggested they would be up for a wrestling match too, were it offered. Only Uncle James seemed distressed, but that was more likely owing to his upcoming responsibilities as host than to any concern for his personal safety during the drive. The rest of us dusted ourselves off, straightened our collars back into place and hurried into the house to help finish preparations for the fifty or so guests who would soon be arriving.

In fact, there was little to do. Thanks to the fine weather and Miss Pritchard, now indisputably in charge, most arrangements had been made before we left for the church. There had also been some assistance from the now invisible Nurse while the family was in church, but to Miss Pritchard went most of the credit that everything was in its place. The tables were prepared, and the food, both sweet and savoury, was on platters in the kitchen covered with cloths to protect it from dust and insects, but ready to serve.

On one end of the veranda, the bride's table was set with the best silver and china, while other tables were arranged on the grass beyond, their white linen cloths anchored with ribbons, which fluttered in the gentle breeze. Chairs and benches were placed either near the tables or on the south side of the house. The men might be able to erect some sort of canvas canopy alongside the veranda to protect against flies and heat as the day progressed, but other than that, only a word from my uncle was needed for the feast to commence.

Uncle James seemed a little uncertain about when the trays should be brought to the tables. Cousin Nettie suggested food should coincide with the arrival of the first guests, but Miss Pritchard said the claret punch should first be served, and this was the plan that was adopted. Guests wandered at their leisure, punch cups in hand, through the front rooms of the house and onto the lawn. By the time they were settled, the bride and groom had arrived.

Uncle James, himself again after his flurry of self-doubt, made a little speech of welcome to all the guests, and Mr. Bird offered a toast to the bride. The guests all raised their glasses. It was now Mr. Maltby's turn to respond, and he rose with glass in hand, but then was so overcome by nervousness or emotion that he was unable to speak and quickly sat down again. My uncle rose again in his place, bowing and smiling as if it were nothing out of the ordinary.

"It is customary at times such as this," said Uncle James, "for the groom to express himself overwhelmed by his good fortune in winning the heart of such a bride." He paused, but seeing that Mr. Maltby was still overcome, went on, "As usual, Mr. Maltby's actions speak more loudly than words."

The guests responded generously with both smiles and laughter, and my uncle continued. "Let me then take the opportunity to express my gratitude and that of my dear wife and helpmate. As you know, Mrs. Humphrys is unable to be with us today, but her thoughts are with her beloved daughter, and she has expressed her desire to join me in officially welcoming Mr. Malty into our family."

During the applause that followed, Uncle James sat down again, and none seemed to feel anything was amiss. The toasts then continued in a more spontaneous fashion, and, for her part, Cousin

Mary bowed and smiled very prettily whenever called upon to do so. In a few minutes, Mr. Maltby had also recovered sufficiently to join her. These well-wishes continued even after the food appeared, and there seemed some danger that the bridal couple would not have any leisure to eat.

Miss Pritchard, now dressed in her best cap and apron, served the bride and groom and all those at the bride's table—my uncle, Cousin Ernest and Cousin Nettie, Mr. Robert Bird, Mr. and Mrs. Harry Bird, Dr. Hardy (who arrived rather late) and even myself. The rest of the family and guests helped themselves from what Miss Pritchard had called a *buffet*. It consisted of neat piles of plates, utensils and napkins on a side table and platters of food and assorted condiments arranged attractively on another much larger table, which looked as if it might have been a wooden door under the linen cloth.

To prevent over-imbibing, the punch bowl had been removed to the kitchen. Miss Pritchard had enlisted pretty Cousin Dora and Mr. Cuthbert as her seconds and had given them the responsibility of refilling glasses, which they did in a fastidious, unhurried fashion. I did not, in fact, see where Lionel Cuthbert sat to eat—or whether he sat at all, since he appeared to be much occupied with his duties. Perhaps Miss Pritchard had set aside plates in the kitchen for her assistants. If so, this would be yet another reason for Miss Pritchard to congratulate herself. The buffet and all her other arrangements were a great success, and even the weather cooperated.

While the others continued to enjoy their refreshments, the bride and groom graciously visited each table. No doubt they must repeat to each party in turn that their wedding trip, to Winnipeg and then to the resort at Lake of the Woods, would only last for six weeks. After all, Mr. Maltby had responsibilities to his business as well as to the Canadian postal service, and Mary had a house and garden to tend.

They also reported that Cousin Ernest's additions to the house were going well and might be completed before they returned. Mary mentioned the need to choose curtains and other decorations and

received many offers of assistance. She said how much she looked
forward to being mistress of her own house, though she would miss
her family.

Some guests would be sure to ask after her mother, and Mary
would report that her mother would be home in time to welcome
them back from their wedding journey. My cousin's warm manner
would correct any impression of less than cordial relations between
mother and daughter. It would become clear that the circumstances
preventing the former from attending her daughter's wedding had
been out of the power of either to change.

All these things I was sure must be recited many times in answer
to neighbours' questions and good wishes, though all the information was common knowledge, for such are the ways of friends and
neighbours. Conversation is a way of communicating good will and
interest. Nothing much is remembered from one occasion to the
next.

I must also have been the subject of friendly inquiries, for I
could see heads occasionally turned in my direction. When this
happened, I followed Mary's earlier example: I smiled and inclined
my head, then turned back to my plate with as much ease as I could
muster. I knew what Mary would be saying of me, that it was but
seven days before I must depart, that she was grateful I would be
there as company to my cousins and uncle after she departed, and
that she would be very sorry not to see my face among the others
upon her return. As for my own feelings, I tried not to think of how
much I would miss her.

After all the guests had been visited, Cousin Mary and Mr. Maltby returned to the bride's table. Mary put her hand on my arm and
smiled sweetly at me.

"We must get ready to leave," she said. "Perhaps Cousin Florence
will help me change for the journey?" She included the others at
the table, "As you know, Mr. Maltby and I must be in Moosomin to
board the train tonight."

I looked quickly at Cousin Nettie. Though pleased at this opportunity for a few minutes alone with Mary, I didn't wish to wound my

younger cousin by taking her place. Cousin Nettie smiled at us both and turned her attention back to the gallant Dr. Hardy.

Relieved that I wasn't usurping the rights of another, I followed Mary upstairs to her chamber, where I could see there was very little left to be done. The boxes, bags and suitcases for her wedding trip were already packed. Her travelling costume was laid out on her bed, with her freshly cleaned and polished boots on the mat beneath. Several other trunks and a few small pieces of furniture were beside the door, awaiting delivery to her new home, and the furniture that remained was almost bare—in preparation for the next occupant. Only the box for Mary's wedding dress lay open.

As we set about the business of removing one set of garments and donning the next, I realized I was not accustomed to dressing and undressing anyone other than myself. However, I dutifully detached the train from my cousin's gown, folded it and placed it and her lovely Indian shawl in the box. Once she had stepped out of the layers of silk, I folded the gown as well and packed it. Then she asked me to help her adjust her stays so she would be more comfortable travelling. In such close proximity, I could not help but notice the swell of her breasts under her lacy chemise, the silky smoothness of her skin, the soft, dark tendrils of hair that had escaped from her chignon during our operations.

"Oh, dear, do you know how to fix this?" she asked, capturing the straggling curls in her fingers and attempting to tuck them back into the smooth roll at the nape of her neck.

I admitted that I did not.

"Well, perhaps it does not matter so very much," she said, gazing into her looking glass. Then she turned towards me, opening her arms so the womanly shape of her whole scantily-clad body was revealed.

"Do you think he will like me?" she asked, her expression appearing for once to be perfectly serious.

This, perhaps, was why she had asked for my company, but I did not know how to reassure her. Surely she could see as I could that she was breathtakingly lovely, but the tastes and pleasures of men were still, for the most part, a mystery to us both.

Fortunately she didn't wait for an answer but immediately became herself again, laughing away her insecurities, giving me an affectionate hug, reaching for the skirt of her grey travelling costume. I helped her step into it, as we didn't want to risk further damage to her coiffure. Then came the satin blouse with its many tucks across her bosom and the matching linen jacket, both with tiny buttons to attend to, plus bows and buckles. Finally only the hat was needed to complete her costume, and at that moment, there was a knock on the door and Cousin Nettie entered.

"You look very nice," she said to her sister, sitting down on the bed with a somewhat proprietary air, as the room was soon to be hers.

Nettie's example gave me the courage to say what I hadn't managed a few minutes before, "If Mr. Maltby could be any more devoted to you, this costume will *capsize* him completely."

We all laughed, and Mary sat down beside her sister. "Don't worry about anything. You will find you can manage very well without me until Mother returns," she said. Then suddenly they were tickling each other and ignoring the possible damage to Mary's hair and costume by rolling on the bed. Mary held out her hand to invite me to join them, but I could not, though I smiled wistfully down at them.

When the sisters had righted themselves again, I was pleased to see no great damage had been done to the bride's appearance. Nettie performed a little of her magic in restoring Mary's tousled curls to their proper place and set the jaunty hat on top of them, and then the bride was ready to lead the way to the stairs while her sister and I followed with the luggage for the wedding journey. Mr. Maltby and the others must have been waiting in the hall, for Mary paused at the top of the stairs, struck a pose, threw a radiant look back at us, then lifted her chin and straightened her shoulders before she proceeded down.

There was still a photograph to be taken of the bride and groom with the rest of the bridal party, and on this occasion I was included in the number. Then there were the formal good-byes, the kiss on the cheek that marked my cousin's departure, not only to board the train for her honeymoon, but on the voyage into matrimony. Yet again I found myself in tears, in spite of my resolutions to the contrary. When would I see my dearest Mary again? And even when I did, would not the differences between us now be too great to bridge?

Soon Mr. Robert Bird had taken his place in the driver's seat of the barouche, and the bride and groom were smiling from inside the carriage. The whole family and most of the guests stood at the front door to wave them out of sight. Uncle James then invited everyone back to their tables for more food and visiting, and only a few excused themselves. Though, as one of the family, I did not have the option of leaving, I would have preferred to retire to my room with my thoughts. Humphrys House would not be the same without Mary's presence.

Chapter 31

-

MEANS OF SURVIVAL

Aware as I was that I would be leaving very soon, I had resolved to experience each of my last seven days fully. But I could not escape the spirit of listlessness that had descended over the whole family. Not only was Cousin Mary immediately missed, but we lacked occupation. In place of the industry required for wedding preparations, there was a feeling of absence. Even the prospect of seeing Dr. Hardy and Mr. Fleming again for Sunday supper and a long-awaited invitation to dine at Didsbury on Monday—long-awaited by me at least—could not stir us to any particular enthusiasm.

I did start to pack my few belongings. Into my trunk went the scrapbooks Cecily and I had begun and then abandoned, a pair of boots that might be saved from the dust heap by a good shoemaker and a dress box containing the lavender gown and hat I had worn to the wedding. Little else could be spared for the remaining days. So this project, like others I might have accomplished in my final week, was also abandoned.

On Sunday morning, in the midst of the general *ennui*, Uncle James brought up a plan for butchering a pig and selling it piece by piece in the village to gain extra cash. Though his tone was matter of fact, the announcement reminded me of his monetary concerns.

Since he had already refused the little assistance I could offer, I felt a wave of helplessness coupled with frustration.

The recent loan from Dr. Hardy, it seemed, must already be spent. Perhaps wedding costs were higher than my uncle anticipated. And there was the food bill, not to mention Martha's wages, as well as those of the stonemason; Mr. Cuthbert; and other occasional workers. Though no definite time was set for Nurse and her baby to leave—Mr. McClure's intentions were as yet unclear—there would at least be one less mouth to feed when I departed.

My uncle admitted butchering a pig was not generally the kind of subject discussed on the Lord's Day, but he insisted it was always good to have a plan in mind, and I observed an immediate improvement in his spirits. This somewhat relieved my concerns. He seemed to have found a way forward.

"Does not the Lord help those who help themselves?" he declared, smiling at the family ranged about him. "And, after all, it is no more or less than Mr. Turton does on occasion, travelling about the country with his meat wagon. Why should we be too proud?"

He also explained that he would not put the plan into action until the morrow. Even then, he must ensure that Mr. Morrison, the butcher, was available.

"I trust *you* will not build a cover and paint the wagon black, so it looks for all the world like a funeral wagon," said Cousin Ernest, rather unkindly, I thought. Ernest was often away from home on his various building projects, but he spent his Sundays with the family. Unfortunately, neither his presence nor his frequent absence had helped him appreciate his father's constant efforts to strengthen the family's economic position.

"I thought merely to scrub the wagon and cover the meat with a clean cloth," replied Uncle James, not rising to the taunt. "Nor should we laugh at good Mr. Turton. He is master of his own house and does not care for anyone's opinions."

Ernest smiled but said no more on the subject. However, I did notice, on the day of the butchering, that he was there to help his father load the meat into the box of the buckboard. Perhaps, as eldest son, he did not intend to be disrespectful, but merely felt it his role to periodically test his father's resolve.

Of all the family, Cousin Nettie seemed not to have lost her sense of purpose. For all her earlier protests that she couldn't replace her sister, she actually seemed well able to manage domestic affairs. Not long after breakfast, she and Martha Pritchard sat down to plan the menu for supper, this time opting for cold meat and boiled vegetables. After all, the meal would follow the 7:00 o'clock evening service, and it wasn't wise to eat heavily so late in the evening. Like the others, I would regret the absence of Martha's pastry, but I understood the wisdom of Nettie's decision, especially when Uncle James so frequently suffered from gout.

Young Cousin Cecily appeared to miss her eldest sister the most, as she showed no desire to do anything but sit on my lap, and more than once I caught her thumb about to creep into her mouth. I was moved by tender gratitude that my little cousin chose my embrace and reflected, as I stroked her soft but unruly hair, how it was that little children in seeking solace often give solace themselves. Perhaps the sense of loss when I left would not be mine alone. For some reason, this knowledge comforted me.

There was little Cecily or I could do but get in the way as Miss Pritchard and Cousin Nettie discussed their supper preparations. Everything would be prepared before church, so there would be little to do but cut and serve on our return. Nettie had also assigned Dora to dust the front rooms, though little dust was evident so soon after the wedding. There was certainly not enough of such work to occupy three of us. I focused therefore on distracting Cecily from her thumb and her pout, and suggested we visit the baby. Though Cecily still spent much of the time when she wasn't in school with Nurse, it would be my first visit since the baby's birth.

We happened on Nurse and baby just at feeding time, and I was no less fascinated than the child to watch the baby take the breast. Any thought I might have had to ask Nurse about negotiations for the future of the little family were forgotten.

When she saw that it wasn't just the children visiting, Nurse had attempted to disguise the feeding process with a piece of toweling, but the infant tended to thrash his tiny arms as he suckled, so the towel was repeatedly pushed aside. I finally reached across to help the mother replace this modest covering—it being difficult for Nurse to manage that while also assisting the baby at his task. She seemed to be holding the bottom half of her swollen breast between two fingers of the opposite hand so that the boy wouldn't lose his place. As I reached to adjust the towel, the tips of my fingers accidentally brushed against the woman's smooth, warm skin. I withdrew my hand quickly to cover my embarrassment, and thought longingly of leaving the room.

"Would you like to hold him?" Nurse asked. For a moment I stared at her in open-mouthed surprise, then nodded dumbly.

Passing the baby to me, however, was a complicated manoeuver. First, Nurse handed me a blanket to put in my lap, tucking her gaping nightdress closed as she leaned forward. Then she patted the baby over her shoulder until he emitted a little pop of air. Finally, she handed the boy to me, guiding the smooth little head with its scattering of downy hair into the crook of my elbow. Though such a tiny morsel, his warm weight in my lap was active and substantial, and when the tiny mouth immediately sought further nourishment within the folds of my bodice, I felt a curious thrill of surprise. It was the same thrill of half ache, half pleasure that I had felt when I heard his first cry on the day he was born.

To cover my rush of feelings, I turned him towards Cecily, and she too laughed as the baby's tiny seeking mouth bumped insistently against the several layers protecting my breast. She gently stroked the boy's head, and when he turned toward her touch, I was both relieved and bereft. After a few moments of sitting in this way, I felt my awkwardness keenly and handed the child back to his mother.

Nurse smiled kindly at me. "Dinna worry," she said. "Someday you'll be having a wee'un of your own. It will all come easy to you then."

I did not know how to respond. It was not that I wanted her to be always dwelling on her shame, but neither did I expect her to be offering such advice to me. Whatever her intentions and however gently she spoke, there was an unspoken implication that in this experience of motherhood she had become my superior, and I found such an implication unseemly. It was my place to pity her, not to be patronized by her. Again, I would have left the room, had not Cecily chosen that moment to climb back into my lap.

Nurse placed the baby back in his basket, but he kicked and squalled out his opinion on that, and so she began to nurse him from the other breast, this time making no effort to cover herself. To avoid looking at her and to disguise my awkwardness, I looked about the tiny room. To my surprise, since she spent most of her days within those walls, I saw few personal touches there, other than some scattered infant nappies and other accessories. Even I, a mere visitor to the house, had found myself dropping scarves, belts, hairpins, books, and writing equipment about the room I occupied—consciously or unconsciously putting my mark upon it.

Again, I felt a movement against me, and—looking down—I noticed Cecily had reached up to rest the back of her hand with apparent unconsciousness against my breast, the same breast from which the baby had tried so frantically to nurse. Again, there was the jolt of physical surprise and—I suppose—pleasure, and then I placed Cecily's hand firmly in her own lap. In a moment I lifted her down and moved toward the door.

"It is time for the baby to sleep," I said.

Cecily pulled away, went over to where Nurse was sitting on the end of the bed and kissed the baby's now gently bobbing head. After a slight hesitation, she also put her lips to Nurse's bare arm, and Nurse responded by stroking her cheek. Then the woman turned her gaze back to the infant she held in her arms, and Cecily and I left the room, closing the door gently behind us.

Chapter 32

-

A STRANGE LEAVE-TAKING

The morning after our visit to her chamber, Ruthie Ford and her baby left the house very early, before the sun had fully risen. I would not have seen them leave had I not suffered a restless night and dressed early with the intention of walking in the garden before it came time to help prepare breakfast. For the moment, the house was quiet. Even Nettie and Miss Pritchard, usually the earliest to rise, were still abed.

No doubt the family was recovering from the previous evening when Dr. Hardy, having no pressing engagements, had favoured them with his company and that of Mr. Fleming later than usual. Not only had he administered some advice to Miss Pritchard on the subject of teeth, but the card table was brought out and a game of whist proposed. With Miss Pritchard on hand, there were two foursomes without me, so I begged a headache—a mild one, with no need for restorative powders—and retired. Now, hours later, here I was, halfway down the stairs, gazing out the window in the landing, when I saw a stranger's wagon come up the drive.

When the wagon pulled up at the side of the house and the driver did not alight or even look toward the house, though he seemed to be waiting for someone, I guessed that the stranger might be Mr.

McClure. He could have sent a message to Nurse while the family attended Evening Prayer.

Neither did the man give any other sign of welcome to the mother of his child, the woman whom I hoped would soon be his wife. He simply continued to wait, and Nurse must have been expecting him, for she stepped forward and began to put her few bundles and bags in the wagon box. She accomplished it all with one arm, for in the other she cradled the living bundle that was responsible for her downfall.

How could a man be so hard? No doubt Cousin Mary, if in my situation, would have run down the steps to help Nurse with her bundles. But I only stood and watched.

It was when Nurse had loaded her meagre belongings and was about to get into the wagon herself that I realized I was not the only observer. Lionel Cuthbert suddenly stepped into the scene. He walked over to where Nurse was struggling to climb onto the seat of the buckboard while holding the baby, and he put his hand below Nurse's elbow, just as he had done several times for me. He did not step back until Nurse and the baby were safely in place. At that point, Mr. McClure turned in his direction and the men seemed to exchange a glance. Did they speak? There was no appearance of it.

Would the man see Mr. Cuthbert's gesture as interference and punish the woman and child for it? I did not know that either. But I did feel grateful on Nurse's behalf. In the simple gesture, Lionel Cuthbert had told her she too was worthy of care. I could only hope that, in whatever joy or grief her future held for her, she would remember this. A moment later, Mr. McClure lifted the lines from their resting place on the horses' rumps and snapped them, then the team and wagon began to move out of the yard. Neither man nor woman looked back.

For an instant I hesitated, transfixed by the sight of the wagon moving slowly away, by the image of those straight backs and the space between them. But only an instant—and then I knew what I must do. If only it was not too late.

I tripped a little as I rounded the turn in the stair and had to stop and rub my ankle. But not long. Soon I was down the hall and at the door, rounding the corner of the house to where he must have stood to watch them leave—my words of gratitude only half formed in my mind. But I found no Lionel Cuthbert standing there, and I did not see him in the yard beyond. It was almost as if I had imagined his presence.

After a moment, I turned and, limping slightly, walked not towards the garden as I had planned but back into the house and down the hall to the kitchen.

Chapter 33

-

INVITATION TO DIDSBURY

Though I had been introduced to Didsbury folk on several occasions—at dinner, at church, at the Pierces' party and at the wedding—and dining with them had been mentioned each time, the invitations had been general rather than specific. Therefore, I had begun to doubt that the visit would take place before I left the district, and this disappointed me. I had heard much about their fine home and lavish lifestyle, about their racehorses and stables, but hearing such stories was not the same as observing for myself.

For all these reasons, I was both surprised and pleased when Mrs. Jessie Beckton linked her arm with mine as she was leaving the wedding breakfast. She had shown no particular friendliness to me before this, but weddings seem to inspire feelings of affection all round. Therefore, I tried to make my manner as easy as hers. It turned out that her purpose was to ask my uncle, my cousins Ernest and Nettie and me to dine at Didsbury on the following Monday.

"We hear you are leaving us soon," she said. "What a short stay this has been! But we cannot have you disappear without a visit."

I could not answer for the others, though I expressed my pleasure at the invitation, so I took her to my uncle. He was in his element and had maintained his convivial form all day. As I expected, he accepted Mrs. Beckton's invitation on behalf of all of us and without the slightest delay.

"You must tell your father of this," he said, meaning I supposed, that I should report the honour of being singled out by the wealthiest matron in the community. I did not totally understand his constant wish to impress my father. And yet, when I examined my own motives in the privacy of my chamber, I also wondered at my eagerness.

For all the democratic ideas I had learned from reading authors such as Mr. Charles Dickens and the Rev. Mr. Jonathan Swift, I was also raised—thanks to my parents—with an appreciation for gracious living. And of all the families settled at Cannington Manor, the Becktons were undoubtedly the most aristocratic in their tastes. The Humphrys and the other country families—the Pierces, the Turtons, the Piggotts, the Stainers (and others)—were also hospitable and tried to maintain their formal "English" manners. However, they were still primarily farmers and took agriculture seriously.

From what I had heard, the Becktons, though they had a large tract of land and called their estate the Didsbury Stock Farm, seemed to have no penchant for seriousness. They had brought fox hunting and polo to the community, not to mention Race Days and a gentlemen's club. Furthermore—from my understanding of the district and the country—it was their glamorous, impractical lifestyle that led English promoters to describe Cannington Manor as "a little bit of English country life in the Canadian North West".

Not everyone appreciated this uniqueness. I doubted, for instance, that Canadians such as Lionel Cuthbert approved of the playful attitude of the Becktons and others like them. Even Sergeant John Geoghegan of the Northwest Mounted Police, stationed at Cannington Manor in 1888 and 1889, had said "many of them [the English aristocrats] were not fit for what they came out for."

When my uncle repeated this speech, he seemed to take the remark personally. According to Cousin Ernest, the sergeant had also described the English settlers as "very progressive and a fine class of people," but this was not the epithet my uncle remembered. Nor did he remember the sergeant's description of Cannington Manor as a "valuable stopping place, not only for those moving north and south, but also for travelling judges, who must go from town to town to preside at various trials." These compliments were poor comfort when the officer seemed to consider the Cannington Manor aristocrats mere dabblers, and it was doubly mortifying that the policeman who made the patronizing comment was someone of consequence.

During his time in the district, Sergeant Geoghegan had patrolled eight reserves every month. He must have been respected, for no crimes took place during that time. He was most famous, however, for earlier deeds. Apparently, it was he who had escorted the legendary Chief Sitting Bull back to his reservation in South Dakota a few years before the Riel uprising of 1885.

I suspected my uncle's offended feelings had more to do with his own self-doubt than with the words themselves. His fear the description might be apt would have made it rankle all the more, though perhaps the officer only meant to suggest the settlers faced a very challenging landscape; it being quite unlike what they had known in England. Furthermore, the English settlers I had met — aristocratic or otherwise—said as much themselves.

Even before the date to visit Didsbury was set, I was familiar with many details about the Becktons. Two of the brothers, Ernest and William, had first arrived in the community a year or so before my uncle and Cousin Ernest. The Becktons were a well-to-do industrial family from the north of England, but the sons had become rather irresponsible young men, accustomed to a certain lifestyle and constantly overspending their allowances. Since their parents and wealthy grandparents wished them to take hold of some occupation, they were enrolled as agricultural students of Captain Pierce.

Whenever I heard this story, I wondered where a retired army captain and former bank trustee would have gained his own farming experience, but I said nothing, since my uncle made much of the likenesses between himself and the captain. Besides, industry, imagination and capital make many things possible.

A "family emergency" took the Beckton brothers back to England in the fall of 1887. When they returned to Cannington Manor a year later, it was with their brother Bertie and a substantial fortune between the three of them. The *emergency*, it turned out, was the death of their maternal grandfather, Sir John Curtis, cotton baron and former mayor of Manchester, and the reopening of a long discredited iron mine. Since the brothers benefitted greatly from both events, it was a true "windfall," the stuff of dreams for commoners and aristocrats alike.

An additional irony about the Beckton story was the fact the brothers had once offered their shares in the iron mine as collateral for a loan, and the Moosomin bank manager had refused to accept them. By 1888, however, everything had changed. The brothers bought their land outright and started construction of their stock farm, becoming at the same time the community's major employer. With no qualms about spending their new resources in the manner of aristocrats, they spared no expense in building their home and furnishing it in kind. They also invested in pedigreed race horses and fox hounds—even fighting cocks for a time—and sponsored many sporting events.

Within a few years, all three brothers were also married—Ernest, to Jessie Pierce; Bertie, to Florence Stanier, from another well-to-do local family; and William (Billy), to Edith, whose family name my uncle did not recall. He did know, however, that Billy had gone back to the old country to wed her.

I wondered how the wives got along and hoped Mrs. Bertie Beckton would attend the Didsbury dinner, as her condition often exempted her from social occasions. She was sister to one of the more successful cattle farmers in the neighbourhood—Mr. Jack Stanier had come to the district the year before my uncle and had managed to build a large log house before his parents and nine siblings arrived. I hoped that Florence Beckton—or "Florrie," as her husband called her—was not the neglected member of the family. With her brother's industry in her blood, she deserved to be appreciated somewhat more than Bertie Beckton's behaviour had yet demonstrated.

From my cousins' stories, it did seem that the Beckton brothers retained many bachelor traits. As I have already mentioned, one wing of the famous Didsbury was still called *The Rams' Pasture* and was dedicated to gatherings of gentlemen for food, drinks and cigars after various sporting events. One whole room apparently was needed to accommodate the large billiard table and trophy cupboards. I had no doubt Mr. Maltby and Cousin Ernest were familiar with these gatherings, but was less sure my uncle had partaken, as visiting the Ram's Pasture seemed to be a young man's activity. Neither was it likely that ladies were included in these masculine entertainments.

Uncle James may not have been a frequent visitor to the Didsbury gentlemen's club, but Jessie's dinner invitation could not have been a surprise to him, and his insistence it was a tribute to me must be a sign of his kindness alone. As we prepared to depart, I noticed another sign of his kindness. Though not specifically asked to do so, he had bundled up his flute to bring with him. I smiled to see this, for I knew he liked to give pleasure.

Chapter 34

PRELUDE AND PROMENADE

Cousin Ernest would be our driver, as Cousin William was not to go, nor, I suspected, was Lionel Cuthbert. Not only did Mr. Cuthbert seem to disapprove of the Becktons—or of Bertie Beckton at least—but they might well think him beneath their notice. And who is to say which impression came first!

Since it was to be another evening affair, we would take the closed carriage. My uncle had also explained that, even in June, the evenings could be chilly, so I should be sure to take a shawl. I kept that suggestion in mind as I planned my costume and finally chose a skirt, bodice and jacket that were more akin to a travelling costume than an evening gown.

As I made these preparations, I regretted having no Mary to advise me. She and her husband would be enjoying the cultural adventures available in Winnipeg or happily ensconced in their guesthouse at Lake of the Woods. I thought of them often, as did the rest of the family. Uncle James had apparently read brochures about the well-known resort and fishing village and enjoyed speculating about what sights they might be seeing.

I, however, found myself at unguarded times imagining their marital relationship. I also vividly remembered Mary standing in the centre of all her bags and boxes and asking, with her arms open to reveal her half-garbed loveliness, "Do you think he will like me?"

Since Didsbury and Humphrys House were a similar distance from the town, and there was no direct route between the two houses, we must first travel to Cannington Manor to take the road to Didsbury. The trip, therefore, took almost a full hour, and it was fortunate we had made an early start.

We arrived, however, at an opportune time. At seven o'clock in early June, it was not yet sunset, so we could admire the approach to the house before the bay windows and ornate veranda that faced us were hidden in shadow. My uncle looked for signs of special artistry about the grounds themselves, as he understood Mrs. Jessie Beckton had recently hired a professional landscape architect. For my part, I imagined the intoxicated young men who had gamboled about this lawn on the occasion of Jessie and Ernest Beckton's wedding party three years earlier. If Cousin Frankie had been of this party as well, no doubt he would have told us the story again. Both my uncle and I were initially disappointed, however, as there was very little landscaping in evidence as the carriage rolled up to the fine fieldstone house.

Though all three couples welcomed us from the veranda, it was immediately clear Jessie Beckton, as wife of the eldest Beckton, was the lady of the manor. She and her sisters-in-law were gowned as appropriate for any elegant summer evening affair—though Mrs. Bertie had also draped a voluminous shawl about her person, no doubt to modestly camouflage her condition. While more elaborately attired themselves, the Beckton ladies didn't seem to mind that Nettie and I were simply dressed. (I had hastened to apologize for what might have seemed a slight.)

"I perfectly understand," said Jessie, "when travelling, you must dress to avoid dust and chills." She pressed my hand, beamed at Cousin Nettie and continued. "I wished to avoid being outnumbered by gentlemen; that is why I didn't invite your younger brothers." No doubt she meant Billy and Frankie. The younger children would not have expected an invitation.

Jessie continued, "I had also thought to invite my mother, who would have enjoyed seeing you all again, but it seemed she was engaged elsewhere. I hope you will not find us too dull, especially after the gentlemen retire for cigars and billiards."

All the Beckton ladies laughed at that. It was clear they did not consider themselves dull, even though the brothers seemed to have retained many of their bachelor habits. At least, since there were three of them, they could be company for each other and ensure that women weren't too much ignored in the household. On the other hand, if there were feelings of competition between them, these were well-hidden during their greetings.

Jessie linked her arm in mine and smiled over her shoulder at Nettie, who followed us.

"Would you like to visit the garden first," she asked, "since it will soon be too dark to see?"

We all agreed, my uncle taking up his position between the other two Beckton ladies, while the younger men disappeared in the direction of the stables. We who remained followed the stone path leading around the corner of the house and immediately saw quite a different aspect of the yard. First, we were struck by the fragrance of lilacs, for there was a bush nestled against every corner, and some already boasted their aromatic purple and white plumes.

I also noticed a scattering of purple iris in bloom and evidence of other perennials in the wide beds—more than could be found at Humphrys House. I expressed my appreciation for the order of the beds and commented on the profusion of fragrances there must be when the roses, evening scented stock and baby's breath were in bloom. Jessie agreed that it was early yet, that the garden would not be at its best for at least a month. She also mentioned a gardener, though it seemed she shared my uncle's interest in horticulture and possibly even did some part of the work herself.

While making it his business to admire all that Jessie Beckton drew to his attention, my uncle did not neglect his other duties. As our lone male escort, he gallantly replaced Mrs. Bertie's shawl when it slipped from her shoulders to reveal the pregnant mound of her stomach. Glimpsing this, I thought of poor Nurse, whom I hoped was now legitimately titled Mrs. Mary Jane McClure.

I had also noticed two or three other expectant women at the Pierce family's party, not just young brides like Florence, but more mature women as well. It would seem that there was quite a lot of baby making in the community; in this way, women for all that they were frailer perhaps carried the greater responsibility for the community's growth. I could imagine Cousin Mary slyly suggesting this came from having not much else to do in the winter evenings when it was too frigid to leave one's own fireside and stifled a smile at the thought.

After we had admired the arrangement of flower beds and the prospect from across the lawn, Jessie Beckton led us to the kitchen garden, which was behind the house. Again, my uncle showed his gallantry, by ensuring that Mrs. Bertie took his arm and by watching for any uneven stones and stray twigs or suckers that might trip her up. He was also walking more erectly than he generally did, which must have cost him a great deal. At home he seldom walked any distance and even when sitting often winced with pain. Most evenings he spent with his gouty leg propped up on a cushioned chair.

The vegetable garden boasted many neat rows of tiny green seedlings and promised to be more than adequate for the needs of all three families. I stole a glance at my uncle. Would he be disappointed to see the family already so well-served? No doubt he had hoped to eventually supply the neighbourhood with produce of his own. On closer examination, however, he did discover some varieties of vegetables were absent and volunteered to bring leeks, Windsor beans and turnips for Jessie and the others, if his crop was good.

Jessie thanked him, then suggested we too visit the stables. These were some distance away, however, and the other gentlemen were already approaching from that direction. Though I was a little disappointed to miss the famous Beckton racehorses and the stone stable that was reputedly finer than a good many houses in the district, I suspected Florence Beckton must find long walks somewhat

taxing in her condition, as would my uncle in his. I was able, therefore, to stifle my curiosity and describe myself quite satisfied—in
fact, delighted—with what I had already seen.

Entering the house from the lawn, we first walked through the
conservatory, where various delicate plants were housed, though
one or two of them had been upset, which was no wonder, considering that several dogs appeared to have the run of the house.
Jessie and Ernest Beckton had as yet no children, but our hostess
had earlier taken the time to introduce us to David and Jonathon,
two Aberdeen Terriers, and a smaller, whitish terrier she called Vic.
None of the short-legged but sturdy dogs had seemed much interested in the tour of the garden, but they all trotted back to the door
to welcome us into the house.

With a rueful laugh, Jessie commented on the spilled plants.

"It's impossible to keep anything safe here," she said. "The dogs
consider this room their personal territory. They like to sit by the
windows and watch everything that's going on outside."

At that, Florence Beckton confessed she was not much used to
dogs in the house. The Staniers had always had dogs to work the
cattle, she said—especially in England—but her father felt house-
dogs could easily be spoiled by too much of the wrong kind of food
and attention.

"We do not have any dogs ourselves at present," she added,
"though I am certain Bertie will turn up with something utterly impossible one day. I only hope he waits until the baby is old enough
to play with it."

These were almost the first comments Mrs. Bertie had made,
and I looked at her with interest, prepared to like the woman who
shared my name.

Jessie shrugged.

"I admit it was a case of self defense," she said. "Any number of
fierce-looking dogs had the run of the house before Ernest and I
were married. I really do not like bull terriers, however much one
hears of their courage and loyalty. But now I have my Scotties—and
they're just as courageous for all their size—I can insist the men

keep their dogs in the other wing. Otherwise, we would be completely over-run, and they would always be scrapping."

I secretly applauded her for developing ways to solidify her position in this still masculine household. While Mrs. Bertie had obviously found other but equally effective methods of coping, if Edith Beckton had an opinion about dogs, she kept it to herself, as did my uncle. Nettie, however, ventured to say she would like a dog "about this size," as she knelt down to scratch the shaggy white coat of the one they called Vic.

A maid appeared and relieved us of our wraps. I noticed Uncle James relinquishing his flute with some reluctance and wondered whether Jessie had noticed and might mention music. From the conservatory, we entered the drawing-room, one of the most appealing features of which was a broad staircase that curved elegantly up to the second floor. There was also a choice of comfortable lounges, chesterfields and easy chairs, and our hostess invited us each to take a seat while we waited for the gentlemen. No sooner had she said those words than she started and glanced at my uncle, as if she feared she had wounded him by implying he was not one of the gentlemen. If he noticed her *faux pas*, he didn't show it, as he was engaged in admiring the expensive appointments.

For my part, I found the style of the large room less to my taste than I had expected. Whereas the garden owed its extravagance to the natural profusion of growing things—or would later in the season—the grandeur of the drawing-room was entirely devised by man. I could not help but find the latter somewhat lacking in comparison, no matter how fine the furnishings. The opulence of the room also reminded me of my own home, a place where much was for show and little was conducive to comfort.

The other gentlemen soon arrived, and there was a certain amount of confusion as the dogs were disentangled. I tended to agree with Jessie Beckton about the bull terriers. They weren't overly large, but even their names were aggressive—Flesh, Fury and The Devil. They also had a pugnacious appearance, with their aquiline noses, broad chests and bowed legs. I wondered briefly if the brothers had for a time invested in bull baiting or dog fighting as well as fighting cocks, as these appeared to be that sort of dog. Eventually, however, they were all safely shut into the Ram's Pasture.

Chapter 35

THE CONVERSATION
AT DINNER

When Jessie Beckton led us to the dining-room, I found myself not only seated beside our host, but with Mr. Bertie Beckton on my right. I was flattered by my proximity to the first—arranged no doubt by his wife—but would not have chosen the younger as a companion. He had, after all, been somewhat too attentive to me during my first dinner party with the Humphrys. Would he attach himself to me again—even in the presence of his expectant wife? For the umpteenth time I worried that I had in some way invited his attentions on that day, and the memory again brought a blush to my cheeks.

On this occasion, however, Bertie Beckton's remarks and attentions were quite appropriate to the situation, and I was relieved of any residual embarrassment for my original error in thinking him a bachelor. Furthermore, Mr. Beckton's conversation and that of the others was so lively, I had little time to fret. Any awkwardness that arose came from other sources.

Midway through the dinner, my uncle responded to a question about the role of a Justice of the Peace.

"There is a certain similarity," said Uncle James, "between all the cases I see, as most disputes arise because young men have imbibed rather too well. I am called upon to intercede when differences cannot be settled through minor fisticuffs in the backyard of the hotel."

"That I believe," said Ernest Beckton, who had asked the original question, and several around the table nodded, which caused me to wonder whether they had personal experience of such disputes.

My uncle continued, no doubt flattered to take the lead. "Generally the parties are sober enough by the time I hear their case that they are able to admit their guilt or innocence, make restitution and resolve to avoid such excess in future. At least they shake hands in apparent good will."

"Until the next time," said Mr. Beckton.

I then noticed that a somewhat uneasy stillness had come over some of the gentlemen at the table. William Beckton in particular was suddenly very taken with the weave of the tablecloth, and I remembered a story Cousin Frankie had told of whiskey camps on Cannington Lake. He implied that, until very recently, one or two of the Beckton brothers helped run such a camp. Frankie admitted he had never seen it for himself, as his eldest brother would have "pounded" him had he discovered him in such a place, but he thought it sounded "great good fun."

Eventually Bertie Beckton broke up the awkward silence by venturing to suggest that perhaps young men might be forgiven for indulging their own high spirits and rather foolish hobbies.

"Think of brother Billy's sailboat, for instance," he said. "Poor Edith lives in fear of him drowning himself some day."

Edith Beckton merely smiled and reached across the table to pat her husband's hand, but William Beckton spoke up for what seemed the first time.

"It's no small feat to build a sailboat," he said, "or to be the first boat on the lake, when the rest of you have only your rafts or wagon boxes." He bent forward to look directly at Bertie. "You just wish you had come up with the idea first."

Bertie was about to respond when my uncle, whose mind did not travel as quickly from subject to subject as those of the younger men, interrupted. He obviously hadn't finished with his earlier topic, though he seemed to guess that he might have touched a sensitive cord when he spoke of spirits.

"Of course," said Uncle James, "almost without exception, such difficulties can be settled with a gentleman's word and handshake."

After a pause to catch his meaning, the company agreed, grateful no doubt for the reprieve from awkward subjects. My uncle went on to say he was by no means as certain of his ground when similar disputes happened on the reserve. These disputes too were possibly caused by intoxication, but the ways of the Cree were very unlike the ways of the English.

"Perhaps," said Edith Beckton, in her crisp, cultured English voice—it was also one of the few times she hazarded a comment during the meal—"the peace pipe might be seen as a kind of gentlemen's handshake."

"I think you are right!" cried Jessie enthusiastically. "My father often spoke of having smoked the pipe with Chief White Bear and some of his—ah—companions. It was—is, as far as I know—taken very seriously, a question of honour. Smoking together makes them brothers, and one does not make war on one's relations."

Again, one could almost hear the sigh of relief as another awkward moment was bypassed. Ernest Beckton—if he had been part of or privy to the whiskey business—now felt sufficiently forgiven to insert himself back into the conversation. He smiled mischievously at his wife as if to signal a familiar game.

"If your family hadn't missed its opportunity to be part of Chief White Bear's family, he might have been sitting at this table with us. Then we could have asked him the question ourselves."

Jessie laughed and blushed at the same time. "Oh dear, yes," she said. "I should of course allow Lily to tell the story, since she must really take the credit. But since she is not here and Miss Southam may not have heard the tale…"

Hearing my name, I indicated my interest in hearing the story.

"Do tell," said Bertie Beckton. "Lily would not mind. She has laughed about it herself." The feeling appeared to be unanimous.

Jessie placed her utensils on her plate and signaled for the serving maid.

"It was in 1883, before we moved into the Great White House," she began, "so we were still living in a tent, as we had all summer. Though, believe me, a tent was a great improvement on that wretched sod shelter where we spent our first winter." She shuddered, then went on. "There had been a violent hailstorm, and the hailstones—I vow they were large as eggs—broke through the canvas. We had to put everything we could lay our hands on over the stovetop to save it from cracking."

"Your stove had a porcelain top?" interjected Cousin Nettie, obviously hanging on every word.

"Yes, we had brought it from—"

"Jessie, my dear," this from her husband, "one story at a time please."

"Oh, yes," Jessie glanced at him before she continued. "Well, the storm had finished—hailstorms are like that, only last for five or ten minutes, though in that time they can do considerable damage. We almost had everything back in order. Then we turned around, and there he was."

"Who was?" breathed Nettie. Edith and Florence Beckton exchanged glances. They had obviously heard the story before.

"I have forgotten his name, but he is the grandson of Chief White Bear—though we didn't know it then. He was dressed in all his finery—red jacket, beads, feathers—braids shiny with grease. He didn't look at us or speak to us; he just sat down, with his head bowed and his rifle on his knees, and seemed prepared to stay that way."

"What did he want?"

Ernest Beckton chortled heartily, and this time Jessie's smile was rueful.

"Well, it turns out—but I'm getting ahead of myself. We didn't know what he wanted. Lily offered him tea, biscuits, one of the cakes we had baked for our supper—after all, Lily knew her position as the eldest Miss Pierce—while I cowered behind the table. When nothing else would interest him and he didn't even look at her, Lily would have offered him tobacco, but we didn't know where Father kept his store of such things. Finally we decided to continue with our work and just pretend he wasn't there. We didn't wish to be discourteous, but what else could we do?"

Cousin Nettie and I nodded sympathetically. All a woman could be expected to do was her best—and then carry on with her work.

Jessie continued, "It was rather difficult to ignore the fact there was a strange man—a—heathen, as far as we knew—sitting a few feet from us while we worked. So we were quite relieved when the Rev. Mr. Baldwin and his sister arrived. Mr. Baldwin spoke to the young man in Cree, and the young man responded. In fact, there seemed to be quite an amusing conversation going on between the three—at least the Baldwins appeared amused, but they didn't share the joke with us."

"Lily, however, might not have thought it quite such a joke," supplied Ernest Beckton.

"Hush," said Jessie, by now engrossed in her tale. She went on, "Finally, Father and Duncan returned. The young man immediately stood up, appeared to make a speech and then held out his rifle to Father. Father, not knowing what the chief's grandson was talking about and thinking it but an expression of friendship, was about to accept the rifle, but Mr. Baldwin stopped him and explained what the young man had said."

All the Becktons and Cousin Ernest were laughing by this time, Jessie so much that she could scarcely manage the words. I began to worry whether she would ever reach the point of her story.

"Mr. Baldwin," continued Jessie, when she could catch her breath, "explained that the young man had come to pay court to Lily. Because our visitor was the eldest grandson of Chief White Bear, he thought it right he should marry Miss Pierce, the eldest daughter of the 'Soldier Chief'—that's what they called Father."

Nettie gasped. "What did you do?" she asked.

"Well, Lily of course went absolutely white, and I thought she might collapse, had not Miss Baldwin and I been there to catch her. Our father hustled the young man and his rifle outside as quickly (and politely) as he could manage and made it very clear he was not accepting a trade for any of his daughters. After the young man had mounted his horse and ridden away, Father came back inside. He was very upset, and when the Rev. Mr. Baldwin explained how some other Cree braves had told him the chief's grandson was on his way to *a courting sit* and how he—Mr. Baldwin—and his sister had come along to 'see the fun,' Father was angrier still. What if he had accepted the rifle?"

Even my uncle was nodding in sympathy at this point, though he might have heard the story before. Perhaps he was imaging himself in the same situation, having to protect his daughters from the strange proposals of those whose ways he did not understand.

"Father did not forgive the Rev. Baldwin for a long time," added Jessie. "And Lily—well, Lily spent the summer and fall in a very nervous condition. Even now she cannot bear to be left alone."

"Oh, dear," sighed Nettie.

I shared my cousin's distress. It reminded me of the occasion Mr. Cuthbert warned me not to walk to Cannington Manor alone. Not only was this way of life still foreign to me, but all women seemed vulnerable. The men could well laugh, but they often had recourse and influence that women did not.

"Now, tell them how your father earned the name 'Soldier Chief'" suggested Jessie's husband.

"Oh, I know that story. Let me tell it," said Florence Beckton. When Jessie had given her nod, her sister-in-law continued. "Was it not because your father had given flour, potatoes and other food to the chief one winter—because the Indians were starving? And did not Chief White Bear and one of his wives and some others—perhaps even Lily's beau—" she stopped to laugh, "make a ceremonial visit in order to thank Captain Pierce? And did not the chief offer to give your father his tattooed skin when he—the chief—died?"

"Yes, that is all true," said Jessie sadly, "and yet my father was the first to die—not that he wanted the chief's skin, of course."

"Oh, no!" All the ladies squirmed at the thought of that, and I would have wished for a gentler, more domestic topic.

I could see, however, that the gentlemen had more harrowing stories to tell, for they were leaning forward in their chairs. Cousin Ernest took the initiative. Perhaps he felt he had been part of the audience long enough. First, he commented that women had many things to fear besides unwanted marriage proposals. Then he went on to tell the pitiful story of Mrs. Elsie Dallas.

Apparently this tragedy was very recent. On October 27, 1891, Mrs. Dallas, wife of Alex Dallas, and her two little boys, George and James, were caught in a prairie fire. James, the baby, was just a year old, and his brother was less than three. Mrs. Dallas had been tending a neighbour, Mrs. William McQueen, who was recovering from childbirth. Naturally, the two little Dallas boys were with her, as their father was working in the field at some distance from their home. When she had done some cleaning, prepared a meal and made certain that Mrs. McQueen and the baby were comfortable, Mrs. Dallas gathered up her boys and started for home, cutting across open country to save time, as her own family needed supper.

Before long, however, she became aware of smoke and could actually see the approach of a prairie fire. Since there was a high wind, she wasn't sure if she could make it home, so she turned back to the McQueens, hoping to reach the fireguards around their buildings, where she and the children should be safe. The wind, however, was strong and the fire moving too fast, so it caught up with her. When she realized she could not outrun it, she noticed a slight depression in the ground. She bade her frightened children lie down in this low spot and attempted to shield them with her body.

All was for naught, however; the fire showed no mercy to the helpless little family. William McQueen was working near Wawota and headed home when he saw smoke, but Ernest thought it was Sam Hodgson, who worked for the Pryces, neighbours of the McQueens, who discovered Elsie and the boys. Everyone, including Dr. Hardy, who was immediately summoned, did what they could. Within a day, however, both children died of smoke-inhalation and serious burns. Though the mother lived for two more wretched days, she could do little more than whisper out her story to her grieving husband, before she too succumbed.

It was a tragic case that once heard could not be forgotten, and its conclusion was greeted with silence all around the table. Both Bertie and William Beckton had moved closer to their wives during the telling—in fact, William had come around the table in order to hold Edith's hand in his own—and there were tears in the eyes of all the other women, as there were in mine. In fact, I felt in danger of weeping openly. For the first time since my arrival in Cannington Manor, I yearned for the relative safety of my own home in England.

"And then there are the blizzards," said Cousin Ernest with admirable lack of compassion, hoping no doubt to keep his audience now that he had them in his thrall.

"Oh, no," cried the three Beckton wives simultaneously. "No more."

My uncle tried to bring back a happier topic by asking if Jessie had learned to say "Soldier Chief" in Cree. She thought it was something like *Okeemo Shimogonisa* and that Chief White Bear was *Wapemaqua*. Everyone tried to imitate her, though none very successfully, which led to a return of merriment. However, it was by now quite late, past time for the group to move out of the dining room and let the long-suffering maids clean up after them.

The gentlemen retired to the bachelor's quarters, this time with my uncle among them, and the ladies continued their tour of the rest of the house—or rather Jessie, Nettie and I continued. Edith and Florence Beckton went back to the drawing room.

Chapter 36

A DIFFERENT TASTE IN ROOMS

I was especially pleased when Jessie Beckton escorted us up the beautiful curved staircase to the second floor. Though the rooms on the main floor were very fine, I wished to see the house in its entirety. At the top of the stairway, a cosy sitting-room and a number of smallish but beautifully-appointed bedchambers were reserved for families and female visitors. Jessie, it seemed, had sought to balance the masculine atmosphere in the gentlemen's quarters by giving full rein to her very feminine taste in the spaces under her direction. Again, I admired but did not envy.

Jessie also showed us the nursery, where excess—some seemed inevitable—was quite appropriate. The room had already been supplied with two small beds, one with high sides that would protect an infant. From this second bed, the young child could be observed from a distance, as the sides were composed of decorative spindles. Neither had Jessie forgotten the benefits of a bassinet with a rocker underneath. This woven item appeared to be a family heirloom, for it showed signs of wear for all its bright paint, new frills and plumped-up pillows. I thought it the nicest piece of furniture in the room and knelt down to give it a gentle push.

I had seen little of babies in my life, but it was easy to imagine an infant in such a bed—dimpled limbs, downy hair and smiling rose-bud lips. As this image floated before me, I was again reminded of Nurse's tiny boy and ashamed I had paid so little attention to him or to his mother. At the same time, Nurse had not appeared to expect much attention from the family. Other than Cicely, Noel and, to a smaller extent, Dora—for they could not have been prevented from visiting the baby—the family had practically ignored his existence, and the baby's mother had seemed to accept this.

Such would obviously not be the case with any Beckton babies. It seemed ironic that Florence Beckton, the most recently married, would be the first to make use of this very comfortable nursery, if only during her visits to the main house. On this too, I refrained from commenting, in case it was the cause of envy for the women of the family.

One never knew whether couples were well-suited to each other, whether they simply chose not to have children for a time, or whether there was some physical or emotional impediment that kept them childless. On the other hand, Jessie and Edith were still but a few years married, so there was sufficient time for such things to unfold. What a complicated business it all was, this marrying and giving birth!

It also struck me that all three Beckton women might be younger than I was. Indeed, it was quite possible I would never marry, so would never have a child, in spite of poor Nurse's words to the contrary. I brushed the thought quickly aside, as there was nothing to be achieved by dwelling on it. Furthermore, it came with other thoughts and imaginings, all equally rebellious or discomforting.

Jessie next showed Nettie and me her own dressing room and sitting room, and the wonders of her indoor water closet. This tiny, narrow room was very clean, and as far as I could detect, carried no odour to proclaim its purpose. There was another downstairs, our hostess said, so much more convenient in this climate than the usual outhouses. But perhaps not as convenient for the maid or footman who must empty these thrones, I thought, surprising myself with my lack of kindness. However, it would obviously be a most fortunate concession to one who was in the family way. Did Florence Beckton, I wondered, have such a convenience in her home— which I understood was little more than a homesteader's shack?

Jessie also pointed out the door to the attic, where the maids had their rooms, but she didn't volunteer to display them. As in most grand houses, the servants had access to the second floor—perhaps the door was positioned here in order for them to easily tend to both water closet and baths—but a separate stairs to the kitchen. Though I had noticed a democratic flavour permeating much of the organization of this pioneer community—and perhaps had even been a little influenced by it—the better class of families must obviously still retain some distinctions.

There was another closed door in this wing, the door to Jessie's bedchamber, which I presumed she must share with Ernest, her husband. Another important distinction, it seemed.

Much like her father, Cousin Nettie was expressing great admiration, even awe, for everything that was introduced to her, and I hastened to add my voice to hers as we followed Jessie back down the grand stairway. As we descended, our hostess seemed disappointed to see only her two sisters-in-law in the drawing room. She turned to us with a mischievous look.

"Shall we visit the gentlemen?" she asked, leading the way across the room to the heavy carved door of the gentlemen's wing. Edith and Florence Beckton rose from the settee where they had been reclining and came to join us.

I was grateful Jessie knocked before entering, as I had no wish to disrupt the gentlemen unduly in their quarters, though I was curious to see the well-known haven. Ernest Beckton immediately opened the door and invited us in, apologizing for the smoke and the commotion. Indeed, it was smoky and noisy, and somewhat thick with alcohol fumes as well, though at our entrance, the gentlemen immediately put down their brandies and snuffed their cheroots.

The men also put aside the long, slender wooden rods, which I believe were called "cues." I supposed these were what they used to knock the billiard balls about on the long table—which at least explained the noise. The men's dogs, meanwhile, must have been accustomed to such commotion, since they continued to ignore the visitors and were dozing contentedly in whatever cushioned spaces were unoccupied.

The smoky air made me somewhat reluctant to go beyond the doorway, but I did want to examine the unusual hand-carving along the edges of the full-sized, marble-topped billiard table, so I stepped in to take a closer look. When I did so, Bertie Beckton offered to teach me the game, but I declined, glancing somewhat guiltily at his wife. I was certain he meant no disrespect to either of us, but I liked neither his manner nor the strong smell of alcohol on his breath.

"We will join you directly, ladies," said my uncle, indicating that at least one of the gentlemen felt they had been neglecting us. I was quite happy to retreat back to the fresher air of the drawing room. And though I am sure my uncle was disappointed, I was not sorry there was no mention of music, because this would have extended our visit.

For all that I had looked forward to seeing Didsbury, I was not comfortable there. Indeed, it was a beautiful house, our hostess agreeable, and the others—as much as I had seen or heard them—pleasant enough. Yet there was about the estate—for all the good will of the people who lived there—a certain forced ostentation, as if the Becktons were sparing no expense in order to support their reputation for wealth. Was it appropriate to indulge the hobbies and pretensions of an old world in the new? I could not have said for certain, but I knew that, in comparison, Humphrys House felt much more like a home.

As to the similarities between Didsbury and my father's house, it remained to be seen whether I would feel at home again in the latter. Since I was almost at the end of my visit to Cannington Manor, I would soon know one way or the other.

Chapter 37

-

DISCUSSING THE FUTURE

As we drove home from our dinner at Didsbury, Nettie suddenly spoke up from her corner of the carriage.

"Pa," she said, "can you do nothing to persuade Cousin Florence to stay longer? It seems just too cruel to have her leave us so soon after Mary is gone."

I was startled at what was nearly an echo of my own thoughts. Though I had that very evening longed to be back in South Norwood, where forest fires, blizzards and dangerous wild animals were virtually unknown, I was again regretting that I must depart the district in a mere three days. How would I be able to readjust to life in England? If only there had been a serious invitation to stay on at Cannington Manor, at least until Aunt Jane returned.

My uncle, sitting in the shadows across from Nettie and me, must have been dozing or lost in thought, as he didn't at first seem to understand my cousin's meaning.

"What's that you say?" he asked, clearing his throat and shifting his body into a more alert posture.

"Cousin Florence—we mustn't let her go away so soon. The house will be so dull if she really must leave."

Though reluctant to share my feelings until I was privy to those of my uncle, I felt I must speak up at this point. "Indeed, I am sorry to go. But my passage out of Halifax is booked." I might also have said, "My parents will be expecting me," but I suspected this was not the case. Neither had they been much in my thoughts for the past eight weeks.

"Pa," said Nettie again, and this time her voice was pettish, "is there nothing we can do? Cannot a passage be cancelled?"

"Nothing easier," he responded, though he did not offer any practical suggestions as to how such a change of plan might be managed.

Trying not to set too much store in a vague possibility, I must press the point. "Would we send a telegram to the port authority?" I asked. "Or must one contact the shipping line? I am due to sail in ten days and must first take the stage and then the train."

"I will look into it," said my uncle, "but indeed we must not allow you to leave so soon. With Ernest mostly away, Mary and her husband gone, Nurse and her baby too, we begin to feel quite a small party."

"That's settled then," said Nettie, nestling back into her corner.

Excited though I was by the possibility, I could not take it as quite so certain. While I had found my weeks with the Humphrys more felicitous than I could begin to say, I was afraid of becoming a burden and had to break in again.

"Dear Nettie, dear Uncle, you are too kind. Even if it were possible, I could not accept your hospitality unless you let me pay my way, or at least give me an occupation."

"Oh, that's nothing," said Nettie. "We are finally to start spring cleaning tomorrow, and you are welcome to help us if you must—though I dare say Miss Pritchard could manage quite well without our interference."

I smiled. It was the kind of comment Mary would have made, and I felt a spasm of longing for her. If I were to stay for another six weeks, I would see her return—see her surprise, feel her embrace. And what reason, after all, did I have to hurry home to England? Of course, it would prolong my confusion over Mr. Cuthbert, but those feelings would be there regardless.

This time it was my uncle who announced it settled, and I was unable to say more, as that would suggest I did not trust him. I determined, therefore, to seek the advice of Cousin Ernest, whom I had reason to believe was more a man of the world than his indulgent parent. After we had alighted from the carriage and my uncle and Cousin Nettie were turned toward the front door, I announced a desire to enjoy the fresh air a few minutes longer.

I wrapped my shawl more closely about my shoulders and throat to provide some protection from biting insects, of which there were many that evening. Then I made as if to follow Cousin Ernest, for he had already unhitched the carriage and was leading the team toward the barn. He accepted my company without comment, other than to warn me to never walk behind a horse nor even close to its back legs, but always near the front quarters of the animal.

If there had been light enough, he would then have seen me blush. Indeed, I knew nothing about horses. Unlike my sister, who had even ridden to hounds, I had never professed an interest in riding and had no mount of my own at home in England. Other than my sister's horse and one kept for the use of my father when riding the estate, we had only carriage horses, and they were handled exclusively by groom or stable boys. In fact, it struck me now that I had never actually touched a horse—which was yet another area where my education appeared to have been lacking.

"If you wish to be helpful, you can open that gate," said Cousin Ernest, when we reached the fence that separated the house and driveway from the barnyard. I moved to comply, but was unable to see how the gate could be released. He meanwhile stood with the team and somewhat impatiently described loops of wire at both the top and bottom of the gateposts. Apparently these cinched the gate to the main part of the fence and when lifted and lowered allowed the gate to drop open. Once open, it must be dragged to the side to clear the way for the horses.

Eventually I found the topmost loop of twisted wire, but my hands had not the strength to pull it up over the top of the post.

I pulled and scratched frantically at wood and wire with my fingernails, but could not make the loop budge. When it seemed that Cousin Ernest must leave the horses in order to rescue me, I felt an arm brush against my shoulder. Someone had placed himself directly behind me, with strong hands clamped over my own, pressing them into the wood and wire.

It was but a brief moment of possession. In the same instant that I jerked my head around to see my captor, Lionel Cuthbert stepped away from me, released his pressure on my hands and motioned me aside.

"Please stand back, Miss Southam," he said, and I stumbled from the gate. If I had stayed to observe, I might have seen him embrace the gatepost with his arms so he could release the tension on the top loop and lift it. That I would have seen if I had stayed, but as was my habit, I turned and fled to the house, my errand gone completely out of mind.

Needless to say, the pressure of those hands on mine and the very proximity of Lionel Cuthbert's body were not so easily forgotten. I also remembered how that very morning I had gone in search of Mr. Cuthbert, wishing to thank him for his kindness to Nurse. Would it always be thus? Would I always run away from that which I wanted the most and miss the opportunity to do what was right and good? And yet . . . and yet, in such circumstances, how could I be sure of what was right and good?

In spite of my failure of courage the night before, I did remember my errand in the morning and found occasion at breakfast to ask Cousin Ernest whether it would be difficult to change my date of passage. To my relief, he did not tease me about my sudden disappearance the previous night. He was also less inclined to gallantries than my uncle, so he said he did not know but would ask. He thought there must be a way, however, for surely such occasions must arise—perhaps even frequently. I reminded him I had only a short time to change my arrangements, and he said he would make inquiries that day, as he was on his way to the Pages, having almost finished his work for them.

After talking to Ernest, I was much relieved and able to face my uncle and Cousin Nettie with more tranquility. As for Mr. Lionel Cuthbert, there was no possibility of tranquility in regards to him. How foolish he must have found me, with my constant blushes and my inability to either face him or put him in his place. Therefore, I could only hope he would not be among those who came to the kitchen for breakfast and lunch. Since my hope was granted, there was no rational explanation for my disappointment.

Chapter 38

-

SPRING CLEANING IN SUMMER

Nettie and Miss Pritchard did not start spring cleaning the day following the dinner at Didsbury as they had planned. Apparently Nettie, claiming a great weariness from having been out the night before, had managed to put it off once again. In fact, it might have been delayed indefinitely, had not Martha Pritchard the very next day resorted to making one of her less than diplomatic remarks about the *filthy state* of the house and how poorly it compared to her last establishment. That settled matters, and we began the job as soon as the breakfast dishes were cleared. Even so, Miss Pritchard was still complaining.

"'Tis a disgrace to call it spring cleaning!" she sniffed, "'tis past spring cleaning. In the middle of June—'tis summer cleaning! At my last place, they were particular. Cleaned and polished all the windows in April, we did."

Since her last place was in England, I wondered if she had taken account of the differences in climate. But, like the rest of the family, I was by now much in awe of Miss Pritchard and her abilities. I therefore kept my council and obediently found an apron, a cap to cover my hair, a scrub brush and a bucket filled with warm water and lye soap. With these weapons at my disposal, I prepared like

Cousin Nettie to do Martha Pritchard's bidding. After all, there was some urgency about getting started, as the house had many dark corners, and we could accomplish very little without the benefit of daylight.

Some of the tasks were also unpleasant. When scrubbing the shelves in the kitchen and larder, for instance, I not only found what I believed were mouse droppings, but also discovered little nests of tiny beetles and their larvae. At first I recoiled in horror and was certain I could not continue the task. I was certain my mother had never seen such an unwholesome sight, and perhaps it was the thought of my mother and her refusal to see the harsher parts of life that gave me the courage to review the situation again. I also wished to repay the family's kindness to me—Cousin Ernest had by that time telegraphed the shipping company to arrange for an extension of my ticket—so I would be able to enjoy the Humphrys' hospitality for several more weeks, perhaps as much as two or even three months.

When my feelings of shock and revulsion for my discoveries in the larder had passed and I was able to return to my task, my temptation was to dispose of the offending bags of flour and meal and start anew. After all, the open bags had attracted the vermin and were no doubt contaminated with them. However, considering the economic situation of the family, this would be an unconscionable waste. Therefore, I contented myself with putting old broadsheets on the freshly-scrubbed shelves and tying the tops of the bags more tightly.

Could one purchase large containers with tight seals and lids that would better protect the mealy contents? I would have to consult Martha to see whether this was possible or if there was anything else that could be done to prevent infestation. I would no doubt be favoured with lectures on the superiority of her old place, but surely this was something I could endure in order to find a solution.

Having done what I could with the kitchen and pantry shelves, I emptied my bucket out the kitchen door, refilled it with fresh water and soap, and followed the others to the front rooms. Martha

Pritchard had already taken the hall rugs outside and hung them to be beaten when the children came home from school. Where the rugs had been, there was a great deal of feathery dirt and clutter, all of which must be checked for items of value, then carefully swept before the scrubbing began. This created a choking dust, and when we opened the doors and windows to bring in fresh air, numerous flying insects assumed they were invited as well, so we had to close windows and doors quite soon after.

Miss Pritchard naturally took the opportunity to observe that in her old place all the doors and windows were fitted with netting, so one could have abundant fresh air without allowing insects into the house. Of course, she assured us (as if we were somehow responsible for this annoyance) England also had fewer flying insects. Cousin Nettie and I, by now both on our hands and knees on the slivery floor, exchanged a glance and struggled to suppress our laughter at such a ridiculous statement.

In that shared glance, I also noticed the foolish and somewhat improper picture we presented. Not only were our faces and necks dripping with most unladylike perspiration, but our sleeves were rolled up over our elbows to avoid having them fall in our buckets. Worse still, though we kneeled daintily on old straw mats to protect our knees, when we stretched out to get our scrub brushes into the corners and along the edges of the mouldings, our bottoms must of necessity lift and wiggle vigorously in unison with our scrubbing.

What if my uncle, one of my male cousins or even Mr. Cuthbert should happen to come into the kitchen and glance into the hallway where we were working? My heart began to pound in the most unreasonable fashion at the thought I could thus be seen. On the other hand, no one could then accuse us of thinking ourselves above hard work. Neither were we *likely* to be surprised in this way. Nonetheless, I took care afterwards to position myself so that my bottom faced the wall and never the centre of the room. However slow and awkward such self-consciousness made me, I felt less vulnerable.

I could not help reflecting how a good many poor girls had no choice but to spend a large part of their lives on their knees. Furthermore, many of them would only have one dress and must hitch up their skirts and ragged petticoats to protect it as they worked. How difficult they must find it then to maintain a proper respect for their own persons. And if they did not respect their own persons, how could they prevent men from taking advantage of them?

I wondered idly if Mr. McClure had ever discovered Nurse in such an undignified position, and suddenly there arose in my mind's eye a picture of groping hands, soiled clothing and rumpled skirts such as I had never before imagined. The image was so vivid and shameful that I was forced to stop and rest my forehead on my hands while I caught my breath and stilled the pounding of my heart.

According to Cousin Mary, my Aunt Jane felt situations such as the one in which Nurse Ford had found herself could never have happened in England, but it was well known that many young women of the lower classes had shared her fate. The workhouses were full of them and their offspring.

Perhaps Nurse was better off as she was. With other children to feed, a poor widower such as Mr. McClure had little choice but to legitimize his union with the mother of his youngest, unless he chose to lose himself and his family in a city such as Winnipeg. And how could a poor man afford a move like that? Living together otherwise would have isolated him, and all pioneers had need of their neighbours.

By the end of the day, Miss Pritchard, Cousin Nettie and I had, with the added convenience of ladders and a few long-handled brushes—both of which were relegated to Miss Pritchard, she being the most experienced—washed all the ceilings, walls, mouldings, window frames and door frames on the main floor. We had also cleaned the kitchen shelves; scrubbed, waxed and polished all the floors—or as much as we were able, because most of the flooring was rough and inclined to slivers; aired the rugs and washed and polished the windows—a tremendous job in itself, since there were so many.

The children had also beaten the rugs (and occasionally each other) with riotous consequences.

On the following day, we must proceed upstairs and repeat the exercise, but I was content to think about what we had already accomplished and to worry about tomorrow on the morrow.

Even more to our credit, these tasks were accomplished alongside laying out breakfast and lunch. By suppertime on that first day, we were a bedraggled lot and my body felt as wrung out as a used dish rag, but—somewhat to my surprise—I was physically exhilarated as well. This was a revelation to me, since other than walking, I was not accustomed to vigorous exercise.

I also enjoyed the feeling of common purpose with my cousin, and any lingering reservations I had about Martha seemed resolved. Whatever our stations in life, we were first of all women, and what's more, women working together to accomplish a goal of value to us all. I smiled to think that Mary Wollstonecraft-Godwin might actually approve of such communal effort.

We must tidy ourselves, however, for the men would soon be in for their supper. Dora had begun to peel potatoes, as directed, but there were a number of other tasks to be done. And some assistance might be needed with the potatoes as well, since they were small and soft (with occasional spoiled ones among them), which made Dora even slower at the job. I patted Dora's shoulder and because she was so impressionable, tried not to show my own fear of the stinkish-sweet smell of decay.

Cousin Nettie appeared to share my sense of accomplishment and good will after our day's work. After descending to the cistern and pulling up several pails of water that she would heat on the stove so we could both bathe after supper, she impulsively stopped to give me a hug as she was brushing by.

"Is that a smudge I see on your cheek, Cousin Florrie?" she asked. I knew she used the particular diminutive simply to tease me, as it was Bertie Beckton's name for his wife and Nettie had never addressed me in that way before. She also rubbed her thumb across my cheekbone in such a way that if it had not already been smudged, it would now be. "And hair falling out from under your cap? Heavens above! What is the world coming to?"

I glanced at the door then, afraid yet half-hoping a certain blue-eyed man might suddenly appear within its frame and see us all working together in such good humour. Would not even such a one as Lionel Cuthbert appreciate both our ease and our industry at that moment? However, Mr. Cuthbert did not come to the house that day, nor for several days after, and as usual, though I told myself I did not wish to see him, I found it most annoying that he did not appear.

I had yet another revelation that evening, after Cousins Billy and Frankie had carried the bath up the stairs to my chamber—Cousin Nettie had generously suggested I take my turn first, while the water was hot. When I was alone and had, with some self-consciousness, shed all my clothing and stepped into the bath, I experienced a feeling of relaxation greater than I had ever previously experienced. The water seemed to caress my skin. In particular, when I bent my knees so my back was flat against the metal bottom of the tub, the warmth lapped over my bosom and belly and I was aware of the most wonderful sense of abandon. This feeling was no doubt intensified by the physical labour I had earlier undergone and the special care I took to clean myself, even those parts I seldom touched.

So great was my enjoyment of my bath that I spent some minutes in this supine position and might have fallen asleep had there not been a knock on the door. This interruption caused me great consternation and some spillage, as I clambered out of the tub and attempted to slip into my nightclothes without drying myself.

"It's only me. May I come in?" came Nettie's voice.

"Just a minute," I gasped, finding I must after all dry my back and legs so my nightgown did not stick to me.

Another knock and Nettie entered. She smiled in a conspiratorial way that reminded me of Mary, but rather than teasing me for my modesty as her sister might have done, she merely commented that I seemed to be ready for bed. Could I put on my wrap as well, she wondered, and help her move the tub to her room? Sensing my hesitation, she explained that everyone else had gone to bed. If this had not been the case, we could have had the boys move the tub for us.

The task was not as easy as it seemed, perhaps because we had to stifle our laughter. The water was deep enough that the tub was very heavy, even for two to carry a short distance, and it sloshed wildly and threatened to splash over the edge with every step we took. In spite of our care, we must have spilled some water, as we half dragged, half carried the bath to the large room that was now Nettie's domain.

Finally, we accomplished our goal and said good-night, and I scurried back to my own room, where I took time only to dry my feet and blow out the lamp before I burrowed into the luxury of my bed. Almost immediately, I slept.

Chapter 39

-

THE PRAIRIE FIRE

That night, in spite of my physical exhaustion, I had a most vivid and memorable dream.

I suppose the tragedy of the woman and children who had died in the prairie fire the previous fall, the family whose story Cousin Ernest had told during the dinner party at the Becktons two days previous, had affected my imagination while I slept. This in itself did not seem unusual. Along with fears of other natural disasters—such as blizzards and floods and swarms of locusts (though not all of them were as real a possibility in this community as fires)—the terror of prairie fires must have a nightmarish persistence in the minds of most pioneer women.

Nor was it unusual for me to dream. In fact, I had had a number of unsettling dreams since I arrived at Cannington Manor. Many of them had involved Mr. Lionel Cuthbert, as this one did. What was unusual, however, was the coherence of the dream and how much I recalled when finally I woke.

In the dream, I had never known such pain in my shoulders and back, and I felt my arms must soon pull out of their sockets, but I also knew I couldn't stop and rest. Lionel Cuthbert and I, it seemed, were beating out the fire along the fireguard, and we had been there a long time, hours perhaps. Despite our efforts, the wet sacks and hunks of blanket in our hands seemed poor weapons against the wisps of smoke and flame that kept bursting up all around us. As far as I could see, the dry sod with its bits of prairie grass, not to mention the garden and the tennis court, had been reduced to char. Though there was nothing visible for the fire to catch hold of, yet there was always another puff of smoke, another flash of light and heat.

Each time I felt my agony unbearable or my strength completely sapped, I looked at the man ahead of me and found the energy to carry on. His shirt abandoned, he laboured on in his under-vest, which perspiration had plastered to his shoulders and back, and I could see his muscles working steadily under their thin, grimy covering. Though the wind had gone down a little by this point, there was still enough to first make a jaunty sail of his blackened trousers and then to flatten them against his strong legs and buttocks.

I stumbled after him as one fascinated, and yet my mind wandered even as I doggedly persisted at my task. I was reflecting on how much this man had begun to occupy my waking thoughts and on how he intruded into my dreams—in the dream I did not consider the irony of this realization. And now, for all my physical agony, I felt a kind of elation to be teamed with him against this common natural enemy. His presence gave me a feeling of safety whatever the immediate danger.

Now, the scene changed. I was in my bedchamber when he called my name. I heard him first from a distance and then much closer, for he came inside and crossed the room to rouse me. And in the dream, I was not surprised to see him there.

"No time for ceremonies," he said. "Some brush fire's gone out of control." And as I still gazed at him without understanding, his hands clamped down on my shoulders, shook me a little. "I need your help!" he said.

Then he was gone, out of my chamber. I heard his heavy boots clattering down the stairs and thumping across the floor.

What was I doing in bed in the middle of the day? It must have

been because of the headache, for the afternoon had been unbear-
ably hot, the sound of the wind adding to the throbbing pressure
against my temples.

In fact, I must have taken a powder. Perhaps that explained the
layers of dream—and as I struggled to wake, I was still uncertain
which layer I inhabited. Had he actually been in my bedchamber an
instant ago—and me with my stays flung aside and nothing but a
few thin layers of muslin covering my skin?

The scene changed again. "Too windy to work," Uncle James
was saying, suggesting a trip to town for supplies and to collect the
post. The family might also drop in on the Maltbys, who apparently
had returned from their wedding trip. This possibility had sent my
cousins and even Martha Pritchard skittering in all directions to
prepare themselves for an outing. While I would dearly have loved
to see Cousin Mary, my headache would only get worse, so I had
begged to be excused.

But I knew I was wasting time with this remembering. With
great difficulty, I sat up in bed. Lionel Cuthbert had said he needed my help, and as I looked to the window, I could see it, the fire.
There, beyond the lawn and vegetable plantings, it loomed enormous in the southern sky and seemed in danger of blocking out the
afternoon sun. The fireguard, encircling the buildings like a moat,
appeared a mere footpath holding back a dragon's breath. (How I
could see all of this from my bed in spite of the curtains on the window, I did not question.)

But still I was wasting time. Why didn't—couldn't—I move from
the bed!

Then the scene changed again. Mr. Cuthbert had fetched one
of the horses and was attempting to hitch it to the plough, but the
animal was terrified and threatened to trample him. Finally Lionel
Cuthbert dragged off his shirt and wound it around the horse's eyes.
I had run out of the house in an old shirt and waistcoat and had
stocking feet because my borrowed boots were too cumbersome,
and now I stumbled across the furrows to reach Mr. Cuthbert's side

"Where are your shoes, lass?" he hollered, then tore off the handkerchief he had over his mouth and held it out to me. "Put this on. Get blankets, gunnysacks, anything. Dunk them in the rain barrel."

What did he mean? Where would I find the things he wanted? Then I was hurtling back to the house, grabbed some blankets from Nurse's bed—in my dream I interrupted her sewing but she didn't seem to be upset, for she smiled at me. Outside again, I found the rain barrel near the kitchen entrance and dumped the blankets into the water, wrenched one out and dragged it behind me.

"Leave it. We need to turn more sod, so the fire won't jump the guard."

He hooked my hand around the reins close to where they met the horse's bridle. (Just as I remembered that I had never touched a horse before, I remembered the compelling force of those hands holding mine captive.)

"Just lead him," he said. "Hurry, lass! Florence! We haven't time to waste."

It was the first time I had heard my name on his lips.

When we had added several rows to the fireguard, Mr. Cuthbert unhitched the horse, pulled off the rough cotton shirt that had blinkered it and let it go. Even as I watched it gallop away from the fire, who knew where, I felt no need to question the man beside me. Then we were back to beating out the flames in the old guard.

"Just stay behind me," he said. "Watch for any I might have missed."

It all seemed futile, but then the wind must have shifted, because the wall of flame began to move away from us. Though he didn't stop right away, Lionel Cuthbert seemed to ease up. Finally he turned to look at me, and to my amazement, there was a smile on his blackened face.

"We have done it, Florence. I believe we have done it."

If he had opened his arms to me at that moment, I would have stepped into them and thought it the most natural thing in the world. Instead he threw himself flat on the grass, while I gazed down at his blue eyes, brilliant in his grimy face, his under-vest sag-

ging open and his chest streaked with soot and sweat. I was suddenly dizzy and collapsed on the ground beside him.

He reached over, pulled the handkerchief from my face, began
to laugh. "Oh, lass, . . . if you could see yourself."

I sat up, untied the handkerchief and handed it back to him.

"And look at your poor feet that have never been dirty before."

Then I saw that my feet had poked through my ruined stockings
and were now completely bare, except for their covering of dust and
ash. In a minute, I became aware Lionel Cuthbert was no longer
looking at me, was in fact avoiding looking at me. Looking down,
I saw that my shirt and waistcoat were gaping open, leaving my
bosom scarcely covered. Burning with humiliation, I started to pull
my clothing together.

Suddenly his manner changed. He sat up and his face moved
closer, as if . . . as if . . .

"Miss Southam," he said. "You'll be wanting to tidy yourself. The
family have returned."

I had heard neither horses, nor wagon, nor voices, but now I
fumbled to follow his advice. It did not help that I was close to tears.
Mr. Cuthbert for his part sprang easily to his feet and stood with
his back to me. I knew he was trying to shield me from the others.

"Thank you," I said, when I had buttoned my shirt and waistcoat
and was finally able to struggle to my feet.

He gave me a little bow and strode ahead to reassure the family, and as I limped along behind him, I was suddenly aware of my
scratched and blistered feet and all the other parts of my body that
gave me pain.

When the layers of dream finally parted and I awoke, my aching
joints and muscles were real. The tears started again, but they were
not for any physical discomfort. It seemed that even my dreams, my
unconscious mind conspired against me.

Chapter 40

-

PREPARATIONS FOR RACE DAY

Since Cousin Ernest's quick action in telegraphing both the port authority in Halifax and the Allan & State Line shipping company, it seemed certain my ticket and visit were now extended another three months, and even that I could change if I wished. All I must do is write my parents with the news, and then I could participate wholeheartedly in the community event of the season, and even help with the preparations. These began a full month before Race Day itself—which would be held on Thursday, the twenty-first of July.

The preparations also threw light on the significant differences between English settlers and the Canadians. The Canadians, among them Lionel Cuthbert, apparently gave Race Day little thought and were reluctant even to commit themselves to attending. They would "see how it went," they said—possibly meaning the weather and how much haying they could do before that date. It had been hot and dry for weeks, so was a good time for cutting and curing the long grass that would provide winter feed for the animals. Besides, very few of the Canadians owned race horses, so they could partic-ipate only as observers, were they to attend.

John and Adelaide Turton were perhaps an exception. From

what I had heard, they appeared to be on the cusp of being English and Canadian as well. Though both English-born—he from Yorkshire and she from Essex County—they had spent their adult lives in Canada and much of them on the Manitoba prairies, where they had met. Married in 1879, in Poplar Point, Manitoba, they had two children when they settled on the north side of the Cannington Manor district, in 1882. Like the Pierces, they essentially "squatted" until the title to their land was delivered in 1883. Since then, Mrs. Adelaide Turton had borne a child a year, though some had died as babies. Alfred, their third child, was the first boy born in the district and the first child baptized at All Saints in Cannington Manor.

Since John Turton had brought cattle and horses with him when the family moved from Manitoba, he now had large cattle herds and the resources to invest in pure-bred horses for entertainment. I had also heard that he sometimes took part in the hunts organized by the Becktons, and that some of his horses were fast and would almost certainly be entered in the races. In this way, the Turtons appeared to have a foot comfortably in both camps—if there *were* separate camps—which was a subject under some debate.

Another exception to the Canadian pattern of more work and less play would be those who worked for the Becktons. Though most were Canadians and couldn't afford racehorses of their own, they must have some interest in the performance of the Didsbury horses, as did I. Having heard much about them from the beginning of my visit, I could admire the beauty of the horses and the aesthetics of horsemanship from afar. Others, I knew, invested their money as well as their hearts.

I had heard—from Cousin Ernest this time—that the Beckton brothers always bet heavily on their own horses to win. This troubled me. Like the Natives who could not make war on those with whom they had smoked a pipe of peace, I could not help but care about those with whom I had shared a meal. Though the Becktons appeared to have an unlimited supply of funds—judging from their beautiful home and their lavish habits—I knew appearances were sometimes deceiving. In my time at the Humphrys, I had also become more sensitive to the value of money, and I trembled to hear of it being squandered.

On the other hand, I realized part of the glamour of personalities such as the Beckton brothers was their ability to take risks. They were, as in Mr. Kipling's poem, able to "make one heap of all [their] winnings and risk it on one turn of pitch-and-toss . . ." Perhaps it was only my being a woman that made me cautious. Weren't all men of the same ilk and needing to test themselves, even cautious and moderate persons such as Mr. Lionel Cuthbert? And was not farming, any kind of farming, of sheep or pigs or cattle or horses or grain—or any business for that matter—any endeavour that engaged a man's heart and mind and resources without guarantee of success—a risk?

This I reflected, on the day the Cannington Manor Ladies Guild met at Selsley, the home of Mrs. Frances Page, to organize the social activities that were an essential part of Race Day. As it happened, my reflections were to be prophetic, though I did not realize it until later.

The Becktons were not alone in their commitment to Race Day, officially titled the *Annual Meeting of the Cannington Manor Racing Association*, though they invested the most money. Many other English families were also involved with the planning. As Cousin Mary had once said, they considered Race Day the highlight of the year and talked of little else for weeks beforehand and weeks after.

There were certainly many things to arrange. For instance, the ladies guild must make decisions about the ball, the first being who would host it. After all, previous fairs and Race Days had sometimes brought visitors from the community of *La Rondèrie*. Known as *the French Counts,* these colourful aristocrats from the Pipestone Valley south of Whitewood Township would surely attend again. It had been said that they "brought Ascot to Cannington Manor," and the guild wished to be worthy of such a comparison.

Mrs. Pierce, the first to speak of the French Counts, grew even more poetic as she described two-seater coaches with frilly tops and uniformed footmen. The horses were matched pairs and high steppers at that, often two pairs to a carriage. Since the counts brought their ladies as well, the Cannington Manor ladies relished the chance to admire the latest Parisian fashions in gowns, parasols and long white gloves.

"They were indeed something to see at the fair last April," whispered Nettie. "Until it started to snow, and then everyone was forced to seek cover. You were fortunate not to be here, as it snowed all afternoon and made for very little show."

After other members of the guild had shared their stories of the French Counts, Mrs. Pierce, though responsible for the digression, blandly suggested the group return to the matter at hand. Where would the ball be held? Though the Humphrys, the Pierces, the Becktons and others had all hosted dances—and Didsbury boasted a fine ballroom—a larger number might wish to attend than could be accommodated in a private home.

"Would not the town hall be a wiser choice?" asked Mrs. Pierce. "It would mean less worry about being forced to welcome guests of unknown character into one's home, and possible damage to furniture and other appointments by intoxicated revelers."

Some further points were made, but there was general agreement that the guild should, with the agreement of the racing association, claim the town hall for the ball. Then the ladies must discuss decorations, since they wished to give plain walls and functional furniture a festive air. Jessie Beckton suggested everyone bring bouquets of flowers from their gardens, and the others agreed, though aware Jessie's gardens were far superior to their own. The Becktons would also supply streamers and rosettes for the doors.

"In orange and black, no doubt," said Lily Pierce, and in the laughter that followed, Cousin Nettie explained that those were the Beckton colours.

"Have you a better suggestion, Miss Pierce?" asked Jessie, laughing along with the others. Observing the Pierce sisters, I felt the same admiration and envy I experienced watching the Humphrys, and again I regretted the lack of sisterly feeling between my sister and me. Since I was the elder, it must have been my fault. Perhaps

I had, as a child, been unable to see past my own grief at losing the affections of my mother—if there had ever been affections to lose. If I had been more loving to my sister regardless, she and I might have become friends who comforted and supported each other.

The discussion continued.

"As to entertaining the French counts between the races and ball," Jessie Beckton went on, "with Mrs. Humphrys still in England, surely it would be most appropriate for the Becktons to invite them for a race supper?"

She explained that she could call on her sister-in-law, Edith, and a houseful of servants, including a French cook, to help her, as well as her mother (Mrs. Pierce beamed and nodded at this) and her sisters Lily and Frances. Nettie Humphrys, on the other hand, had only her two young sisters and her cousin.

"And Mrs. Maltby and the indefatigable Miss Martha Pritchard," interjected Mrs. Bird, who seemed anxious Nettie not feel slighted by any hint that such a party was beyond the capabilities of her household. Nettie smiled gratefully at the pleasant woman who had so recently dined with the Humphrys, but did not argue the point herself. No doubt she had already discovered the mixed benefits of hosting large gatherings.

"I expect to still be here, but cannot be certain," I ventured. It was the first time I had spoken during the meeting, and I did not do so to draw attention to myself. I did, however, wish to make certain Cousin Nettie wasn't persuaded to take on more than she felt she could manage.

"That settles it then," said Mrs. Pierce. "Though it is kind of the Humphrys to be willing, it would be much easier for Jessie and the Becktons to host the supper."

"Do the Turtons never host community events?" I asked, not to challenge Mrs. Pierce, but as a matter of curiosity. I had heard the Turtons now had a fine fieldstone house as well, after years of living in more modest accommodation and adding makeshift rooms as necessary for their growing family. Apparently, the Turton house even boasted a tower and bell for use in emergencies or for calling the men in from the fields for their meals. Mrs. Turton was not present at the planning meeting and might not, in fact, have belonged to the Cannington Manor Ladies' Guild, so I felt someone should inquire on her behalf.

About the possibility the Turtons might wish to play host to the French counts, Mrs. Pierce suggested it would be a burden for Mrs. Turton, simply because of the size of her family. At present she had both an infant and a toddler, as well as several older children, to care for.

Mrs. Pierce hastened to add that she knew the family—and Mrs. Turton in particular—to be hospitable and generous in every way. In fact, it was the Turtons' famous hospitality the Pierces had thought to emulate when they put up their welcome message. She repeated it for the benefit of those who didn't already have it memorized: "Welcome all who enter this hospitable gate, none can come too early, or stay too late."

"I would myself have gladly played host to any dignitaries when the captain and I lived in the White House," added Mrs. Pierce sadly. "And we often did. As it is now, with Ted's growing family, there simply isn't enough room."

"That's fine, mother," said Jessie Beckton. "We are happy to do it, and I will rely on your advice—and your being at my side to welcome them."

For a moment there was silence. No doubt others in the room wondered who else would be invited to the supper, which promised to be the finest of the season. Jessie may have sensed this, for she laughed rather too heartily and said, "I don't wish, of course, to be claiming all the honours for myself, I simply thought…"

At that, everyone hastily assured her of their agreement. Didsbury was the perfect location, and all knew her capabilities as a hostess.

"Indeed," said Jessie, "I think I must have at one time or other, had all of you—in fact, everyone in the neighbourhood—to dine. We seldom dine alone, and I don't believe in class distinctions. Neither does my husband nor his brothers. One of the reasons we came to this country was to be free of all that nonsense."

She paused. As much as I liked Jessie Beckton, I felt certain she was mistaken about the lack of class distinctions. Surely many of the English had come to the community because they wanted to continue to live in a style they could no longer afford in England. Not only that, but my uncle and others like him often expressed their satisfaction at being able to mix with "the best sort of people." Every advertisement that mentioned the word "aristocratic" or "gentry" was further proof that class mattered, and the presence of other English families of their own class was what brought new settlers from England to Cannington Manor.

I did not give voice to these thoughts, however, for did not I share such pretensions? Had I not worried when I noticed the more democratic feeling here, the lack of distinctions? After all, I still came from a class-conscious society, and it was not something that could be put aside lightly, though my feelings about certain persons who worked for the Humphrys—namely Miss Pritchard and Mr. Cuthbert—had undergone a remarkable change. Though I did not speak my mind, Jessie apparently thought it necessary to strengthen her point, for she went on.

"From the time Didsbury was built, Ernest and his brothers have made a point of inviting gentlemen home after every sporting event—those, as they say, 'of high or low degree.' This includes all dog handlers, beaters and grooms. They *all* come back to Didsbury to drink and smoke and visit. And yet even the Beckton brothers have been accused of making class distinctions.

"One such occasion happened a year or so before we were married. It was winter, and I don't recall what had brought them together, but the men were lounging about, having a friendly drink and perhaps playing billiards in the 'Ram's Pasture.' Suddenly someone—Mr. Frank Kidd, I believe it was—took offense at something that was said. It might have been Bertie who was responsible, for he is somewhat careless of his speech when he has been drinking. Whatever it was and whoever said it, Mr. Kidd felt someone was being 'uppity' and believed others were looking down on him for being nothing but a 'poor Canadian farmer'.

"Mr. Kidd then left, grabbing his hat and coat as he went. After he had donned his outerwear and stepped out into the frigid air and high winds, however, he thought better of the idea and returned to the billiard room. 'It is too—darned—cold to be independent,' he said."

I could not resist laughing with the others. Though I was not certain Jessie had proved her point, it did demonstrate how the pioneer experience could make all men fellows. I could also picture the good humour with which the Beckton brothers would have welcomed Mr. Kidd back and offered him more libations against the cold.

Cousin Nettie also had a story to tell.

"I remember hearing Mr. Harry King tell a story about class distinction—or rather about the lack of class distinction," she said. "My sister's best man, Mr. Robert Bird, had once been accused of snobbery—Mr. Bird, who is so quiet and mannerly at all times!" She smiled at Mrs. Harry Bird, sister-in-law of the gentleman in question. "Yet Mr. King, who has many dealings with him because the stage coach often brings deliveries to the store, says Mr. Robert and his brother are always polite and friendly. 'Why,' Mr. King said of one such occasion, 'after leaving the store, speaking to Bob, I didn't know if I was Harry King or *King Henry*.'"

Again the group of women laughed heartily, and I along with them. Another woman, one to whom I had been introduced, but whose name I did not recall, then recounted a story her husband had told of the generosity of the Beckton brothers. It was apparently soon after they returned from England with their fortune. They were riding into the village one day and happened to see a team and wagon hitched to the rail outside the Moose Mountain Trading Company store. They immediately noticed the harness on the team was in bad repair and that the wagon was in even worse condition.

"Oh, yes," Jessie Beckton nodded, "I remember them speaking of that. They noticed it partly because they had just replaced all the harnesses for their own teams and were about to purchase new wagons. They would have liked nothing better than to march into the store, find the owner and give him the money to replace his harness and his wagon."

"But they couldn't do that," said the first woman.

"Of course not," said Jessie.

"They must consider his pride. No man wants to be pitied," said another.

"Men!" added Mrs. Pierce in a way that seemed to sum it all up.

"So, what did they do?" I asked, since I had not yet noted any gesture of particular generosity, admirable as it was that they considered the feelings of one who was poorer than themselves.

"They organized a runaway," said Jessie, "but I shouldn't be the one to tell the story. It seems too—ah—self-congratulatory—though it was before I was part of the family—"

The first woman then went on to describe how the brothers spoke to one of the "dudes"—in other words the young agricultural students who seemed to spend much of their time lounging outside the Mitre Hotel. Accepting the money as the windfall it was, the dude untied the team from the rail and startled the horses enough that they stampeded all the way out of town. In fact, they might not have been caught for miles, had not a wagon wheel buckled, tipping the wagon and smashing it into a ditch. When most of the men in town, including the owner of the vehicle and horses, had gathered around, they could all see that the wagon and harness were damaged beyond repair. This was where the Becktons stepped in and insisted that they had caused the accident by frightening the horses. Therefore, as the runaway had been their fault, they must be allowed to replace the harness and the wagon.

"And so they did," finished the woman. "With the encouragement of all the witnesses, the man could accept a new set of harness and a new wagon from McNaughton's in Moosomin without any damage to his pride."

I thought the action more than a little reckless, as surely the horses could also have been injured. I was also unsure how the man's pride could be salvaged if everyone knew why the Becktons had done what they did. Mr. Cuthbert, I was sure, would have been humiliated by such a gesture, and the fact he had benefited from someone else's foolishness would be no comfort. Yet, again, I kept my own counsel. I was a mere visitor here, after all.

Now that the pattern had been set, a number of other women added their stories. All were determined, it seemed, to demonstrate either the lack of class distinction in the community or the generosity of the gentry, ending with the Pierces' benevolent relationship with Chief White Bear and his people. This brought them back to Race Day, for they remembered how the Natives were always part of the celebration. Their bright feathers and beads mixed very well with the finery of the French gentility and other more exotic guests. In fact, many from Cannington Manor wore their Norfolk jackets and riding breeches in honour of the occasion. It was always a colourful and exciting affair, they said, and everyone was equally welcome.

I also learned that most Race Days ended with a pow wow, featuring drums and dancers from the White Bear reserve. They performed in front of the Moose Mountain Trading Company store, generally between the supper and the ball. There were reports, in fact, that the tom toms could be heard and huge bonfire seen from many miles away.

"And at the end, a white dog is boiled for their feast," finished one woman.

This extra information was followed by an enthusiastic chorus of both shudders and laughter.

"A dog?" I asked impulsively. "Why a dog? Don't they have any other meat?"

"But it is their tradition!" said the chorus, "just like the Jewish people and their unleavened bread and sacrifice of young lambs and goats."

Or perhaps because they have no choice, I thought. Because they don't raise cattle and our farms have taken away their game. For some reason this unsettled me greatly. Perhaps I was naïve, but I suddenly saw how one culture could, with the best of intentions, misunderstand and therefore exploit—even destroy—another. I wondered what Mr. Cuthbert would have to say about this. He had been born in this country. Would he too feel the Native people were an exotic race to be exhibited for our entertainment?

There was no opportunity to ask his opinion, of course, and I could not appear to criticize any of the well-meaning women of the Cannington Manor Ladies Guild. Neither would I be likely to see Mr. Cuthbert, as I had heard he would be spending most of the month of July on his homestead. It was haying time, after all, and as long as the weather held, he was unlikely to sacrifice his future for the sake of either paid employment or idle entertainments.

Because of his absence, it would be several weeks before I would hear him admit how much he lost in the hailstorm that was to devastate many of the farmers two days before Race Day.

Chapter 41

-

RETURN OF THE
BRIDAL COUPLE

My recent dream had been premature in its prediction that Mary and Ernest Maltby had returned already from their wedding trip. In fact, they came home to Cannington Manor as planned, six weeks after their wedding. Cousin Ernest, who was still working on their additions, reported having seen them. Apparently, they had promised to be in church on the following day, so Uncle James expected them for supper afterward.

It would be an emotional reunion. Cousin Mary had not been apart from her family since she had returned from her studies in Germany the year the family moved to Canada, and most recently she had been more mother than sister to her siblings. Every one of them had missed her keenly during her trip, while, after several months, they had become accustomed to their mother's absence. Though they realized Mary would no longer be living at home, there was still the sense that she had returned, even if only to live in the village.

In fact, since Ernest had not yet completed the Maltbys' additions, Uncle James might have had the notion the newly-weds would stay with the Humphrys for the time being—though with such a large family, there was the problem of how they could be accommodated. After all, Nettie had graduated to Mary's room and was very comfortable there, and I still occupied one of the larger rooms. I worried that my presence might be the impediment to such a felicitous plan, but reassured myself by remembering that Nettie and Uncle James had been most insistent I stay. On top of that, I had begun to make myself more useful in the kitchen, and the children would need more supervision now that it was their summer vacation from school.

Whether or not notions of the Maltbys staying at Humphrys House were cherished in some hearts, we were of one mind in that we had missed our Mary, and we all wished her to see us at our best. Therefore, I was not the only one who dressed with special care on that Sunday in mid July when she would be at church.

The Service of Evening Prayer was to be at three in the afternoon. The change of time was to accommodate the Rev. Mr. Cartwright, who now resided in Moosomin but was staying at the rectory in Cannington Manor for part of the summer. During that time, he would replace the Rev. Mr. Dobie as well as serve his two regular parishes. On the twentieth of June, Mr. Dobie had himself been married to Miss Frances Brockman, and the couple were away to Winnipeg on their wedding trip the same day.

At first, the choice of wedding dates had seemed rather unfortunate, as the Maltbys could not attend the Dobie wedding. On the other hand, if the Maltbys had attended the Dobie wedding as newlyweds themselves, they might have stolen some attention away from the new Mrs. Dobie on *her* special day.

After church, the Maltbys were expected to follow us back to Humphrys House. In preparation for this visit—the Maltbys' first as husband and wife since their actual wedding day—Miss Pritchard, under Cousin Nettie's direction, had prepared a meal that would rival the wedding breakfast, except in number of guests. This time the table was laid for eighteen only. Besides the family and Mr. Cuthbert—I had been flustered but pleased to hear his name mentioned—there would be the visiting Rector, Mr. Cartwright. Mr. Bob Bird was also invited; as he was best man, he had also fetched the couple back from Moosomin after their trip. Dr. Hardy and Mr. Ned Fleming might almost be taken for granted, and if Nettie happened to see them at church, Mrs. Jessie and Mr. Ernest Beckton would be invited to repay them for their hospitality to us.

This was to be Cousin Nettie's first large supper party as hostess, and she was anxious to do everything right. She had, therefore, issued most of the invitations several days ahead and then suffered agonies that the newlyweds might be unexpectedly delayed. In fact, the only reason she had not already invited the Becktons—and all three Beckton couples at that—was because Florence Beckton had given birth to a son three weeks before, near the time of the Dobie wedding. Because of this event, Nettie was uncertain what members of the families might be available.

With all the excitement about seeing Mary again and wondering how much she might have changed after six weeks of marriage, there was also a little confusion about seating for the trip to church. It was not until the teams were hitched up and the vehicles and drivers were ready to leave that everything sorted itself out. Uncle James and Cousin Nettie would ride in the Victoria, with Billy proudly driving them, and the others would happily make do with the wagon. I found myself in the back seat with Cousin Ernest— and the children wedged between us—almost before I knew it had happened. In fact, I was unsure whether it was a position I had chosen or whether it had been chosen for me.

Miss Pritchard, I noticed with a small pang, sat beside Mr. Cuthbert, with Frankie on her other side. It was no wonder that she was in the happiest humour I had yet seen her display and exclaimed a good deal over the springiness of the wagon seat. This seemed to be causing her to bounce against both her companions a good deal and to claim that she was about to break her neck. Cousin Frankie, no doubt because he was somewhat young and foolish himself, appeared to be highly amused by her antics, but Mr. Cuthbert paid her little attention.

The ride to the village was without incident, though the children were fretful, and about midpoint in the journey, I took Cecily on my knee to prevent her complaining that Noel and Dora were crowding her. Indeed, it would have been impossible for her not to feel crowded. I tried not to watch Miss Pritchard's trim little back—she held herself very well for a maid—and the smiles she was bestowing on both Mr. Cuthbert and Frankie at every opportunity. Surely she must have contrived her position, and with what encouragement? However, I had seen no evidence of mutual attraction between her and Mr. Cuthbert.

Such is the way with jealousy; it can be fed or appeased by very small things. And so it was that I forgot all about Miss Pritchard when Mr. Cuthbert handed me down from the wagon, for there could be no mistaking that he held my hand unnecessarily long—and even walked by my side to the church door. I had no idea how this had come about either, yet so it was. Ernest or Frankie had already clambered down from the wagon to tie the team to the rail and then disappear, and the other members of the family had run ahead, which left only Lionel Cuthbert and me. We did not speak as we made our way across the uneven ground; nor did I take his arm, though he was close enough I could have reached out to him for support if necessary. He seemed no more at ease than I was, so it was difficult to actually take pleasure in his company. Yet I sensed something of significance had occurred.

When we reached the church door, Mr. Cuthbert left me to take his place in the choir. For this too I was grateful, as my emotions by this time were in turmoil—I could not have said whether I had most welcomed or regretted our strange proximity. Sitting side-by-side in church would also have looked very odd to outsiders, tantamount to announcing an engagement, in fact—and there was assuredly no possibility of that.

I soon saw Cousin Mary in the vestibule—she and her bashful husband were surrounded by various Pierces, Humphrys, Birds and others, and one could not pass by without seeing them. There was, however, at that time no room or opportunity to embrace, nor even to greet, Mrs. Maltby myself. This caused me another pang, though I assured myself such a loss of intimacy must have been inevitable upon her marriage, since I was neither her closest family nor a member of her community.

As I passed the couple, Mary did look up and see me. Her expression suggested some surprise, and she seemed about to speak, had not Mrs. Pierce reclaimed her attention. Something about that worthy woman's pose gave me another cause for concern and allowed me to forget my own disappointment. What if, after all Cousin Nettie's arrangements, the Maltbys accepted another invitation? Fortunately, Nettie was by Mary's side and no doubt able to defend her prior claim to her sister's company. Would she perhaps take the opportunity to extend her invitation to Mrs. Pierce?

Before long, foot shuffling in the front pews suggested it was time to take our seats before Mr. Cartwright greeted the congregation with those beautiful and customary words: "The Lord is in his holy temple: let all the earth keep silence before him." I felt a sense of loss when Mary and Mr. Maltby did not slip into the Humphrys' pew but chose to take seats ahead of us; however, I was comforted when my beautiful cousin turned around and bestowed her particular smile on me. This told me that whatever surprise she might have felt when she saw me, it should not be understood as dismay. No doubt Mary too was self-conscious and perhaps uncertain how joining the esteemed company of matrons should affect her behaviour to those who belonged to her earlier station.

Comforted by this thought, I was able to concentrate on the rhythms of the familiar prayers and to be moved by the singing; I even recognized the lovely new hymn "The Day Thou Gavest, Lord, is Ended." Though Uncle James, who was conducting the choir, indicated that the congregation should join in, few took the invitation. Listening generally afforded greater pleasure than joining in, and this time I was sure I could pick out Mr. Cuthbert's sweet tenor. I did not, however, allow myself to look at his face.

After the service, the conversational groups were much as they had been before the service had begun, though this time the clusters were in the church proper, not crammed into the vestibule. And when Mary and her retinue moved outside, I was at least able to find a spot near Jessie Beckton. Jessie had apparently accepted the invitation for supper with alacrity, without even bothering to consult her husband.

They would be grateful, she said, for the opportunity to talk of something other than the care of infants. She was happy to report that both her sister-in-law, Florence, and the baby had come through their ordeal without mishap. Three weeks after the event, they seemed to be thriving and were enjoying a great deal of attention from both families and all the staff. Since Florence had spent most of her lying-in at Didsbury and no date for her departure to her own home had been set, her concerns and the baby's demands did rather dominate the household.

Mary asked whether Bertie and Florence had chosen a name for the child.

"Herbert Stanier," answered Jessie, "a fine stroke of diplomacy, as neither family can feel neglected."

At this moment, Jessie's mother, Mrs. Pierce, interjected that the child had been born on the anniversary of her dear husband's death four years before. Mary gently apologized for having forgotten. Though only her father and Ernest were living in Cannington Manor at that time, as she reminded Mrs. Pierce, her father had been grateful for Captain Pierce's friendship and guidance as he too was striving to establish himself in the community. Indeed it might well have been the Captain who suggested he invest in hogs and not sheep.

I recalled at once that Uncle James had attributed this advice to Mr. Cuthbert, but I had no wish to contradict Mary. There is a natural human tendency to alter stories to suit one's audience. Furthermore, Mary—besides being instinctively kind—now lived in the village and would understandably want to bolster her alliances with Mrs. Pierce, who was still, after all, the first lady of Cannington Manor.

"Times have changed since then," sighed Mrs. Pierce. "It will never be as it was when the Captain was alive. Now, I often see people in the street that I don't know."

I pondered these words. Perhaps Mrs. Pierce's greater—though unconscious—concern might be that such strangers would not know who she was and would not treat her with the deference to which she had been accustomed. In that way, it might well seem that the Pierce era was finished.

Jessie Beckton patted her mother's hand. "Father would have welcomed such change," she said. "The presence of strangers means the community is growing, and that means greater stability. No one will forget that the Pierces were here at the beginning. Why, the very land under our feet was Pierce land."

"God's Little Acre, as your father would say," murmured Mrs. Pierce, apparently comforted.

Nettie, who must have missed the opportunity to do so earlier, took this moment to invite Mrs. Pierce as well to the supper party at the Humphrys. When the older woman seemed to hesitate, Jessie Beckton volunteered a space in her carriage. She and Ernest would also convey her mother home after supper; in fact, they would take their leave whenever Mrs. Pierce was ready to go. Again I was somewhat surprised that Jessie could know her husband so well that she would make such offers without consulting him.

Lily Pierce at that moment appeared in the company of the Pages, and Nettie began to look a little worried. Perhaps she wondered if she now must also invite Lily and George Shaw Page, who appeared to be Lily's beau, as well as Frances and Spencer Page and the third brother, Willie. To add even one body was slightly awkward, as it changed the arrangement. To add six was another matter entirely. She visibly relaxed, however, when Jessie told her sisters she would be taking charge of their mother and would return her in the evening. That seemed to suit Lily, as she apparently had been invited to spend the rest of the day with Frances.

The rest of us watched the happy group walk away in the direction of their carriage. George Page had come to Cannington Manor much later than his brothers and had a separate homestead, which he had given the charming name of "The Dovecoat." The Pages seemed to have a penchant for naming things, I reflected. Had not

Spencer and Willie Page named their homestead "Selsley" after the district in Gloucester where their father was rector—as I had been reminded more than once?

Jessie appeared to have been thinking along the same lines I was. "They make a very pleasant couple," she said, "and Lily would like nothing better than to settle down with a husband on their own farm. No doubt she would raise exotic breeds of chickens and take all the prizes at the Agricultural Fair, since she is such a stickler for doing things right."

"Yes," laughed Mary, with a spark of her old self, "I can imagine her putting all her hens through the wash and hanging them out to dry, so they would be sparkling clean and fresh for the judges to see."

We all joined my pretty cousin in her mirth, though Mrs. Pierce's expression was a little uneasy. "Mr. Page is a very pleasant gentleman," she said, obviously referring to Lucy's beau, since *Spencer* Page was already husband to her daughter Frances. Mr. Willie Page, the third brother, as I recalled from my wagon trip to Cannington Manor, was rather sullen, definitely not the kind to be called "pleasant."

I remembered Noel telling a story of him. Not only did he drive freight back and forth between the village and Moosomin, but he was famous for being rough with his oxen. According to Noel, he bragged of tying them up and beating them soundly every Friday night, "for the good of their health." I shuddered again as I remembered the story. Though oxen were not appealing animals, being heavy and stolid in both appearance and manner, the idea of anything being beaten deliberately was repulsive to me.

Mrs. Pierce, however, had continued on the subject of her daughter Lily's prospects. "Not only is George a farmer, but he's also an athlete, captain of the cricket club. And did you know that his brothers were guests at Rideau Hall, in Ottawa, before they first came to Cannington Manor?"

We all nodded. Even I had heard that story several times before.

By that time, Nettie was anxious to depart. Not only would Miss

Pritchard have resented a half-dozen last minute guests, but she
would also be difficult if the supper were spoiled because the company was late. We bade each other good-bye for the time it would
take us to travel to the Humphrys. Again, I had no occasion to extend my own greeting to Cousin Mary, but I trusted there would
still be a time to do so, just as there would be time for us all to continue sharing our stories about our neighbours.

Chapter 42

NETTIE'S SUPPER PARTY

Nettie's supper party was undoubtedly a success. Excusing ourselves and following Miss Pritchard to the kitchen, we discovered the meal was not spoiled in any way. Though the fire in the kitchen stove had gone out while we were in church, it had only done so after the crowning glory of pork and kidney pies were thoroughly cooked. Miss Pritchard shook up the coals, added wood and soon had it lit again, so the early potatoes and other vegetables she had left soaking in cold water would boil in a few minutes. As for dessert, the plum pies would take less than an hour in the oven, and then they would be garnished very prettily with a few wild strawberries and served with a pot of Jersey cream.

Finding things so in order, Nettie and I needed only to remove our jackets and dust ourselves off from our journey before we could join the others in the drawing room. There we found a well-chosen company—seventeen people disposed to be pleased with each other. The Maltbys were the centrepiece; Cecily was sitting on her eldest sister's knee and Noel hanging over Ernest Maltby's shoulder. Dr. Hardy, as usual, was spinning a yarn.

When I glanced quickly at Mr. Cuthbert, I noted that, though he spoke little himself, he listened as attentively as any to the doctor's story. There was no hint of the animosity that had seemed to exist between himself and Mr. Bertie Beckton. I assumed, therefore, that he considered Dr. Hardy a man of dedication and worth and forgave him for his frivolous interests and his tendency to dominate all conversations in which he had a part.

When it was time to move into the dining room, I had been talking to Cousin Ernest and Mrs. Pierce, so we walked in together. Other than the fact that Uncle James and Nettie led the way, followed by Mr. and Mrs. Maltby and then the Becktons, there appeared to be little concern about precedence. I showed Mrs. Pierce to her place at the table, whereupon Ernest helped her with her chair, then me with mine—and finally placed himself between us.

When I was seated and took the time to survey the rest of the company, I found myself sitting almost directly across from Mr. Cuthbert at the long table. From there I could observe that his table manners were equal to those of any others in the company—perhaps superior to some. Once or twice he made so bold as to appear to be studying me from across the table, perhaps recalling our early supper conversation. Each of these times, I immediately lost the thread of the general conversation and could only pick it up again after I had concentrated on my plate or my lap for several minutes.

For this reason, I almost missed Dr. Hardy's reminder that he was to be part of an evening "concert and miscellaneous entertainment" being hosted by the Cannington Manor Ladies Guild in a few weeks time. Were others involved? He asked. Among those who nodded were my uncle, Cousin Ernest and both the Maltbys. I had difficulty imagining Mr. Maltby playing any part unless with a tennis racket or a cricket bat in his hand, and others may have had similar doubts, for there was a certain amount of teasing. However, neither Mary nor her husband would reveal anything further, and my uncle and Cousin Ernest were similarly unforthcoming.

Dr. Hardy had no such delicacy. He informed us he had a part in a farce called *A Silent Woman*, and his fellow players were Alan Troughton and Mrs. Scarfe. At that, he turned to Cousin Nettie, who was sitting on his left, at the foot of the table.

"Capital fellow, Troughton," he said, "and left to his own devices of a Sunday. You ought to have invited him."

For some reason Nettie coloured at this comment. Perhaps she was simply imagining the difficulties of accommodating yet another at the table. After appearing to watch her keenly for a couple of seconds, Dr. Hardy mentioned to the whole company that Mr. Dobie was to sing a song or two for the concert, and he hoped Mr. Cuthbert would be doing so as well.

At this, Lionel Cuthbert also reddened, his sun-burned skin becoming even brighter about his collar, a transformation that had the mysterious effect of taking my breath away.

"I have not been asked," said Mr. Cuthbert, "and had not decided whether I would attend."

"Then you will soon be asked," said Dr. Hardy decisively, and everyone at the table agreed. It was now Mr. Cuthbert's turn to keep his eyes fixed carefully on his plate, and he ceased to gaze across the table at me. As often occurred in my interactions with Mr. Cuthbert, I was both relieved and disappointed by this absence of notice.

Soon the first course was cleared and Miss Pritchard brought in the dessert. As usual, her fruit pies were a great success, and Dr. Hardy promised he would both show his appreciation and earn his keep by helping with the dishes. After the door had closed behind the maid, he added that he might also have time for another look at Miss Pritchard's back tooth, since he hadn't been able to extract the whole of it on his last visit.

"You are very good to us," said Uncle James, whose expression was suddenly melancholy, so that I wondered whether his gouty leg was giving him particular pain.

"Yes, very good," Frankie piped up, "willing to torture one or the other's teeth nearly every week."

Dr. Hardy responded by making a threatening gesture that looked for all the world like a gigantic pincered creature about to pounce. "Just you wait," he said. "I haven't yet had the opportunity to practice my dentistry skills on you."

"Nor are you likely to have the opportunity, if I have a say about it," said Frankie. "Pritchard said you nigh pulled her head off last time."

Dr. Hardy only smiled, obviously very relaxed with the family and feeling no need to explain his methods.

"Miss Pritchard must be very sure of her position here," said Mary, catching my eye. I could do little but smile and shrug in response to Mary's insinuation. I had indeed ceased to care as much about certain distinctions.

Nettie spoke up, however. "You would be surprised to see how much she has improved," she said. "Well, perhaps not her temper. She still complains there is no society, nothing here for servants to do, and that she will never again take a position where there is only one girl. And she said such a lot about *our* not being very particular about the house that we—she, Cousin Floss and I—spent two whole days spring cleaning. Even the children helped by beating the rugs."

"I did notice right away how very bright and clean everything seemed," said Mary hastily, perhaps wishing she had not brought up the subject of Miss Pritchard.

"She also bakes bread twice a week, churns butter once a week, and makes her own barm."

"Then we should certainly keep Miss Pritchard happy," interjected Dr. Hardy, "which reminds me that I intended to have you all come out to see my lambs. They are growing fast, though the grass has been a little dry from all this hot weather. Of course we must always be on the watch for coyotes, eh Miss Dora?"

Ned Fleming, who had been eating his plum pie with admirable concentration—no doubt he had heard many of Dr. Hardy's stories before—looked up when he heard mention of coyotes and nodded his head.

Cousin Mary then appeared to have another thought. "Ernest," she said, then laughed because she realized there were three of that name at the table—"*brother* Ernest, that is—do you think we could have some music?" She looked at Uncle James. "Father, Mrs. Pierce, would you mind, though it is the Lord's Day? After Dr. Hardy has done his duty in the kitchen of course. And Lionel—Mr. Cuthbert—I don't want to see you stealing away on us. We must have you sing as well."

No one could resist such requests, not so soon after Mary's return. There would obviously be no dentistry performed in the kitchen that night. In fact, Miss Pritchard seemed in danger of losing her kitchen help as well when the company moved to the drawing room and Ernest brought out his banjo. Mary accompanied him on the piano for several humorous songs, among them *Ta Ra Ra Boom De Ay*, which set the children to prancing about the room.

Others, among them the Becktons, Nettie and Dr. Hardy, appeared to be quite ready to dance as well, so Mary and Ernest soon had them on their feet for a lively American folk dance they called the *Virginia Reel*, which seemed to involve a lot of swooshing down the length of the room. I did know a few dances—that part of my education not quite so lacking as some other areas—and might even have joined in for *Corn Rigs* and *The Barley Hay*, but for the lack of partners. Neither Mr. Fleming, Mr. Maltby nor my cousins Willie and Frankie seemed inclined to dance, and I would not have been able to stand up with Mr. Cuthbert—even had he invited me to do so.

It was some time before Uncle James remembered that the children—Dora, Noel and Cecily—should go to bed, even though they were now on vacation. Because they protested it was unfair they be sent away in the middle of so much merriment, I went upstairs with them. It took some time to oversee their preparations, including the washing of hands and faces and the saying of prayers.

When I had finally tucked all three in their beds and was coming down the stairs, the dancing seemed to have stopped. Instead, I could hear Mr. Cuthbert singing *Ye Banks and Braes of Bonnie Doon*. The words and notes were so plaintively sweet that I sat down on the landing the better to hear them. When he had finished, I hurried back to join the company, but it seemed he was finished singing for the night, and soon after that the company began to disperse.

Then I felt rather like the children—that I had missed the best part of the evening, or at least the part of the evening I most wanted to experience. I was also heartsore that no one had apparently taken much account of my absence and waited for my return. Nonetheless, I stayed with the family to bid everyone good night. Then, I felt Mary's kiss on my cheek, and heard her say how happy she was that I was still in the country. We must try, she added, to have one of our talks very soon. I smiled at this, for the truth was that there had been few long, intimate conversations with her during my stay, and one of those few had focused almost completely on Mr. Cuthbert.

I hoped she would find some time to spend with me, but realized I should not count on it. In fact, considering how easily I had been forgotten by the whole family and their guests, I could not help but wonder whether it had been wise to extend my visit. I might already have overstayed my welcome.

Chapter 43

THE VIEW FROM A PONY CART

Falling two days before Race Day as it did, I expected the hailstorm on the nineteenth of July, a Tuesday, might put a damper on the annual event. Even so, I had little idea how much damage could be done by hail, nor how capricious such destruction could be. All the crops on one farm could be flattened, while the next homestead was untouched. One field could be destroyed and the next be passed over in a way that seemed almost Biblical.

This was the case at my uncle's, and fortunately it was the field of wheat that was taken and not the oats, since oats were needed to feed the animals. Therefore, the loss need not slow down his plans to finish his hog barn and efforts to seriously start up his pork-packing business. Losing the wheat, however, would mean having to buy flour—it was too late in the growing season for the crop to recover—and it also dashed my uncle's hopes of having grain to sell.

When Miss Pritchard dropped what she was doing in the kitchen and ran upstairs as soon as the thunder and lightning started, I looked quizzically at Cousin Nettie.

"Martha is afraid of thunderstorms," Nettie explained. For a minute I looked at my cousin in surprise; then we both began to laugh. It was uncharacteristic of that busy, bold and frequently intimidating little person to be afraid of anything. Yet, here she was, like a dog that cries to be let inside during storms, and when the door to his master's house is opened, scrabbles into the darkest corner to hide.

Perhaps Miss Pritchard's fear came from the fact she could not understand and control this huge mystery. Or perhaps the key to her strange behaviour was some event in her past, about which we had made so little inquiry. Again, I felt a twinge of shame. Did I, who had imagined myself altruistic and superior when among the Cannington Manor ladies, see a servant only in terms of her function, with no thought to the life that had moulded her?

For our part, Cousin Nettie and I huddled at the kitchen window, watching the tiny—and not so tiny—balls of ice hit the ground, some springing back again as if they were made of India rubber, others landing with a plop and staying to melt where they lay. I had never seen anything like it. When the storm was over a mere fifteen minutes later, the sky was devoid of clouds and seemed an especially brilliant blue. Yet, when we opened the door, we were met with a blast of Arctic air.

Still, I followed the children outside, where they used twigs to scatter the piles of ice marbles heaped against corners, in doorways and windowsills, or on any ledge or crevice they had been able to find. When I picked up one of the magical baubles in my hand, I found it was indeed ice, which in the heat of my palm rapidly shrank to the size of a tiny bead, then disappeared altogether. Around me, the other hailstones had also shrunk, and in a short time there was nothing left of them but puddles of water.

I did not think then of destruction, but merely marveled at the mystery of it, this playful taste of winter in the midst of summer. Though I refrained from dancing and running about like Cecily and Noel, I was very much tempted to do so. Instead, I took deep breaths of the fresh smell after so much hot, dry weather and marveled that the brittle grass seemed to have been transformed in an instant into brightest green.

After a time, Uncle James and the others came to the house from the new barn, where they had sheltered when the storm hit. Though he tried to put a good face on it, my uncle's obvious distress was my first signal the storm might have serious rather than playful consequences. He had not yet seen the fields, but he was already concerned about the vegetables. The timing of the storm was unfortunate, he said, with the cabbage and cauliflower just beginning to head.

We all trailed out to the garden through now spongy grass—and mud where there was no grass, and we did indeed witness much destruction in the vegetable beds so lovingly designed by my uncle and tended by all of us. Not only were cabbage and cauliflower considerably beaten—most of the leaves as well as the beginnings of heads stripped from the stems—but the tomatoes, the corn and all the vines—melons, cucumber and pumpkin—had suffered as well. There would be no vegetables for sale here. Only the root vegetables might still produce a decent crop.

I could hardly bear to look at my uncle's face. How could he maintain his optimism when he described this loss to my aunt? And he must tell her of it; his plans for a market garden had been so hopeful and ambitious. Furthermore, she would be home in six weeks, so she would see for herself, even if we had by that time harvested or discarded the evidence. Could some of the plants regenerate themselves in that time? Could we plant anew? It seemed unlikely to me, as I gazed at tomatoes beaten to the earth and vines where all the promise of fruit was battered.

I began to fill my apron with tiny tomatoes and cucumbers that were loose on the ground. Parts of the small cucumbers might be usable, and the tomatoes, though green and tiny yet, might make pickles or ripen on warm window sills. By bending over to do this, I also avoided looking at my uncle's face. In a minute, Nettie and Dora had followed my lead.

Uncle James spoke then. "We can do that in the morning," he said, "so as to avoid packing the soil when it is so wet." And he led the sad little group with our few muddy gleanings back to the house, while Billy and Frankie went to check on the fields. Lionel

Cuthbert, apparently, had already left, for he had hay drying in the field as well as crops to think of. I heard his name with a little start, as I had not seen him for several days.

It was later that we learned we had not been the hardest hit. Nettie and I also realized that we had been foolish to stand, and to allow the children to stand, so close to the kitchen windows during the storm. At some of our neighbours' homes, hail had lashed windows so fiercely it broke them. At Didsbury, for instance, the staff counted 18 broken panes. Fortunately none were in the front of the house, so there was no need to change the location of the Race Day supper.

This I learned on the day itself, when Jessie Beckton found me strolling about the village on my own and offered me a ride in her pony cart.

"I hope you don't mind sharing with my dogs," she said, and I bent to pet little Vic as well as a Fox Terrier Jessie called "Spotty." She explained that Spotty could help out if any of the horses bolted, though she didn't explain what form that help would take. She also insisted on introducing me to "Dolly Creighton," her jaunty little pony.

Somewhat to my surprise I enjoyed the introduction. Dolly Creighton was a small, sturdy bay with somewhat lighter mane and tale, and she seemed to respond well to me, going so far as to reach up and nuzzle my straw hat and then to thrust her pert nose into the basket in which I was carrying a picnic lunch for Nettie and myself. Encouraged by the owner, I stroked the pony on her forehead, under her chin and along her neck, even under her coarse, heavy mane. To my even greater surprise, she stretched out her chin and bobbed her head almost as if she were nodding. Indifferent to the effect on my white gloves, I scratched her more energetically, until her very skin seemed to ripple with pleasure and she bumped her head playfully against me.

At this Jessie jerked the reins a little. "Dolly, behave!" she said sharply, and that's when she asked me again to join her and the little dogs. I accepted, though it was not a large cart and promised to be a tight squeeze.

"You have obviously made a friend," Jessie commented when I was safely seated and she had urged Dolly Creighton into a walk. "Dolly does not respond so well to everyone. She will take advantage, though, if you let her."

I was uncertain of her meaning, though my ignorance was typical of many of my experiences in the community. Pleasures there were, but one was always in danger of doing the wrong thing, especially around animals.

I had another reason to feel awkward in Jessie Beckton's company, and that was the race supper. Not having an invitation myself, though I knew my uncle, Cousin Ernest and the Maltbys would be there, I was somewhat reluctant to ask about the preparations. It was not that I had expected to be part of that number—after all, even the Becktons could not accommodate the whole neighbourhood in their dining-room. Neither could they be sure how many from *La Rondèrie* would attend the races; the French gentry might not appear at all and there might be as many as a dozen. That number combined with the Pierce and Beckton families already totaled close to forty, if Duncan Pierce and his wife came from the Crooked Lake Indian Reserve to attend the races, as they usually did. No, I did not expect an invitation.

I finally asked how the Becktons had fared in the hailstorm, and Jessie told me about their windows. She also mentioned that they had immediately sent a man to Moosomin to order replacement panes, which would arrive within a day or two. In the meantime, the maids had cleared up the glass and covered all the broken panes with cardboard and netting. Everything, therefore, was well in hand, and Jessie seemed unperturbed. This was the difference when one had money to spare. Problems were easily solved, costs were shouldered, and one went on as if nothing had happened.

Neither did Jessie seem overly concerned about damage to the crops, though she thought there had been some. She was rather more concerned about her perennial borders, which were considerably beaten down, forcing her to make do with a few bouquets of daisies for the town hall—along with red and white stocks and blue and purple delphiniums. Her lack of concern for crops did rather confirm my suspicion the Becktons were primarily hobby farmers, though I immediately reproached myself for my lack of kindness. What right had I to sit in judgment—I, who had no commitment at all to this country?

To make up for my unkind thoughts, I tried to show more interest in what was going on around us. I already knew some of the history of Cannington Manor's Race Day, including how, in 1887, the year of Her Majesty's Golden Jubilee, Mr. Amos Kinsey laid out what was the first hurdle track in the West. My cousins had described how Mr. Kinsey drove a team around the spot, first testing for a level surface for the track, then plowing a furrow to mark the inside boundary. Now bordered with railings along both sides, the track boasted a grandstand and a judges' booth.

I even knew—thanks to the Humphrys—that this same Mr. Kinsey once worked on the railroad at a place with the unpleasant name of Rat Portage. While at Rat Portage, Mr. Kinsey had rescued a pair of young elk from the wild, broken them and trained them to pull a cart. When I first heard this, I was reminded of the reindeer in children's Christmas stories. Furthermore, when the first locomotive pulled into Fourth Siding, Mr. Kinsey and his pair of elk were on board. Before long, the talented fellow had claimed a homestead in the Cannington Manor district. This was early in 1882, before even the Pierces had settled.

Because the elk were still very fast, though domesticated, Mr. Kinsey was sometimes called upon to transport serious medical cases to the doctor in Moosomin—this was before Dr. Hardy came to Cannington Manor. Eventually, however, one of the elk became lame, and Mr. Kinsey took them both to the Moose Mountains and released them back into the wild. Not long after, he and his wife moved to Moosomin, where they built a fine house and Mr. Kinsey's horsemanship was still much appreciated. The people of Cannington Manor, however, did not forget him or his experiment. They liked to imagine that any elk they saw around the lake or anywhere in the Moose Mountains were descendents of the pair Mr. Kinsey had trained.

After a short silence during which I cast about for another topic, I mentioned that I had seen a number of what appeared to be racehorses in the town, though there were two or more hours to be passed before the first race.

"Possibly so the horses get accustomed to the crowds," said Jessie, "or the owners just want to show them off."

"Horses are affected by noise then?"

Jessie nodded. "Most of our horses tend to take it in stride"—we both took time to smile at her little witticism—"since they have racing in their blood."

I also commented on the range of sizes I saw among the horses. Surely the larger ones would have an unfair advantage. Jessie Beckton smiled again at this. It seemed I had provided an opportunity for my companion to display her knowledge, and she spent the next several minutes explaining that there were different heats; as well as the differences between ponies and horses, between thoroughbreds and quarter horses and between Shetland ponies and Welsh, Fell or Highland ponies. She also named all the horses and ponies the Becktons had entered in the day's races.

This was far too much for me to take in, so I was relieved when we saw Edith Beckton with her own pony cart a little distance away and began to move in her direction. A minute or two later, we also came upon Nettie, apparently strolling towards the store. Therefore, I thanked Jessie Beckton for the visit and the very pleasant ride in her pony cart, said goodbye to her menagerie and joined my cousin.

Chapter 44

RACE DAY AT GROUND LEVEL

Nettie had also been looking for me and had decided I must be at the store. There was yet another fortuitous turn, as not long after Nettie and I were reunited we happened on the Maltbys, both wearing their riding costumes and on horseback, and they invited us to be their guests for dinner at the hotel. (Our picnic lunch could wait.)

Mary smiled down on us as she issued the invitation, and I was, as always, amazed by how her beauty seemed to fit every occasion, just as her tight black jacket and pleated riding skirt fit her trim but womanly figure. She sat upon her horse with ease and grace, and I could well imagine her being part of the regular hunt days. Few of the women and not all of the men—possibly not even her husband—would ride so well.

Dining at the Mitre Hotel was another new experience for me. As in England, a respectable woman would have no occasion to venture into a hotel except to dine with a family party or perhaps if she were travelling, and she would be unlikely to travel alone. Hotels attract some odd types, and I had already noticed the rowdy young men who tended to congregate on the porch of this hotel. It was as if they had nothing better to do than make sport of each other or of the passers-by.

Entering the establishment in the company of Mr. and Mrs. Maltby, however, we were not likely to be exposed to any such disrespectful behaviour. One young gentleman went so far as to take his pipe out of his mouth and jump up from his chair to open the door for us, and the other men greeted the Maltbys very cordially. They also lifted their hats for Cousin Nettie and me as we passed. Cousin Mary, as she was now a married woman, acknowledged all their greetings with a smile and a bow, while Nettie and I kept our eyes cast down. I did notice, however, that my young cousin allowed herself to bestow a slight smile on the young man who had opened the door.

"That was Mr. Alan Troughton," she whispered to me when we were safely inside. The young man's name meant nought to me until I remembered Doctor Hardy having mentioned him, though I did not recall in what context.

The scene that greeted us from the hotel foyer looked peaceful enough, though the general atmosphere was noisy. The dining room was obviously through the open door on our left, and the gentlemen's beer parlour on the right. Though we could not see the latter, as it was separated from us by a partition running along one side of the central staircase that appeared to give access to the upper floor, we could hear the rattle of glasses and loud conversation through the thin walls.

The dining room also appeared busy and somewhat raucous, perhaps merely on account of the number of bodies in the room. Most of the sporting community may have had a similar notion to take refreshment there, and I could not see a table available. However, Mr. George Dicken, the proprietor, hurried over just as if he had been expecting our party all along. Mr. Dicken even found us a quiet corner and after laying our table with a fresh cloth and utensils, offered to take our order himself.

I was amused to recall at that moment Cousin Ernest's disdainful comments about the hotel cuisine. "It doesn't matter what part of the beast it is, it's always beefsteak," he had said, "and always cut thin and fried, and it is as tough as old boots . . . the frying pan is about the only kitchen implement used." With this in mind, I suspected the wisest choice might be not to have meat at all. Mr. Maltby, however, relieved us of our worry by asking for the proprietor's recommendation. We all nodded our approval of beef stew with biscuits, and Mary's husband proceeded to order for us.

As we waited for our meal to arrive, I found myself somewhat awkward in the company of Cousin Mary and her husband. She seemed so poised, so sure of her powers—far from the blushing young woman who had wondered on her wedding day whether her charms would please her husband. I, on the other hand, was nothing more than what I had been—a woman past her bloom and possibly doomed to be a childless spinster. And there I forced a stop to such musings. It was not like me to dwell on such things, though I was becoming aware of the disadvantages of visiting such a vital community. However kind people were, I was not really a part of it, nor blossoming and multiplying like everything around me.

It was while I was reflecting thus that I realized Mrs. Maltby was talking of Lionel Cuthbert, and I am sure she intended me to hear, though she was, perhaps deliberately, not looking at me. Cousin Ernest had told her, she said, that Mr. Cuthbert's losses during the hailstorm had been considerable, not only his wheat and his oats flattened, but his hay now sodden as well. It would take weeks to dry, and mildew was more than likely to set in, making the hay unfit for either horses or cattle. Not only did this mean Mr. Cuthbert's hard work of the past fortnight was wasted, but it could put him in a desperate situation for winter.

"Perhaps," said Ernest Maltby, "it is for the best. Grain is selling very poorly just now. Wasn't Tony Purser telling us of hauling a load of wheat to Moosomin and earning barely the cost of feed for his horses? Wouldn't Cuthbert be better off just working for your father?"

"Oh, Ernest!" said Cousin Mary, revealing a trace of irritation. "Father cannot pay him for more than odd jobs, not enough to live on. And if he has to find work with others as well in order to live, then he will be less available when we—when my father—needs him. Not to mention that he has no love for the Becktons." Here she lowered her voice and looked somewhat sheepishly around her. "Besides, if he lost his homestead after all this time, it would break his heart, and he would possibly leave Cannington Manor."

"And we do not want any persons leaving, do we?" Mr. Maltby smiled at his beautiful wife and touched her cheek lightly with his fingers. If he had noticed her second of irritation or wondered at her passion, he did not acknowledge it. I looked away, not wanting to intrude on this moment of intimacy.

But then Mary was beaming directly at me, so I must look at her. "No, we certainly do not want anyone to leave, as Cousin Floss well knows," she said. "In fact, from the moment they arrive, we will do everything we can to ensure that they stay."

"Here is our dinner," said Cousin Nettie, more concerned apparently with the physical necessities than with any awkward play of emotions around the table. And I had no choice but to follow her example. I could not allow myself to dwell on Mr. Cuthbert and his losses, as the simple fact was they had nothing to do with me and there was absolutely nothing I could do about them. And in the meantime, Mr. Dicken had indeed arrived with four steaming plates of stew and fresh potatoes, one of which he balanced on the napkin over his arm.

Because my expectations had not been high, I found the meal surprisingly good, certainly good enough to distract me from any dangerous thoughts. This enjoyment of the food might also have owed something to the fact I had spent a good part of the morning out of doors and therefore had developed an appetite. The conversation during the meal was somewhat truncated, as might be expected, since we must not dally and miss the first race.

In fact our timing could not have been better. When we had finished our luncheon and made our way to the track, we found Cousin Ernest had had the forethought to reserve grandstand seats for the Humphrys family, so we had both convenient accommodation and an excellent view. And there we were enthroned for most of the afternoon, so engaged in all that was happening, we scarcely noticed how quickly the time passed. For all that might have distressed me, it was my first time at the races, and I was wondrously caught up in the noise and excitement.

As Jessie Beckton had promised, the first heat of the day was the pony race, and the Welsh pony Cora was on the field. She and the jockey perched on her back—whom Nettie whispered was in fact Tony Purser, considered "one of the best riders available"—both proudly displayed the orange and black of the Beckton stables. Though the prettiest in the lineup, Cora did not win her race. Instead it went to an ungainly animal by the name of Rooster. I thought the name quite fitting, but was disappointed by the results.

When I expressed my feelings to Cousin Nettie, she laughed at my excitement and reminded me it was just the first heat. Unfortunately, the pattern of Rooster first and Cora second repeated itself, even in the second heat, which was called because of a poor start, though Rooster and Cora had run the whole course. There was no disputing, therefore, that Rooster was clearly the winner and Cora destined to be the runner-up. I hoped neither the pony nor her owners and handlers would be too disappointed, and also that the Beckton brothers had not wagered a huge amount on the results. This thought brought Mr. Cuthbert to mind, of course, for I was certain he would see it all as foolish.

In fact, many incidents contrived to bring Mr. Cuthbert to mind. When I commented about the noise, Cousin Ernest told a story about Scottish bagpipes at one of the community's agricultural fairs. Apparently Mr. James Beattie from the Scottish settlement of St. Andrew's, which was south of the town of Wapella, had come to enjoy the show. When there was a lull in activities so the judges could examine the entries, Mr. Beattie felt entertainment was in order. He had generously brought along his bagpipes in case of just such an occasion, so he now brought them out, filled his lungs with air and began to blow. According to Cousin Ernest, the result was about what might have been expected.

"Horses and cattle broke loose," he said, "fowl escaped from their coops and everything scattered. It was one h—l of a mess."

Apparently Mr. Beattie, confounded by this reaction, was heard to mutter that the livestock had no more taste for music than the Sassenach who owned them. However, he thought it wise to pack up his bagpipes and make his departure as quickly as possible.

"Oh, Ernest," protested Nettie, "I do believe you have invented the whole story. And do hush. It's the second heat of the three-eighth mile and there was that business of interference by one of the horses in the first heat. Remember—Sangaree won, but the judges gave it to Paddy Flynn because Paddy Flynn's jockey complained."

This brought our attention back to the horses moving towards the starting gate, and we noticed that the horse named Chuck had a different rider. Ernest went down to inquire and discovered that Mr. McAbee, the horse's owner, had been asked to ride Chuck himself, since the judges felt the jockey was unable to control him at the post. Soon the horses were off. When they rounded the bend with Sangaree in the lead, both Cousin Nettie and I voiced our approval in a most unladylike fashion, and we both felt vindicated when our favourite not only won that heat but the next as well. Paddy Flynn placed second and Chuck third.

In spite of all these delicious distractions and sometimes even because of them, I was still every now and then conscious of a sudden pang of fear and concern for Mr. Cuthbert, much as I tried to turn my thoughts away from him. Though I reminded myself repeatedly that he and his welfare were not my concern, I fervently hoped he would not be overly discouraged by his losses. At the same time, I knew if any man were capable of persisting through adversity, it would be him.

It seemed a great shame he could not be part of this community activity, as it was his community far more than it was mine, but it was inevitable that he be absent. Surely he was the kind of man for whom work would be the best medicine when he had suffered a loss. He might even be breaking more land, since that might be done without added expense and would give him a head start on next year's work.

Just as I had become reconciled to not seeing Lionel Cuthbert that afternoon, I was almost certain I did see him, at a distance—a sturdy-looking man of average height standing on his own behind the rails that stretched along the outside of the track. A man who carried himself well and wore a woolen cap on his sandy hair in spite of the summer heat. Had he allowed himself an hour or two from his work, an hour or two to watch the English at their play? If it were Mr. Cuthbert, I was never to know. Though I saw the same man watching the races from behind the rails two more times that afternoon, he came no nearer to where we were sitting.

-

Chapter 45

THE FRENCH COUNTS MAKE THEIR APPEARANCE

It was after we had seen the third heat of the pony race that we observed the arrival of the party everyone called the "French Counts" and about whom there had been so much speculation. Because of this, we didn't observe much of what the organizers called *the two-fifths trot*, though we later learned it was the most exciting race of the day, with five heats required to determine a winner.

The newcomers indeed had an air of elegance, though those who hoped to see the newest Paris gowns were certain to be disappointed, the ladies of the party having apparently donned travelling coats for the journey from *La Rondèrie*. There were parasols and top hats aplenty, however, and that must suffice. No doubt the gowns and long white gloves would be in evidence at the Becktons' dinner party.

When the French aristocrats arrived, both Cousin Ernest and Cousin Nettie seemed suddenly to have acquired remarkable eyesight, as they identified Count Yves de Roffignac, Count Jumilhac, Baron de Brahant and their ladies, all at a distance from which I could not have observed any particular air or distinguishing feature—it was a similar distance to that from which I observed the man who might have been Mr. Cuthbert. The newcomers did move to the grandstand, with a train of people who had gathered around them—no doubt including Jessie Beckton and other members of her family. However, there were always too many people and too much movement around us for us to be able to see them clearly. Neither did we have any excuse to approach them and be introduced. To do so would have been an imposition.

My cousins, however, also seemed to have accumulated a substantial body of knowledge about the community of *La Rondèrie* and the interests of those who lived there. They explained that these gentlemen were involved in the cultivation of sugar beets and were building a factory for refining them into sugar. They also raised chicory, which they mixed with their coffee or drank as an inexpensive substitute for coffee.

I had little knowledge of coffee, having always drunk tea, but I had heard that the French and other Europeans set great store by it, so no doubt the aristocracy of *La Rondèrie* had come upon a lucrative idea. Apparently chicory was very difficult to grow and manufacture, but they possessed the secret recipe and would grind the roots themselves and sell their product to buyers in Lower Canada, France and the United States, under the trade name *The Bellevue French Coffee Company*.

My cousins also reported that Count de Seyssie and Monsieur Jammet owned large tracts of land and raised cattle—quite large herds they thought, perhaps even larger than those of Mr. John Turton. Count Jumilhac, in addition to his coffee ventures, also raised sheep, and others—Monsieurs De Soras and Wolf perhaps—had large flocks as well. With so much enterprise in one community, it was no wonder my cousins and in fact the whole of Cannington Manor felt that a connection with *La Rondèrie* would be profitable and one of equals—more friendly at least than the relationship between the parent countries of England and France had ever been.

Not only was I impressed my cousins were able to recognize and name the visitors so rapidly and at a distance, but I also noted that they named more than there were bodies to match. I saw only four or five men and three women disembarking from the two carriages, and I'm sure my cousins named at least a dozen. I was also uncertain whether they had actually met any of the French aristocrats themselves.

This difficulty, however, was soon to be rectified, as Uncle James arrived with the rest of the family and began to talk of arrangements for the evening. He seemed convinced that the invitation from the Becktons had included all of the family but the three youngest. Young Dora pouted a little at this, and her father chucked her playfully under the chin.

"You will have your opportunity for evening parties soon enough, my beauty," he said. This attention seemed to comfort her a little, but I noticed that she still jabbed Nettie with her elbow. Nettie made a face in response.

The older of the two young ladies was, of course, overjoyed by the expanded invitation and immediately began to fret about what gown she should wear and how soon the family could depart, as she must have time to change her dress and rearrange her hair. So distracted was she that she missed the Cannington Manor Stakes, which the Becktons' Empress did not win as expected; instead, she took second place to Cottingham's Dinah.

When there was a break in the action on the track, I asked Uncle James to extend my excuses to Jessie Beckton, as I felt unable to attend the supper. I had already decided I would not attend the ball and, much as it would have been interesting to observe the company at supper, I was less sure than my uncle that I had actually been invited. Furthermore, it had already been a very eventful day, quite eventful enough for someone of a naturally retiring disposition, someone more comfortable being a watcher of events than a participant.

Soon after, Nettie's attention was arrested, along with the attention of everyone else in attendance, by the so-called "Indian" race. There were a large number of entries, and the jockeys had adopted what they considered appropriate costumes for the event. Many wore feathers in their caps or in bands about their heads, along with brightly-coloured beads, other decorations and blankets swathed around them in various ways. One jockey had even managed to devise a kind of dangling, feathery headdress. There was also a lot of whooping, both before and during the race, which must have confused many of the horses and might have caused serious bolting and injuries.

If I was concerned about what the horses thought of this foolishness, I was even more troubled when I saw that some of the Natives from White Bear Reserve were also watching. What did they think, I wondered, of this kind of show? Did they take it in good humour, or did they see it as a mockery of things that were sacred to them? This as well was something I would never know for certain.

When the "Indian" race was completed, with no very clear decision about the winner or winners, the crowd began to disperse. Our party now included all of the Humphrys and even Miss Pritchard, so it took some time before we had organized ourselves and made our way to our vehicles. By that time, the famous two-seater carriages with "very frilly tops" and liveried footmen had already departed, no doubt on their way to Didsbury.

After the Humphrys contingent had arrived home, done their evening chores and been sorted out according to who would stay and who would go to the supper at the Beckton estate, those who were of the evening party made the necessary alterations to their costumes and took their leave. I, on the other hand, spent a restful evening with Miss Pritchard and the children.

We all ate our evening meal informally at the kitchen table, and when that was cleared away, we all retired. In fact, I was in danger of falling asleep while supervising the children's prayers. When I was alone in my room, I could hear the deep rhythmic heartbeat of the tom toms in the distance, accompanied by a kind of high, melancholy wailing, but it didn't frighten me or interfere with my sleep. Neither did I wake when Nettie and Ernest returned, which must have been in the wee hours of the morning.

Only Uncle James, Billy and Frankie were present for breakfast. My younger cousins had apparently enjoyed the supper but had brought my uncle home before the ball. They could not, therefore, report at breakfast on the success of the whole evening, though they had much to say about the supper. Uncle James again praised Mrs. Jessie Beckton's powers of hospitality—which did not surprise me, though I suspected she had taken little part in the preparations. Nor was it a surprise to hear that Jessie's mother, Mrs. Pierce, and Jessie's own siblings were a considerable help to her in keeping the conversation flowing. Of the English company, only Spencer Page and Mary Maltby spoke any French—my uncle mentioned this with some understandable pride—and even they found their education did not take them much beyond basic greetings and comments upon the weather. Similarly, the French ladies spoke little English, though their husbands were somewhat more proficient.

When I asked about their persons, Cousin Billy thought the French ladies rather old, though he supposed they were fine enough. I smiled at this, as it seemed to suggest my cousin, whom I had never before heard express any interest in women, had cherished some hope there might have been young ladies among them. My uncle, on the other hand, praised the elegant appearance and manners of both counts and countesses, though he admitted it was rather difficult to judge the ages of the latter. French matrons dressed in quite a different manner from my aunt Jane and the other English ladies he knew. For one thing, they did not wear collars. I wondered if this was my uncle's way of referring to a certain amount of *décolletage*.

My uncle had not, however, spent the entire supper either admiring or being shy about ladies' bosoms. He had also learned quite a lot about the counts' progress with their various industries. They too had suffered from hail that summer, but they hoped for good yields of both beets and chicory, which were essentially root vegetables. Count de Jumilhac also spoke with regret of the distance from markets—a problem about which I can imagine my uncle having a great deal to say—and the absence of a railroad. Apparently this was a particular problem with sheep, as they tended to huddle so didn't travel well in vehicles. The best way to deliver sheep to market was to herd them, as they would have done in France.

From what part of France had the French aristocrats come? I

wondered, but no one offered the information, and there was no opportunity to ask. Now that I was rested and had learned there would have been an opportunity to come home before the ball, I regretted my decision to spend the whole evening at home. Observing the French counts and countesses would have given me more opportunity to learn and to speculate about the similarities and differences between the two communities.

Chapter 46

-

THE ENGLISH AT PLAY

There were among the English settlers those who wanted to draw out the excitement of *Race Day* into *Race Week*. "There is simply too much entertainment for one day," they said. Races, supper, ball and other activities must all be crammed into a few hours, which meant there was never enough time to partake of everything. Furthermore, wouldn't it be a good thing to incorporate a hunt? It was no surprise, however, that most of the Canadians were not in favour of expanding the holiday in this way. They even looked somewhat aghast at those of their neighbours who would risk the loss of their winter's supply of hay—in fact the loss of their livelihoods—so they could spend a whole week at play.

My uncle had mixed emotions on the subject, as he explained on a number of occasions. On one hand, he saw how bringing people together built up their sense of community and favoured alliances of all sorts. On the other hand, he was often short of ready funds, and the extra entertainments meant extra costs. Most important of all, he still hoped to have his stone buildings finished before the winter, since his hog business was dependent on their completion. Though he wasn't physically involved in the building of either cow stable or pork factory, he was responsible for supervising the work of the others—among them his sons Billy and Frankie, when they weren't busy elsewhere; and Lionel Cuthbert, when he was available. It was especially important that he be there when Mr. W. Anderson, the stone mason, was on the job.

I noticed that since the hailstorm had done its damage to the crops, the pork processing factory seemed to occupy more of my uncle's attention. He no longer spoke of market gardening, and this saddened me. I was learning that few things are more painful to watch than a man losing his dreams. Furthermore, the larger the dreams, the greater the disappointment seemed to be. And Uncle James was a great dreamer—as my father had pointed out on more than one occasion.

I wondered as I was musing on this change in my uncle whether Lionel Cuthbert was also a dreamer. In one sense, he must have been. Had not he left his parents' farm in Upper Canada in search of better opportunities in the district of Assiniboia? At the same time, his dreams were more modest, the kind of dreams that could be attained by one man, provided he kept his health and strength and was able to persevere through the various setbacks. In this country it seemed there would always be setbacks. It was still, in so many ways, untamed.

Because of his responsibilities, my uncle chose to spend the next few days at home—except of course for the usual trip into the town for the Sunday service. Though Mr. Cuthbert did not drive with us nor come back to the house for supper afterwards, he did appear in time to meet us at our vehicles and walk with the family. I was accompanying my uncle, as he walked somewhat more slowly and sometimes needed an arm to lean on. Therefore, when Lionel Cuthbert matched his steps with my uncle's—rather than with mine as he had done on that previous occasion—I could still overhear their brief conversation.

They compared the damages to their crops in the recent storm, and I was surprised at how calmly both could speak of such things. Either both had regretted their losses in private and were now determined to think only of the future, or their losses had not been so great as first was feared. Mr. Cuthbert did say, however, that he would be available to work on the barn in the coming week, as his hay was still too wet to stack. My uncle expressed his appreciation. He was somewhat disheartened, he said, with the lack of progress on some of his enterprises, and he was sure Mr. Anderson would be grateful for Mr. Cuthbert's strong back.

In a completely illogical fashion, I then wished my uncle had not referred to Lionel Cuthbert in this manner, almost as he might have referred to a work horse. Mr. Cuthbert, however, didn't seem offended. In fact, he may even have held himself a little straighter, so his strong back was more in evidence. No doubt my uncle had meant to compliment his companion, or had been reflecting with some chagrin on his own reduced physical capacity.

By this time, we had reached the vestibule, and both men nodded to me before proceeding inside to don their surplices. As usual I found the service satisfying, though probably more because of the pleasure to my senses provided by the music and the rhythm of the familiar words than because of any moral or spiritual lessons I received. The service also offered me the sweet and secret pleasure of listening for Lionel Cuthbert's voice as it rose and fell among the others. Any sense of thanksgiving I might have felt was also suspect and was at least partly owing to the anticipation of encountering Mr. Cuthbert at my uncle's during the following week.

Much as I was preoccupied with such imaginings, I did try to pay attention to the homily. Seeing the Rev. Mr. Cartwright in the pulpit, I remembered that he had been rector of the parish a few years previous and was said to be very tolerant of the agricultural students' excesses and even of their indolence. However, he did not tolerate their absence from church. As the story goes, when he approached one particular young fellow about not attending, the "dude"—in Cousin Ernest's vernacular—said he lacked appropriate church-going attire. Mr. Cartwright immediately made it known that clean overalls and shirts were certainly good enough for the Lord and therefore the Lord's people.

According to Cousin Ernest, the reverend gentleman may have

issued this strong invitation out of self-interest, as the $5.00 per year donation each young man was expected to make was part of the rector's stipend. Whatever the reason, the invitation had the desired effect. From that time, most of the young Englishmen attended services regularly, frequently wearing overalls, work shirts and the inevitable red neckerchiefs.

Perhaps the "dudes" had a vested interest as well, as church was where they received their invitations to Sunday supper from the various matrons in the community. For all their *foolishness*—and this was my thought, not that of Cousin Ernest—the young men were no doubt homesick and not accustomed to eating well nor caring for themselves in an orderly fashion. Sunday suppers with families such as the Pierces or the Humphrys were their only experiences of family life since they had left England.

Besides the trip to church on Sunday, Uncle James made another trip to town on Tuesday, taking Cousin Ernest and Cousin Dora with him. The rest of the family knew only that they were rehearsing a "surprise entertainment" related to the Cannington Manor Glee Club concert to be held at the Town Hall on the first of August. This was the same concert Dr. Hardy had mentioned, and the involvement of Uncle James and Cousin Ernest was not unusual, but the inclusion of Cousin Dora was a recent development. Every Tuesday, she came home from rehearsal with sparkling eyes and secrets begging to be told, and Cousin Nettie and I must actively prevent her from giving everything away, so great was her excitement at being part of it.

Another activity that could not be missed was the tennis tournament organized by the Cannington Manor Lawn Tennis Association on Thursday, July 28. Mr. Maltby was the village's acknowledged tennis champion, and naturally, the whole Humphrys family was there to support him. For my part, I hoped to see Mr. Maltby exhibit the grace and form that had won Cousin Mary's heart in spite of her reservations. Furthermore, since he was so recently married, it seemed a most auspicious time for him to retain his title.

This, alas, was not to be, as a Mr. Godwin came all the way from the town of Lethbridge in the far West to take away Mr. Maltby's cup. After the match, I happened to overhear a gentleman suggest to Mr. Maltby that marriage must be draining his strength. Mr. Maltby chuckled, but I noticed Cousin Mary, who had also overheard the jibe, bristle a little. I was glad, however, that she said nothing, as I think any protest from her might have embarrassed her husband.

How complicated marriage was! The expectation that two people should always be united in hearts and minds was so persistent and yet so unreasonable. When, however, I approached Mary to express my distress and comfort her if necessary, she had regained her humour.

"Perhaps it is more difficult for a man to focus on other interests when he has a wife," she said. "I cannot say I regret offering him some distraction. Surely that might be expected."

She then went on to talk of Mr. Maltby's past athletic achievements, for instance his outstanding number of runs in a cricket match against a team from New Zealand. When Mr. Maltby was up to bat, the game actually had to be called, as the New Zealanders simply could not put him out.

Chapter 47

-

A SILENT WOMAN

Though for Cousin Dora the entertainment being held at the Town Hall on the first day of August contained only one act of major importance, for me it was an evening that would offer many delights and call forth a deeply emotional response. In the first place, I did not often attend the theatre or variety concerts, and I had certainly never attended an event where so many of the participants were known to me. Furthermore, all those who were involved made up in enthusiasm and energy what they might have lacked in sophistication. In all, it was a production well worth waiting for.

Because I had little experience of the theatre, I knew nothing about stage nerves, so I was not prepared for the emotional performance Cousin Dora gave before she was even attired for the concert. Usually so gentle—even docile—in manner, she could not sit still to eat her supper. Nor could she find any costume that pleased her, though she was momentarily distracted by Cousin Nettie's suggestion she don some of her brothers' clothing and pretend to be a boy. When she had finally chosen a frock, it had a stain, and she wept for her mother and for Nurse in such a storm of tears that when it subsided, Nettie had to repair her ringlets and wash her face all over again. Meanwhile, I was as helpless as Cecily and Noel in the face of this uncharacteristic behaviour.

Finally Dora was ready, comforted in part by wearing one of Nettie's own capes over her prettiest dress and smiling bravely through the remnants of her tears. The next difficulty was Uncle James, who also seemed to be having an uncharacteristic attack of nerves. His gouty leg was giving him trouble as well, especially on the stairs. Eventually, he was forced to put a tea tray on the banister and prop his suffering leg in it, then essentially slide down the two flights of steps. At last, he too was ready and ensconced in the carriage, his leg sufficiently recovered that, with benefit of a cane, he could muster a dignified walk.

It was fortunate for Cousin Dora, and indeed for all who trembled for her, that she did not have long to wait before it was time for her to perform. The "surprise entertainment" turned out to be The Cannington Manor Tunatic Band, a kind of toy symphony orchestra, and it was the first item on the programme. It contained every conceivable instrument, from the prosaic piano and violin to the more unexpected banjos, bongo drums, triangle, bones and musical combs. The combs were indeed hair combs, played with tissue paper.

Dora, now her pretty, glowing self, played the triangle, and one could tell by her intensity that she was following the directions carefully, though even occasionally remembering to smile. Some of the other players, Mr. Maltby among them, appeared to have a more carefree attitude to timing. He rattled his bones with reckless abandon within their frame and was positioned so he could frequently catch the eye and nod of his wife, who sat at the piano, but did not have to look at the audience that packed the hall. Cousin Ernest, meanwhile, played his banjo and took the lead, while several others plinked and bonged as the spirit moved them. As conductor, Uncle James kept the whole reasonably in time if not in tune, and the overall effect was not unpleasing.

At the end of the band's rendition of *My Grandfather's Clock*, the audience applauded so enthusiastically at the band's novelty and the skills—or lack of skills—of the various performers that the band played their encore number, the ever popular *Amazing Grace*. When it too finished, with a rattle and a bong and a tinkle (the last from the triangle), the audience again applauded enthusiastically and would possibly have welcomed further tunes. Uncle James, however, bowed and left the stage, and the members of the band followed suit. When they come back, it was to play softly in the background when Mr. Campbell sang *See Saw*, the well-known children's swing song.

The Rev. Mr. Dobie and Mr. Scarfe both sang early in the programme, and I half hoped Mr. Cuthbert might be next until Mr. Campbell came on stage. In fact, I found myself anxiously anticipating Mr. Cuthbert for at least half of the evening, which meant that I missed every opening. I noticed, however, that Mr. Campbell had devised a tableau as a setting for the simple children's song. Though it took some time for him to set up the limelight, the effect was impressive, as were the muted sounds of the band, and the audience expressed its appreciation for the extra effort.

It also took a few minutes to clear the stage for a recitation of *The Three Young Maids of Lee*, also known as *A Bird in the Hand*, which was especially entertaining as two of the three were of unusual proportions for maidens. Even Cousin Nettie, who sat beside me, could not identify them, though she thought the smallest of the three maidens was a Miss Romboldt. We later learned that the others were Mr. Scarfe and Mr. Campbell, both of whom managed to transform themselves very quickly from regular gentlemen to simpering maids.

I had seen the poem performed before, though perhaps never with quite so much enthusiasm. Owing to my recent reflections on possible spinsterhood, it also caused me some twinges of discomfort, as it is not kind to those who do not marry. It involves three young maidens—often played by three men to even more hilarious effect—who think themselves too fine and find fault with every beau who comes their way. They get their come-uppance when they become the three old maids of Lee. This illusion is created when, for the second stanza, the three maidens turn their backs to the audience, for on the backs of their heads they wear crone masks. Not surprisingly, the three crones are not nearly as choosy as they were when they were young.

Though all the acts were quite entertaining, I expected the highlight to be Mr. Hardy's farce, *A Silent Woman*. When the play began, I noted with interest the entrance of the young man who had shown such particular attention to Cousin Nettie on our visit to the hotel for dinner. Being one of a particular type of tall, blonde young Englishman whom one always sees leaning against doorways or smoking his pipe, Alan Troughton was a good choice for the part of Arthur Merton.

In the play, Merton is engaged to Marianne Sandford (played by Mrs. Scarfe in this production). At first I wondered that a married woman had been cast as a maiden, but then remembered there is a kiss between the young couple at the end. No doubt it would have been considered improper for a bachelor to kiss an unmarried girl. Even in England, that would have been frowned on—except in professional theatrical circles, since they were known to be rather careless of decorum.

The plot of the story is very simple. Mr. Merton is out of the country when he receives a letter from a male friend, who turns out to be a false friend perhaps envious of Mr. Merton's privileged position. The friend intimates that Mr. Merton's betrothed (Miss Sandford) has become very loquacious; in fact, writes the friend, she "never stops talking." Much concerned but unable to come right out and express himself to the lady in question, Mr. Merton writes to Mr. Sandford, Marianne's father, played with the aplomb we had all come to expect from Dr. Hardy. In his letter, Mr. Merton says he "longs for that impossible thing, a silent woman." In writing this, Mr. Merton did not realize Mr. Sandford would share the letter with his daughter or that she would be outraged by what she feels is her suitor's impudence. She decides to teach her beau a lesson and enlists her father's help.

When Mr. Merton calls upon his fiancée after their long separation, he finds that she has had an accident that has rendered her deaf and speechless. Naturally, he finds it very difficult to communicate with her, and the father and daughter show him no mercy until Arthur Merton declares aloud that he would give the world to have his beloved hear him and speak to him again. These are the magic words. Miss Sandford relents and reveals the deception. To show that she has indeed forgiven him, she must kiss him, and her father kindly turns his back to offer the young couple the opportunity.

I stole a glance at Cousin Nettie at that point and saw that she was quite absorbed but did not appear to be dismayed. In fact, her expression told me nothing. If she had developed a romantic interest in Mr. Troughton, I thought she might have blushed to see him kissed by Mrs. Scarfe (though it was rather a chaste kiss, as appropriate when a young woman has been wronged).

The applause, not surprisingly, was more whole-hearted than the kiss, and the actors must return for a second and then a third bow. It seemed unlikely that the audience could be more pleased. And yet, there was an "exhibition of mesmerism" still to come. Apparently, a Professor Kennedy had heard of good reports of Cannington Manor and had bethought himself to come all the way from New York especially to perform for all the gentlefolk there. Even though it became obvious that the professor was actually the talented Mr. Scarfe in yet another incarnation, the audience cheered and responded appropriately. In fact, most of those who attended reported that Professor Kennedy "kept everyone in roars of laughter until the close."

It seemed then that the evening's entertainment was truly over, and that there would be no song from Lionel Cuthbert. But then he appeared, dressed for the occasion in what must have been his best Scottish regalia. I had seen gentlemen in their kilts before, as my family occasionally travelled to Scotland, but that was always at a distance and never someone I knew. I found myself quite overcome by emotion to see him thus. He always held himself well, though his carriage was more functional than self conscious. His costume, however, lent a most attractive swagger, and the total effect was—was—I could not have expressed it. I did know, however, that if

Cousin Nettie were then to glance at me in an effort to read *my* heart, as I had earlier glanced at her, she would not have found me so composed and difficult to read.

Mr. Cuthbert's presentation was modest, as always, and as always he offered the audience too little rather than too much. He first sang the light-hearted *I Love a Lassie* and then finished with Mr. Robbie Burns' beloved *Auld Lang Syne*. It seemed a perfect end to the evening, and I would very much have liked to sit for a while, both to still my heart and to replay Mr. Cuthbert's performance in my mind. Instead, however, we were all obliged to rise dutifully and finish with *God Save the Queen*.

Fortunately, all my companions seemed as happily exhausted as I was after such a full evening, so I doubt that my utter lack of conversation was noted. This trance-like state continued as the large company shuffled out of the hall and wended home. There would be time enough tomorrow to discuss and recall all that had taken place.

Chapter 48
-
AUNT JANE RETURNS

Though I looked forward to Aunt Jane's return and that of her youngest child, James Barnet, who would soon be five years of age, I was far from the most excited by that event. Uncle James was almost beside himself for the week before she arrived, and most of the rest of the family followed suit. Cousin Nettie was perhaps an exception. She carried on with most of her activities as usual. Though she might have attended a few more house parties and dances—perhaps imagining her mother's presence would curtail her activities in future—she also made a special effort to keep the house more in order.

One of Nettie's efforts was her difficult-to-enforce rule about the removal of outside footwear. For instance, the boys—meaning Frankie, Billy, Ernest (when he was home) and any other workmen—and the children—Cecily and Noel—must leave their boots by the kitchen door. Others might merely clean boots on the mats at either front or kitchen entrance, provided their footwear wasn't overly dusty or soiled. After much persuasion, Ernest brought in one of the rough benches from outside, painted it and placed it beside the kitchen door to aid in the removing of boots. Two of the better chairs were stationed at the front entrance for the same purpose.

We did not attempt another wholesale cleaning, but did wipe

down the entrance hall and the kitchen and larder again; having acquired a few metal containers, I was able to face the larder with slightly more courage. Nettie was sure the kitchen would be of special interest to my aunt, and the entrance would be her re-introduction to her home. For these reasons, we also shook out and washed the doormats.

In addition, Nettie began the habit of gathering bouquets of flowers and putting them in vases about the house. One of her favourite spots was atop the newel posts at the bottom of the main stairs. This, however, turned out to be an unfortunate location, as Uncle James inevitably knocked over one or other of her vases when he stumped heavily down in the morning. My uncle had given up using a tray for his leg, but he needed a great deal of support from the banister as he made his way to and from his chamber. It might have been easier for everyone if a room for him had been devised downstairs, but he refused to be treated like an invalid, especially as his condition was intermittent, not constant.

In all, I thought him somewhat reduced by his losses over the summer, though I had considered him healthy and hearty when I arrived. He obviously missed Aunt Jane, Mary and even Nurse McClure, for so we had begun to think of her. Though Nettie did her best to fill the roles of housekeeper and companion, she was also young and needed her entertainments, which meant she frequently rose very late in the morning, so my uncle had only Miss Pritchard and me, respectively, to lay out his breakfast and keep him company while he ate. Though he tended to rise early, he sometimes needed encouragement to greet his day.

Aunt Jane and little James were to leave England on August 26, so we expected they would reach Halifax by about the seventh of September. Then there would be four or five days by train and one day by carriage, as Ernest would meet them in Moosomin, so if all went well, they would be home by 13 September. There might of course be delays, as none of these modes of travel was entirely reliable.

The piano and chair they brought with them, final gifts from the almost legendary great aunt, would accompany them as far as Halifax, but would have to be shipped and fetched later, as there was still some uncertainty about shipping costs. Uncle James had written a special letter to the Minister of the Interior, Mr. Edgar Dewdney, asking that he "use his influence with the Commissioner of Customs to let these things come in duty free." I knew this as Uncle James had discussed it with Cousin Ernest over supper one evening.

"I still think I should go with you," said Uncle James, ruefully rubbing his swollen leg.

"Oh, Father, you know how you suffer during long journeys!" exclaimed Nettie, while Ernest barely managed to hide his irritation.

"But surely your mother, my other and better half, would expect it of me."

"I think," Nettie said gently, "that she would be far happier to see you rested, not tired and rumpled from travelling."

"That's right, Pa," said Ernest, "and remember that neither ships nor trains are entirely reliable as to time. There would be no point our both having to wait in Moosomin, uncertain when Mother and little James will actually arrive."

"Still, I'm sure your mother—"

Ernest, I could see, was making some effort to stifle his exasperation. "Would it help," he asked, "if I sent a telegraph to the Moose Mountain Trading Company when we are set to leave Fourth Siding?"

Uncle James did persuade Ernest to take the phaeton and to make sure he remembered the special carriage rug. This was one Uncle James had designed and had made for my aunt out of fox skins; it was now a little worn, but still quite pretty.

Having reconciled himself to greeting his wife on their own doorstep, Uncle James carefully planned the costume he would wear for the homecoming and spent several hours writing prayers for her safe journey home. These he would give to the Rev. Mr. Dobie to be used during services. He also wondered if Mrs. Hanson would play *Eternal Father, Strong to Save*, with its chorus of *O hear us when we cry to thee for those in peril on the sea*. If Mrs. Hanson were not available on the Sunday Ernest left to fetch his mother and brother, then no doubt Lily Pierce or even Mary would be able to take her place.

The children too made special preparations for their mother's and little brother's return. Dora and Cecily started new memory books especially for their mother. This time they need not paste and press their grasses, flowers and other discoveries over the stories in ladies' magazines. Instead, they used actual scrapbooks that I had purchased for them at the Moose Mountain Trading Company out of the small purse I had brought with me when I came from England—the same purse I had attempted to give to my uncle. There had been little need for it—and very little that I could find at the town store, anyway. My purchases, therefore, were limited to thread, needles and thimbles (to replace those I had lost), a pair or two of cotton stockings, some hairpins and the scrapbooks.

For his project, Noel had scorned his scrapbook and started a collection of rocks, feathers and remnants of birds' eggs after the babies had hatched—I had finally been able to persuade him not to frighten the parent birds away in order to steal eggs that were intact. He also tried to add grasshoppers and small live frogs, such as could be found in any marshy area, to his collection, but they refused to stay in the tiny houses he made for them out of grass and sticks. Usually they escaped his collection box entirely, and when they did not, it might have been most humane to have ended their lives in the first place.

All in all, Noel's collection seemed designed to cause distress to everyone, especially the wild things he tried to collect, and I was sorry I had encouraged it. Neither did I know what he did with it in the end—whether he ever showed it to his mother. I suspect he did find a way to torment his little brother with it, once the excitement of the return had faded. Noel must certainly have felt some animosity towards this younger sibling who had enjoyed their mother's exclusive attention for so many months.

Whether or not there was an important event coming up, Billy and Frankie had little time for family meals, for they were now cutting, binding and stooking the grain that had survived the hailstorm six weeks before. Ernest was sometimes available to help them, but most often not, and Lionel Cuthbert had his own harvest to attend to. When my cousins came home from their long hours in the fields, they were generally dirty, tired and bad-tempered, for which one could scarcely blame them. I sometimes wondered if they thought themselves treated as little more than hired labourers, and all that for nought but board and room. I tried, therefore, to treat these young men with special consideration and encouragement.

For all their hard work, they still had spirit, and I overheard them use their mother's imminent return as an occasion to re-tell the story of the first time Aunt Jane entered the house. Miss Pritchard at least was impressed. We also noticed afterward that there were certain parts of the hall floor where she would not walk and certain closets she would not open.

Two weeks passed in this state of expectancy, and on Sunday, the twelfth of September, Cousin Ernest set off to fetch his mother and little brother. If all went according to plan, they would spend the night in Moosomin and start back Monday morning. Not surprisingly, it was difficult on that Monday for anyone in the household to focus on any task for long, and the sound of a horse and vehicle in the distance would bring everyone running to the window expecting either a message from the store or perhaps the travelers themselves. Most often the vehicle was only Dr. Hardy driving by with his buggy and his faithful Sue, as the doctor's place was only a mile or two up the road. It did seem that the doctor made an uncommon number of visits back and forth to patients that day; however, he finally came in the drive and handed Uncle James the telegram from Ernest. The travelers had "arrived in good time," and all had "started early this morning—stop—expect to arrive home before eight in evening."

This knowledge heightened the tension and excitement even more, as it was by then past three. Cousin Nettie and Miss Pritchard set about preparing a special evening meal, and Nettie invited Dr. Hardy to stay or to return to dine.

"I wouldn't dream of intruding on a family reunion," he said, smiling. "I will go home to my lonely abode and my usual bread and water."

Nettie, of course, threatened to hit him with the dishtowel he had at hand. He pretended to duck and wince. Then he turned to Uncle James, who appeared preoccupied and unable to make any sensible conversation.

"I'll pay my respects in a day or two, after your good wife has had the opportunity to rest from her exertions."

I thought again that this sensitivity was typical of his character. For some time it had been apparent to me that I need not worry over Cousin Nettie's attentions to Dr. Hardy. Not only was it appropriate when he had been for months practically as a member of the family, but perhaps the difference in their ages was not so remarkable. Many a young woman has married a man fifteen or even twenty years her senior. That was certainly the case when Uncle James married Aunt Jane, and even when Mary married Mr. Maltby. Then I recalled Cousin Frankie's teasing suggestion that it was actually Freda the doctor admired. With Freda only fifteen or sixteen—a liaison was somewhat less customary. In fact, I wondered if signs of such an attachment might have influenced Aunt Jane's decision to take her middle daughter to England with her in order to enrol her in an English boarding school.

Would this not solve the mystery of why Freda and not Nettie was chosen for the privilege of spending time in England? And yet, the decision may have been made on the basis of age alone. Nettie had been fifteen when the family left England, but would now be deemed too old for a finishing school. Another party might also have been involved in the decision—Great Aunt Peg, for instance— and she might have made the choice, as it was unlikely Uncle James could afford such an extra expense. Whatever the reason, the arrangement must have had advantages to both Cousin Freda and her parents.

When I was in the company of Dr. Hardy, I saw why he might make a young girl's heart flutter and sometimes wondered that he did not have the same effect on me. Not only was he kind and gentlemanly, but also well-favoured, talented and amusing. These would be pleasant attributes in a partner. On the other hand, a love of society could be detrimental if it kept him away from his own hearth. And what of his enjoyment of the drink—about which I had heard such rumours? Had the Humphrys considered this tendency when looking at him as a marriage candidate for one of their daughters?

The fact that I could look at all these factors with such a dispassionate eye was clearly evidence of a lack of feeling for him on my part. I also knew my lack of interest was not because of such practical considerations, but more likely influenced by the fact he had never shown any particular interest in me. There had been no speculative glances, no smiles meant for me alone, no awkwardness if our eyes happened to meet, and these small things are often the deciding factors for a woman.

Mr. Cuthbert and I, on the other hand, had been thrown together from the first. Whatever my initial reluctance to admire him, I could not ignore that his personal attributes, both physical and moral, were from the beginning those that pleased me. Although our initial greeting had been awkward and no words of mutual regard had ever been spoken—in fact, very few words of any kind had been spoken—I remembered every occasion when he had seemed to be looking at me with interest and every time he had offered a hand to help me. Though I had no proof he was attached to me, I was convinced that it was so. And this was enough for me to both long for and dread his company.

Cousin Mary's words during our walk in the meadow may have influenced my feelings, but for the most part, she merely spoke truths of which I was already half aware. The fact that there was no future in the attraction between Mr. Cuthbert and myself—as I told myself at least once a day—could not diminish my feelings or my conviction that my feelings were shared.

Not long after Dr. Hardy left with his horse and buggy, the Maltbys arrived with theirs. I wondered just a little whether Cousin Mary might have had a difficult time persuading her husband to come. Though naturally his wife would want to welcome her mother back after such a long absence, Mr. Maltby must surely feel some nervousness over this reunion with the woman who was now his mother-in-law.

I could only speculate about Aunt Jane's satisfaction with the match, though Nettie had once confided that Uncle James initially had reservations about Mr. Maltby. I believe he had found him somewhat austere. On the other hand, my uncle's esteem for his son-in law had grown in the past few months. In fact, he had often been heard to say that he thought they—Mr. Maltby and Cousin Mary—"would do very well and would be good for each other."

The travellers did eventually arrive and not much later than Cousin Ernest had predicted. Since Cousins Billy and Frankie had come in early from the field and had also spent some time making themselves presentable, the whole family was arranged about the foyer, poised to dash outside when the carriage came up the drive. For my part, I stood a little back from the group.

Uncle James had stationed himself by the front door, and I was touched by his determination to be the first person his wife saw as the carriage came to a stop outside the door. No doubt it was difficult to achieve such a feat in such a large and vibrant family, but he managed it. As the carriage arrived, Uncle James stepped forward, though still moving with some difficulty, opening the carriage door for his wife and offering his hand to help her descend. Then he put his hands on her shoulders, and they gazed directly at each other for a moment. I think he may have had tears in his eyes, though she merely looked tired.

It was only a moment, however, before they were bowled over by the greetings and demands of all their children at once. Ernest was waiting to unhitch the horses. From the carriage came a wail from Cousin James, who must have been sleeping. Cecily and Noel both threw themselves at their mother; Nettie, Dora and even Frankie—

though he was more reticent—all had tears in their eyes; Mary and Mr. Maltby were pressing close, waiting to be acknowledged; Billy, though he stood somewhat aside, was a picture of pride, awkwardness and desire. Poor Aunt Jane tried to respond to all of them at the same time. Meanwhile, Uncle James stepped back a little to avoid the danger of being knocked down by the urgency of the others. He had had his moment.

Eventually, exhausted as she obviously was, Aunt Jane found a word and a touch for everyone. Uncle James again offered his arm, this time to lead her into the house, though she was somewhat impeded by little James clinging to her skirts. The rest of the family followed behind. My aunt had not yet acknowledged me; quite possibly she did not even see me, or if she did, she didn't realize who I was. In fact, she may have thought me either a neighbour or even the maid, since Martha Pritchard was hanging back in a similar fashion. Oddly, after Uncle James brought me to her attention, he almost immediately introduced Miss Pritchard, who curtseyed politely. Aunt Jane acknowledged us both with a nod and a closed-mouth smile.

I confess that I felt just a little slighted by this, until I remembered my own mother's recent letter. There had apparently been some communication between the sisters, though no personal visit. According to my mother, Aunt Jane was to have her teeth pulled prior to leaving for Canada. My mother had described it as a barbaric treatment, but perhaps, considering that Dr. Hardy was entrusted with the dental as well as medical care for a very large area, it may also have been a way to avoid greater suffering.

I suspect Aunt Jane might have preferred to immediately retire upon her return, but the fact the meal had been prepared in her honour gave her little choice. She did, however, forget herself for a moment when she wondered why Nurse wasn't there to greet them and asked Cecily to fetch her, as James must be put to bed. Cousin Cecily turned white, then crimson. She would dearly have loved to do this service for her mother—whom she suddenly remembered she had missed so much—but she clearly didn't know what to do.

I stepped forward quickly and offered to put him to bed, but little James would have none of a stranger, and his fretful cries only became louder and his grasp of his mother's skirt tighter.

Cousin Nettie had greater success. James allowed his big sister to pick him up, and after encouragement and a few extra embraces from her mother, Cecily took Nettie's hand and retired as well. I was uncertain whether I should follow the group or not, so I concentrated on Noel, since it was usual for him to retire at the same time. He was more reluctant, and his nine-year-old face as he avoided looking me in the eye became as sulky and unfriendly as that of his younger brother. It was as if we had suddenly become strangers. Dora then took the initiative and asked whether he might be allowed to eat supper downstairs on this occasion. Perhaps she was thinking of her own interests as well; nonetheless, she earned smiles and a pat on the cheek for what appeared to be generosity.

When Nettie returned from nursery duty, the rest of the family was already seated and Miss Pritchard ready to serve. Aunt Jane, having taken the opportunity to adjust her toilette, appeared in a fresh blouse and was seated in her proper place at the foot of the table, with Mr. Maltby on her right and Mary on her left. I had seated myself in my usual place on my uncle's right, but when I noticed my aunt gazing thoughtfully at me a couple of times, I began to wonder whether she questioned the arrangement. As it would have been difficult to find another seat, I tried to believe she was merely re-acquainting herself with the features of her niece and smiled back as dutifully as I was able. She responded each time by looking away.

Again, I felt hurt and disappointed. For all her gentleness, there was also a firmness about her that suggested she would correct whatever she did not approve of, and for a reason I had yet to discover, she did not appear to approve of me.

In the privacy of my room that night, I tried to persuade myself that my sense Aunt Jane disliked me, or at least disliked my being there, was unfounded. Could her response be put down to fatigue? It was obvious throughout the meal that she had great difficulty attending to all the news my uncle had to share. She also studied each of her children very carefully, perhaps with no more favourable a gaze than she had cast on me. It was as if she were consciously remembering each of them. Meanwhile, her manner to Mr. Maltby was almost as gracious as to her own husband, so it seemed there would be no difficulties on that account. She did, however, succumb to her fatigue and excuse herself after the main course, but not before complimenting Miss Pritchard on her steak and kidney pie about which, she said, she had heard so much, and it did not disappoint.

Uncle James rose as if to escort her to the stairs, but she must have known how that would cost him physically, as she asked for Cousin Ernest to accompany her instead. The family stood to watch her go, and then settled back to eat dessert with an almost visible sense of relief.

Chapter 49

-

BUSH FIRE

Not long after harvest (such as it was) a fire started in the bush around Fish Lake, and most of the men and older boys from Cannington Manor and its environs went to help fight it. Even Uncle James joined the effort, though I am sure riding in the wagon over bumpy trails, not to mention all of the other hardships, must have cost him dearly. He felt, no doubt, that it was important he as well as his sons be seen to take part.

No doubt the men were able to react so quickly because of all the precautions taken after the tragedy a year ago. In fact, following the new fire regulations had given the families of the district some relief from the grief and fear they still felt after the deaths of young Mrs. Elsie Dallas and her two boys the previous fall.

As with most communal efforts, Uncle James had thrown himself whole-heartedly into following the new regulations. Even without the incentive of increased fire security, he saw such initiatives as another way of transforming Cannington Manor from a raw "prairie frontier" to "a prosperous agricultural community."

He had, therefore, approved the territorial government's designation of the whole township as a "fire district" in the July just past. This had meant all the farmers in the district, both small homesteaders and large property owners, must contribute either money or labour and equipment to the construction and maintenance of adequate fireguards. The Humphrys portion, Uncle James explained, was "three-and-one-half days of ploughing with one team and one man, or one-and-three-quarter days with two teams and two men."

Though the regulations about fireguards had been adhered to for the most part, it was more difficult to create fireguards and control fires in the densely wooded areas around the lakes, especially as these fires were generally caused by lightning strikes. My uncle also explained that in the days before the "Whiteman" came, the Natives believed fires were a good thing, as they burned the old, dead wood and gave room for the young to grow.

With so many farms and lives to protect, however, settlers needed to stop the fires before they grew too large to be contained. Neither did the settlers want to lose the acres of dead wood around the lakes, as they needed the fuel for their stoves and furnaces. Yet, when my uncle spoke about Native practices that honoured the cycle of life, about the old dying to make room for the new, there was a certain wistfulness about him. For all his ideas about progress, he appeared to regret interfering with the natural evolution of the land.

Fish Lake was deeper in the woods beyond Cannington Lake, yet we could smell the smoke from home, even with the windows closed. Neither could we stay long indoors where the smell was muted, as we must tend to the chores while the men were away. Women must also take supplies—food and drinking water, as well as axes, digging implements and extra gunny sacks—to the men on the fire line. Nettie and I claimed that task, leaving Aunt Jane and Miss Pritchard in charge of the farm.

I was surprised at Nettie's ease around the horses. She must at some time have received instruction from her brothers or at least have watched them very carefully, as she hitched the team to the wagon herself and drove quite successfully, though the smoke made the horses nervous. The animals seemed to sense the threat, perhaps even more than we did. Where our trail was intersected by a trail from the north, we saw Mrs. Turton and another woman, apparently on a similar mission, for they had a barrel of water in their wagon. How they had been able to load it, much less fill it with water, we could not imagine.

We did know, however, that Mrs. Turton had possibly driven horses and worked with other livestock even before she married. In any case, it seemed a good idea to wait for her and let her wagon take the lead.

At any other time, I would have admired the winding trail, with its hills, sharp curves and deep hollows, but with such a threat in the air, stinging our eyes and noses and giving the sky a strange orange hue, we could not see the beauty, though we were caught up in the excitement. When Mrs. Turton finally pulled her wagon to a halt in a flat, open space, we followed suit. We could see neither men nor flames, though the smoke seemed thicker and I thought I heard shouting in the distance, as well as an ominous crackling that must have been the fire.

"This is as far as the horses will go for me," said Mrs. Turton, when I had stumbled over the underbrush to her wagon. "All we can do is wait for one of the men to come our way." I noticed that the portion of her face and hair I could see beneath her large straw hat was dusted with soot.

When I climbed back aboard our own wagon, Nettie and I looked at each other and saw that our faces too—especially about the eyes and mouth—were blackened by dust and ash. At any other time, we would have laughed at the appearance we presented.

"This is my neighbour, Mrs. Peterson," Mrs. Turton called out by way of introduction. Her companion—a large-boned, rather rough-looking woman—scarcely acknowledged our greeting, though she turned to Mrs. Turton and said something I couldn't hear. Mrs. Turton listened but didn't respond, and I decided I didn't like Mrs. Peterson.

The men must have set a lookout, as we didn't have long to wait. A team pulling what the men called a "stone boat" and balancing a

wooden barrel much like that in Mrs. Turton's wagon came gallop-
ing out of the bush. Two men stood with legs spread for balance on
the flat surface of the crude platform, one of them Cousin Ernest
and the other stranger, though possibly one of the Canadians.

"Wait here. We're sending Father back with you," shouted Ernest
to Nettie. Then he and the other man managed, though with some
difficulty, to transfer the barrel from Mrs. Turton's wagon to the
stone boat. It must have been very heavy, and quite a lot of water
spilled.

"Will you want more drinking water?" called Mrs. Turton.

"No," said Ernest. "This should be enough for now." Then the
team and their load were off again, and I realized we had been
watching so intently we hadn't given them the supplies we had
brought with us, our reason for being there.

"They've forgotten their lunch," said Nettie.

In a few minutes, another team appeared, this one pulling a wagon. When these men pulled their handkerchiefs from their faces, I
saw that Lionel Cuthbert had been driving, with Frankie beside
him. My uncle was in the back, holding onto the sides of the wagon
and dangling his feet out the end. Mr. Cuthbert and Frankie supported him as he stumped over to our wagon. While Nettie and
Mrs. Turton were getting my uncle settled in our own wagon box, I
watched Mr. Cuthbert gather up the sacks and various tools. His appearance discomposed me even more than usual. It had been several days since he had taken a meal at the house, and seeing him now,
covered with sweat and smoke, gave me a strange feeling. In fact, I
might not have recognized him had I not, in my dream, fought a
prairie fire at his side.

In reality, he was even more blackened with smoke and dust than
he had been in my dream, and he too may have been feeling the
strangeness, as his expression and manner was abrupt, even angry.
In a minute he was walking quickly back to his team and wagon.

"Cuthbert!" hollered Cousin Frankie, running after him, and I
could hear the indignation in his voice.

Mr. Cuthbert stopped as he was about to mount the wagon, and

I heard him say something to Frankie about not wanting the women left on their own. At that moment, I remembered the wicker lunch basket we had made up with such care and our jam pails of drinking water, which seemed foolish now. I grasped them and hurried to where the hired man appeared to be giving directions to the master's son. Frankie didn't look pleased, but it appeared he was going to do as he was told.

With some difficulty, I put the basket and the pails under the seat of Mr. Cuthbert's wagon. Just as I was about to return to Nettie and the others, Lionel Cuthbert looked straight at me.

"You," he said, "get yourself home, and don't let me see you up here again!"

Then the man and wagon bounced away over the uneven ground. I tried to cover my embarrassment by reaching out to Frankie. If only I had at least kept a sandwich for him! When I put my arm around his shoulders, however, Frankie shook me away and stalked back to the wagon, where he climbed into the back and sat beside his father. I followed him, with my eyes cast down to avoid tripping, though I happened to look up just as I passed Mrs. Turton's vehicle. Mrs. Peterson seemed to have been watching, and I noticed that her head was tossed back and her mouth open, as if she were laughing.

In a moment, Mrs. Turton was turning her horses around and heading back over the trail, so again we followed her, with the teams moving much faster away from the fire than they had when approaching it. In fact, our horses were acting as if they were in a race, and Nettie was having difficulty controlling them. Soon, I was aware of Cousin Frankie scrambling to the front of the wagon, grabbing the lines from her and pushing between us and onto the seat. When he had slowed the team sufficiently, Nettie managed to hitch up her skirts and climb back the same way he had come, so she could sit with my uncle.

Whether Uncle James needed support or not, I was uncertain, for all this was accomplished without speaking. I was glad in fact that we didn't attempt to talk, as I for one would have found nothing to say. My mind was too much focused on the sooty face, bare throat and half-blackened, half-bared chest and arms of Mr. Lionel Cuthbert.

Though we travelled at a more reasonable pace with Frankie holding the lines, we still arrived back at our own yard more quickly than I had expected. Aunt Jane came rushing out of the house and began to fuss over Uncle James, though he kept assuring her he was all right, just a little winded. Frankie unhitched the horses and took them to the barn, glad no doubt to have redeemed himself and proved his manliness by demonstrating his greater skill with the horses. I didn't know what had happened along the fire line, but Mr. Cuthbert was obviously concerned about my young cousin and wanted him out of harm's way, so much so that he had stepped out of line and opposed the wishes of his boss's son.

After Aunt Jane had settled her husband in a chair by the entrance, she looked more closely at Nettie and me. "Why, look at you," she said to Nettie, "you're black as a sweep."

Miss Pritchard, who had no doubt come along to see what the excitement was about, turned quickly and hurried back to the kitchen. No doubt she anticipated my aunt and was starting water for baths, a duty that would keep her busy for some time, since there were four of us in obvious need of cleansing. Neither were we alone, as Noel and Dora had been feeding the chickens and pigs, and when they returned to the house, the smells and some of the grime of the barns came with them. In spite of this—or perhaps because of it—they carried themselves with satisfaction.

Chapter 50
-
AFTER THE FIRE

When all those who had been outdoors had cleaned themselves sufficiently to appear at table, we were more than ready for the meal Miss Pritchard had managed to prepare even as she was heating water for baths. The group at the dining table seemed sadly depleted, however, and I wondered when Ernest and Billy would return.

"The fire will keep them busy well into the night, no doubt," said Uncle James. "There is so much undergrowth to feed it. But they should be able to douse it eventually or drive it into the lake."

In my mind I not only saw the figures of my two cousins, but also that of Lionel Cuthbert silhouetted against flames that lit up the night sky until it seemed almost day. While Uncle James gave the blessing over the food, I winced at the vividness of my imaginings, and when I opened my eyes, Aunt Jane was looking at me in surprise.

As well as being a smaller group, we were also a quiet group, though both my aunt and uncle described the prairie fire the previous fall. It must have been the same one that cost Mr. Dallas his wife and sons, though everyone was careful not to mention them.

"There was fire all round us that day," said Aunt Jane, "and the smoke so dense, no one knew exactly where the fire was and dared not go out of doors."

Eventually, however, some must have ventured out, for Uncle James described how the flames had spread to the grass, and how with "half a gale" blowing, they soon had a roaring fire coming down towards the house. The family had been in danger of losing everything and they had no choice but to fight the blaze.

"We got horses onto a plough," Uncle James continued, "and immediately drew a line on the west side of the bluff to the east of the house and to the north of the fire. And then, having dispatched Noel on the pony and Frank to call up the neighbours, we set to work as hard as we could to beat it out.

"Ernest, Willie, Frank Bird and I—and Mary and Nettie also lent a hand with sacks. We stopped it on the north side, and the sloughs stopped it on the west. By the time the neighbours began to arrive, it was conquered, and we soon made an entire finish of it."

Shortly after my uncle finished his version of the incident, I heard the other men at the kitchen entrance—stopping even under these circumstances to remove their outdoor shoes before they came down the hall and appeared in the dining room doorway. Cousin Ernest was first, but Billy and Mr. Cuthbert were close behind him. In order to stop myself from leaping up and going to them, I became very interested in checking for dust and smoke that Cousin Frankie might have missed when he washed his neck and ears. He pushed my hands away just as he had earlier pushed away my comforting arms.

"I thought you would want to hear, Father," Ernest began, his voice somewhat hoarse, no doubt because of the smoke and wind, "there were enough of us that we were able to drive the fire into the lake. A few men will watch tonight, but with luck that is the end of it and not nearly as much damage as last year." He prepared to sit down in his usual place. Aunt Jane gave a barely audible gasp.

"You will be wanting to wash up," interrupted Uncle James smoothly. "Miss Pritchard has warm water in the kitchen. And, Lionel, if you would join us? You worked like a tartar and must be exhausted. It is far too late for you to drive home tonight."

And so it was, though I suspect Aunt Jane might not have approved. The men cleaned themselves as much as they were able with the water available and, despite their smoky clothes and hair, came to eat their supper in the dining room. They appeared to be too tired to talk much, though Frankie blurted out that "Cuthbert here" had sent him home "as if he had the right." Ernest spoke up in Mr. Cuthbert's defense.

"It is well he did, as you were about to drop on your feet—an accident ready to happen—though you were a good scout all afternoon."

Somewhat mollified, Frankie went back to eating his supper.

That night, tired as I was, I found it difficult to sleep. I had not been one of those fighting the fire; nor had I driven the horses, like Nettie or Frankie. Still, it had been an adventure where suspense and strong emotions can be almost as exhausting as physical exertions. Neither could I prevent myself from imagining Lionel Cuthbert lying on his straw mattress in the bunkhouse, with no more than a rough blanket over him. Or perhaps he slept in the bed of his wagon—his limbs stretched out or curled up in sleep. For now, however, danger was over. The family was safe and all together.

Chapter 51

-

ANOTHER WALK IN THE MEADOW

The day after the fire, I found myself exceedingly restless and unable to focus on any domestic task. After the morning meal was cleared away, therefore, I took the first opportunity to go for a walk in the meadow. As it happened, my path was the same that Mary and I had taken when we strolled out together before she was married, now more than three months previous. Though the path skirted the piggery and stone barn (now almost finished), there did not appear to be any workmen there, and I remembered the talk at breakfast of Uncle James and some of the boys taking a trip to the town.

Cousin Ernest would also be gone to his current building project, since he had finished the Maltbys' addition. As for Mr. Cuthbert, he had not appeared while I was at breakfast, so I thought him far away, perhaps taking his turn checking on the site of yesterday's fire.

Remembering all the drama of the previous day, it seemed extraordinary there was so little evidence of it. Other than some smokiness in the air and a somewhat hazy sky, one could have believed the threat had never existed. According to Ernest's report, there had been no casualties this time—not man nor beast nor buildings nor even haystacks—but there could easily have been.

There were still some homesteads that lacked adequate fireguards, and bush fires and prairie fires were opportunists with the ability to catch one unprepared.

I had reasons besides the drama of the previous day to make me restless. I knew I should by now have planned my departure from Cannington Manor and the Humphrys—the lack of a warm welcome from my aunt made it obvious I should leave as soon as possible—but I now seemed incapable of decisive action. Some part of me would be wrenched away when I left this place—even apart from my feelings for Mr. Cuthbert. Knowing this, it would have been wiser to hasten rather than delay such an action—to get it over with—and yet I hesitated.

Since changing my initial departure date, I had not written again to my parents, and I had received nothing but brief messages from my mother, so they obviously had no urgent need to see me. Still, I knew I had reached a point where I must act.

Deep in these reflections and hardly aware of where I walked, I thought I heard some unexpected sound from the direction whence I had come. I stopped to listen, looked back and saw nothing behind me or around me—not that I could see any distance. Though I stood in a clearing, I had recently passed through a dry creek bed followed by a small rise, so much of the path I had followed was hidden. Not far from me, however, was a thick stand of bushes, which could harbour unknown creatures. Instantly I regretted not having invited one of my cousins to accompany me. Not only was conversation a good way to dispel fear, but I had been told it was a protection against real dangers. Wild animals, apparently, often attack simply because they have been taken by surprise.

Now that my reverie had been disturbed and my nerves unsettled, I was uncertain about continuing my walk. Cousin Mary and I had followed the cow path that ringed the bush and opened eventually into a beautiful clearing, where a few weeks ago Miss Pritchard, the children and I had gathered wild strawberries. And yet, I did not know what might lurk in the shadows between the trees. It was as I stood in this state of nervous uncertainty, contemplating whether I would turn back or continue on, that Mr. Lionel Cuthbert came up the rise out of the creek bed and approached me.

As was typical of all my encounters with Mr. Cuthbert, I hardly knew what I felt. There was some surprise and embarrassment, even some apprehension. I remembered the night when he had come silently up behind me in the dark as I was struggling to open the gate for Cousin Ernest. That time, his hands had been neither gentle, nor gentlemanly. They had closed over mine with a kind of forceful possession that had shocked me, not only because I was startled, but also because he seemed impatient—displeased with me—as if I were intruding on him and causing him trouble.

His angry words to me during the fire had given the same impression. "You, get yourself home. Don't let me see you up here again!" He had spoken to me, touched me, as if it was his right to do so.

How little I understood men—what made them angry, or happy for that matter. I did not fathom the way their minds worked anymore than I understood their physical yearnings. Even men such as Frederick Corby were a mystery to me. I had admired Mr. Corby's appearance and manner, enjoyed his attentions, wished to please him and expected that we would marry. Yet I had failed him in some way, for he had withdrawn his affection.

At the same time, I had never been conscious of Mr. Corby in the way I was aware of Mr. Cuthbert. I had never felt there was any danger in Mr. Corby, nor this strange, masculine presence and authority that Mr. Cuthbert appeared to have over me.

Though I was conscious of the old turmoil, even alarm, when I saw Mr. Cuthbert approaching me, I determined to hold my ground and felt on the whole more gratitude, even pleasure, than fear. In his company, I no longer imagined wild creatures or lurking strangers. Neither was the man himself a threat standing as we were, for now that he had come up the rise, we were both in sight of the house.

Realizing this, I allowed myself to consider the possibilities. Had he actually sought me out? Even followed me? If that were so, how was I to respond to him? No matter how much my feelings had changed, our difference in station remained. Mary had spoken of the need to consider his feelings and had hoped he would not be disappointed again. Though she had seemed to encourage me to care for him rather than not, I was obliged to see it the opposite way. Clearly, I should politely end his hopes—if hopes there were. But as usual, Mr. Cuthbert caught me by surprise.

As he came within a few feet of me, he took off his woolen cap and stuffed it in a pocket of his trousers. His longish, sandy hair, therefore, was somewhat ruffled, and he had to toss his head to clear it from his eyes. There was something about this boyish gesture that affected me, caused me to feel a swell of tenderness towards him.

"I do not like to see you walking alone, Miss," he said, in a tone that was calm and matter-of-fact.

"Oh," I said, "I did not intend . . . it was to be a very short walk." I blushed a little at the falsehood. Then I felt dismay that I was forced to justify my behaviour.

"Nor did I like to see you in the hills yesterday. A fire is not for entertainment."

Again I tried to protest, but he pressed on with his own thoughts regardless of what I might have to say. "Have you not heard," he said, "that a woman and her children died—who would have been safe had they stayed where they were? Had she not set off across the fields on her own—"

He was talking about Mrs. Dallas of course, but how could he be comparing me to that poor woman?

"It was on my aunt's advice. We took supplies," I said, still wondering why I was making excuses to him.

"But did you not know the danger? Did you not know I sent Frank home more for your sake than for your uncle's or his own? And he did not thank me for it."

I was angry now, for Nettie's sake as well as my own. How dared he judge our good sense! Who was this Lionel Cuthbert that he should presume so much! Yet I found myself unable to speak, unable to challenge his presumption.

"And there are not just fires to be feared. A woman named Mrs.

Ramage was lost in a blizzard not long ago, because she took to wandering about on her own."

"What happened to her?" I asked.

"She was travelling home from Fourth Siding with a neighbour named Evans when they were caught in a blizzard. They managed to find some protection by unhitching the horses and turning the wagon over to make a shelter. Eventually, Evans decided to go for help, telling her to stay where she was. But after a time, she too crawled out from under the wagon and wandered about trying to find help. Naturally, she succumbed to the cold.

"Evans was found half frozen but alive, and a huge search party went out, but because she had left the wagon, her body wasn't found until July, several months after the blizzard. The wonder is her body was found at all, not torn and scattered by wild animals."

I shuddered at the picture he presented. Yet some part of me wondered why it would have been better for her to freeze to death under the wagon than to die while trying to find help herself. After all, it's doubtful that the search party went out during the blizzard. I didn't want to argue Mr. Cuthbert's logic, however, as the story was still very frightening and obviously seemed significant to him. His tone when he finished was not angry but desperately sad. I think I might even have heard a break in his voice.

He was silent for a moment, perhaps to regain his composure, and then he said, quietly and firmly, "Miss Southam, there are dangers here such that a woman should not be on her own." He paused, then said abruptly, "I believe you need someone to take care of you."

Again, he had silenced me, and my faithless heart was moved from anger to gratitude. How sweet such words were to the ear. To know that someone—that he—had such concern for my welfare.

But he still hadn't finished. "A man," he said, "also needs a woman. A man needs a woman to hold him when times are hard and remind him of warmth and hope."

When he said this, I thought of his recent losses and felt for him such a flood of tenderness that tears came to my eyes. I would almost have touched him, had not some instinct warned me it would not be a simple thing to touch Mr. Cuthbert, even if reaching out in sympathy. One could not touch Mr. Cuthbert and expect him to keep his distance. So, difficult as it was, I let the moment pass, though I made no move to silence him or to depart from his presence.

Still standing as we were, there on the hill a little past the dried-up creek, I listened to him talk about his dreams. He had given no fancy name to his homestead, as many of the others had done, but merely called it "the farm." Yet it was for this he had left his family in Ontario. And he was well on his way to building his dream. He would soon have met his homestead requirements and would have clear title to his land. And his house was plain and built of logs, but solid.

Like him, I thought. Not that he was *plain*, but there was no falseness or foolishness in him.

"No windows in *my* house were broken." (Was this to reassure himself, or me, or to compare himself to the Becktons, with their fine house and many broken windows?)

And still he talked.

"I have a few good Angus cattle and will invest in pigs, when I have a crop of wheat to sell." He paused, as if he was again remembering how the hailstorm had dashed his hopes. But obviously he wasn't giving up. He was talking of the future.

"And I would break sod for a garden, if ye wished it."

If I wished it! Mr. Cuthbert was making his intentions clear. There could be no mistaking him.

Mr. Cuthbert paused, perhaps allowing that I might wish to encourage or protest. Yet I did not know what to do or say. I had never been in such a position before. Mr. Corby, though he had spoken of love in a vague, flowery fashion, had not in all the years I had known him said so much.

When Mr. Cuthbert went on to speak of children, my face must have turned scarlet, as I felt the heat of it. He dearly wanted children, he said, a family of his own. His heart was sore whenever he spied a man among his children. There was no life without children, and for them and the wife who bore them, he would never spare himself, but labour until the end of his days.

Again he was silent, and I knew it was my turn to speak, that he had a right to some kind of answer. The birds and insects had suddenly hushed around us, as if they too were waiting, at least to hear me say "wait," or "I cannot," or "let me think about it." But, I could not manage even that.

"Oh—" I said. And then, to my shame, instead of saying anything more, I turned and ran, as fast as I could manage in Frankie's heavy boots. Across the clearing, down the hill, across the dried-up creek bed, back to the house and without thinking to remove or clean my boots, back upstairs to the room I had come to think of as mine.

He must have followed me, though at a distance, because a short time later I heard a wagon on the drive, and when I went to the window at the bend in the stairs to check, I saw that he was leaving. There was no backward glance, but only the sight of his head and shoulders as he drove away.

Chapter 52

MY ACTIONS RECEIVE SCRUTINY

Nettie suggested later that day that she and I might dig the last of the potatoes. It was a sensible plan, since one never knew how long the autumn days would last. Or so the settlers said. October would soon be upon us. This too made it important for me to plan my journey home. Soon it would be too late in the year for ships to cross safely, and what then would I do? I would have no choice but to remain for the whole winter where I had already overstayed my welcome.

It was while we were in the garden that Nettie told me her mother would like to know my plans, and I felt that sinking of heart one has when a hidden error has been discovered or long-awaited bad news arrives. I had to admit I had as yet no plans.

"I, of course, would have you stay forever," said Nettie, smiling at me from under her large straw hat, "but mother feels it would not be right. She worries—about how it looks. A young woman with no visible purpose—there are those who might take advantage."

So here, it seemed, was proof I had been deluding myself. I was not part of the family, however much I might wish to see myself that way. Hurt made my face and my words feel stiff.

"I did not realize," I said, "that I have been a burden."

"No, no, it is not that," Nettie was all affection now, patting my arm and gazing intently into my face. "As I said, I would have you stay forever. But Mother says your family must be missing you, and—"

"—and?"

Nettie's words came out in an awkward rush. "And you should be spending your time with young men of your own station."

"I don't understand. I am not spending time with any young men—"

"What of Lionel Cuthbert?"

"Mr. Cuthbert?" In spite of myself, I blushed. "I am not spending time with Mr. Cuthbert."

"But mother saw you meet with him this very morning. Are you saying you were not in the meadow—that you did not arrange to meet him there?"

"He surprised me on my walk. That is all. Nothing was planned." And yet I knew as I said it that my face betrayed me.

"You did not discourage his company then—for Mother said you were speaking together for some time."

I could not disagree.

"Mother worries, you see, because of Ruthie."

"But I would not—"

"Of course not, but you understand how it looks, and mother is concerned about the impression you are making on my young sisters—and me. Being seen walking and talking with a young man who is someone—who is not someone you could marry."

By now, Nettie seemed almost in tears herself from her efforts to make me understand. I pitied her sincerely, but I also felt the unfairness to myself. There was no help for it. I must speak to Uncle James right away, must arrange for the earliest possible passage. When I said as much to Nettie, she reminded me Uncle James had recovered sufficiently from the exertions of the previous day to take Billy, Frankie and little James to the village. Therefore, I must wait.

In silence, we finished digging the rest of the potatoes and piling them in bushel baskets.

Chapter 53

-

WORD FROM HOME

After my conversation with Nettie, I felt I should at least try to speak to Aunt Jane, if only to reassure her I would be leaving before the winter. It was difficult, however, to find a quiet interlude that offered sufficient time and privacy. After all, I expected the conversation to be awkward, if not actually unpleasant.

That very day would have been preferable, had it not taken Nettie and I most of the afternoon to finish digging, piling and transporting the baskets of potatoes to the bins in the cellar. Had there been brothers to help, no doubt the job would have gone faster, as Nettie and I could only carry small amounts at a time. However, there was no help available until Dora and Noel were home from school, and they were much less dedicated and no stronger than we were. Therefore, by the time the job was done, the hour had come when we must clean and tidy ourselves thoroughly before helping Martha Pritchard prepare the evening meal.

After the meal, which the boys continued to eat in the kitchen (no doubt to the enjoyment of Miss Pritchard), Uncle James mentioned there was a letter for me. He had picked up the mail during his visit to the store. I supposed that it must be from my mother and also that it would contain nothing of much importance. I therefore accepted it from my uncle, put it in my pocket and went back to helping clear up after the meal. When that chore was completed to everyone's satisfaction and Miss Pritchard and the children were gone to their rooms, I found a piece of sewing and followed my aunt to the sitting-room, where I intended to instigate the conversation I had been dreading.

We were not, however, alone, as it was one of those rare evenings when both my uncle and Cousin Nettie were home. Both looked up from their usual places as I entered the room and seemed to have no intention of moving. This would prevent the intimate conversation I had hoped to have with my aunt. Neither was there any plan to go visiting later, though it was only about eight o'clock; in fact, Frankie and Billy had already retired for the night, no doubt still exhausted from their exertions of the previous day.

After an hour spent peacefully in this manner, with quiet talk between my aunt and uncle and appropriate comments or replies from Cousin Nettie and me, I too retired. As I was undressing, I remembered the letter from my mother, but even so, did not hurry to open it. Instead, I sat for a time by the open window, gazing out into the growing dark and letting my sense of loss be fed by the hint of fall in the slightly chilly air. Finally, I closed my window to a mere crack, took my lamp to a small table by the bed and propped myself against the pillows so I could read.

My mother's letter began much as I had expected, full of meaningless details of visits, parties and balls she had attended with my sister and vaguely hurtful comments about how much my sister was admired. As usual I wondered about her purpose in telling me these things. Did she plan to wound me with these constant reminders that I mattered so little to her?

There had also been some changes in the staff. For one, the kindly maid whom I had liked had been dismissed, as she appeared to have formed a liaison with the new groom. Marriages between members of the household staff were still largely forbidden; in fact, most live-in servants were expected to be and stay single, as this supposedly helped them keep their focus and prevented jealousies.

This made me think of Mrs. McClure, for I had discovered that Nurse was indeed Mrs. McClure now. She had even attended the recent concert in the village in the company of her husband and child. I did not speak to her, nor I think did anyone in the Humphrys family, but I was very happy to see her appearing in public. Or I would have been, had I not been so distracted by the appearance of Mr. Lionel Cuthbert in his kilt!

It now seemed that Ruthie Ford for all her disgrace—and she had certainly suffered for her vulnerability or her lack of wisdom, whichever it was—had eventually found for herself a fuller existence than she would have enjoyed had she spent all her days in respectable service. How odd and strangely comforting that was! I no longer had to upbraid myself for what was at best my lack of attention and at worst pure prejudice.

Though much of my mother's letter was predictable, the ending was anything but. After hoping that my visit with my uncle and aunt and cousins was still going well, she wondered whether I might perhaps be spending the winter there. I would be interested to hear, she wrote, that Mr. Frederick Corby was again visiting regularly. This time, he was addressing his attentions to my sister and appeared very devoted. In fact, the relations between him and our whole family were "perfectly amiable, as if there had been no breach."

I wondered for a moment about my mother's use of the word "breach" and whom she held responsible for it, but the most devastating lines were yet to come.

"*This is a rather sensitive time,*" she said. "In fact, it would be best if you do not plan to return home for some months. No good would come of distracting Mr. Corby at this time or perhaps reminding him of interviews that were less than pleasant."

I was so astonished by the conclusion of the letter that I must read it through several times to be sure of its meaning. Then I was by turns indignant and amused, and it was not until I had snuffed my lamp, put on my nightcap and prepared to sleep that I recognized my situation. It seemed that I had overstayed my welcome at my uncle's house, and at the same time was not wanted in my own. I had often been lonely as a child, and I was not always happy with myself as an adult, but I could not remember ever having felt so desperate and unwanted as I did that night.

Chapter 54

PICNIC AT CANNINGTON LAKE

When Mrs. Turton first introduced me to Mrs. Peterson near Fish Lake on the day of the fire, I decided very quickly I did not like Mrs. Turton's neighbour. I felt then that there was something slighting about the woman's manner to both Cousin Nettie and me.

At closer quarters on the day of the picnic at Cannington Lake, I liked her even less. For one thing, I did not like the look of her hands, which were large and red. Nor did I like her conversation, which seemed unforgivably coarse. At the same time, I did not wish to put myself above her and the other "Canadians" by staying very carefully with members of my own set, as my aunt seemed to do. It was quite clear to me by now that the community was divided into two camps: my aunt's "particularly nice people" and the more "rough and ready" Canadians.

Though only a generation, if that, away from the old country themselves, the Canadians seemed freer of affectations and more likely to simply go ahead and do what must be done. I had admired this quality in Lionel Cuthbert, and I saw it in these industrious women as well. While my aunt fanned herself in the shade and chatted with Mrs. Pierce, Mrs. Turton and the women of the Canadian group were preparing the huge picnic lunch.

Many of the women were quite mannerly and helpful, but Mrs. Peterson was anything but. From the time I approached the table where she was slicing cucumbers and other fresh vegetables onto a huge platter, she seemed determined to make me feel as uncomfortable as possible.

First there were comments to the other women at the table about my aunt and her "hoity-toity" manners. "Wouldn't expect her to do the scrubbing or to dirty her fingernails scratching in the dirt," said Mrs. Peterson.

"Now, Hilda—" said Adelaide Turton, who was also tall and rather large-boned, but with a much pleasanter face. Though it and her figure showed the kind of wear and tear that grief, hardship and frequent child-bearing might create, her experiences seemed not to have hardened her. In fact, I had thought on one or two earlier occasions that if I were in desperate need of a friend, I would seek her out. Had not the Humphrys and others spoken of her acts of kindness to both settlers and Natives? And her kindness to the latter seemed quite independent of her husband's contract to supply meat to White Bear Reserve.

After ten years in the Cannington Manor district, the Turtons were known for both hospitality—it was often said that farmers cutting wood on Turton land were sure of getting supper and a bed for the night—and their well-established herd of beef cattle. As to the size of his herd, the number was difficult to judge, for Mr. Turton was a great teller of tales, an extra benefit for those who bought their meat from him.

Though I had learned much about the Turtons and would in my now tenuous position with the Humphrys have been grateful for a confidante (and perhaps even occupation as a nanny were there not already a grandmother on their premises) there was no occasion to make overtures of any kind on the day of the community picnic. All the women were bustling about, intent on their tasks, and Mrs. Turton had the additional challenge of having to organize her large family and encourage them to find other places to play than around her feet.

I noticed little Gertie in particular, a dark-eyed child of around two years. She had somehow inveigled her mother's large straw hat and would not give it up, though it repeatedly slipped down and covered her eyes. In fact, I once or twice moved her away from the table where her mother was sawing huge slabs of roast beef from a succulent joint in front of her on the long trestle table. The little girl only tipped her head back and gazed at me in wonder from under the overhanging hat, and then she went back to the game of tag with her siblings.

The fact that I interfered seemed almost to encourage Gertie's rather dangerous game, so I joined the other women working behind the table, stationing myself quite by accident beside Mrs. Peterson. When I realized what I had done, I could see no easy way to escape her without giving offense. Eventually, she handed me a knife and some carrots to scrape into a barrel behind me.

"See what you can do with these," she said in her gruff way. Then she gave a nod towards Mary, "You're fine enough, but you don't have your cousin's sparkle, so you'll have to content yourself with being useful."

Trying not to wince at her rough manners, I followed her glance towards my cousin. Lovely as ever in a summery frock and parasol that she must have bought in Winnipeg, Mary Maltby was reclining on a blanket under a tree, while her new husband seemed to be plying her with tidbits to tempt her appetite.

"No doubt a bun in the oven already," observed one of the other women, and Mrs. Peterson made an obscene gesture with a large cucumber. I blushed while the other women laughed, and that brought Mrs. Peterson's attention back to me.

"And here's a miss acting like nothing of the kind has caught her fancy." To my horror she made the same obscene gesture toward me; I felt the nudge of the cucumber against my thigh through my skirt and undergarments. Not only that, but as I put down the knife and the carrots and began to walk away, I could hear a reference to blue eyes.

"No doubt the little Scotsman would be happy to teach you a

thing or two—given a bit of encouragement," said Mrs. Peterson.

"Hilda, I'm ashamed of you," said Mrs. Turton. But she did not come after me or offer me any comfort.

I made my way with as much dignity as I could muster to Cousin Mary's side and joined her for a time on her blanket, but she was obviously feeling unwell.

"No doubt they all have it that I am in the family way," she said, "when I merely suffer from too little sleep and a little too much sun. Who would have thought it would be so hot at the end of September? And I am tired. There is still so much visiting to be done—and furniture to arrange and curtains to hang now that Ernest has finally finished the addition." She smiled up at Mr. Maltby, who had suddenly appeared above her. "I mean brother Ernest, of course," she said. "*My* Ernest is perfect in every way."

He folded his long legs and sat down beside her, finally making a few selections from the plate he had brought her—she appeared to have eaten very little—and eating them himself. She stroked his hand and turned back to me.

"Being newlyweds is like suddenly becoming community property," she said. "Everyone wants a piece of us, and they are always speculating, insinuating—. How can you bear that Mrs. Peterson? I never spend any more time than I have to with her sort."

As usual, Mary had found a way to deal with her changed circumstances, and as usual, I wished I could be more like her. But I was not her, nor could I be. Furthermore, I found myself both pleased and embarrassed by the couple's frequent caresses—pleased because they seemed so comfortable together and embarrassed because I had thought such affectionate gestures to be a private thing. Neither did I know how to look at them when they had eyes only for each other. After a few minutes, I bade them goodbye.

It seemed again that afternoon that my world was getting smaller and smaller, almost as if there were no place for me. I wondered where Lionel Cuthbert was spending his afternoon. He had helped drive our family, so he must be somewhere about. Not that I would have sought him out—I simply wondered where he was. I doubted he would be among the young men who had donned bathing costumes in order to splash about in the lake or lie on blankets on the beach. Not only was it late in the season for such adventures, but such a public display would surely not suit someone with his reserve. Rather, it would be the province of the callow young agricultural students to parade their masculine physiques for the edification of the chore girls. Few of the young ladies would be watching them; even Dora had more sense, especially under the watchful eye of her mother.

I also considered seeking out my aunt, though I suspected she saw me more and more as an interloper, however useful I tried to be and however outwardly gracious her manner. She had not, fortunately, become perceptibly colder since she had witnessed my conversation with Mr. Cuthbert and delegated Nettie to make her disapproval known. Neither had I found occasion to speak to her or my uncle about leaving—my mother's letter had shattered that plan for the moment. Furthermore, since I felt I was imposing on my aunt, I certainly could not continue to seek friendship and support from my uncle.

I looked for Mrs. Pierce, but I no longer saw her. Perhaps she was chaperoning the female bathers. It seemed, therefore, that there was no one to whom I could go for companionship, much less advice. In fact, I would have been grateful even to see Miss Pritchard's face, not that I considered her a companion. But she—for all that she complained there were no entertainments to be had for servants—frequently refused to take advantage of what was offered and had chosen to stay at home. No doubt she was at this moment lying on her bed writing a letter, as she seemed to have quite a number of correspondents. I wished with all my heart I had made the same choice.

The situation at the Humphrys had become nearly impóssible, and it seemed I must disregard my own mother's suggestion to extend my visit and allow my younger sister her opportunity with Mr. Frederick Corby. What other choice did I have? Perhaps I could pretend I had not received her letter.

In another place and time, I could perhaps be a companion to someone such as Mrs. Pierce. At the moment, however, the founding lady had more than enough family support at her son Ted's home. Even were she to return to the Great White House, she still had Lily, her last unmarried daughter, to be her companion, though the attentions of Mr. George Shaw Page did seem to suggest that Lily's situation might be soon to change.

Even this vague possibility was of no use to me. I had no time to wait for such a solution or to nurse my unhappy heart. How everything had changed in such a short time! How quickly, in little less than a month, I had gone from favourite cousin and niece to the unwanted guest!

Mrs. Turton happened to come by as I was standing there undecided. She patted my hand, but she was carrying an infant and herding a group of other youngsters and did not stay or speak to me. I began to feel as if the word "outsider" was written on my forehead, and anyone who might have approached me was afraid of being tainted by it. Finally, an idea came to me. I had heard it said the Humphrys homestead was a mere seven miles from Cannington Lake and that the trail was clearly marked. It was but mid-afternoon, so there would be several hours of good walking time before night began to fall, and as the afternoon went on, it would no doubt be cooler and more pleasant. Now that I had a plan, I felt less desperate. I also thought to retrieve my shawl from my aunt.

Aunt Jane made little comment when I told her I was taking a short walk, other than to say I should take care not to lose my hat or I would freckle. She and Mrs. Turton now seemed engaged in conversation, and my younger cousins were for the moment out of sight. Perhaps they had taken their little brother James and the Turton children down to the water, as generally Aunt Jane did not let her youngest out of her sight. To have no questions asked added to my conviction that I was no longer wanted. Perhaps in spite of my resolve I had hoped to be prevented.

So I struck out, wishing, as I did whenever I went for a long walk without adequate preparation, that I had Cousin Frank's boots with me. Though I was wearing my sturdiest female footwear, it could not compare with that of a man. And that reflection of course got me to thinking I should have been born a boy. At least then my father might have had more to say to me.

As I wandered down the broad trail I had chosen because I believed it to be that taken on our inward journey, my troubled state of mind did not prevent me from noticing the beauty of my surroundings. Owing to the quick efforts by the men of the district, the recent fire had not spread to Cannington Lake, so the birch trees retained their white bark and the aspens their tinkling golden leaves. Meanwhile, the wild roses, choke-cherries and some of the other bushes had crimson plumage, and some of this gold and crimson had scattered on the path and crunched under my feet. I knew it would not be long before these trees were bare and the only colour would be the dark green of the evergreens that were scattered around and through the mostly-deciduous forest. Yet it was hard to believe such beauty would ever end.

Every now and then I heard a sound I didn't recognize, a sound that seemed larger than the birds that gathered intermittently in rushes of tiny wings, collected for a conference and then sailed away together. When I heard these unknown sounds, it was difficult not to imagine the animals that might lodge in the woods, and not to be aware I was one woman alone and not a large woman at that. It gave me some comfort to pick up a smooth branch that was almost as tall as I was. I liked the polished feel of it, for its bark and smaller twigs had long since fallen away, and yet it seemed sturdy.

After walking for some time, I came upon a fireguard and began to be a little alarmed, for I did not recall having seen it on the inward journey. Could it be that I had somehow missed a turning or intersection of trails and followed the wrong one? Was it possible that in my worship of my surroundings I had overlooked such an important detail?

About that time it also seemed to me the birds had fallen silent—did that mean the presence of a dangerous animal? I remembered Mr. Cuthbert's words and realized again how ill-fitted I was to be taking the risk of walking alone. All kinds of animals might lurk in these woods—not only skittish coyotes, but savage wolves, bears, wild cats, wolverines. I could feel my heart pounding in my ears. I tried to reassure myself that wild animals were still more afraid of humans than I of them—or so I had been told. Besides, I had my weapon, though it was a little difficult to hold both it and my shawl. I stopped for a moment and tied my shawl around my waist. Then I took a firm hold on my stick and marched forward more boldly. I could hear and see birds again, and I convinced myself that the rustlings in the leaves were only the wind or very tiny creatures.

At the next unfamiliar sound, however, I thought of doubling back and trying to find the picnickers again, but the trail behind me, even though I must just have passed that way, did not seem familiar either. How was it that the woods now seemed so thick and endless when before, in the wagon, the way was so simple and filled with the light that flickered through the trees? There seemed no choice but to keep going forward. The worst thing to do, I thought, would be to stop. No, I must continue to walk boldly, but also to make as much noise as possible by shuffling my feet in the leaves along the path. Walking boldly while shuffling my feet was difficult, however, and I was in frequent danger of tripping. How I wished that I could whistle or sing! And indeed I forced myself to hum a jaunty little tune.

The further I went, the more unfamiliar and untrodden the trail became. Spongy spots that would have caused no difficulty for the horses and wagon seemed virtually impassable when on foot. Had we crossed a creek-bed or a dried-up slough? My poor boots were now damp inside and began to carry a weight of mud, but I was afraid to stop and try to clean them for fear of what might then steal up on me. Not only that—which was more than enough—but I was afraid, with the blisters forming and places rubbed raw, if I once removed my boots I would never be able to replace them.

By now I was very tired and more than a little afraid that I was lost. There also seemed to be more dips in the trail, and creek-beds and gullies than I remembered. How was it that I had not noticed before? Still, I knew I must go on, though I was almost certain I had lost the trail. I began to imagine stopping, having to spend the night. I would not be able to continue when I could not see in front of me. Then there would be no hope of keeping to the trail, if I had not already lost it.

I tried not to notice that the light was changing, that the colours were less brilliant, that the shadows were increasing. Again I reminded myself that I must not stop, whatever happened. As long as I could see, I must keep walking.

I tried to pray. But the words "deliver us from evil, for thine is the kingdom . . ." turned into thoughts of the man who had offered himself as my protector, and some part of me began an inner chanting of his name—*Lionel, Lionel*. I chided myself for behaving so foolishly and wondered whether I might have said his name aloud—for suddenly, miraculously, he came.

First I heard the wagon, and I stopped and turned to face it. How could it be? He had found me. I wanted to sink to the ground in relief and gratitude, but instead I waited for him. He quickly knotted the lines about the wagon peg, jumped down, and rushed towards me. A few strides, and his arms—his arms were around me, knocking my weapon out of my hand and my hat to the ground as he pressed my head against his shoulder.

"Florence," he said. "Florence." I could not tell whether it was anger or fear that trembled in his voice. I clung to him, just as I had clung to him that first night.

"Please take me home," I said.

He released me, and I reached down to pick up my hat, took a step, and suddenly the pain in my feet was so intense I cried out. He gathered me to him, one arm under my knees and the other under my shoulders, at first staggering a little under my weight, then lifting me up and carrying me to the wagon. When he had climbed up beside me, I was so overcome by weariness that I could not sit upright, and then my head was pillowed in his lap—not a soft pillow but a warm one, and I was content. I felt the movement in the muscles of his legs as he picked up the lines and began to drive away.

Perhaps I dozed, for it did not seem long before he brought the horses and wagon to a standstill and was helping me down again. I felt no surprise as I realized he had not brought me to my uncle's house. Though I had never visited the small log cabin sitting without adornment in its square of prairie grass, I knew where I was, even as I knew, when he led me inside, what it was he would ask of me there.

Chapter 55

IN LIONEL CUTHBERT'S CABIN

What can I tell of what happened there in Lionel Cuthbert's cabin, of intimacies so unspeakably terrible and sweet? Of stepping first through the rough doorway, bending to remove my shoes, then hearing him enter and pull the door closed behind me. And, spinning around, finding in a minute his hands warm and strong on arms and shoulders, of lips on brow and startled mouth, buried in curve of throat, hands moving down length of back, hands cupping buttocks, buttons popping, laces stretched and breaking, hands cupping breasts—of heart pounding, sweat and softening between thighs, seeing ladder to loft and mounting it, he behind me caressing me still, of collapsing backwards onto straw mattress, struggling with too many layers, skirt above waist, tearing fabric, opening my thighs, both urgency and wonder, pain, fear, oh stop, no more—how can I bear it—but joy—no—yes—joy—yes, deeper, closer, melting in waves of heat and trembling while his body surges against—inside me. Where does he end and I begin? Where do I end and he begin? We are one body. Eyes closed. Unable to look in his face, yet feeling still his panting breath on my throat, my name in his mouth.

"Florence."

My name was a moan and he rested, his weight on me—his shirt, which there had not been time to shed, adhering warm and damp to his chest—my chest. It was as if he, by possessing my body, had forced me to recognize my very self; yearnings I could not have named gathered together where our bodies intersected.

This thing that had happened could never be undone, nor could I be the same again, and yet I felt only tenderness and wonder. I put my hands on his head and found that thick, damp nest of sandy hair so surprisingly soft, yet springy against my fingers. I touched his ears, so neat and shapely, close against his head.

To think I should have come all this way, yet so easily might never have known him, might never have known this. I thought of our first encounters—was it meant to be from the time he lifted me from the wagon? From my first glimpse as he steadied me against the rough, woolen fabric of his coat. From the time I rebuffed him, offended at his presumption. From the offense and the awkwardness to the constant awareness of him and the growing admiration, the inevitable tension and uncertainty. From my shame after Mary's revelations in the meadow so close before her wedding, shame that I had not kept my feelings secret. From my hurt over my parents' neglect, the lack of warmth from my aunt. From the sudden change in my relationship with the Humphrys, the need for reassurance and a place to belong.

But the wonder and mad pleasure could not last. In a few minutes it was replaced by fear. What had I done? How could I face my aunt, my uncle? They would be looking for me even now. What was I to do? I could not simply remain where I was—in his bed, in his cabin. There was still a world outside, and somehow I must face it again.

And yet he slept, in his pure, unquestioning strength and the heat and scent of his manliness. As he took from me, he had entrusted himself to me. There had been no seduction here but a coming together of need and desire that had been building since the beginning—perhaps even from before we knew each other.

Why must there be an accounting for this thing we had done?

Why could the world not let us be? And yet I had obligations to them—my aunt and uncle, even my parents. Otherwise, how was I different? Again I remembered the woman whom I had scorned as much as pitied for most of the days we were under the same roof.

She had fallen under the spell of physical attraction, as had I. No doubt she too had felt sure of her beloved's honour; had I more reason to feel secure? True, Lionel Cuthbert had made his intentions clear when he followed me to the meadow and told me of his plans. Had he not said a man needs a woman and that he wanted children, that his heart was sore whenever he spied a man among his children? These did not seem to be the words of a man who would betray me.

And yet, what if they had been good intentions—no more? Did I know this man whose warm body was heavy on mine, his flesh still nestling against my own? Did he realize that for a woman this step once taken could never be retraced? That I had thrown myself completely on his mercy?

There were also practical and immediate considerations. I must wake him who had bedded me, and I must try to remove from my person all evidence of what had happened. When I had with some difficulty and—it must be admitted—some regret, relieved myself of Mr. Cuthbert's weight, I managed to sit, then stand up. I was conscious of twinges of pain and stiffness, but it was not unbearable, so I was able to examine my clothing. I discovered then that my dress was only a little torn, and this might appear to be the result of my wandering in the woods around the lake. The major damage was to my bloomers and chemise, but that could perhaps be hidden. Of more concern were the stains on the skirt of my dress. I would have to wash my dress, and in order to do this I must enlist the aid of Mr. Cuthbert.

It was not straightforward, however, to wake him. At first he looked at me with astonishment, as if he did not know where he was or even if he were awake. And then I was forced to look quickly away, as I realized he was again in a state of arousal.

"Mr. Cuthbert," I said, gazing at a small captain's chest, which was the only furniture in the loft other than a chair and the straw mattress. "I must avail myself of your washing facilities."

There was a rustle of straw and clothing, and when I dared to look at him again, he was standing with his back to me, apparently fastening his trousers. In a few minutes and with few words, we had both descended the ladder. It was now dusk, but still light enough for me to watch as he lit the small cast-iron stove and put a metal basin of water on it. Then he lit a lantern and set it on a shelf against the wall. Finally, he took a pail and disappeared out the door. I took this as an indication that I could safely disrobe, which I did as quickly as possible, for I did not know how much privacy I would have.

On a table beside the door, where the basin had been, I found what appeared to be a clean rag and some lye soap. I put them both in the basin and slipped out of my dress. With only the light of the lantern and stove, it was difficult to see the soiled portions of my skirt. Uncertain where to begin, I put the whole skirt aside, hitched up my shimmy and removed my bloomers. Then I twisted the rag to remove the water, rubbed a little soap on it and cleaned myself as best I could. Just as I was about to step into my bloomers again, the door opened and Mr. Cuthbert entered.

I sprang to a corner of the room clutching the few clothes I had around me.

"Mr. Cuthbert!" I cried, and I heard him put down a pail of water and back carefully out the door again.

I wasted no time in scrubbing the whole skirt of my dress as thoroughly as I could and then pulling the dripping fabric back over what was left of my undergarments. My stockings and boots were another reason to despair, but at least that damage was consistent with being lost in the woods. I managed to insert my feet back into my boots but could scarcely walk because of the blisters. This time, Lionel Cuthbert knocked before opening the door.

"Enter," I said.

He looked at me, standing wet and bedraggled beside the stove in the middle of his cabin. Though he was in the shadow, I am sure

I saw him smile.

"You look a drowned rat," he said.

"I need my wrap," I said, shivering. We both searched the small room, but there was no sign of the shawl. Mr. Cuthbert then climbed up to the loft and in a minute came back with my hat and a heavy wool blanket. I felt some astonishment that my hat had still been in place when I had mounted the ladder those minutes or hours ago, before my life had been irrevocably changed. Nonetheless, I took the hat, thanked Mr. Cuthbert and placed it firmly on my head. He then wrapped the blanket quite tightly around my shoulders.

"I willna have you catching your death," he said.

Then, seeing how much I was limping, he whipped me up, blanket and all, and managed to plop me rather unceremoniously onto the seat of the wagon. When we were safely on our way again, he put his near arm about my shoulders and forced me to sit close to him. Resisting was of no use; it simply made him hold me more firmly.

"I willna have you catching your death," he repeated, and I found myself leaning into his warmth in spite of myself.

The trip from Lionel Cuthbert's cabin to Humphrys House was somehow shorter than I expected, perhaps only three or four miles. When I recognized the turnoff that marked the quarter-mile or so to my uncle's estate, I found myself wishing the way had been longer. As if he sensed what I was feeling or perhaps shared it, Mr. Cuthbert reined in the horses, then turned to me and tucked the blanket more firmly around me.

"I will be going tomorrow to speak to the parson about a license," he said.

For a time I was silent, though I knew he expected a response. I did not know what emotions were uppermost in my mind—wonder, relief, delight, fear, uncertainty—but I knew what my answer must be.

"No," I said. "Wait."

I think he might have gasped. Whether or not he did, I heard his words very clearly, and I heard the anger in his voice.

"What manner of man do you think I am?" he said. "Do ye think I would bed a woman and not take her as my wife?"

The words alone brought a flood of physical memory. I knew with every nerve in my body what we had done. And here he was, a man of honour, ready to accept his responsibility. His intentions were clear; my feelings only were confused, and I did not know how to explain them to him. My admiration for him had not changed, and I was grateful that he wished to offer me his protection, but I needed time. The very rapidity and willingness with which I had gone to his bed seemed to demand the next step be taken with great care and attention.

There was, however, no opportunity to explain, as the house was alight, and someone appeared to have heard the wagon. We came into the yard to find a rabble of wagons, men and lanterns.

"Please . . . wait," I whispered to Lionel as he climbed down from the wagon and reached up to lift me after him. I don't know if he heard me, but I was grateful he shook off the arms that would have relieved him of his burden, carried me to the house himself and would not loosen his grasp until he had deposited me on a lounge in the sitting room. Then he seemed to fade into all the faces that crowded around me, until he disappeared entirely.

Judging from the number of people in the room, one might have guessed the picnic at the lake had adjourned to the Humphrys' house. I don't know when they discovered I was missing, though I suspected not until after the meal was eaten and the gathering up had begun. It was clear, however, that there had eventually been concern and an extensive search party. How odd I had not thought to ask Mr. Cuthbert about any of that; nor had he thought to mention it.

My aunt took one look at my dirty boots and stockings and told Martha Pritchard to begin heating water for a bath. Martha did so, and someone—it may have been Cousin Mary—kneeled to take off my boots and then removed my garters and began peeling my stockings from my poor feet. Those gentlemen who were still in the room began to sidle to the door. This was clearly women's business now.

"Where did Cuthbert find her?" I heard one man ask no one in particular.

Then I heard Uncle James reply. He did not know, he said, but knew he could rely on Lionel Cuthbert in any emergency. For some reason this provoked a snort of laughter, which was quickly aborted. I heard my uncle continue, and from his words it was clear he felt gratitude only and did not suspect anything beyond the obvious.

Meanwhile, Mrs. Pierce was sitting beside me patting my hand, and Dora and Cecily had both thrown themselves around my neck, where they were clinging and sobbing in such a way that I could scarcely breathe. Cousin Nettie was trying with little success to pry them loose, and Mary gave me a somewhat inscrutable smile as she stood waiting to hand me a cup of tea. I could hear crying in the distance and suspected little James had been sent to bed, though he deeply resented missing all the excitement.

Though I did see Mrs. Turton, I was grateful there was no sign of Mrs. Peterson. No doubt she would guess the whole scenario immediately and spread it with relish among all the neighbours. Even as it was, I must be very careful of my words and behaviour. Remembering Mr. McClure and Ruthie, I knew I was not the only one who could be hurt if the truth were known. I must not even tell Mary. And, in fact, I did not wish to tell her or anyone. My memories of our love-making were far too precious and overwhelming to share.

And as to other consequences that could perhaps arise from this evening's activities, I did still have my home and family in England. It was my parents' duty to protect me in any unforeseen circumstances, no matter how unpleasant it might be for all of us. And if that support were absent, I still had my legacy from my father's aunt. If the need were there, there would be a way to survive and care for that which was mine.

Chapter 56

-

I MAKE MY DECISION

In a week that included several restless nights and much kindness from all the Humphrys, I knew I had made my decision. My difficulty now was how to tell Mr. Cuthbert of it. He had not been to the house for meals; nor had I seen him at work. Since I was actively seeking him, I visited all the places I had ever seen him: not only the barns, piggeries and livestock yards, but also the rose garden and the meadow where he had told me of his home and his plans for the future. It was also the place where, if I had not run away again—I had so many flights to regret—I might have heard him clearly asking me to share his bed and his life. Would my actions and my decision have been different had I given him my answer then?

But such thoughts were not useful. I simply needed to find Lionel Cuthbert, and there seemed to be no alternative but to seek the help of my uncle. This meant I must also tell my uncle of my decision and not allow him to change my mind if he appeared to want to do so.

Uncle James expressed some shock when I told him Mr. Cuthbert, his hired man, had been so forward as to ask me to marry him. And he was more shocked still that I wished to become the wife of a man even he must consider his social inferior. When he had overcome his disbelief, the strongest objection he could articulate was that my aunt would not be pleased. He also warned me it would be a hard life, since Lionel Cuthbert had only a small cabin, little livestock and no more land broken than was absolutely necessary for him to get his title. I assured my uncle that Mr. Cuthbert had told me these things and reminded him of what he had often said about Mr. Cuthbert's abilities.

My uncle repeated that he had always been impressed with Mr. Cuthbert's unfailing energy and farming prowess.

"But he seeks nothing more," he said. "He has no interest in art or music or politics or business—all the things that mark a gentleman. He is not like us."

I smiled. "Dear uncle," I said, "it is true he is not like you, and though—as you know—I admire your ambition greatly, I do not expect it of him. I simply want to be at his side in all that he does."

"But are you prepared for such a hard life? He has no money and no position."

"I have no great need for money or position. I simply want to be—needed and valued, and I am persuaded of Mr. Cuthbert's ability to give me that at least. Besides, I have some resources. Perhaps I could be of some help to him. He too has dreams."

My uncle's response to this was quick. "Does he know about your—resources? Niece, I beg you to be careful."

"I have never told him."

Finally, my uncle said he would have Billy drive him to Mr. Cuthbert's homestead that afternoon, though he would rather Ernest were there to talk to the man.

"Uncle James," I said. "I wish to come too. I very much wish to see him."

"It would be better—"

"Uncle, please. I won't interfere."

My uncle relented, and everything proceeded as he had promised. Billy drove us to Mr. Cuthbert's cabin, and Billy and I waited in the wagon while my Uncle James went alone to the house. He knocked and after waiting a little, he opened the door and stepped inside. We could hear him calling Mr. Cuthbert's name. After a minute he came outside again and returned to the wagon.

"Out on his breaking perhaps," offered Billy, pointing in an easterly direction. My cousin had been silent up to that time. No doubt he wondered what was going on, but he had the grace to wait to be told. My uncle nodded and was about to climb back up to the wagon seat, as usual with some difficulty, when we heard the sound of a team and wagon, and Mr. Cuthbert himself drove into the yard. Mr. Cuthbert quickly reined in his team and came over to our wagon. I tried to say with my expression those things I could not voice in front of my uncle and cousin.

He spoke to my uncle. "Do you have need of me? I had hoped to finish the work I mentioned to you."

My uncle responded with what I felt was totally unnecessary formality. "I wish to speak to you on a matter of some importance that concerns my niece," he said.

I blushed. What must Mr. Cuthbert think from such a tone? Billy looked at me in astonishment, but again he had the grace to keep silent. We watched as Uncle James and Lionel Cuthbert walked towards the cabin. They were well out of earshot, but I noticed that Mr. Cuthbert had shortened his strides to adapt to my uncle's slower and more awkward gait.

Finally, when I felt I could bear it no longer, they came out the cabin door and started back to the wagon. Suddenly Uncle James stopped, said something to Mr. Cuthbert, and the latter turned and went back to the cabin, stepping inside. I stood up and would have jumped down from the wagon and run after him had not Cousin Billy put a detaining hand on my arm. By that time, my uncle had almost reached us.

"Mr. Cuthbert wishes to return something that belongs to you," said Uncle James. "You may speak to him for a minute, if you so desire."

This time Cousin Billy did not stop me, and Uncle James was about to help me alight when suddenly Mr. Cuthbert was there and lifted me to the ground. He did not hold me any longer than was necessary; instead he stepped back and put my shawl around my shoulders. We walked a few steps away from the wagon. In such awkward circumstances, we could do little but look at each other. Perhaps we feared it would be impossible even to touch hand to hand without caressing. It was difficult to express very much by merely looking either, as every time I lifted my eyes to those of Lionel Cuthbert, I began to blush and had to look away.

Finally he said, "Do I now have your permission to see Mr. Dobie?"

I nodded, reddening again. I dared not think what might be the feelings of the Rev. Mr. George Dobie on this occasion, but hoped he would be generous, since he was so recently wed himself. Even if he were not, I was confident Mr. Cuthbert would know what to do. In fact, if the minister at Cannington Manor were reluctant or unavailable, I would not have put it beyond Mr. Cuthbert to drive to Moosomin that very day and engage the Rev. Mr. Cartwright.

"I am sorry," I said, "I didn't mean . . ." I was at a loss to say what I did mean. Even if I had the words to describe what had happened between us in the cabin and my need to take time to think about it and understand it, I could not have spoken those words aloud. But perhaps it did not matter, as he was more a man of actions than words.

Neither did I want to tell him yet that I would go back to England in a fortnight as already arranged with my uncle, for I suspected Mr. Cuthbert would object and that even my offer to pay for his passage to go with me would not reassure him. Perhaps it was for the best that he would almost certainly refuse. Still, I wished to see my parents before we were wed—I owed them that regardless of what their response might be—and I also had to arrange the transfer of my income from my aunt's legacy to the bank in Moosomin. This too I planned to accomplish without discussion.

Mr. Cuthbert did inform me that Uncle James had offered him a share in the pork-packing plant he hoped soon to have in operation. He also explained that he had refused the offer as he had no interest in being a business man. This did not surprise me either.

At about that time I heard my uncle clear his throat, so we walked back to the wagon. Many things were unsaid and it would later turn out that my suspicions about Mr. Cuthbert's reaction to my wish to spend some time in England before the wedding were correct. But I still felt confident everything would turn out as it should. For the moment—for perhaps the first time—I was clear about what I wanted and the steps I would take to achieve it.

When we reached the wagon, Mr. Cuthbert's hand was there to assist me to my seat as always, and he even took a moment to dust a few bits of grass and leaves from the hem of my skirt. I smiled my thanks, again hoping my face would show what words could not. Then we all politely bid each other goodbye, Cousin Billy clucked to the horses, and we drove out of Mr. Cuthbert's yard.

When Billy was putting the horses away and we were about to enter the house, Uncle James cast a glance at my shawl.

"I happened to notice your wrap in Mr. Cuthbert's cabin," he said. "He explained how you must have left it in his wagon when he found you lost in the woods." Uncle James paused. "I think we need not tell your aunt of this," he said.

Chapter 57

ANOTHER MARRIAGE
AT CANNINGTON MANOR

As I had hoped, everything did turn out very well; better, in fact, than I could have expected. I was almost disappointed to find myself not with child, though it was probably for the best, since it was mid-October when I arrived at my parents' home, so I was obliged to spend the winter in England. I had still, after all, some business to attend to, and neither Mr. Cuthbert nor my own father desired me to make the crossing when the Atlantic was most dangerous.

In fact, I was rather gratified and surprised by the concern of both. Mr. Cuthbert wrote that he must visit the Rev. Mr. Dobie again to explain the delay in our marriage plans, but he did not appear to resent it. It was in keeping with what I knew of him that he would consider my safety and well-being before his own desires. He was also a surprisingly faithful correspondent. His letters were not artful, but plain and short and filled with practical things, such as the information that he had broken sod for a garden—south of his house—where it was sunny and yet sheltered from the wind. Yet between the plain words written in his small neat hand, I could read and remember an ardour that required I should read these fortnightly missives in the privacy of my own room, and that I should store them under my pillow.

My father's caution was a greater surprise, as I had never felt he paid much heed to my existence. Suddenly, it seemed that nothing was more important to him than my company. After all, I would soon be residing at such a distance there would be few opportunities to meet. Though this was totally unexpected behaviour, I was sincerely grateful for it.

Through my aunt, the Humphrys had extended an invitation to my parents to stay with them if they came for the wedding or for subsequent visits. Though at first I had some trepidation about how my aunt might describe the man who was to be my husband, I discovered when my mother showed me the letter that there was no cause for concern. Aunt Jane had described Lionel Cuthbert much as I had described him. He was a hard-working Canadian farmer of Scots descent and blessed with a fine tenor voice. He was also known to my uncle and respected by him. She also mentioned that Mr. Cuthbert had at present quite a small house, as was the case with most bachelors, so it would be most comfortable and convenient for guests to stay at Humphrys House.

As I handed the letter back to my mother, she looked thoughtfully at me and wanted to know how small a house and what was Mr. Cuthbert's income. I confessed frankly that I did not know the latter, for a man's value in the Canadian prairies was judged by his character, his good sense and the work of his hands. Then, concerned that these words might have sounded defensive, I also mentioned my uncle's offer of shares in his pork-packing company and that Mr. Cuthbert had refused them, as he had no interest in being a businessman. I am not sure why I told her that—perhaps I simply wanted to keep the record straight. She and my father had said they would not be able to attend my wedding, but they might well visit another time. If and when that time came, they could see for themselves how I lived and draw any conclusions they might.

For the most part, my mother was kind and attentive, owing no doubt to her satisfaction that she would soon have in me a married daughter. Nor did it hurt that I had admitted Mr. Cuthbert was comely, rather in the style of the Scottish poet Robbie Burns—

but in appearance only, he had not the same wanton character. My mother also gave a good deal of attention to my wedding garments, though she was distressed by my preference for gabardine, wool and cotton over silk and satin, and especially by my choices of colour. I reminded her then that I was to be a farmer's wife and would not attend many balls. It would not be sensible to have gowns of a style or colour that I could never wear again. Whether or not she accepted this explanation, she said no more about it. She was in fact so compliant that I began to think I might for many years have misjudged her capacity for affection.

My relations with my sister were also pleasant, as she was guided as always by my mother's behaviour. When she could see I had no interest in Mr. Corby other than welcoming him as her beau, she demonstrated all the sweetness and attentiveness one might expect of a younger sister.

Neither had I experienced any lack of ease in meeting Mr. Frederick Corby, though he might have felt some, since he apparently chose not to visit as usual on the day I arrived. This threw my poor sister into a panic, as she was certain he had abandoned her, just as he had deserted me a year before. If this is what he had considered doing, he must have learned some wisdom in the intervening year and arrived the next day at his usual time.

Neither was there anything in our meeting to suggest we had ever felt anything for each other but disinterest and general good will. It was as if I were a long-absent family member whom he was meeting for the first time. And indeed this is what I felt—other than a vague surprise to find him neither so tall nor so handsome as I remembered. On the other hand, my sister seemed to like him very much, so I endeavoured not to gloat.

By the time I was finally allowed to return to Cannington Manor, I had gone through a number of different stages of accepting my family, appreciating their kindness and then wearying of them. Nothing at my old home seemed as important or as dear as the life that awaited me in Canada. The tedium of the trip, both by ship and by train, was therefore lightened by expectation, and I could only marvel at the difference this made to the landscape. How could I have missed so many beauties on my first journey? Then, in Moosomin, my dearest Mr. Cuthbert met me with all the tenderness one might expect of a lover and future husband—or at least as much as he could demonstrate in the presence of Cousin Ernest and my Aunt Jane, for it appeared that we were to be chaperoned.

Frustrating as this was, I recognized it as a sign of support and affection and tolerated it with as much grace as possible. I was genuinely pleased, however, to watch my aunt treat Mr. Cuthbert with a courtesy that was not condescending. My marital happiness did not depend on there being good relations between our two families, but I certainly welcomed it.

And soon our wedding day had come and gone. I had insisted on a simple service with no attendants as I could not possibly have chosen which of my cousins to favour, but I could not refuse my aunt the opportunity to host the wedding breakfast—with the help of Miss Pritchard, of course. Nor could I prevent Uncle James from giving a speech, though it was the toast to the bride and not the response, as Mr. Cuthbert was perfectly capable of attending to that himself. I would always remember the look on my bridegroom's face, the somewhat heightened colour and carefully groomed sandy hair and mustache, but most of all the sparkle in his eyes as he turned to look at me.

The other thing I remembered about that day was what Cousin Mary whispered in my ear after she had helped me don my wedding gown and was about to send me on my way to where the rest of the family were waiting.

"You are a sly fox," she said. "If I had any advice to give at this moment, it would be 'show pleasure.' But somehow I don't think there is any need."

I looked quickly at her, blushing, for the implication was clear. No doubt she had sensed the truth from the beginning. But I saw no condemnation in her face. I saw only her warm and affectionate smile, and all I could do was laugh. And we were both still laughing as we descended the stairs together.

Chapter 58

THE GREATEST FELICITY

The life is hard here, and I doubt that my dear husband and I will ever know wealth or ease, but, when least comfortable, I am still content with my lot and certain of my importance to him that I love. And when our evening meal is done, the dishes washed and piled carefully in the simple cupboard he has clapped together for that purpose, and my husband lights the bedside candle and holds out his hand to me, I know as I have never before been allowed to know, what it means to be beloved. Not only that, but I follow him up the ladder to our rough bedchamber with a stronger, sweeter sense of delight and anticipation than I have ever known.

THE END

ACKNOWLEDGMENTS

Of the many people who helped this book along the way, the first were my parents, Joyce Kydd and William (Bill) Kydd, of Wapella and Whitewood, Saskatchewan. They introduced my siblings and me to the heritage site that was once the town of Cannington Manor. The legendary British aristocrats who settled the town were gone by then, but their story runs deeper than the few remaining buildings on site or the crumbling mansions buried in neighbouring fields.

The history of Cannington Manor has resonated with many, especially in my family. My sister Janet Blackstock has commemorated buildings and stories in her pen and ink drawings and watercolours. She and another sister, Barbara Vennard, have abetted my research efforts, and my mother accompanied me on a visit to Thomas Beck—author of *Pioneers of Cannington Manor* (1882 – 1984) and several historical booklets—and his wife, Ethel Fripp Beck. Thomas Beck emigrated from Britain to Cannington Manor as a young man and later worked as operator for the historic park and research officer for the Saskatchewan government.

I'm also grateful to the institutions that provided historical records. Most useful were the Regina Public Library's Prairie History

Room and the Administration Centre at Moose Mountain Park, depository for the Cannington Manor archives when the historic park is closed. Marty Halpape, Southeast Area Park Manager when I visited in 2007, was helpful and well informed, and his successor, Joan Adams, follows in his footsteps. Darren Marty, Chief of Interpretation for the Remington Carriage Museum, provided information on modes of transportation used on the prairies in 1892. Finally, my mother's cousins, Melvin and Allan Bowman, escorted me to Fort Edmonton Park in an effort to explain the mysteries of farming with horses rather than tractors.

Other individuals offered time and stories. Some were descendants of Cannington Manor's early settlers, while others simply worked in the area for a time, but all saw themselves reflected in some way by the community and were eager to share what they knew. Among those who shared stories were Harold Beck (son of Thomas and Ethel Beck and custodian for All Saints Anglican Church, Cannington Manor); Jean Hindmarch and Carol Thomas, former guides at Cannington Manor Park; the Rev. Michelle Moore, incumbent at All Saints as well as Carlyle United Church; and Autumn Downey.

I would also like to thank the *Alberta Foundation for the Arts* (AFA) for the writing grant that allowed me time to finish the first draft of my novel and Athabasca University, for a professional development grant that sent me on a research trip to Carlyle, Cannington Manor Park site, Kenosee Lake, Wawota and various other stops. Remembering that research trip also brings to mind Carlyle Motor Products, and the little red car that made my meandering possible.

I am also grateful to the *Writers' Guild of Alberta* and the *Saskatchewan Writers' Guild* for their retreat programs, as most of my initial writing happened at St. Peter's Abbey in Munster, Sask.; Strawberry Creek, near Thorsby, Alta.; and Banff Centre. Not only was the concentrated time provided by the retreats essential, but so were other retreat participants. I will not attempt to name all those who encouraged me to finish this novel (formerly called *Can-*

nington Manor, The Marriage at Cannington Manor and *Means of Survival*). Over the years, there have been many such mentors and friends, and their support and encouragement has been vital. I also thank the arts boards and other funding agencies for both guilds.

Besides feedback from fellow writers during retreats, my evolving manuscript benefitted from the professional readership and advice of Catherine Bush during the 2009 Sage Hill Writing Experience Novel Colloquium and of Betty Jane Hegerat in the following year. I also appreciate discussing the manuscript with Dave Margoshes and Fred Stenson. In fact, Fred Stenson's article "Naming the Dead," published in *Quill & Quire* (September 2008), affirmed my decision to use actual names for real-life characters. Lives are short, and few of us will be famous in the usual sense. By naming people inside these pages, I wish to celebrate their existence.

Also invaluable was the support from other writer friends, among them Myrna Garanis, Audrey Whitson, Astrid Blodgett, Judy McCroskey and many more. I am also grateful to members of Indian Head Library's Book Club, for their interest and encouragement.

Though all these earlier contacts were valuable, this present book is the product of Stonehouse Publishing of Edmonton, and I am immensely grateful to Netta Johnson, publisher, and Julie Yerex, editor, as well as their designers and advisors, for their grace and patience, as well as their insights and approachability. Working with them has been a privilege.

As always, I thank my children, Joy, Niko and Bobby Yiannakoulias and Philipa Hardy, and their spouses, and my grandchildren, Scarlet Fire, Kaeylarae, Arie, Erasmus, Gwen, Thea and Willow. Your faith in me has often been what keeps me going. Last but always first, I thank my partner, Kevin Whittingham. He has suffered my sleepless nights as well as my joys, and yet resists giving advice other than "it will all look better in the morning." I hope you know how much I appreciate you, my darling. Please carry on just the way you are.

A Note on Sources

Most of the characters in this book, including Mary (Humphrys) Maltby, Ernest Maltby, members of the Humphrys family and many other residents of Cannington Manor and environs, actually lived. Only a few characters (Florence Southam and her family, Lionel Cuthbert and the somewhat vulgar neighbor Mrs. Hilda Peterson) are wholly invented. Though I was dealing in large part with actual people, I had to imagine conversations and other details of inter-actions. At the same time, I tried to be faithful to recorded dates, names, relationships and everyday activities, hoping these historical touches would be of as much interest to the reader as they are to me.

In order to be faithful, I relied heavily on a few historical doc-uments. Most useful were the following: *Pioneers of Cannington Manor* (1882 – 1984), by Thomas Beck; historical booklets *All Saints Church, Cannington Manor and Fish Lake (Kenosee Lake)*, also by Thomas Beck; *Historical Report on the Humphrys/Hewlett Property near Cannington Manor for the Period 1888 – 1920*, compiled and written by Garth Pugh, for Historic Parks, Saskatchewan Culture and Youth; letters from Martha Pritchard (employed by the Hum-phrys family) published in *Letters from Canada: Backstairs Gossip from Saskatchewan 1892/1893*, presented to the Canadian National Archives---reference MIKAN 102097 by John Palmer; *Life in Old Country Settlements: the Settlement of Cannington Manor*, by Lily Shaw Page (eldest daughter of Captain Edward Pierce), published in *Saskatchewan and its People*, 1924, Volume II; various letters written by Mary Maltby and others and numerous brochures that are part of the Cannington Manor archives. I also read parts of *Gentleman Em-igrants: From the British Public Schools to the Canadian Frontier*, by Patrick A. Dunae; and *Scoundrels, Dreamers & Second Sons: British Remittance Men in the Canadian West*, by Mark Zuehlke.

Finally, though I have tried to be precise in my editing and fact-checking, it is always possible to make or overlook errors. If that is the case here, I apologize. It has always been my wish to be true to the facts as well as the historical period.